מסורה

ArtScroll Judaica Classics®

a treasury of chassidic tales

on the festivals

VOL. II

פסח / pessach
ל״ג בעומר / Lag Baomer
שבועות / shavuos
בין המצרים / the three weeks

a treasury of chassidic

by
Rabbi Shlomo Yosef Zevin

Translated by Uri Kaploun

ספורי חסידים על המועדים

tales
on the festivals
A COLLECTION OF INSPIRATIONAL CHASSIDIC
STORIES RELEVANT TO THE FESTIVALS

Published by
Mesorah Publications, ltd / New York
in conjunction with
HILLEL PRESS / Jerusalem

FIRST EDITION
First Impression ... February, 1982
Second Impression ... January, 1984

Published and Distributed by
MESORAH PUBLICATIONS, Ltd.
Brooklyn, New York 11223
In conjunction with
HILLEL PRESS, Jerusalem

Distributed in Israel by
MESORAH MAFITZIM / J. GROSSMAN
Rechov Bayit Vegan 90/5
Jerusalem, Israel

Distributed in Europe by
J. LEHMANN HEBREW BOOKSELLERS
20 Cambridge Terrace
Gateshead
Tyne and Wear
England NE8 1RP

A TREASURY OF CHASSIDIC TALES — ON THE FESTIVALS VOL. II
© Copyright 1982
by MESORAH PUBLICATIONS, Ltd.
1969 Coney Island Avenue / Brooklyn, N.Y. 11223 / (212) 339-1700

All rights reserved. This text, the new translation and commentary — including the typographic layout — have been edited and revised as to content form and style.

No part of this book may be reproduced **in any form** without written permission from the copyright holder, except by a reviewer who wishes to quote brief passages in connection with a review written for inclusion in magazines or newspapers.

THE RIGHTS OF THE COPYRIGHT HOLDER WILL BE STRICTLY ENFORCED.

ISBN
0-89906-914-2 (Hard cover)
0-89906-915-0 (Paperback)

סדר במסכרת
חברת ארטסקרול בע״מ

Typography by Compuscribe at ArtScroll Studios, Ltd.
1969 Coney Island Avenue / Brooklyn, N.Y. 11223 / (212) 339-1700

Printed in the United States of America by Moriah Offset

Table of Contents

פסח / pessach		315
הסדר / the seder		353
ההגדה / the haggadah		360
שיר השירים / shir hashirim		373
ל״ג בעומר / Lag Baomer		395
שבועות / shavuos		399
מתן תורה / the Giving of the torah		402
עשרת הדברות / the ten commandments		410
רות / Ruth		434
בין המצרים / the three weeks		455
איכה / Lamentations		461
Biographical Sketches		471
Glossary		515
Source Index		521
Subject Index		537

פסח
pessach

◈§ The Kidnapped Sultan

The Baal Shem Tov, as is known, was on his way to *Eretz Yisrael* — but heaven willed it otherwise, and he was compelled to return when already halfway there. This is how it came about.

עֲלִילוֹת
דָּם
Blood
Libels

After all manner of tribulations that befell him on the way, the Baal Shem Tov arrived at Istanbul two days before Pessach. But there his accustomed heights of spiritual sensitivity vanished; as well, he was in dire want. He sought out the local synagogue and endeavoured to savor the familiar delights of Torah study — but this was denied him. So it was that he and his daughter Adel were distressed indeed.

On the morning before Pessach eve, Adel went down to the seashore to wash her father's clothes in honor of the approaching festival. It was already *erev* Pessach, but there was yet no sign of *matzos*, or wine, or anything else. Blinking away her tears, she looked up and saw a passenger boat drawing near. Among the people who stepped off at the shore was a wealthy and God-fearing personage who had just returned home from his merchandising.

"My daughter, why do you weep?" he asked.

"My father is a saintly man," she sobbed, "but he has been punished by heaven, and he can no longer enjoy the nearness of the Divine Presence as he always does. Right now he is sitting in the synagogue. I don't know what to do, because we haven't got anything at all for Pessach."

"Go along and bring your father to me," said the compassionate stranger. "Throughout the festival you will be my guests, and I will see to all your needs."

With that he gave her his address, and off she sped to the synagogue. She told her father the whole story, and they set out for the house of the merchant.

Their host greeted them warmly, even though he could not discern any mark of especial greatness in the countenance of the Baal Shem Tov. The latter declined to

pessach eat, for it was so late in the morning that he could no longer eat bread or any other kind of *chametz* food, and in readiness for the mitzvah of eating *matzah* at the *Seder* at night, one of course is not permitted to eat *matzah* during that day. But when he was offered wine, he drank without fearing lest he enter the evening's festive meal sated, for as the Talmud remarks, wine in quantity whets the appetite, while a little wine satisfies one's hunger.

Until nightfall the tzaddik slept in the room which his host had given him. When the latter returned from his evening prayers he asked Adel to rouse her father from his sleep, for it was now time to proceed with the *Seder*. This, she said, she would never do. He opened the door himself, and beheld a face all flushed and afire. The eyes were protruding, and tears were streaming from them. Alarmed, the host at once retreated.

By now he realized that his guest was a man of God, and did not return to waken him. After some time the tzaddik awoke and washed his hands. The Evening Prayer which he now began was the worship of a soul in ecstatic union with its Maker — for during his sleep he had been restored to his former stature. He then joined his host at the table for the *Seder*, and read the words of the *Haggadah* with inspired fervor. By the time he arrived at the Psalms of thanksgiving that comprise *Hallel* it was three hours past midnight. One verse in particular he exclaimed aloud and with devout emphasis: לְעֹשֵׂה נִפְלָאוֹת גְּדֹלוֹת לְבַדּוֹ כִּי לְעוֹלָם חַסְדּוֹ — "Praise Him Who alone does great wonders, for His lovingkindness endures forever."

Throughout the entire proceedings the merchant did not allow himself the liberty of asking any questions of the Baal Shem Tov. Once the *Seder* was over, however, he asked him to explain: why had he wept in his sleep, and why had he cried out one particular verse in the *Haggadah*?

"A fearful decree threatened the lives of the Jews of Istanbul," replied the Baal Shem Tov. "I made every endeavor to have it annulled by the Heavenly Court, even if it would cost me my life — and, thank God, my efforts bore fruit. And at the very moment when I was reciting that verse of praise, the decree was in fact פסח quashed. Tomorrow morning in *shul* you will hear what it's all about."

Next morning, when the congregation was ready to start the Morning Prayers, and awaiting the arrival of one of their prominent townsmen, a prosperous wine-merchant, that very man burst in the door and exclaimed: "*Mazel Tov*, gentlemen, *Mazel Tov!* We've all been saved from a terrible decree: the Almighty has saved us!"

※ ※ ※

This is as far as the narrative is related in the published anthologies of stories on the Baal Shem Tov. Of the nature of the decree, and the manner of salvation, there is not a word. These have been passed on to us by word of mouth by the elder chassidim of the intervening generations. Here is their story.

※ ※ ※

There was once a sultan in Istanbul who liked to take an occasional stroll incognito, disguising himself as a common citizen. On one such outing he so much enjoyed the beauty of the countryside that he did not notice how far he had strayed from the town. All of a sudden he found himself surrounded by a noose of malevolent faces: he had stumbled upon a gang of highwaymen, and they dragged him off to their gloomy den. There they emptied his pockets of all his money and valuables. He thought he would now be freed. Instead, they informed him that they would of course have to kill him so that he would never be able to disclose their whereabouts.

After a moment's deliberation he decided not to identify himself — for if they knew that it was the sultan that they were freeing, what hope would they have of not being brought to justice? Rather than give them cause to kill him forthwith, he would leave them in their ignorance, and in the meantime rely on his own resourcefulness as the last spark of hope.

"Look here," he said. "If you kill me, you won't earn anything by it. But if you let me live, I will be able to render you a service that will earn you an enormous amount of money."

"How? How?" they asked.

"I am the master of one craft," said the captive, "and if I engage in it for you, you won't regret it. I know how to make bed-covers out of plain mats. Connoisseurs pay high prices for them. Buy me the mats I need, I'll make one bed-cover a day, and let one of you take it off to Istanbul for sale. The proceeds, of course, will be yours; my gain will be my life."

Duly convinced, they bought him a mat in order to see whether his claim was valid. He spent the next day working on it, and as he handed the finished product to one of their henchmen to be sold in Istanbul, he said: "The fixed price of this bed-cover is such and such; if you are offered less than this, do not sell it on any account. Remember that this is merchandise which is appreciated only by the experts, so don't take it to heart if the first customers you encounter laugh at you when you ask for such a high price. Just keep on walking from shop to shop, until you run into someone who is sufficiently expert to be prepared to pay you this fixed price."

The messenger set out with this odd piece of handiwork, and in each bazaar dutifully demanded the stipulated price. Everywhere he was laughed at — so much so that at one point a whole circle of scoffing merchants thronged around him, calling him a madman.

At this moment a Jewish wine-merchant happened by, and seeing the smirking and snickering crowd, he approached out of curiosity. He was told that this individual was offering for sale an ordinary mat, somewhat reworked, and was demanding an exorbitant price for it, claiming that it was a first-class bed-cover that needed a connoisseur to recognize its quality. "Clearly out of his mind!" concluded the bystander.

The Jew took a long look at the stranger: his face was certainly not that of a madman. He then examined the mat, and noticed that it had one letter woven into it. (The letter was in fact the initial of the sultan's name.)

Suspecting that there might be something behind this odd affair, he invited the stranger to his shop, paid the

set price, and assured him that he was able to appreciate פסח
this fine article at its true value. He went on to ask who it
was who made it. He was told that this could not be
revealed, but if he so desired he could buy one more like
it every day. The Jew agreed.

When the sultan heard the messenger's story and saw
that the price had in fact been paid, he guessed that the
purchaser had detected the letter and was anticipating
some code or message. This of course encouraged him to
apply himself to his work even more industriously.

The next day, when the Jew duly bought another mat
and found in it the second letter of the sultan's name, he
understood exactly what he had to do: he went straight
to the royal palace, and recounted his bizarre story.

Now from the moment the sultan had disappeared, the
palace had been thrown into consternation. His trusty
bodyguards had sought him everywhere. Now, at long
last, they had lighted upon a fruitful clue. The Jew was
ordered to continue with his daily purchases, but to keep
them in strict secrecy. And so it was that day by day, letter by letter, he had spelled out before him the name of
the royal prisoner, and his precise whereabouts. The
palace thereupon dispatched a squad of fearless warriors.
In order to be sure they would find their obscure destination they seized the sultan's hapless messenger and
hustled him along with them. They surrounded the dismal hideout, fell upon the highwaymen by surprise, and
freed the sultan.

Now he was not a man to forget a favor of this
magnitude. Once safely back among the massy arched
colonnades of his palace, he summoned the Jew to whom
he owed his life and said: "What do you request? — For
I shall grant it!"

The Jew demurred: "If Divine Providence has seen fit
to grant me the privilege of saving the life of my royal
master, could I ask for any further reward?"

But the potentate still desired to give fit expression to
his gratitude, and a royal decree was duly signed, sealed
and proclaimed: "By this irrevocable firman be it known
by all men in our invincible Ottoman Empire that to this
Jew and his seed after him throughout all the generations
do we in our wisdom hereby grant and bestow the

Pessach / פסח [319]

pessach privilege of entry and admission to the royal presence at all times and at all seasons, without requesting permit or permission."

✻ ✻ ✻

Years passed and decades rolled by, and the Jew never had occasion to make use of this prerogative. He lived his life as a wealthy and respected member of his community, and was never in need of any particular favor for which he might need to trouble the sultan. In due course the sultan was succeeded by his son, and the Jew too left behind him a son — who inherited this rare privilege.

One day the young sultan went driving in the streets of the capital, accompanied by his grand vizier. Looking through his carriage window he saw groups of Jews bringing home crates of *matzos* by wagon, for it was a few days before the festival of Pessach.

"What are these strange wafers?" he asked.

The grand vizier was a bitter Jew-hater.

"These wafers," he explained, "are the *matzos* which the Jews eat during their Passover festival. And, if it please your illustrious majesty, the most zealous amongst them eat a special kind of *matzah* which in the language of the Hebrews is called *shemurah*. This means that one of its necessary ingredients is the blood of a Moslem child, whom these Jews select and slaughter in preparation for their annual ritual."

The sultan was alarmed. The vizier proceeded to make his libel plausible by advising that his master investigate for himself whether there were in fact Jews who ate *matzah* which was known by the special name of "*shemurah*."

This much was of course easy to prove. The credulous sultan at once believed the whole infamous fabrication — without knowing that *shemurah* means "guarded", and is the name that simply denotes the kind of *matzah* which is baked with extraordinary precautions against the remotest possibility of leavening in the course of its preparation. Following the advice of his vizier, he issued a secret order that an exhaustive list be drawn up of the Jews who baked this kind of *matzah*. They were to be arrested by surprise on the first day of the festival, and פסח rounded up for execution.

The eve of Pessach was still quite some hours off, so the son of the Jew who had saved the late sultan's life lay down for a daytime nap. In his dream his father appeared to him and said: "My son! A fearful threat hovers over the Jews of this city. You alone are in a position to save them. Go therefore to the sultan, in accordance with the privilege which is yours, and tell him that it is a malicious calumny that his grand vizier has concocted concerning the Jews — that they use Moslem blood for the festival. Tell him further that the vizier himself is an impostor: only outwardly does he make a pretense of being a Moslem, for in fact he is a Christian of the Greek church. If the sultan wants to be convinced of this, let him send secret agents to his house, and they will find him in his bed at night with a crucifix around his neck!"

The young man awoke from his dream, and dismissed it from his mind. For does not the Prophet write: וַחֲלֹמוֹת הַשָּׁוְא יְדַבֵּרוּ — "And dreams speak vanity"? He busied himself with preparations for the evening's *Seder*, and planned to go to his synagogue as usual at nightfall. But in the meantime he was overwhelmed by such a stupor that he soon fell into a deep sleep. Sure enough his father appeared to him once again, adjuring him earnestly to fulfill his earlier command, and warning him that if he failed to do so, the bloodguilt of his brethren would forever lie on his head.

When he awoke it was night. The young man understood that such a warning was not to be taken lightly. He hesitated no longer, but set out at once for the royal palace. By the time he reached the spiked iron gates it was so late that he decided it would be imprudent to exercise his hereditary privilege, for it was clear that the sultan had already retired for the night. He therefore requested the court officials that he be admitted to the presence of the dowager queen, the widow of the late sultan.

He told the aged lady of his strange dream, which he was convinced was not to be swept aside. He entreated her to speak at once with her reigning son, in an pessach endeavor to have the malicious decree annulled. Ever since his father had saved the life of her late husband, he reminded her, the right had never been used by himself nor by his father; if now he came to speak with her, it was because the lives of many of their brethren were in peril.

Moved by his pleas, the dowager queen told him to wait, and she went to rouse her son. Now until this moment she had known nothing of the secret decree, so that she was astonished by the words of the young Jew. In fact she was even apprehensive as to whether his whole dream might be a vain imagination, in which case it would be preferable not to mention the Jew or his dream at all. Instead, therefore, she decided at this point to tell her son that his father, the late sultan, had appeared to her in a dream; he had told her that since their son had decided upon a certain course of action which was exceedingly evil, she should warn him that if he did not undo it forthwith, his end would be bitter indeed.

The young sultan listened carefully to his old mother's story, but disclaimed knowledge of any such course of action.

"Perhaps," ventured his mother, "you have contemplated doing something against the Jews?"

"Against the Jews? Yes, mother," he replied, "that I have — but what I plan is something irreproachable. You see, amongst them there is a sect of individuals who on their Passover eat *matzos* which are baked with Moslem blood. I have therefore given the command that this infidel evil be wiped out from our midst."

Seeing the Jew's dream thus verified, the dowager queen went ahead and told her son the whole story of her visitor and his plea, reminding him meanwhile of the eternal debt which the royal family owed the resourceful Jewish wine-merchant and his descendants. The young ruler took her words to heart, and dispatched a lackey to summon the Jew to his presence. The young man fell to his feet, retold the story of his dream, and begged the sultan to put his father's words to the test by sending trusted troops to the mansion of the vizier in order to establish whether he was in fact a Moslem only in appearance.

פסח

This request was granted. A secret squad was dispatched forthwith. They roused the startled vizier, searched his person, and found the hated crucifix around his neck. Their blood seethed with fanatic zeal; they drew their scimitars and slew him.

※ ※ ※

This had taken place exactly at the moment when the Baal Shem Tov had exclaimed the Psalmist's words: "Praise Him — לְעֹשֵׂה נִפְלָאוֹת גְּדֹלוֹת לְבַדּוֹ כִּי לְעוֹלָם חַסְדּוֹ Who alone does great wonders, for His lovingkindness endures forever."

The decree was at once annulled, and the next morning, as the local congregants foregathered anxiously in the synagogue in readiness for the prayers of the first day of Pessach, in burst the beaming wine-merchant with his "*Mazel Tov*, gentlemen, *Mazel Tov!*" And then he went ahead and recounted the whole story of how Divine Providence had given him the privilege of being an agent in the salvation of his townsmen.

⋑ *The Confession*

The saintly Reb Leib Sarahs was well advanced in years, so Reb Azriel of Polotzk — a disciple of the Maggid of Mezritch — undertook to accompany him throughout his travels. So it was that on one occasion they stopped and took up lodgings in an inn which was owned by a Jew of means, some three miles out of Vilna.

Morning came, and Reb Leib sent Reb Azriel to call the innkeeper. As soon as he appeared, Reb Leib addressed him as follows: "Go off to the street of the gentiles and summon for me the duke who lives there. Tell him that there is a Jew staying in your inn at the moment called Leib the son of Sarah, who requests the duke to come to him at once."

The innkeeper was aghast.

"Am I out of my mind that I should do such a thing? No Jew who approaches that street is sure that he will leave it alive. The duke himself, who is of royal blood, has never spoken to a Jew. How can I possible dare to

Pessach / פסח [323]

appear before him and tell him that a Jew summons him to his presence?"

Reb Leib replied harshly: "Do you know who I am? I am Leib the son of Sarah, and if you do not obey me, you will regret it!"

Sure enough, the innkeeper's wife and two sons suddenly fell ill. Seeing the danger in which they stood, he ran to the tzaddik and said: "Here I am, ready for whatever mission you see fit — so long as you remove this plague from my house."

"Then set out this minute to the duke," ordered Reb Leib. "Do not delay: just call him here, and your family will be cured at once."

Quaking from head to foot, the poor fellow made his way on his dangerous mission — but as he passed through the dreaded street nothing whatever befell him. He mustered the daring to knock on the hefty gates of the ducal mansion.

A husky bodyguard snarled at him: "Jew! What business brings *you* here?"

"I need to see the duke," the innkeeper replied.

While the bodyguard marched off to relay this unusual message, the duke himself happened to be strolling by, and his henchmen told him that some Jew was waiting outside to see him.

"Bring him to me!" he ordered.

When this was done, the innkeeper began, "My dread lord! There is an old Jew lodging in my inn at the moment. His name is Leib the son of Sarah, and he told me to summon my lord the duke to see him at once."

No sooner did the duke hear the name of the tzaddik than he replied in alarm: "I'm coming! Just wait a moment until I dress; I'll go along with you straight away."

The Jew could hardly believe his ears. He waited a moment, and then the duke hastened to join him on foot, instead of riding in the splendor of his carriage according to his custom.

As soon as they arrived Reb Leib sent the innkeeper off to visit his ailing family, and closeted himself with the duke for several minutes in his study. Reb Leib next instructed his companion Reb Azriel to harness their horse, and as the duke returned to his mansion, they too went on their way.

Thinking over the events of the morning in the privacy of his home the duke was puzzled. What on earth had come over him that he should run off in alarm at the summons of some old Jew called Leib the son of Sarah? He immediately dispatched a squad of hussars to the inn with orders to bring him the old man who was lodging there. Off they galloped, but had to report back that by the time they had arrived the Jew had departed.

After some time, a little before the festival of Pessach, the gentile servant of this innkeeper disappeared. The local clergy duly spread the libel that the Jew had slaughtered him in order to use his blood in the baking of the *matzos* to be eaten on the forthcoming Pessach festival. The authorities thereupon seized the hapless innkeeper and cast him into a dungeon. There they tortured him unceasingly, in order to extort a false confession from his lips. So cruelly did they rack his body that like the stricken Jonah he cried out: "Better is my death than my life" — and repeated the words of his tormentors. On the strength of this wretched confession the ecclesiastical court condemned him to death; the only detail now missing was the duke's signature to authorize the sentence.

"But I am about to set out for the big fair in the city to buy horses," protested the duke, "and when it comes to choosing horses this Jew is an expert. Let's keep him alive until after the fair: I'll sign for him. When we come back I'll hand him over to your holinesses, and if you still abide by your sentence I will sign it."

The Jew was therefore taken under heavy guard to the fair. One day, while he was busy choosing horses for the duke, he espied the very gentile servant who had disappeared. The servant ran towards him eagerly, fell at his feet, and exclaimed: "Thanks be to the Lord that I see you here!"

"But why did you run away from my household?" asked the innkeeper. "And where have you been?"

"My master," the merchant began, and wept. "You have treated me better than a father and mother. But our parish priest kept on trying to persuade me to journey off to some faraway place where he would give me a

pessach house and fields of my own. I didn't want to take notice of him. But suddenly one night he came along and called me outside, sat me in a wagon, and there they bound me and hustled me off to a distant town. All this time I am a homeless wanderer, without as much as a square meal to eat. I wanted to return to you but it's a long way — and who's got the money for traveling? Even today I wouldn't have managed to make it to the fair — if it were not for some old Jew who turned up with his servant and brought me here in his wagon. All night long I slept in it. When I woke up in the morning he said: 'Look for your master here, because he is here for the fair.' So please, take me back home with you, so that I won't die of hunger."

This encounter breathed new life into the unfortunate innkeeper, and he realized that it was the doing of his remarkable guest, the aged tzaddik with the companion.

"Come along with me," he said to the gentile, "and I will see to it that you have something to eat."

He took him off to a local tavern, paid in advance for whatever the starving vagabond could possibly want to eat, and told him: "Wait for me here, and don't leave until I come here to call you."

He then resumed his work of buying horses for the duke, and in due course their carriage was prepared for the journey home. As soon as they started to move, the horses pranced about wildly and left the road. The duke was afraid that the carriage might even be overturned.

"My master," said the Jew. "I know a firstclass wagondriver who lives here. If you are agreeable I'll call him. I am sure he will want to come with us, for he too comes from the Vilna district and is in a hurry to return there."

With the duke's consent the Jew went off to the tavern to bring his former gentile servant; he promptly climbed up, took up his place out in front in the driver's seat, took the reins in hand, and off they went without mishap.

Once they were on their way home the duke turned to the Jewish innkeeper and said: "You no doubt recall that you came to visit me on behalf of some elderly rabbi who was then staying with you?"

פסח

"I do indeed," said the innkeeper.

"'Very well,'" said the duke, "then I would now like to reveal to you what he told me then — even though to this day I do not understand his meaning. This is what he said: 'I have a small request to make of you. When one day you will be shown a death sentence for this man, tell them that you first want to take him with you to buy horses at the fair, and that afterwards you will do as they request.' When in due course they brought me your sentence, I saw with my own eyes that the spirit of God was upon this rabbi, and I was certain that out of this fair your salvation would come. But here we are, already on our way home, and I undertook to hand you over to the judges and to append my signature to their verdict. So what did the aged rabbi gain through his request after all?"

"When we appear in town before the judges and the witnesses who knew the servant who disappeared, you will understand the intention of that man of miracles," the Jew assured him. "Look: that man out there holding the reins is the very servant who disappeared. He was sent far away by order of the parish priest in order to trump up a libel against me. My lord: ask him yourself, and he will tell you everything that befell him."

The duke was overwhelmed. "Now I know," he said, "that there is indeed a God in Israel! Only one thing I do not understand: what came over you that made you confess to a lie, and sign that you killed your gentile servant, thus stirring up the hatred of all your non-Jewish townsmen?"

The wretched Jew wept and explained: "Their tortures were more than man can bear, so that I preferred to die. It is the same with all the confessions that our enemies extort from us."

The duke crossexamined the servant closely, and when they reached their hometown, he ordered him to repeat his story in the presence of the witnesses who had known him earlier. The parish priest heard the entire evidence and not a word of it could he deny.

The Jew was at once absolved of all charges. As for the parish priest, he too played *his* part in the fulfillment of the verse: צַדִּיק מִצָּרָה נֶחֱלָץ וַיָּבֹא רָשָׁע תַּחְתָּיו — "The

Pessach / פסח

pessach righteous is delivered out of trouble, and the wicked comes in his stead."

∾ A Jewish Blood-Libel

Word reached Reb Levi Yitzchak of Berditchev that the owners of the local *matzah* bakeries were forcing the young women who kneaded and rolled the dough to work from early morning until late at night.

He stood up in the synagogue and cried out: "Gentile anti-Semites always claim that Jews knead their dough for the *matzos* with the blood of Christians. That is an outright lie! It is not Christian blood they use, but the blood of the young daughters of Israel who are being overworked in our *matzah* bakeries!"

∾ Redemption in the Present Tense

שַׁבָּת
הַגָּדוֹל
Shabbas HaGadol
The Sabbath preceding Pessach

Year after year, after searching his house for *chametz* on the evening before Pessach, Reb Avraham Yaakov of Sadigora used to recount the following story.

In a village that lay on the outskirts of Kolbasov there lived a Jewish innkeeper who held his rundown tavern on lease from the gentile squire who owned the village. Business was miserable, and the poor fellow simply could not muster the rental on time. The squire repeatedly demanded his due — but what was there to be done? Even the squire's dire threats could not alter the plain facts.

Finally, on the morning of *Shabbas HaGadol*, the Sabbath before Pessach, the squire found a way to vent his frustration: he sent off a gang of his burly Cossack retainers to the Jew's house, with orders to make their presence felt and teach the Jew a lesson. The tipsy hooligans stormed down the rickety door, emptied the sewage pot over the floor, threw the steaming *cholent* through the window, upturned the table and smashed the chairs, and trampled on whatever they could lay their vicious hands on.

Well pleased with their handiwork they stomped back to the squire, leaving the innkeeper and his family sitting among the ruins, dazed and forlorn. To ease his anguish the unfortunate fellow decided to walk off to the פסח neighboring town to hear the sermon which is traditionally delivered by the rabbi of each town on the afternoon of *Shabbas HaGadol*. Now the *rav* of Kolbasov at that time was none other than Reb Avraham Yehoshua Heschel, the same who was later to become renowned as the Ohev Yisrael of Apta. By the time the villager arrived, the *rav* was already standing on the *bimah* in the midst of delivering his *derashah*, with the congregants crowding around all sides to hear his every word. The weedy villager wriggled his way into a corner near the door, and he too strained to hear.

And this is what he heard in the course of that sermon: "In our prayers we find a blessing that appears in two tenses. In the blessings following *Shema Yisrael* and in the *Haggadah* which we read on Pessach we find גָּאַל יִשְׂרָאֵל — praising Him Who 'redeemed Israel.' In the *Shemoneh Esreh* prayer we find גּוֹאֵל יִשְׂרָאֵל — a blessing addressed to Him Who 'redeems Israel.' The former blessing refers to the redemption from the bondage in Egypt; the latter blessing applies to the redemption which is current at all times, so that even if in some tiny village somewhere there lives a Jew who can't afford to pay the rent, and the squire sends his Cossacks to wreak havoc in his house, and they shatter and destroy every single object they find — then even for such a Jew the Almighty finds a way of bringing him a means of redemption from his woes."

In the ears of the afflicted villager, these words were music. All the way home he pranced for sheer joy, singing away lustily: "The rebbe said *Goel Yisrael!* The rebbe said 'Who *redeems* Israel'!"

Sunset came, and the *paritz* sent his henchmen again, this time to see what the Jew was doing after what had stricken him. To their amazement they found him happy and carefree, dancing about and singing. There was only one explanation possible — and this they reported back to the squire: under the pressure of his misfortune, the Jew had obviously been driven out of his mind.

In the evening the squire called for the Jew whose first thought was that his landlord had devised fresh means to torment him. But then he recalled the rebbe's words about Him Who *"redeems* Israel." He banished fear from his heart and stepped out on his way, all joy and confidence.

"Tell me, Moshke," the *paritz* bantered, "why are you such a ne'er-do-well? You yourself are as poor as poor can be, and you don't pay me a penny, either."

"So what can I do about that?" protested the leaseholder.

"Listen here, Moshke," said the *paritz*. "I'll give you a note to take to the whiskey distillery in town, and they'll give you liquor on account for a certain sum. You'll then sell the stuff and earn a little, and repeat the same story over and over — and then you'll have money to pay me, and enough to feed your family with as well."

The plan worked beautifully. In the few days that were left between *Shabbas HaGadol* and the eve of Pessach the leaseholder managed to buy and sell, buy and sell, until he had earned enough to pay up his debt and to buy all his family's needs for the festival. Then before Pessach began, he tied up a handful of coins in a kerchief, and handed them over as a gift to the *rav* of Kolbasov, saying: "Rebbe, I've brought you some *Goel Yisrael* money."

◆§ Deeds, not Words

"It is the custom among learned rabbis," Reb Zvi Hirsch of Liska would explain, "to go to great lengths in their pre-Pessach sermons to resolve seeming contradictions between various pairs of legal statements by Maimonides. I do the same — but in *practice*. You see, in one place *Rambam* lays down the law as written in the Torah, בָּעֶרֶב תֹּאכְלוּ מַצֹּת — 'In the evening you shall eat *matzos*.' In another place he codifies the law as written in the Torah, לֹא תִגְנֹב — 'You shall not steal.' Now it sometimes happens that the needy folk of our town find a painful contradiction between the fulfillment of these two commandments ... But when a poor man comes to me, I see to it that there is absolutely no room for any contradiction — and both rulings of *Rambam* may be observed simultaneously."

"And that little bit of help constitutes *my* sermon for פסח Shabbas HaGadol ..."

◆§ A Question of Priorities

"One Friday," recalled Reb Zvi Hirsch of Liska, "Reb Mordechai of Nadvorna arrived in a certain town in order to spend *Shabbos* there. Since one of the townsmen was about to leave because he was to be my guest here for *Shabbos*, Reb Mordechai asked him to convey his regards, and to repeat to me the following thought.

מָעוֹת חִטִּין Matzah-flour for the needy

"In introducing the laws of Pessach in his *Shulchan Aruch*, Rav Yosef Caro writes: 'Thirty days before Pessach one begins to discuss and expound the laws of the festival.' Commenting on this statement, Rav Moshe Isserles (known as *Rama*) appends the following: 'And it is customary to buy wheat for distribution to the needy for Pessach.' Now this is problematic. Of what relevance is this comment? For we all know that it is not in the style of this sage to introduce a concept that is unconnected with the preceding words; and this case is all the more surprising since he prefaces his comment with the word *and*, as if to point out just such a connection. Here, then, is what *Rama* is telling us: 'I really don't care all that much whether you do expound and sermonize or whether you don't expound and sermonize — *so long as you buy wheat for distribution to the needy* ...'"

Reb Zvi Hirsch of Liska resumed his story: "As soon as my guest relayed to me the words of Reb Mordechai of Nadvorna, I realized that he must be possessed of divine inspiration, because when sermonizing every year on the *Shabbos* before Pessach I used to come up against this seeming incongruity in the comment of *Rama* — and along he comes and sends me the solution!

"Now just before *Shabbas HaGadol* that year a poor woman came to me in tatters, weeping bitterly because she still had no *matzah*. The words of the tzaddik of Nadvorna immediately came to mind. The trouble was that everyone was busy with their final preparations for the festival. So I sent off my sons-in-law and my daughters, and I joined in too, and we started baking matzos for that unfortunate woman. Now do you think that any of the local householders who saw us on our way just stood by and did nothing? Not at all! They left off whatever they were doing and joined in energetically — and to my delight we had baked her a fine batch of *matzos* within half an hour."

৺ Foresight

In the weeks before Pessach one year Reb Aryeh Leib of Shpola did the rounds of all the surrounding townships, buying up enormous quantities of wheat which he ground into קִמְחָא דְּפִסְחָא — flour to be distributed to the needy. No one could quite understand: for whom had he prepared so much flour?

Three days before Pessach one of the neighboring townships was burnt down, and the unfortunate residents were left homeless and penniless, without the wherewithal for even the barest necessities for the oncoming festival. Only then, as they watched the Shpoler Zeide industriously baking and distributing *matzos*, did his townsmen realize that before the malady struck, the tzaddik had already prepared the cure.

৺ Too Precious to Give Away

מַיִם שֶׁלָּנוּ
The water prepared for matzah-baking

There is a picturesque sight to be seen every year among those who delight in enhancing their performance of every mitzvah to the best of their ability. Such people bake their *matzas* mitzvah — with which they intend to fulfill their obligation of eating *matzah* that evening at the *Seder* table — during the day, after the hour at which the prohibition against *chametz* comes into force. In preparation for this, they foregather before sunset the day before, on the thirteenth of Nissan, and together go out with song and ceremony to draw the water for the baking. This water is called *mayim shelanu* — water which is left to stand and cool down during the night.

One year Reb Meir Margolios took his pitcher in hand, and set out on foot to draw water. Reb Meir was the rabbi of Ostrov, a disciple of the Baal Shem Tov, and the learned author of *Meir Nesivim*. On his way he met

the local preacher, Reb Yaakov Yosef, who is known by פסח
an acronym of his Hebrew name as Reb Yeivi. The latter
was on his way to the same place, pitcher in hand — but
riding in his carriage.

"Rabbi," he called to Reb Meir, "why should you be
trudging through all the mud and mire instead of riding
in a carriage?"

"A mitzvah as great as this," replied Reb Meir, "that I
can fulfill only once a year, I am especially fond of. I
really have no desire to give it away to the horses ..."

Reb Yeivi promptly sprang down from his carriage,
and they continued together on foot.

⋅ട This Year in Jerusalem

On the thirteenth of Nissan one year, while drawing
the water to be used in the baking of *matzah* on the
morrow, the eve of Pessach, a group of chassidim wished
their rebbe, Reb Shalom of Belz, the blessing which is
customary on annual festive occasions of this sort:
לְשָׁנָה הַבָּאָה בִּירוּשָׁלַיִם — "Next year in Jerusalem!"

"Why next year?" queried the tzaddik. "Don't we
believe and wait expectantly every day for the coming of
Mashiach? If so, we should believe and expect that with
this very water which we are now drawing, it will be
granted us to bake *matzah* tomorrow, on the eve of Pessach, in Jerusalem, and to eat it there."

⋅ട How to Become a Rothschild

Reb David Moshe of Chortkov used to relate how בְּדִיקַת
Mayer Amschel Rothschild, the founding father of חָמֵץ
the dynasty of magnates, rose to his legendary opulence *The*
by virtue of an incident that took place one year on the *search*
eve of the fourteenth of Nissan, during the annual *for*
household search for leaven on the evening before *Seder* *leaven*
night.

In his youth Mayer Amschel was an attendant of Reb
Zvi Hirsch of Chortkov, the father of Reb Shmelke of
Nikolsburg. In due course he married a young woman
from Siniatin, where he set up in merchandising and
prospered somewhat.

Pessach / פסח   [333]

pessach   Now Reb Zvi Hirsch had saved up five hundred gold ducats as a dowry for his daughter. Throughout the year he hardly ever opened the desk drawer where it was kept — except for the eve of the fourteenth of Nissan, when in the course of the search of *bedikas chametz* he opened it up. When this occasion came around for the first time after Mayer Amschel had left the household and married, the *rav* duly opened the drawer, and was horrified to find that the wallet containing his entire savings had disappeared. The members of his household hastily decided that the thief could be no other than Mayer Amschel. They cited reports that he had opened a shop and was prospering — indisputable evidence that he was the thief, no doubt about it! The *rav* repeatedly silenced their arguments, and reprimanded them for succumbing to the sin of suspecting the innocent. Had they themselves not been witness to his honest and God-fearing ways during the period of his employment with them? But they gave him no rest, until eventually he was compelled to make a reluctant journey to Siniatin. On opening his door and beholding his former employer whom he so much admired and esteemed, the young man rejoiced exceedingly, and showed the *rav* every mark of respect.

With heavy heart and faltering spirit Reb Zvi Hirsch recounted his misfortune to his trusted former attendant, and through the discreetest of hints intimated to him that there were such as suspected him.

"They are right," Mayer Amschel was quick to confess; "I took the money. At the moment, though, I have at hand only about two hundred ducats, which I will return to you at once. The rest I will return within a short time."

The *rav* returned home with a double measure of relief — firstly, because the members of his family had not transgressed by suspecting an innocent party, and secondly, because the missing amount was now being returned to him. And in fact it all reached him in due course, in periodic instalments.

In fact, however, the young man had stolen nothing. This is how it all came about.

As Pessach approached, a gentile maid from one of the

nearby villages had been hired to whitewash the house of פסח
the *rav*. The locked drawer in his study fascinated her intensely. She contrived to secure a key, and in due course presented the bulging wallet to her admiring spouse. For a long time he kept it well hidden, but when he was satisfied that the whole matter had no doubt been forgotten — and besides, it was high time to begin to enjoy this windfall — he took one ducat with him on his next visit to the local tavern, and ordered vodka in plenty for himself and all his cronies. When it was time to pay, he slapped the gold ducat expansively on the counter and said to the innkeeper: "Look what I found! Here, take it to town and have it exchanged; keep what I owe you for the drinks and give me the change."

This he did. The next week again the humble hostelry rang loudly in the wake of this peasant's generosity, and when the local yokels all caroused a third time he again paid with a gold ducat that he had found ...

The innkeeper was no fool. He went off quietly to the Polish lord and passed on his suspicions.

"Next time he comes around," advised the lord, "surround him on all sides with his favorite drinking companions, and fill him up till he's dead drunk. *Then* we'll hear the truth! As they say, 'In flow the spirits, out flow the secrets.'"

The next time came soon enough, and by now the rustic's quickly-growing circle of friends were intensely inquisitive: where *had* he found all those ducats? And so it was that he confided the whole story of his wife's little escapade to a couple of dozen eager and red-nosed listeners, mentioning for good measure exactly where the treasure now lay buried.

The innkeeper took along a group of witnesses to the lord, and on hearing their testimony he sent off his henchmen to dig in the peasant's back yard. There they duly found just a few ducats less than five hundred. They bound and shackled him and hauled him off unceremoniously to the lord's castle, where he confessed.

The lord now sent for the *rav*. Quaking, the unfortunate scholar prepared himself for the worst: for who could know what new libel had been trumped up against himself and his hapless flock?

pessach	Surprisingly, though, the lord asked him instead how many children he had, how much he earned weekly, and so on — and the *rav* of course answered.

Then came the following question: "And how do you plan to marry off your daughter?"

The *rav* thereupon told him about the five hundred ducats that he had saved up, and that had been stolen; and on being asked further questions, he described the wallet in which the money had been kept. Fully convinced, the lord promptly handed it over to its rightful owner, and told him of the episodes in the local tavern. So it was that the *rav* returned to his home with mixed feelings — joyful at his discovery that his former employee was indeed an upright man, and grieved that he had suspected him.

He immediately set out for Siniatin and asked the young man what on earth had prompted him to admit to an offense which he had not committed, and to return a sum which he had not stolen. Mayer Amschel's explanation was simple enough. He had seen at their previous meeting that his former master was deeply distressed, and had gathered that if he were to return to his family with empty hands both he and they would be in even deeper anguish. He had therefore decided on the spot to say that he had stolen the money; he had given away his entire fortune at the time in order to give the *rav* some peace of mind, and had then sold and mortgaged whatever he owned in order to make up the required amount.

Amazed, the *rav* begged his forgiveness for having once suspected him. He returned him his money, and gave him his blessing — that heaven should grant abounding riches to him and to his seed after him, for many generations.

Mayer Amschel grew to be prodigiously wealthy, and the father of the opulent House of Rothschild.

﷽ Why Worry?

בִּעוּר חָמֵץ
The elimination of leaven

Heilprin, the prominent magnate, once sent an urgent letter to Reb Aharon of Chernobyl: a certain nobleman had threatened that if the Jews did not present him with 200,000 rubles by Easter, he would issue the most fearful edicts against them. The writer therefore requested that Reb Aharon and his saintly brothers endeavor to raise the required sum, part of which he himself undertook to provide.

When the letter was read out to the tzaddik he said: "Why is he bothering me with his imaginings?"

This was too much for his secretary.

"Rebbe," he protested, "this is something that affects the entire House of Israel!"

But the tzaddik merely repeated his earlier comment.

Baffled by this response, Heilprin dispatched an emissary to convey his request to the rebbe in person. The reaction was the same.

"But what shall I tell my employer?" asked the hapless emissary. "Perhaps I could be given the reply in writing, so that he will believe me when I tell him that I was here."

The rebbe obliged, and asked his secretary to jot down a few words. The secretary however was reluctant to write. How could the tzaddik dismiss a weighty request so lightly?

The rebbe now turned to the emissary and said: "Return to the one who sent you, and tell him to keep himself occupied with his business interests and not to worry at all."

A little later the rebbe received a letter from his brother, Reb Yitzchak of Skver, asking him likewise to exert himself in this matter. This letter too was ignored.

Now on the morning of Pessach eve the custom in Chernobyl was that all the townsfolk would bring their leftovers of *chametz* food to the tzaddik, who would throw them into the fire. On this occasion the rebbe took the earthenware bowl containing his own leavened products, and as he threw it into the fire, said to the individual who had been holding it: "My brothers think pessach that edicts are abolished with money. Not so. Edicts are abolished with *this.*"

Perceiving that his words left the man puzzled, he went on: "Did you recite the *piyyut* on *Shabbos HaGadol?*"

"Yes," he replied.

"Then do you remember what it says there in one of those rhymed hymns?" asked the tzaddik. "It says:

וְלָמָה אֲכִילַת חָמֵץ לְשֵׁשׁ שָׁעוֹת?
זֵכֶר לְחִפָּזוֹן הַשְּׁכִינָה לְהַעֲבִיר גְּזֵרוֹת רָעוֹת.

"That is to say:
By the sixth hour to burn *chametz*
Why are we bid?
To recall divine haste
Of edicts to be rid."

Sure enough, in the course of Pessach news reached Chernobyl that the nobleman had died, and his decrees were annulled.

... Neither Slumbers nor Sleeps

Reb Chaim Eleazar of Munkatsch used to tell the following story on Shushan Purim, the anniversary of the passing of Reb Koppel of Likova.

Reb Koppel, who made a comfortable living from his merchandising in spirits, was abundantly blessed with daughters to marry off. (One of them was later to be the mother of the celebrated Chozeh of Lublin.) One year as Pessach approached he had an ample stock of barrels stored in his cellar. They were worth a small fortune — he had no other income — and he was relying on them to provide him with the numerous dowries that he would soon need.

Now the local gentiles had learned from long experience that at this season Reb Koppel, being a God-fearing Jew, would be seeking a gentile neighbor to whom he could sell all his leaven products before Pessach, for the Torah of course would not allow them to remain his during the festival. They therefore agreed among themselves that none of them would buy his *chametz* from him. He would then have no alternative but to declare it all ownerless. They would then help themselves to this ownerless property undisturbed, and become its legal owners in fairly shared portions. Their conspiracy worked beautifully. From early in the morning of the eve of Pessach, Reb Koppel trudged about from the home of one gentile to the next in search for a customer for his stock of whiskey, only to discover that each one declined to cooperate for a different pretext. The time-limit for *biur chametz* arrived: beyond this hour he could neither own his worldly possessions nor sell them. He therefore loaded all his barrels on a wagon, took them to the riverside beyond the outskirts of the township, unloaded them there, and declared unreservedly: כָּל חֲמִירָא וַחֲמִיעָא דְּאִכָּא בִּרְשׁוּתִי ... לִבָּטֵל וְלֶהֱוֵי הֶפְקֵר כְּעַפְרָא דְּאַרְעָא — "All leaven or anything leavened which is in my possession ... shall be considered naught and ownerless as the dust of the earth."

Penniless and propertyless, he drove his empty wagon home with a happy heart, thanking the good Lord that he had been enabled to fulfill the mitzvah of ridding oneself of one's *chametz*, simply and literally: never again would his valuable stock be seen or be found. His family, true enough, were disturbed no end, but Reb Koppel himself enjoyed every precious minute of the festival. The day after Pessach, though they were certain that the gentiles from all around the countryside had no doubt drained the barrels dry, they thought that perhaps they had been left standing empty. Now that the family had been left destitute, the least they could do would be to salvage some meager pittance from the sale of the empty barrels.

They were greeted at the riverside by the taunts of a little group of gentiles: "You're a smart Jewboy, aren't you! What kind of a trick is this, saying that you're ridding yourself of all your whiskey, and at the same time posting a watchman with a sword in his hand to guard your barrels night and day throughout your festival?"

Reb Koppel and his family did not know what they were talking about — until they approached the barrels, and saw with their own eyes that not a drop was missing. Only then did they realize that a watchman had been sent them — from heaven.

As for the barrels of whiskey, now that they were

pessach ownerless Reb Koppel took legal possession of them, loaded them up on his wagon, and stacked them up one by one in their accustomed place in his cellar.

✥ A Lesson from the Garden of Eden

לִבּוּן
Making utensils kosher for Pessach

When he first founded the *Chabad* system of chassidic philosophy, Reb Shneur Zalman of Liadi gathered around him a select circle of gifted Talmudic scholars whom he instructed in the teachings of Chassidism. Each of the three study groups into which they were divided was called a *cheder*.

One of these disciples, who was noted both for his brilliance and for the profundity of his scholarship, had originally been one of the new movement's opponents, the *misnagdim*. However, soon after Reb Shneur Zalman's arrival at Liozna he took up the study of Chassidism with such assiduity that in due course he gained an impressive mastery of its teachings. He was the kind of man who would immerse himself in the contemplation of a certain philosophic concept for hours on end. The following incident, for example, took place one evening at the conclusion of the fast of the Tenth of Teves. Feeling somewhat weak, this scholar decided to retire early. He first walked across to the basin in his room in order to wash his hands in preparation for the *Shema* which is recited before retiring. Then he stood awhile near his window, meditating in tranquillity upon the endless mysteries of the divine Unity that are entwined in the words of the *Shema* — until he realized that it was dawn.

Now the first time this young man entered the tzaddik's study alone for the one-to-one encounter of souls known as *yechidus*, he asked: "Rebbe, what am I lacking?"

"You lack nothing," replied Reb Shneur Zalman, "for you are a God-fearing man and a scholar of repute. Only one thing: you still need to eliminate your *chametz*, the puffed-up leaven that represents the coarseness of a bloated ego; and in its stead you need to introduce *matzah*, the lowly food which symbolizes *bittul*, self-abnegation."

The rebbe then proceeded to cite a straightforward law פסח
that his listener was of course familiar with — though
until now he had understood it only at the level of its
plain and literal meaning.

"Now if say a kitchen utensil that had been used for
Pessach comes in contact with *chametz*," said the rebbe,
"the law lays down detailed regulations as to how to
render it once again kosher for use on Pessach. If, for example, it had been used on the fire, then it now needs to
be heated so intensely that either sparks shoot forth from
it, or it sheds its outer shell ..."

The young scholar came out of that room a changed
man.

As he told his friends: "The rebbe taught me one of
the laws of Pessach the way they study Torah in the
Heavenly Academy in the Garden of Eden. Through this
lesson he gave me the strength to bring this law — of
rendering a utensil kosher — to practical realization in
the conduct of my daily life."

And as he went off to his prayers he added: "Now,
thank God, I have something to ponder over while I'm
davenen."

◆§ Piety and Peace

The *rebbitzin* was busy and flustered in the kitchen מַצָּה
with all the last-minute bustle of preparations for the שְׁמוּרָה
Seder, so someone else answered the knock at the door. *Shemurah—*
Two of the local distributors of alms had come to the *the matzah*
home of Reb Avraham Yehoshua Heschel of Apta with a *which is*
request for *matzah* to give to the township's needy *especially*
families. Seeing a stack of *matzos* wrapped up in a *guarded*
napkin, the person who opened the door innocently gave *against*
them away and hurried back to work. Puffing and *leavening*
steaming, the *rebbitzin* came along soon after and saw
that the *matzos* had vanished. She was appalled: these
were none other than the select *matzos* which had been
baked that same day with devout intentions, and with all
manner of meticulous precautions against *chametz*, especially for the *Seder* table — the rebbe's own *shemurah
matzah!*

She discovered soon enough what had happened, but

pessach it was too late to undo. She felt her heart sag within her: how could she tell her husband of the mishap and cause him spiritual anguish? There was only one thing to do. She took a bundle of plain, ordinary *matzos*, deftly wrapped them up in the very same napkin, and pretended to know nothing of the whole affair. And that same evening, her husband conducted the *Seder* ceremony with the ordinary *matzos*.

Soon after the festival was over, the tzaddik — who is popularly known as the Ohev Yisrael, "the lover of his fellow Jew" — was visited by a couple seeking a divorce.

"What makes you want to divorce your wife?" he asked the husband.

The young man answered that his wife had refused his request to cook for him during Pessach in separate utensils without *shruyah* — for it is the custom of certain chassidim and pious folk to avoid allowing even baked *matzah* to come in contact with water throughout the festival.

Hearing this, the rebbe called for his *rebbitzin* and said: "Tell me the whole truth, please. What kind of *matzos* were placed before me at the *Seder* table?"

The *rebbitzin* was afraid to speak up, so she held her peace.

"Do tell me, please," he reassured her; "have no fear."

The *rebbitzin* mumbled the truth: "Ordinary *matzos* ..." And she proceeded to disclose the whole story.

The tzaddik now turned to the over-zealous young husband standing before him.

"Look here, my son," he said. "On the first night of *Pessach* I ate plain, ordinary *matzah* and pretended not to know nor sense the difference, in order that I should not be brought to expressing hard feelings or harsh words, God forbid — and you want to divorce your wife because of *shruyah*?!"

The tzaddik then restored harmony between them, and they left him in peace.

פסח

◆§ The Theory of Relativity

Every year when Pessach came around, Reb Yechezkel of Kozmir used to go to extraordinary lengths in avoiding the remotest contact with *chametz*. Before the festival he would go out in his carriage to a well outside the town in order to personally supervise the drawing of the water which was being prepared for the needs of all eight days of Pessach, and to keep an eye on the loading of the huge barrels onto wagons for the journey home. He would allow nothing which would be needed for Pessach to be placed on the floor. When it once happened that someone stood a bottle of wine on the floor he did not drink that wine, even though he had made a point of brushing out any possible crumbs between the floorboards with a feather. On another occasion — it was Yom Kippur — someone offered him a chair so that he could rest a little. He did not sit down until he had checked that there were no crumbs on it, for the same white *kittel* that he then wore he would be wearing six months later at the *Seder* table.

The wheat which was harvested for milling into flour for the baking of his *shemurah matzah* was kept in a sack, which was in turn placed in a cask. This cask was deposited for good measure in another sack, which was tied up and suspended by a rope from the ceiling. One year the time came to send the wheat off to be ground. Someone promptly took hold of the nearest knife — one of those used in the kitchen for *chametz* food throughout the year — and reached up to cut the rope.

"God forbid!" the tzaddik cried out. "Take a knife from the Pessach set!"

One of the bystanders thought that with the precautions evidenced by this *chumra* the tzaddik was going just a little too far.

Sensing this, Reb Yechezkel turned to him and said: "In defining the minimal quantity with which one transgresses the prohibition of *chametz* on Pessach the Sages say, חָמֵץ בְּפֶסַח בְּמַשֶּׁהוּ. Now in their plain meaning, these words of course indicate that this prohibition applies to even the minutest quantity — בְּמַשֶּׁהוּ. But listen

pessach again: the prohibition applies to each individual בְּמָה שֶׁהוּא — *according to what he is*. According to the spiritual level which each man attains, to that degree of stringency does the prohibition of *chametz* apply to him."

❃ ❃ ❃

When his grandson, Reb Yisrael of Modzhitz, would relate this incident, he used to add: "My grandfather's comment is in full harmony with a rule we know in the laws of impurity: בְּחוּלִין פּוֹסֵל רִאשׁוֹן, בִּתְרוּמָה — שֵׁנִי, בְּקָדָשִׁים — שְׁלִישִׁי, וּבְחַטָּאת — רְבִיעִי." (That is to say: in Temple times, objects which the Sages list in *rising* order of sanctity could be defiled respectively by contact with sources of impurity which are listed in *inverse* order of intensity. Thus the least sanctified objects, such as food which even a non-*kohen* may eat, could not be defiled unless by a source of the most intense impurity, and the *most* sanctified objects, such as certain sacrificial offerings, could be defiled by contact with even the slightest degree of impurity.)

৺১ Baked under Supervision

From the moment flour meets water, *matzah*-baking is always carried out with the utmost dispatch, so that the dough will be thrown into the oven before it gets a chance to leaven. When Reb Yechezkel of Kozmir used to bake his *shemurah matzah*, he was so insistent that no time be lost that after the kneading he would barely allow any time for rolling the dough flat. In fact the raw *matzos* were so thick that it was impossible to perforate them in the usual way with a spiked wheel. Instead, holes were roughly pricked with a wooden splinter, and the *matzos* were tossed at once into the oven where they would be safe against becoming *chametz*.

Fearing that this might not be true if the *matzos* were too thick, his chassidim once asked him: "Wouldn't it be better to make them thinner so that they'll be better baked through and through?"

"It is written," said the tzaddik, quoting the words which King David in his distress addressed to the

פסח נָפְלָה נָּא בְיַד ה׳ כִּי רַבִּים רַחֲמָיו וּבְיַד אָדָם אַל" ,prophet Gad
אֶפֹּלָה — 'Let us fall now into the hand of God for his mercies are great, and let me not fall into the hand of man.' Better to rush the *matzos* into the oven even though they are thick, and thus fall into the hand of God — for once they're in the oven they bake away alone under God's own supervision, because his mercies are great — rather than have a lot of people meddling with them."

⋖§ A Presumption of Integrity

Surrounded by his learned sons and a retinue of elder chassidim, Reb Avraham of Chechanov would go out to the countryside year by year to supervise a group of Jewish farmers as they reaped a quantity of wheat expressly for *matzas* mitzvah.

It was his custom to walk all the way home with one hand holding onto the side of the wagon which was piled high with sheaves, so that his attention should not be distracted even for a moment from his task of watching out against the remotest chance of contact with moisture. Once the wagon came to a deep puddle. In order to skirt it the tzaddik was forced to take his hand off the wagon briefly, while its huge wooden wheels splashed their way straight through the middle. When they came home he said nothing, and his chassidim proceeded as usual to thresh and winnow and sift, and then stored the wheat away in the granary. Not long before Pessach, however, the tzaddik instructed his son, Reb Yaakov of Yazov, to write to a certain individual in nearby Pultusk requesting him to send him wheat for *matzas* mitzvah.

His son was amazed: "But we have our own wheat, on which we've all worked so hard in preparing and supervising!"

His father answered: "That moment at which I took my hand off the wagon constitutes a distraction of my attention. That was הֶסַּח הַדַּעַת, and I can't call *matzah* made from that wheat *shemurah*."

The son was insistent: "And what makes you think that when that individual in Pultusk watched over his wheat *he* did not have even one moment's inattention?"

His father silenced him curtly: "If a Jew comes along

pessach and tells me that he has properly-supervised *shemurah matzah*, then I can rely utterly on the presumption that he is telling the truth. He is בְּחֶזְקַת כַּשְׁרוּת. But as for me, I *know* that my attention was distracted."

ᴈ Opportunity Knocks

A hungry wayfarer came to the door of Reb David of Lelov, but the tzaddik did not have as much as a mouthful of food to give him. He therefore took down the *shemurah* flour which had been carefully stored away and guarded in readiness for Pessach and handed it to his wife, asking her to cook some humble dish out of it for their guest.

Reb David later explained himself as follows: "The whole point of guarding *shemurah matzah* is to guarantee that there should be no possibility of its becoming *chametz*. In giving us this instruction the Torah writes: וּשְׁמַרְתֶּם אֶת הַמַּצּוֹת — 'And you shall guard the *matzos*.' Now this last word can also be vocalized הַמִּצְוֹת, the commandments; and the word חָמֵץ is also the root of the verb which means missing an opportunity through delay. Accordingly, the Sages understood this verse to be intimating an additional lesson: מִצְוָה הַבָּאָה לְיָדְךָ אַל תַּחֲמִיצֶנָּה — 'If the chance to perform a mitzvah presents itself, do not let it lapse.' Today the mitzvah of hospitality presented itself, and by not delaying the opportunity of fulfilling *it* I am fulfilling the commandment of 'guarding the *matzos*' just as the Sages said one should.

"As for what to eat on Pessach, I'm sure that by then the Almighty will bring some other *shemurah* flour my way."

ᴈ Facelift

זֵיעָה
שֶׁל מִצְוָה
Perspiring for a mitzvah

The preparations for Pessach in Lubavitch used to swing into momentum as early as the preceding summer.

The farm from which the wheat was harvested for the rebbe's *shemurah matzah* — the Cherbiner farm — was thirty *viorsts* away, on the road leading to Dubrovna. Its

[346]   *A Treasury of Chassidic Tales on the Festivals*

owner was a chassid called Reb Zalman, a man who was פסח
noble both in intellect and character. He was master of
the Babylonian Talmud and very much at home in the
Jerusalem Talmud and the *Turim*, and expert as well in
the *Zohar*, the writings of the Arizal and all the works on
Chabad philosophy that had appeared in print. In addition, he was a most generous philanthropist. Despite all
this he retained a simplicity of conduct which was
reflected even in the way he was addressed: Zalman
Cherbiner — Zalman from Cherbin.

The first step towards producing the flour for the rebbe's *matzah* was a thorough examination of all his fields
to see which would yield the finest grain. Then the day
for the harvest was chosen according to three criteria —
clear weather, a hot sun, and three dry days preceding it.
The wheat was reaped from twelve noon until two or
two-thirty in the afternoon.

When the grain was almost ripe Reb Zalman would
pay a visit to Lubavitch to organize matters. Since no one
could know in advance exactly which day would answer
to all the requirements, he would come with a number of
wagons in which he would take home the men who
would be doing the reaping. In fact most of the work was
done by Reb Zalman and his suntanned family, together
with other Jewish farmers who lived on his estate. But
for good measure these were always joined by several of
the full-time scholars studying in the *beis midrash* of the
rebbe, who saw to their modest requirements. These
learned young men were known by the unassuming
name of *zitzers*, which is Yiddish for "sitters." Together
with them Reb Zalman usually took home to the farm a
number of the chassidim from other parts of the country
who were visiting Lubavitch at that season. Sometimes
they would all wait together at Cherbin for a week or
more — until the ideal day arrived.

As for Reb Zalman, this was a time of threefold joy.
First of all was the fact that it was time to reap wheat
for the rebbe's *shemurah matzah*. Secondly, he gained on
the side the mitzvah of providing hospitality for so many
members of the convivial brotherhood. Thirdly, he
would soon be privileged to have as his guest the rebbe
himself, who always came in person to participate in the

Pessach / פסח [347]

pessach reaping. In his younger days the rebbe was Reb Shmuel of Lubavitch, the son of the author of *Tzemach Tzedek*, and after his passing, his son and successor, Reb Shalom Ber.

The day that Reb Zalman set out for home with his wagonloads of eager helpers, the whole township of Lubavitch was abuzz with dozens of earnest speculations as to the next day's weather. Day by day everyone watched out for the messenger from Cherbin who would bring word that this was indeed the day. And when the day did in fact arrive, the rebbe himself set out for Cherbin.

The reaping and threshing were carried out in a spirit of joyfulness — but tempered by a sober awareness that this was a responsible activity of great moment. Every man there wore his black hat, and a *gartl* around his waist, as he would for any solemn mitzvah or prayer service. Despite the heat everything was done energetically as if the workers were all accustomed to this kind of activity. Reb Zalman himself, even when he was advanced in years, would dart in and out among the workers, sickle in hand, as if he were the youngest man present. So light on his feet did he appear, in his black shoes and white socks, that it was as if the very soles of his feet experienced delight in their performance of the mitzvah just as his mind and heart did — as if they too were animated by the same joy ...

Some men reaped while others sang, and all around the sunny steppes their lusty song resounded. At a modest distance stood the local womenfolk in reverent awe, their toddlers prancing around their somber long skirts. They were all decked out in their *Shabbos* best, and in honor of the occasion wore their finest starched white kerchiefs.

As soon as the reaping and threshing were over, some of the men, ruddy and glistening, joined Reb Zalman in a quick plunge in the nearby river. He would then put on the black silk frockcoat which was normally reserved for *Shabbos*, and would proceed to lead that tired and happy little congregation in the afternoon *Minchah* prayers — but to the vigorous rhythms of the prayers of Simchas Torah. And in keeping with the festive mood of the day, it goes without saying that they omitted the penitential פסח verses of *Tachanun*. Reb Zalman reserved a special rollicking melody for the concluding passage of *Aleinu* and for the four verses which follow it, and after the concluding *Kaddish* the little *minyan* broke into a lively dance to the rhythm of his song. They danced with such abandon that their venerable host would even somersault over and over for sheer joy.

In a clearing between his fruit trees Reb Zalman's family always had prepared a long table covered with a rich assortment of dairy products for a festive *seudas mitzvah*. In the course of this afternoon meal the rebbe would deliver a *maamar*, expounding on some topic in chassidic thought. When night gathered over the little orchard they would recite the *Maariv* prayers together. The rebbe would retire to rest in a room that had been prepared for him, while his chassidim gathered again around the table in tranquil camaraderie, humming familiar melodies and exchanging favorite stories until daybreak.

After morning prayers the rebbe would return to Lubavitch. Reb Zalman would bring the chassidim there late in the afternoon, when they would take the sack of wheat for *shemurah* and suspend it from the ceiling in a room that had been set aside for the purpose.

※ ※ ※

Years passed, Zalman Cherbiner passed away, and the wheat for the rebbe's *shemurah* was now harvested from the farms in the Jewish colonies of the Kherson region. The estate chosen was usually that of a wealthy chassid called Reb Nachman Dulitzki, nicknamed Nechyevke, and the work was supervised by Reb Zvi Sanin. From 1897, when the *Tomchei Temimim* yeshivah was established in Lubavitch, all the stages of preparation of the *shemurah matzah* that follow the reaping and threshing were entrusted to the students of the yeshivah.

In the early years the wheat was ground in a watermill. Every possible *hiddur* was undertaken to ensure that the flour would be unquestionably dry and fit for making *shemurah*. For example, only new millstones were used. But when the local miller succumbed to the *pessach* pressures of progress and introduced mechanized rollers, the chassidim abandoned his newfangled equipment and set up their own handmill to grind flour for *shemurah*.

After sorting and examining the wheat three times over, the milling would start on Rosh Chodesh Adar, six weeks before Pessach. The senior students of the yeshivah were now given detailed instructions for each detail of the subsequent stages — the drawing of *mayim shelanu*, the water which was kept cool in readiness for the baking; the heating of the oven to ensure that it was kosher for baking *matzah*; and the kneading and baking of *matzas* mitzvah on the eve of Pessach.

Now it once happened that a prospective student arrived at the yeshivah — an intelligent and erudite young man — and the heads of the institution accepted him willingly. At the beginning of each academic year a list of all the newly-accepted students was drawn up. The rebbe's son and eventual successor — Reb Yosef Yitzchak Schneersohn — was the director of the yeshivah, and it was his task to present this list to his father, Reb Shalom Ber. Each name on the list was accompanied by a comment by the board of examiners, as well as by other confidential advisors.

The rebbe interested himself in every single student, but in particular in this young man, whose talents showed promise. There was only one problem: the confidential comment pointed out a certain lack of refinement in the young man's character, and this coarseness was reflected in his features.

Reb Shalom Ber pondered the report at length, read it over again, and said: "We should accept him, but we'll have to take him well in hand."

As soon as the list of students was approved — at about the middle of Cheshvan, soon after studies were resumed — the rebbe's son set up an individually tailored program for this young man. This program he brought to the attention of the two supervisors, one of whom was the *mashgiach* responsible for the Talmud studies — which were known in the yeshivah as *nigleh*, the revealed plane of the Torah — and the other of whom was the *mashgiach* in charge of the studies in the ethics and philosophy of *Chabad* Chassidism.

On Rosh Chodesh Teves that year the rebbe traveled פסח abroad. A couple of months later, when it was almost Rosh Chodesh Adar and time to begin sorting the wheat to be used in baking, he wrote to his son instructing him to entrust all the hard work in the preparation of the *shemurah* to that young man, and to write back reporting on how he performed his tasks.

The rebbe's son duly obeyed. For two solid weeks that student was kept busy — sorting wheat, setting up the handmill, grinding —in such a way that he would not detect that all his exertion came as the result of an order from above.

Baking time arrived, and again he found himself loaded with the heaviest work — so, too, during the baking of *matzas* mitzvah late in the morning of the eve of Pessach. In addition the rebbe's son had entrusted him the evening before with the task of searching for leaven in the long wooden synagogue, as well as *bedikas chametz* in the yeshivah building. This had kept him occupied until two or three in the morning — and at seven he had to be on duty at the bakery in order to stoke the heavy brick oven for just one more kashering in preparation for the last batch of *matzah*.

The tasks of *erev* Pessach were finally completed, and the hardworking young men had returned to their quarters after immersion in the *mikveh*, refreshed and neatly dressed in anticipation of the festival. The rebbe's son now called for this same young man. Firstly, he was to diligently study the chassidic discourse on the verse שֵׁשֶׁת יָמִים תֹּאכַל מַצּוֹת — "Six days you shall eat *matzos*" — which appears in the *Siddur* edited by Reb Shneur Zalman of Liadi. Having mastered that, he was to come to the rebbe's son at seven the next morning, the first day of Pessach, and before the daily prayers the rebbe's son would study this same *maamar* together with him, one to one — a singular privilege.

But even on *Seder* night he had no rest. For on Pessach the hundreds of students would all eat together at numbered tables set up in the big study hall — known as *der groysser zal* — where each student had his traditional regular seat. Each table was waited on by one of its students, and this young man found himself on duty until two in the morning, without a free moment for study.

At seven o'clock nevertheless he duly appeared as arranged, with all the scholarly and mystical intricacies of that discourse digested and ordered in his mind. For the whole intention of the exercise to which he had been subjected was to test to what extent the study of *Chassidus* mattered to him — and he passed his test with flying colors.

When the rebbe's son later reported on this whole episode to his father, Reb Shalom Ber said with visible satisfaction: "We have, thank God, planted a tree that will bear fruit. I hope that one day he will be able to benefit others. It will take a long time, but ultimately he will sprout forth with vigorous branches bearing fruit, whose seed will in turn yield further fruit."

It was the custom in Lubavitch that on the last afternoon of Pessach the students would invite the rebbe to grace their festive table with his presence. The meal would extend until late at night. The rebbe would deliver an erudite and inspirational discourse on a subject in chassidic thought, and the whole assemblage would later break forth in spontaneous dancing. When this occasion came around that year the rebbe motioned to his son and said: "Yosef Yitzchak! Just look what a powerful thing is *perspiring for a mitzvah!* Look — he has acquired different features altogether. His countenance is no longer coarse: he now has the face of a *mensch* ..."

הסדר
the seder

~§ The Colonel's Seder Night

Quite soon after the wedding the bride detected that something was amiss. The young couple had recently married in some obscure township in the Vilna district, and now she observed the oddest behavior in her husband. He would rise at midnight like some chassidic mystics do and lament the exile of the Divine Presence, while reciting the passages of *Tikkun Chatzos;* at dawn every day he would immerse in the *mikveh;* and he was fond of reading a certain book which he kept hidden under his pillow. The young girl reported these phenomena to her father, who strode straight into the bedroom to discover for himself what dread secret lay hidden under his son-in-law's pillow. The shock was greater than his worst nightmare: the book was *Toldos Yaakov Yosef,* the work of one of the leaders of "the Sect" — Reb Yaakov Yosef of Polonnoye, the disciple of the Baal Shem Tov! It could not be denied: his own son-in-law had become ensnared by the growing chassidic movement ...

By the time he found the young man he was a seething cauldron of wrath and abuse — all of which he poured forth over his son-in-law's head. But this left no impact whatever. He therefore tried another approach, and deployed instead all the arts of gentle persuasion in an effort to implore the young fellow to desist from his evil ways. The effect was the same. He now tackled the problem from a third direction, and demanded that the recalcitrant fellow give his bride a divorce. The young man would not cooperate: on the one hand he was bound to the chassidic movement with all his soul, and on the other, he did not want to divorce his wife.

THE SEDER

Helpless and frustrated, the father-in-law turned to his townsmen for advice as to how to rid himself of this embarrassment in the family. This threw the little town into turmoil, as one by one the local *misnagdim* vied with each other in advising their unfortunate friend. Some held that pressure should be applied to force the depraved young wretch to divorce his wife. Others pointed out that a divorce issued under duress would only lead the poor young woman into an endless labyrinth of legal disputes and rabbinic responsa as to whether it was in fact valid. The only way out, therefore, was to offer the husband such sums of money that he would agree to give the divorce of his own free will.

These consultations simmered away for so long that word of the episode eventually reached the ears of the squire who owned that region. This *paritz* was a retired military officer. When he heard that the whole uproar was sparked off by a book, he asked who its author was. He was told that this was an individual who misled his fellow Jews from the path of their traditional Law; his name was Yaakov Yosef HaKohen, from the town of Polonnoye. Hearing this, he asked at once to see the book, and there he was able to read for himself the title and the name of the author printed in Russian at the foot of the title page. He now summoned before him the parties to the dispute together with all their friends and relatives.

"The time has now come," he began, "to relate an incident which happened in my youth. Listen carefully, please.

"Many years ago, when I was serving as a colonel, I was encamped late one winter with my unit near Polonnoye. We received the order to move. The procedure for such occasions was a full parade before dawn at which the men were given their marching orders. At roll call, three soldiers were missing. So I ordered a few of their friends to go to the nearby town to locate them and bring them back. After a little while they returned, but with the weirdest report. They said that they had found the three soldiers in a certain house which was lit up by candles. At the table inside sat a venerable gentleman of impressive appearance. And our three missing soldiers

were standing there, speechless and motionless, as if they הסדר
were paralyzed. I, of course, couldn't believe such a
strange story, so I sent off a different squad to check up
on this report. But they repeated exactly the same story. I
decided to go and find out the truth for myself. I took a
few of my men with me, but as soon as I walked into the
room and saw that old man looking like an angel from
heaven sitting at the table deep in thought, I literally
shuddered from awe. And the missing soldiers, sure
enough, were standing there petrified in their places as if
they were nailed to the floor.

"I finally mustered the daring to disturb his sublime
meditation, and said: 'I see, sir, that you are a holy man.
You see, my soldiers here have to leave this district today
together with the whole unit. So could you please do
something so that they will be able to leave your house?'

"The old man answered: 'No doubt they have stolen
something. If you remove the stolen objects from their
pockets they will be able to leave.'

"We searched their pockets, and found that they were
full of silver vessels of all kinds. As soon as we took
them out two of the men began to walk away, but the
third was still stuck to the floor. His friends said: 'He
must have hidden something in his boot.' They were
right. We took out a small silver goblet, and then he too
walked away."

❊ ❊ ❊

Now all this had taken place on the first night of Pessach. When the *Seder* was over the family had all gone to
bed, leaving the head of the house — Reb Yaakov Yosef
himself — sitting at the table in holy meditation. The
door of the house had of course been left open, for this
night is *leil shimurim*, a night guarded against all harm.
The three soldiers had passed by, and seeing through the
windows that the whole household was asleep — apart
from the old man at the table, who seemed to be as good
as asleep — had walked straight in through the open door
and helped themselves to the *matzah* and remnants of
food which had been left on the table. They had then
stuffed the pockets of their greatcoats with silver utensils which had been taken out according to custom in

the honor of the *Seder*. And it was then that they had dis-
seder covered that they could not budge.

The retired colonel continued his story: "Now when I saw this miraculous thing I asked the holy man to give me two blessings. Firstly, children — for I was childless until then; secondly, long life. He obliged, and blessed me. Then I asked him to tell me when my days on earth would come to an end.

" 'The end of man is hidden and cannot be revealed,' he said. 'But listen: towards the end of your days an occasion will arise through which you will make my name known amongst Jews who did not know me.'

"The old rabbi's blessing has been fulfilled. The Almighty blessed me with children, and as you see I have been spared to a ripe old age.

"Now tell me, gentlemen," concluded the old squire, "is there any man amongst you who would still dare to say an evil word against a holy man like that? Is there anyone here who could see it as a sin that a young man should study a book written by a man of God? I am now ordering you to make peace between yourselves at once — and let no one say a harsh word to this young man here!"

After listening to his narration, all those present solemnly undertook to follow his instruction.

"It is now clear," the aged *paritz* added, "that my end is near, for I see that the last words of the holy man have at last been unfolded. Nevertheless I am pleased that I have been able to bring peace between you, thanks to the name of the holy man who now reposes in the Garden of Eden."

And indeed, a few months later the old man passed away and was laid to rest.

✑§ The Seder of Chaim the Porter

Looking back over the *Seder* he had just completed, Reb Levi Yitzchak of Berditchev noted with satisfaction that he had succeeded in suffusing each of its successive stages with the light of kabbalistic meditation — that he had indeed done justice to each of the mystical *kavanos* at their respective moments.

But at that moment a voice from heaven intimated to הַסֵּדֶר him: "Be not proud of the manner in which you conducted your *Seder*. In this town there lives a Jew called Chaim the Porter: his *Seder* is loftier than yours."

Reb Levi Yitzchak turned to address the chassidim who had completed their *Seder* at home and had come to observe how the tzaddik conducted the final stages of his *Seder*.

"Do any of you know Reb Chaim the Porter?" he asked.

One of them knew him, but did not know where he lived.

"If it were possible to call him here I would be most pleased," said the tzaddik.

The chassidim immediately fanned out over all the streets of Berditchev until they found his dilapidated cottage.

His wife opened the door gingerly and asked: "Why do you need my husband? He's in there snoring, dead drunk."

The chassidim ignored her, walked straight in, succeeded in waking him up, and just about hauled the burly fellow on their shoulders to the home of the tzaddik.

Reb Levi Yitzchak offered him a chair, and said: "My dear Reb Chaim! Did you recite *Avadim Hayinu* on *Shabbos HaGadol*?"

"Yes," blinked the porter.

"Did you search your cottage for *chametz* last night?" asked the tzaddik.

"Yes," said the simple fellow.

Reb Levi Yitzchak had one more question: "And did you conduct the *Seder* tonight?"

Flushed and flustered, the poor man unburdened himself: "Rebbe, I'll tell you the truth. I heard that a man's not allowed to drink vodka for eight days on end. So this morning I drank enough to last me for eight days. So of course I was sleepy, and I went to bed. When it was night-time my wife wakes me up and she starts nagging me. You know how. She starts saying like this: 'Chaim,' she says, 'why don't you make a *Seder* like all the other Jews?'

"So I said to her, I said: 'What do you want from me?

Pessach / פסח [357]

the seder I'm an ignoramus, and my father before me was an ignoramus. I haven't got a clue what it's all about. The only thing I know is this — that our fathers' fathers were in exile amongst the gypsies. But we've got a God, you see, who took us out of there and made us free. And now we're all in exile again. But God will bring us out again, for sure!' Then I saw that on the table there were *matzah* and wine and eggs, so I ate the *matzah* and the eggs, and I drank up the wine. And then I was so exhausted that I had to go back to sleep."

The tzaddik told the chassidim that they could now take the porter home.

After they had left he said: "Heaven was exceedingly pleased with this man's words, because he said them with all his heart, without any ulterior motives. His sincerity was unblemished — for he knows nothing more than what he said."

◆§ Adjust your Altimeter

Though he lived in abject poverty, Reb Shmuel of Karov — a chassid of the Chozeh of Lublin — decided that he would ask nothing from the hand of man, even if it would cost him his life: he would accept only whatever the Almighty roused the hearts of his brethren to give him of their own free will. He remained steadfast in his principle for quite some time, even when Pessach came near. He was distressed, to be sure, that he did not even have the wherewithal to buy a minimal *kazayis* of *matzah*, nor wine for the Four Cups of *Seder* night. But he breathed no word to a soul, trusting instead that the Almighty would no doubt find a way to raise him out of his anguish.

Now a short time before Pessach a wealthy chassid called Reb Shlomo of Kanskivli visited his rebbe, Reb Yaakov Yitzchak of Lublin, who was known as the Chozeh ("the Seer") because of his far-reaching vision. On his arrival the Chozeh asked him to send Reb Shmuel whatever a family needs for Pessach. Late in the afternoon of Pessach eve, sure enough, an overloaded wagon trundled along the dusty track to Reb Shmuel's derelict cottage. It was packed high with vessels and utensils of every kind, and food and drink and delicacies galore.

Reb Shmuel was so overwhelmed at the sight of this gift that he sat down at his *Seder* table in high spirits and with a happy heart. So intoxicating was his joy that the All-Merciful One had enabled him to remain faithful to his principle of never asking for help from a mortal intermediary, that he soared to dizzying spiritual heights. Indeed, as he performed the various *mitzvos* in the course of the evening, he had the sensation of flying through the very heavens. Never, so it seemed to him, had he been privileged to experience a *Seder* as lofty as this.

The next evening he lay down to rest just a little before the second *Seder* — but when he awoke he found that it was almost midnight. Now all his years Reb Shmuel had made a point of eating the *Afikoman* before midnight, on the second night as on the first. He now felt compelled therefore to hurry through the reading of the *Haggadah*, the meal and all, in order to be able to maintain this practice. Never, so it seemed to him, had he conducted a *Seder* as lowly as this; probably no one in the whole world had ever conducted one like it. In brief, he was humbled no end.

After Pessach he made the journey to his rebbe in Lublin. As soon as he walked in, the Chozeh greeted him and said: "Now let's see what kind of *Seder* Reb Shmuel conducted on the two nights of Pessach. The first night — lowly, very lowly. Flying in the sky ... What kind of business is this, flying in the sky? ... The second night — beautiful, very beautiful. There's no one in the whole world who can conduct a *Seder* as lofty as the one that Reb Shmuel conducted on the second night ..."

ৼ§ This Year — Free Men

For chassidim the *Seder* of their rebbe is always a cherished experience, a time to crowd around the rebbe's own table in awe and expectation, eyes and ears alert to absorb how the tzaddik explains and practices every ceremonial detail. What a yearly disappointment, then, for the chassidim of Reb Avraham of Sochatchov! For he would never permit his chassidim to be present during

the his *Seder,* and rarely would he allow one of the
haggadah venerable disciples to join him at the table. Once a
number of chassidim mustered the daring to ask the rebbe for the reason. In fact they were certain that they almost had the answer, for no doubt at this time the rebbe was granted a blissful measure of divine revelation that was far beyond their sensitivities; and if they could not share in the experience, then at least they would like to hear it described.

But the rebbe's explanation was different: "On *Seder* night every Jew has to feel that he is a free man — and no chassid standing in the presence of his rebbe can properly enjoy the taste of freedom."

הַהַגָּדָה

the haggadah

◆§ Dancing in the Dark

קַדֵּשׁ For the last thousand years the fifteen stages of the
Reciting *Seder* service have been introduced by the chanting of
Kiddush a rhyming mnemonic: קַדֵּשׁ וּרְחַץ — "Recite *Kiddush* and
at the wash hands" — and so on. According to time-honored
Seder custom, when schoolteachers prepare toddlers for the
table *Seder* they teach them to recite by heart a simple explanation of each item in homely Yiddish phrases. The first item, for example, which refers to the blessings to be pronounced over the first of the Four Cups of wine, runs like this: "*Kadesh* — When Father comes home from *shul* on Pessach eve he has to recite *Kiddush* straight away, so that the little children will not fall asleep, and will ask the Four Questions beginning *Mah Nishtanah*." Then, as the family reaches each successive stage of the ceremony on *Seder* night, the youngster who asks the Four Questions explains in his quaint singsong what is about to take place.

[360] *A Treasury of Chassidic Tales on the Festivals*

הההגדה

On the first *Seder* night one year at the home of the Shpoler Zeide, his young son announced — "*Kadesh*," and proceeded to explain: "When Father comes home from *shul* on Pessach eve he has to recite *Kiddush* straight away" — and at that point stopped short.

"Why don't you carry on?" his father asked him.

"That's all my teacher taught us," said the little boy.

His father thereupon told him that the explanation must be added — "so that the little children will not fall asleep, and will ask the Four Questions beginning *Mah Nishtanah*."

At the next day's midday meal the child's teacher was one of those invited to the rebbe's table.

"Why don't you teach the little ones the reason given in *Kadesh*," he asked, "as has been the custom since the distant past?"

"I thought that there was no need to go to such lengths with small children," the teacher answered, "especially since this is not really an important reason — for this requirement of making *Kiddush* early in the evening applies uniformly to everyone, even if there are no little ones in the house."

The Shpoler Zeide protested vigorously: "How dare you contend that this is not an important reason? Are you wiser than the schoolteachers of all the past generations? You simply don't begin to understand why our forefathers required children to be taught this way. Don't you ever take it into your head to diverge from the customs of our venerable forebears by following the dictates of your own reason!

"Listen now to the inner meaning of these words.

"These words — קַדֵּשׁ וּרְחַץ: 'Recite *Kiddush* and wash hands' —serve as an introduction to the entire *Seder*. Now in the *Zohar* it is written, 'Rabbi Chiyya opened his discourse and said: אֲנִי יְשֵׁנָה וְלִבִּי עֵר — אָמְרָה כְּנֶסֶת יִשְׂרָאֵל, אֲנִי יְשֵׁנָה בְּגָלוּתָא. The words in the *Song of Songs*, "I am asleep but my heart is awake," are the plaint of the entire House of Israel, which says: "I am asleep during the exile ... " ' We see then (continued the Shpoler Zeide) that during the exile Jews are as if asleep, bereft of the higher reaches of spiritual sensitivity, for they are afflicted and pursued. And this is the mystical truth that *the haggadah* explains why our forefathers instituted the custom that toddlers recite their introduction to the *Seder* — for it resembles the introductory teaching of Rabbi Chiyya in the *Zohar*. This, then, is what it all means.

"*When Father comes home from shul on Pessach eve* — that is to say: When our Father in heaven returns from *shul* after the evening prayers to his abode On High, having seen that even though every single Jew was exhausted from the heavy work of preparation for Pessach they all nevertheless came to *shul* for the evening prayers, and poured out their souls in the recitation of the thanksgiving psalms of *Hallel*, each man according to his level of worship; then, —

"*He has to recite* Kiddush *straight away* — that is to say: He straight away has to renew his betrothal of Israel, his *Kiddushin* with His forlorn bride, according to His promise brought to us through his prophet, Hosea: וְאֵרַשְׂתִּיךְ לִי לְעוֹלָם — 'And I shall betroth you to me forever.' And why must he redeem us from our exile straight away?

"*So that the little children will not fall asleep!* For out of their Father's love for them the People of Israel are sometimes referred to by His prophets as small children. Thus Amos asks: מִי יָקוּם יַעֲקֹב כִּי קָטֹן הוּא — 'How shall Yaakov stand? For he is small!' And so too the prophet Yirmeyahu: הֲבֵן יַקִּיר לִי אֶפְרַיִם אִם יֶלֶד שַׁעֲשׁוּעִים — 'Is not Ephraim my beloved son, a precious child?' So the Almighty *must* act quickly, lest these children fall too deeply into the slumber of exile, and despair (God forbid) of ever being redeemed. He *must* act quickly, —

"*So that they will ask the question:* Mah Nishtanah? *Why is this night different from all other nights? Why is the long dread night of this exile being prolonged more than all the dark exiles which we have already endured?*"

With these words the Shpoler Zeide broke out in tears. He threw his arms heavenward and cried out: "Father Above! Redeem us quickly from exile while we are still only in the kind of sleep in which our hearts remain awake! Do not let us fall into a deep slumber!"

Every man present was moved to tears, every mind was fired with thoughts of repentance; some men fell to the floor, and quietly sobbed.

But their rebbe soon roused them: "It is time to *glad-* den our Father just a little. Let us show him that his toddler can dance *even in the dark!*"

With a thump and a clap and a clicking of heels, the air sprang alive with a rollicking tune; and to the rhythm of the song of his chassidim all around, the tzaddik began his accustomed dance, describing sweeping circles of inspired ecstasy.

⋑ Stature is Self-Evident

Early in the *Seder* the middle one of the three *matzos* on the table is broken into two unequal parts, the larger being set aside for the *Afikoman* to be eaten later in the evening.

During the *Seder* at the table of Reb Menachem Mendel of Lubavitch in 1865, one of the guests took his own broken *matzah* in hand and examined it carefully in order to determine which was the bigger part to be put aside for *Afikoman*. The rebbe noticed this, and in his comment exploited the fact that in addition to its usual meaning — "big" — the word *gadol* is used in Torah circles as a noun to denote a scholar of outstanding stature. He said: "If a great one (a *gadol*) needs to be measured, then a small one is greater than he is ..."

His grandson, Reb Shalom Ber, then a child of five, was present and heard the comment. Years later, when he himself was rebbe, he once said: "From that day on I developed a distinct dislike for the kind of *gadol* who has to be *measured*."

⋑ As Prescribed by Physician

Among the chassidim of Reb Shneur Zalman of Liadi there were three doctors, one of whom, known as Reb Avraham Doctor, lived in Riga. He used to be sent the crumbs remaining from the rebbe's third *matzah* together with other morsels of food from the rebbe's *Seder* table — the vegetables used for *karpas* and *maror*. He would then grind them and add them to the medicines he made. It once happened that he was summoned to the bedside of a patient whose own doctors had *the haggadah* all despaired of saving. The chassid administered the powders which he himself had compounded and the patient recovered. A prominent physician who observed this phenomenon asked him how he had succeeded in curing this patient whose heart and lungs were barely functioning. The chassid saw that the questioner was an upright and honest man, so he told him his secret.

Years passed. In due course, when Reb Shneur Zalman of Liadi was imprisoned in Petersburg under capital sentence due to the slander of those who opposed his teachings, the file containing the record of his cross-examination was forwarded to the censor at Riga. There the same prominent physician was called upon to give evidence. He affirmed that the accused was an honorable man, and his testimony was treated with respect.

✑§ Illuminating This World

"יְמֵי חַיֶּיךָ" — הָעוֹלָם הַזֶּה
"The days of your life" refers to This World

In the *Haggadah* there is a passage in which the Sages explain that the words in the Torah, יְמֵי חַיֶּיךָ — "the days of your life" — refer to life in This World. When he arrived at this passage at the *Seder* table one year, Reb Yosef Yitzchak of Lubavitch recounted the following episode regarding his grandfather, Reb Shmuel of Lubavitch, who is known as *Maharash*.

Reb Shmuel once observed that his two small sons — Reb Zalman Aharon and Reb Shalom Ber, the latter his eventual successor — were playing under the trees near his summer study, and debating earnestly. They were too shy to tell him the subject under discussion, so their sister Devorah Leah explained it for them. It transpired that their teacher, Reb Shalom, had said that it is written in *Likkutei Torah* that there is an intrinsic difference in the character attributes of a Jew and of a gentile. Reb Shalom Ber, then a child of five, could not understand that there could be such a difference, despite the attempts of his older brother, Reb Zalman Aharon, to explain it to him.

Their father the rebbe thereupon called for Ben-Zion, his simple but pious attendant, and asked him: "Have you eaten today?"

"Yes," replied the *meshares*.

ההגדה

"Did you eat well?" the rebbe continued.

"What do you mean, 'well'? Thank God, I am satisfied," the attendant replied.

"And why did you eat?"

"In order to live."

"And why do you live?"

"So that I'll be a good Jew and do what the Almighty wants of me" — and the good man sighed.

"Please send me Ivan the coachman," said the rebbe. When the latter entered the rebbe asked him: "Have you eaten today?"

"Yes," replied the gentile.

"Did you eat well?" the rebbe asked.

"Yes," he replied.

"And why do you eat?"

"In order to live."

"And why do you live?"

"So that I'll be able to fill up with a mug of vodka and a mouthful of something good to go with it."

When they were left alone the rebbe said to his sons: "Look now at the difference between the natural life of this man — and of that."

❊ ❊ ❊

Having concluded his story, Reb Yosef Yitzchak resumed his exposition to those seated at his *Seder* table: "This is what is meant by the words of the Haggadah — יְמֵי חַיֶּיךָ הַיָּמִים, כָּל יְמֵי חַיֶּיךָ לְהָבִיא הַלֵּילוֹת. [In their plain meaning these words refer to the statement in the Torah that one is obligated to recall the story of the Exodus "all the days of your life." In one of its interpretations of these words the *Haggadah* says: " 'The days of your life' refers to the days; *'all* the days of your life' adds the nights."] The word לְהָבִיא (here translated 'adds') literally means 'to bring in.' What the Torah obliges us to do is to *bring life into our days* and to *bring life into our nights*. And to this interpretation the Sages add: יְמֵי חַיֶּיךָ הָעוֹלָם הַזֶּה — that we are required to bring life into our contacts with all the material things of This World, so that our 'This World' should be the world of a Torah-observant Jew."

Pessach / פסח [365]

the haggadah

◆§ For Whom the Bell Tolls

All the days of your life: "These words," says the *Haggadah*, "are intended to include (lit., 'to bring') the days of *Mashiach*." All the days of a man's life ought to be directed to bringing about the Messianic era *(Traditional)*.

לְהָבִיא לִימוֹת הַמָּשִׁיחַ
To bring the days of the Mashiach (Haggadah)

The Chozeh of Lublin had passed away, and the time came to apportion his worldly possessions. His silken *Shabbos* garments, his belt, and the clock that always hung on his wall — these fell to the lot of his son, Reb Yosef of Torchin. On his way home from Lublin such a heavy rain pelted down that his wagon could not struggle along any further, and he had to spend the night in the house of a certain Jew who lived in a nearby village. When the downpour finally stopped some days later the villager requested payment for the lodgings.

"I haven't got a solitary coin in my pocket," explained Reb Yosef, "but I do have a number of sacred possessions."

He opened up his sack and displayed his treasured inheritance on the table, inviting the villager to choose an object of the value required. The host asked his wife for advice, and she replied: "The clothes are of no use to us; neither is the belt. The clock, though, could be useful: every morning it'll tell us what time to milk the cow."

So they took the clock in settlement of the debt.

Years later another tzaddik passed through that village. This was Reb Yissachar Dov, the Sava Kaddisha of Radoshitz, and because it was very late he too spent the night at the house of the same couple — in fact, in the very room in which that clock hung. But he did not sleep a wink. Instead he danced and sang all the night through. In the morning his host asked him why he had not slept, and what had made him so joyful.

The tzaddik answered with a question: "Tell me, please, where does this clock come from?"

The villager explained that he had received it in lieu of payment from a man who had no money.

"As soon as I heard this clock tick," said the Sava

[366]   *A Treasury of Chassidic Tales on the Festivals*

Kaddisha, "I could tell that it had belonged to our **הההגדה** master, the tzaddik of Lublin. You see, every clock sounds the message to its owner that he is one hour nearer to his passing. Now this is, to be sure, an important message — but the fact is that its sound is melancholy. The clock of the Chozeh of Lublin is different. It ticks away exultantly, and tells those who listen that we are one hour nearer the coming of the *Mashiach* — so of course I was so happy I couldn't sleep, and I danced instead."

✥ Creating a Prayer

Reb Yissachar Dov of Belz once recounted an unusual   אֶחָד חָכָם
custom of Reb Zvi Elimelech of Dinov. Before begin-   *One wise*
ning his own *Seder*, this tzaddik used to do the rounds of   *son*
the cottages of the local townsfolk to see how they conducted their *Seder*. As he walked down the cobblestoned alleys of Dinov he could hear from all sides the voices of his simple brethren singing and reciting the narrative of the *Haggadah*. He once stopped still near the wooden shutters of one of the cottages and heard a voice reading aloud: כְּנֶגֶד אַרְבָּעָה בָנִים דִּבְּרָה תוֹרָה — אֶחָד חָכָם, וְאֶחָד רָשָׁע...—"The Torah speaks of four sons: one wise son, one wicked son, one simple son, and one who does not know how to ask questions." And every time the reader came to the word for "one" — אֶחָד — he would cry it out aloud with prolonged concentration, just as people do when they say *Shema Yisrael*.

Reb Zvi Elimelech was delighted, and commented later that this simple householder had made out of the Four Sons of the *Haggadah* — including even the wicked son — a sublime prayer, a prayer as sacred as *Shema Yisrael*.

✥ A Breath of Life

While reciting the *Haggadah* on *Seder* night, when   מַצָּה זוּ
Reb Levi Yitzchak of Berdichev came to the words   *This*
מַצָּה זוּ — "This *matzah*" — he was so swept up in the rap-   *matzah*
turous ecstasy of *dveikus* at the prospect of fulfilling the mitzvah of eating *matzah* that he literally fell off his chair onto the floor under the table, upturning the *Seder*

Pessach / פסח [367]

the haggadah

plate, *matzos* and all. By the time he came to, the table had been set afresh. As he put on the long white *kittel* which was now handed to him to replace the one which had just been stained with wine, he mouthed the beloved words with the visible delight of one who has fainted and now draws a deep breath of smelling salts: "Ah ... This *matzah!*"

⋙ Drink to your Health

אַרְבַּע כּוֹסוֹת
The Four Cups

Not long before Pessach a certain chassid fell ill with a certain disease which caused him to hemorrhage. On the one hand he desperately wanted to fulfill the mitzvah of drinking the Four Cups of wine on *Seder* night; at the same time, his health was in danger. While still troubled by this dilemma he was surprised to receive a bottle of wine which had been sent to him as a gift by Reb Avraham Mordechai of Ger. Attached was a note which simply quoted a brief Aramaic text from the Talmud: "בְּרֵישׁ כָּל מַרְעִין אֲנָא דָם, בְּרֵישׁ כָּל אַסְוָון אֲנָא חֲמַר — At the head of all maladies am I — blood; at the head of all remedies am I — wine."

The chassid was amazed to read this note, and more than pleased that his rebbe had resolved his doubt without having been asked. On *Seder* night he duly poured himself Four Cups, and was cured soon after.

⋙ Torn Between Two Loves

יוֹם טוֹב שֵׁנִי שֶׁל גָּלֻיּוֹת
The additional festive day of the Diaspora

The chassidim were perplexed. It was the second night of Pessach and they had all arrived at the *beis midrash* in high festive spirits; they were now expectantly waiting for their rebbe to lead them in the evening prayers. But when Reb Yitzchak Aizik of Zhidachov entered, they noted at once that he was wearing his weekday *tallis*. Besides, it was clear that his prayers were not fired by the kind of enthusiasm to which they were accustomed. After the silent recitation of *Shemoneh Esreh*, instead of proceeding at once with the exultant praises of *Hallel* he paused awhile — again giving cause for wonderment. The anxious silence was broken at last as the rebbe's voice broke forth as always in the joyful rhythms and grateful psalms of *Hallel.*

At the festive meal that followed, the tzaddik spoke to the chassidim who crowded around his long table: "During the *Maariv* prayers this evening I found myself utterly deprived of all spiritual sensitivity. Not only that, but they dressed me in the *tallis* that I normally wear only on weekdays. I could not understand what the Almighty had done to me — until it was revealed to me from Above that all this came about because I had decided to make the journey to *Eretz Yisrael* after Pessach and to settle there. The sanctity of the additional festive day of the Diaspora therefore applied to me no longer. And that is why the heightened sensitivity of *Yom-Tov* was taken away from me, and the *tallis* that came to hand was the weekday one. I then weighed which of the two situations was to be preferred, and concluded that it would be a pity to actively deprive myself of the sanctity of the Diaspora's additional day of *Yom-Tov*. I decided therefore not to go to *Eretz Yisrael*. The moment I made that decision, the spirituality of *Yom-Tov* was restored to me — and that is when I said *Hallel*."

The tzaddik then turned to his son and said: "Reb Eliyahu! Please put some wine on the table and we'll appease *Eretz Yisrael.*"

❈ ❈ ❈

And indeed, so ardent was his love for the sanctity of the additional festive days which are celebrated only in the Diaspora that he never settled in the Holy Land. But through all the days of his life, his eyes and his heart were drawn towards it. In Safed he had a synagogue built which in bygone years bore his name. He used to say that his prayers ascended heavenward through that spot. Indeed he once said that every day before the morning prayers he went out alone on a little excursion to *Eretz Yisrael* ...

On his table always was the charity box of the Fund of Rabbi Meir Baal HaNess, a foundation for the support of pious scholars who study Torah on the holy soil. And if while immersed in the mystical teachings of the *Zohar* he encountered a phrase whose light eluded him, he would rest his forehead on this cherished box, and whisper the

the haggadah words of the Talmud: אֲוִירָא דְאֶרֶץ יִשְׂרָאֵל מַחֲכִּים — "The very air of the Land of Israel makes one wise." The gates of illumination would be flung wide open, and his soul would be suffused with the light of the *Zohar*.

◆§ A Gift to Make Amends

One of the celebrated guests at the *Shabbos* table of Reb Yisrael, the Maggid of Koznitz, was Reb Yaakov Yitzchak of Pshischah.

In the course of the meal the Maggid turned to him, addressing him by the name by which he is best remembered, and whose meaning is "the holy Jew": "Yid HaKadosh! Perhaps you could tell me why it is that on the additional festival day which is peculiar to the Diaspora I experience a sensation of spirituality greater than that of the first day?"

In his reply the Yid HaKadosh made use of the metaphor beloved by the prophets, in which the Almighty is the husband, Israel is His bride, and exile is the estrangement which follows Israel's infidelity. And it will be recalled that the addition in the Diaspora of a second day to each of the three Pilgrim Festivals only came about in the wake of the dispersion of the House of Israel.

The reply of the Yid HaKadosh, then, was simple: "When a husband quarrels with his wife, and afterwards they make peace, their love is stronger than formerly."

The Maggid kissed him on his forehead and said: "You have revived me!"

◆§ The Way to a Man's Soul

חָמֵץ בְּפֶסַח
The prohibition of eating leaven on Pessach

The father was understandably distraught. His son had not only cast off the yoke of the commandments, but now wanted to apostatize, God forbid. He hastened to the home of Reb Avraham Yehoshua Heschel, the Ohev Yisrael of Apta, and begged him to do something so that the young man would relent while there was yet time.

The tzaddik replied: "If you know for a fact that your son has never eaten *chametz* on Pessach from the time that he became a freethinker, then it is possible to save

[370]   *A Treasury of Chassidic Tales on the Festivals*

him; if not — not. For two phrases appear in the Torah הַהַגָּדָה side by side: אֱלֹהֵי מַסֵּכָה לֹא תַעֲשֶׂה לָּךְ. אֶת חַג הַמַּצּוֹת תִּשְׁמֹר — 'You shall make yourself no molten gods. The feast of *matzos* shall you keep.'"

➳ Principled — but Polite

As an extra precaution on Pessach, some people refrain on principle from drinking any whiskey, even that which has been prepared especially for the festival. One such chassid was Reb Mordechai Schatz of Zaslav, a disciple of the Baal Shem Tov. One day during Pessach he had occasion to call on a certain renowned scholar who offered him whiskey. Reb Mordechai had to find an inoffensive way out of his predicament. So he said: "The *Zohar* refers to *matzah* as מֵיכְלָא דְאַסְוָתָא — 'the food which is a remedy'; and people who are taking medicine are not allowed to drink whiskey …"

➳ A Home Away from Home

A certain chassid from Lvov once inadvertently drank something on Pessach about which there was some doubt as to whether it contained an admixture of *chametz*. As soon as he realized what he had done he consulted Rabbi Yosef Shaul Natanson, and requested a course of penance to atone for his carelessness. This sage recommended that he take his request to Reb Yehoshua of Belz. When he arrived in Belz the tzaddik told him that the appropriate way for him to repent in this case was to make the journey to *Eretz Yisrael*. The chassid returned to Lvov and told the sage what the tzaddik had instructed him to do. Somewhat surprised, the sage wrote to Belz to ask for the textual authority on which this recommendation had been made.

Reb Yehoshua wrote back: "In the Book of *Lamentations* it is written, גָּלְתָה יְהוּדָה מֵעֹנִי — 'Judah was exiled because of affliction.' On this verse *Midrash Eichah* comments: 'Because they ate *chametz* on Pessach.' From this we may derive that the punishment for transgressing the prohibition of eating *chametz* on Pessach is going into exile. If so, should I tell him that he should exile himself from this country to another country in the Diaspora? Better that he should betake himself to *Eretz Yisrael!*"

◆§ Guiding the Hand of Providence

A certain conscientious *rav* was concerned lest he unwittingly mislead any of his townsmen when they turned to him for guidance in questions of the law relating to Pessach — the removal of *chametz*, and the like. He therefore journeyed to Radomsk to see Reb Shlomo, the celebrated author of *Tiferes Shlomo*, and handed the tzaddik a *kvitl* on which he had written out his request for a blessing for success in this matter.

"If you want a dependable *segulah* which will guard you against giving any such questionable replies," the tzaddik advised, "you should study through the entire section in the *Shulchan Aruch* which details the laws of Pessach, from beginning to end."

"But what is the connection?" the *rav* ventured to ask.

"It is well that you should know," the tzaddik explained, "that every law codified in the *Shulchan Aruch* petitions heaven that it be studied. If someone does not study a particular law, then heaven so arranges things that he will be compelled to study it — through making complex legal queries come his way, so that he will be forced to consult his books. My advice to you therefore is that before Pessach arrives you should study through all the laws of the festival that appear in the *Code of Jewish Law* — and then Providence will not bring unwanted queries your way."

שִׁיר הַשִּׁירִים
shir hashirim

The Song of Songs (Shir HaShirim) is read aloud in many synagogues on the Sabbath which falls on the Intermediate Days of Pessach (Shabbos Chol HaMoed Pessach).

↞§ Kiss of Life

In days gone by it was the custom of God-fearing householders on Friday afternoon to take their seats in the synagogue quite some time before sunset. Once in that haven they could savor a foretaste of *Shabbos* in tranquil anticipation. This was the time when fathers would listen to their young sons reciting the *Song of Songs*, the lyrical allegory in which King Solomon sings of the love between Israel and her Bridegroom.

On Friday afternoon the synagogue of Vloshchov was honored by the visit of Reb Yaakov Yitzchak, better known as the Yid HaKadosh ("the holy Jew") of Pshischah. The tzaddik looked around until he saw a certain little boy reading to his father. After listening for a few minutes he said: "*Nu, nu!* This little fellow reads *Shir HaShirim* rather like King Solomon did."

Those who heard this comment were awestruck — the more so when the tzaddik walked over to the singular child and kissed his head.

Years later, when this little boy had grown up to be the renowned Reb Shlomo of Radomsk, he recalled: "I felt the power of that kiss until I became *bar-mitzvah* and placed my *tefillin* on that very spot. It was then that I realized that the kiss of the Yid Hakadosh was just like putting on *tefillin*."

↞§ Unheard Melodies are Sweeter

Reb Yisrael Dov of Vilednick once set out with a group of his disciples to spend Rosh HaShanah with his rebbe, Reb Mordechai, the Maggid of Chernobyl. The

shir hashirim

evening before the solemn festival their wagon creaked to a halt outside an inn in a village not far from their destination. They climbed down, intending to enter and rest a little — but the tzaddik stood still as if bewitched, for near the door sat a beggar with an old violin, playing the most wistful of melodies. When they came to an end the tzaddik asked him to continue playing. The beggar agreed, but only on condition that his hearer buy him a little vodka. This arrangement was repeated several times over. The chassidim were growing impatient: they wanted to arrive at Chernobyl in time for the early morning *Selichos* prayers on the eve of Rosh HaShanah. Nothing, though, could be done. The tzaddik was wholly involved with his fiddler, and it was clear that they could not set out and leave him here alone.

At long last the beggar came to the end of his last melody. By the time they reached Chernobyl it was well past dawn and everyone in town had already completed the *Selichos* prayers — everyone, that is, except for the Maggid himself, who was waiting for them. As Reb Yisrael Dov and his travelling companions entered his *beis midrash*, the Maggid greeted his distinguished guest warmly, and the chassidim realized that he was not at all displeased with their delay. After each of them had also received his greeting of *Shalom* the Maggid addressed their teacher: "Yisrael Dov! I see that in the village you received from the beggar the entire secret of the *Song of Songs!*"

The chassidim now realized that their delay had not been in vain: there was more in the beggar's melodies than had met their ears.

✥ The Same Love

יִשָּׁקֵנִי
מִנְּשִׁיקוֹת פִּיהוּ
*He kisses me with the kisses of His mouth
(Song of Songs 1:2)*

Before the Baal Shem Tov became known as a tzaddik he worked as an assistant to a teacher of small children. One of his duties as a *bahelfer* was to escort the pupils to their *cheder* and back home again. And on the way home he would give each child a kiss — out of love of a fellow Jew.

In later years his disciple Reb Dov Ber, the Maggid of Mezritch, once said: "If only I could kiss the *Sefer* Torah with the same love that the Baal Shem Tov used to show a little child who had begun reciting his *aleph-beis!*"

שִׁיר הַשִּׁירִים

◆§ Sense of Smell

Reb Yaakov Yitzchak, the Chozeh of Lublin, who in earlier days had been a student in the yeshivah of Reb Shmelke of Nikolsburg, once revealed that when that tzaddik sat before his open volume of *Orach Chaim* and expounded its teachings on the proper daily conduct of a man in This World, he smelt the fragrance of the Garden of Eden. Reb Shmelke did not want this to be known. He therefore placed various sweet-smelling herbs on the table so that if any of the disciples discerned that other fragrance, they would conclude instead that it was simply the aroma of the herbs.

לְרֵיחַ שְׁמָנֶיךָ טוֹבִים

The fragrance of your fine oils (1:3)

◆§ Superior Merchandise

Reb Shmuel, the young son of Reb Menachem Mendel of Lubavitch, once sought to travel to Belz incognito. He therefore dispensed with the somber garb of the rabbinic scholar, and dressed as if he were a traveling merchant.

At sunset on Shabbos, when it was time for the mystic meal of *Seudah Shlishis*, he made his quiet way to the *beis midrash* of Reb Sar Shalom, and stood in an obscure corner. The tzaddik of Belz was blind in his old age, so as soon as he appeared at the door of the packed hall a passage would cleave open from the entrance to the head table, so that he could walk there in a straight line. On this occasion the tzaddik paused a moment as soon as he entered, and remarked that he smelt a beautiful fragrance. He then turned at once in the direction of the guest who was later to be revered as the rebbe Maharash of Lubavitch, and walked towards him, following the scent which had first captured his attention.

When he reached him he said: "Young man! From me one can't hide!" And he led him to a place of honor.

Some of the chassidim thought that because their rebbe was blind he had simply erred. Seeking to correct him they whispered to him: "Rebbe, this guest is a

Pessach / פסח [375]

shir hashirim

merchant!"

The Hebrew word they used for "merchant" was *socher*.

The tzaddik was quick to agree — but not quite as they expected, for in his reply he alluded to a hymn sung on Simchas Torah in praise of the Torah: כִּי טוֹב סַחְרָהּ מִכָּל סְחוֹרָה.

He simply said: "You are right. A *socher* he certainly is! — 'For the merchandise of the Torah is superior to all other merchandise ...'"

~§ A Debt of Gratitude

מָשְׁכֵנִי אַחֲרֶיךָ נָּרוּצָה
Draw me, we shall run after You (1:4)

When Reb Shmelke the son of Reb Moshe Leib of Sasov was still a young man he set out once for Mezhibuzh. There he wished to study at the feet of Reb Avraham Yehoshua Heschel, the Ohev Yisrael, who was later renowned as the *rav* of Apta. As soon as the *gabbai* informed the tzaddik that the son of Reb Moshe Leib had arrived, he was instructed to bring a chair next to that of the rebbe, to light extra candles in the suspended candelabrum, and to bring the tzaddik the coat which he usually wore only in honor of Rosh Chodesh. When the young guest was admitted to the rebbe's presence he was virtually embarrassed by the honor being shown him: the tzaddik approached him and extended a cordial welcome, and invited him to sit next to himself. He could hardly decline, so he carried out the wish of his illustrious host.

The tzaddik explained himself: "I am under obligation to show you respect because it was your father Reb Moshe Leib who brought me to the true service of God. Let me tell you how it all came about.

"I was once the *rav* of a small town called Kolbasov, where my life consisted of the uninterrupted study of the Torah. One day when I was sitting with my books I observed two men approaching my house. I saw at once that they were men of stature. But so intense was my thirst for increasing my knowledge of the Torah that I did not ask them who they were: I only greeted them, offered them a drop of vodka and some light refreshments, and returned to my books. They stayed on after they had

שִׁיר הַשִּׁירִים

partaken of what was on the table, and continued talking to each other. Their conversation of course distracted me a little from my studies, but since they were clearly no common folk I said nothing, and simply concentrated harder. I gained the impression that they were speaking of lofty matters, but I told myself: 'What's all that have to do with me? For this isn't *my* accustomed path in the service of the Creator.'

"Late in the afternoon it was time to go off to the synagogue for *Minchah* prayers and then for the *Maariv* service. I went, and they went too. They then asked me if there was a place to sleep. I certainly had no free space, but somehow we managed to find them a nook. When I rose at midnight for the lament of *Tikkun Chatzos* they rose too. We then continued as on the previous day: I sat and studied alone, and they resumed their discussion. At daybreak they took their leave and took to the road.

"Just before it was time for the morning prayers I spent a few quiet minutes on my veranda, reflecting over this strange visit. 'Whatever came over me?' I asked myself. 'Why didn't I ask them who they were and what brought them to my home?' I then recalled snippets of their conversation that I had overheard while I was studying. These were sublime thoughts indeed. Day by day more of their conversation came to mind. The ideas they spoke of were as sweet as honey, and enabled me to pray more earnestly. I regretted intensely my not having made their acquaintance.

"Two weeks later, likewise before my morning prayers, when I had just taken off my hat and was only wearing my *yarmulke*, I was again relaxing on the veranda deep in thought. Suddenly I saw a wagon trundling past with those same two men seated in it! I never go out of doors with my head covered only by a skullcap, but I was at once so overjoyed and overawed that I quite forgot that I wasn't wearing my hat. I ran after them to greet them with *Shalom*. They did return my greeting — but very coolly. They said they were in a hurry. I asked them what I could do for them; they said I could buy them some bagels. Forgetting everything, I ran down the street myself to buy them, and while running I saw that they had already resumed their journey. I called *shir hashirim* out towards my home, asking that someone should quickly bring me my hat and my *tallis* and *tefillin*. Then I ran after them, calling them to draw their reins. But they didn't want to stop, and the wagon lurched straight ahead. The horses galloped ahead, and there was I, drawn after them, running as fast as I could behind them, for quite a long distance — until at long last they had pity on me. They drew to a halt and waited till I caught up to them, and then helped me to climb up to join them.

"When we reached a nearby village we first stopped there to pray, and then they wanted to send me back home. 'No,' I said. 'Wherever you go, I shall go.' They refused my request, and said: 'Your place is not with us but in Lyzhansk, with the saintly Reb Elimelech. Make your way there, seek him out, and find peace in his protective shadow. We came here only in order to show you the path which you should follow.'

"I followed their advice and eventually found my place in the circle led by the tzaddik of Lyzhansk."

Reb Avraham Yehoshua Heschel now concluded his story: "Those two men were Reb Levi Yitzchak of Berditchev and Reb Moshe Leib of Sasov. And now, my dear Reb Shmelke, since your father was one of those who guided me to the chassidic path in the service of God, I am under obligation to show his sons every possible mark of respect."

Fanning a Spark

The learned Rabbi Yeshayahu of Pshedborz once asked his chassidic contemporary, Reb Yitzchak of Vorki: "What special power belonged to your rebbe Reb Simchah Bunem of Pshischah that makes you chassidim extol him so highly?"

Reb Yitzchak replied: "Reb Simchah Bunem could do to people what the prophet Eliyahu did. Elijah found Elisha ploughing with his oxen, like any peasant tilling the soil, and speaking to his oxen like peasants do. But when Eliyahu cast his mantle on him he was at once inspired. He slaughtered his oxen and burnt his plow, cooked the meat and gave it to the people. And when

Eliyahu asked him: 'What have I done to you?' — he answered: 'You have done a great deal to me.' He left his father and mother and was drawn after Eliyahu, and ran after him; it was quite impossible to separate him from his master until he had received from him a double portion of prophetic power. שִׁיר הַשִּׁירִים

"So too with Reb Simchah Bunem. When he took a man's hand in his own, that man was at once inspired: his heart was ignited with a burning love of his Maker; he was drawn vigorously toward the study of the Torah; he ran with all his might to master it out of sheer love — until he kissed its very letters, and was literally prepared to sacrifice his life, if called upon, for the sanctification of the Divine Name."

◆§ Digesting One's Books

Chassidim are always reminding themselves and each other that the mere study of sanctity will not suffice; even meditating on one's study will not suffice — unless one then toils to *realize* these studies in one's own life.

There was once a chassid — a businessman, not a professional scholar — whose coat pocket always held his well-thumbed copies of *Shaarei Orah* and *Shaar HaEmunah*, two abstruse works of *Chabad* philosophy written by Reb Dov Ber of Lubavitch. One day in about 1873 he entered the study of Reb Shmuel of Lubavitch for a *yechidus*. The rebbe asked him what time he was accustomed to rise in the morning, and what he did before he began his morning prayers. The chassid duly replied that in preparation for prayer he spent some time studying the classic works of Chassidism. He added that in the course of the prayers he also paused at appropriate stages to meditate on what he had studied, and that after his prayers he studied further. The rebbe then asked him how he approached the recitation of *Shema Yisrael* before he retired at night; the chassid replied that this too was accompanied by meditation on divine themes.

Said the rebbe: "So far you've been telling me about how you think about divinity. When do you think about *yourself*?"

The chassid heard, and fainted.

shir hashirim The rebbe remarked: "There's no need to faint — but there's plenty to *do*." And he ordered his attendant to help the chassid out of the room.

As the chassid was being led out, the rebbe quietly sang his own distinctive melody to the words of the *Song of Songs* in which Israel speaks of her rapturous desire to cleave to her Beloved: מָשְׁכֵנִי אַחֲרֶיךָ נָּרוּצָה — "Draw me; we shall run after You."

The rebbe's son, Reb Shalom Ber, was about the age of *bar-mitzvah* at the time, and the attendant called him to come and hear how his father sang that melody. In later years, when the lad himself became rebbe, he once expounded in terms of chassidic thought why his father had chosen to sing that plaintive melody at just that moment.

⋅§ In the Eye of the Beholder

שְׁחוֹרָה אֲנִי וְנָאוָה
Black am I, but beautiful (1:5)

Heartbroken, a woman appeared before Reb Yisrael, the Maggid of Koznitz, and wept bitterly: the husband of her youth had deserted her, saying that she was of homely appearance.

"Could there perhaps be some truth in that?" said the Maggid.

"Woe is me!" cried out the poor woman in anguish. "When we married, wasn't I beautiful in his eyes? Why then have I now become black?"

The Maggid heard her plaint, and cried out: "Master of the Universe! When Israel at Sinai accepted Your commandments without hesitation and declared נַעֲשֶׂה וְנִשְׁמָע — 'We shall do and we shall hear' — and You took them in marriage as Your bride, they were then beautiful in Your eyes, and You chose them from among all the nations. Why do You now (Heaven forfend!) reject us? O Rock of Israel: arise and save Israel!"

⋅§ The Mind is its Own Place

כְּשׁוֹשַׁנָּה בֵּין הַחוֹחִים
Like a rose among the thorns (2:2)

A tavern would seem to be a most unpromising place in which to serve one's Maker. So, at least, was the contention of the chassid who came to pour out his heart to Reb Aryeh Leib, the Shpoler Zeide, or Grandfather from Shpola. Since he earned his living by pouring drinks for all kinds of vulgar folk, and had no choice but to hear their coarse language and see their unseemly conduct, he was afraid that he might become coarsened by his contact with them. The Shpoler Zeide smiled and said: "It seems that you want to fulfill your function as a Jew by being given a sack full of gold dinars, being seated in a clean and splendid palace, dressed in silken garments with an impressive fur *shtreimel* on your head, with shelves on all sides filled with sacred volumes — and then you will be able to serve the Almighty with your prayer and study proceeding from a clear and pure mind. But you may take my word for it: if the Almighty wants individuals to serve Him without any distractions or obstacles — why, for that he's got hundreds of thousands and myriads of angels! The *real* delight that He finds in This World comes from those who are hedged in from all sides with obstacles and hardships, until it almost seems to them that they have been confined in a gutter — and despite this their minds cleave firmly to their Creator, and they anxiously yearn for the happy opportunity of one solitary moment when they'll be able at last to address just a few words to Him. This longing no angel can experience! Do not complain, therefore, regarding your livelihood. On the contrary, give thanks to Him for having given you the privilege of serving Him in this manner — to stand all day long in a place of impurity, and yet in your heart of hearts to cleave to the fount of sanctity!"

שיר
השירים

➢§ *Sweeter than Paradise*

From province to province and village to village the young Reb Yitzchak Aizik of Zhidachov wandered in self-imposed exile. He arrived in Zanz one day, and lodged in the humble household of Reb Chaim of Zanz. Since heavy snows prevented him from leaving he stayed there for about a week, which he utilized by immersing himself day and night in the study of the Torah in the *beis midrash* of his host.

One night the tzaddik left his home and heard the singsong of his guest proceeding from the House of Study as he strove to master and be illuminated by the

כִּי קוֹלֵךְ
עָרֵב
For your voice is sweet (2:14)

Pessach / פסח [381]

laws detailed in *Orach Chaim.* Rapt and motionless the tzaddik stood for over an hour outside the door, pressing his ear against it, listening to the sweetness of that music. And so bitter was the frost that night that the locks of his beard were covered with ice and frozen firm to the doorhandle.

Some hours later his family realized that the tzaddik was not at home. After a brief search they found him — bent over the doorhandle and listening to the sounds from within. When they called him to come home they realized that they would have to bring warm water to melt the icicles before he could join them.

On the way home he excused himself to his family, saying: "I heard the voice of the words of the living God, the voice of Torah studied for its own sake, proceeding from the *beis midrash.* The words of that man's study so stole my heart away that if at that moment the gates of the Garden of Eden had been opened before me and a voice had said, 'Enter within!' — I would not have left my place."

◆§ *A Bed of Bricks*

רְפִידָתוֹ זָהָב
Its bedding is of gold (3:10)

When Reb Yisrael, the Maggid of Koznitz, was a young man, he earned his livelihood as a resident tutor in a remote village household. On his arrival there he asked that no one should enter his room to make his bed: he would prefer to do this himself. After a long period someone happened to see his bed in his absence, and discovered that in place of a straw mattress he had laid out a layer of bricks. The family realized that their *melamed* must be a holy man. And as soon as the Maggid sensed that they were now regarding him more reverently than before, he fled.

◆§ *The Right Qualifications*

The bed of Reb Menachem Mendel of Rimanov was a perforated wooden frame with cords drawn across its length and breadth, after the style of the beds used by the Sages of the Talmud. One particular attendant was responsible for preparing it daily for the tzaddik, and he was not allowed to pass this task on to another.

In due course the household was joined by an individual who became known as Reb Zvi Meshares ("the Beadle"), the same who was eventually to succeed Reb Menachem Mendel. On his first arrival he was assigned a variety of menial tasks — stoking the oven, sweeping the house, and so on. He repeatedly asked the other servants to allow him to prepare the tzaddik's bed, but they were afraid of the tzaddik's reaction. One day however it so happened that the particular *shammes* who was meant to prepare the bed had to leave on some urgent business. He called Reb Zvi and explained that this time he had no choice but to ask him to make the tzaddik's bed ready for his midday nap. At the same time he warned him repeatedly not to alter any detail in the regular arrangement of the straw, the sheets and pillows, so that the tzaddik should not discern any difference. Reb Zvi was elated. He leapt to the task with joy and alacrity, thanking the Creator for having given him the privilege of performing this humble service for the tzaddik.

Reb Menachem Mendel sensed at once that something was different. When he rose he called for his *gabbai* and asked: "Who made my bed today?"

"No doubt the man who always does," replied the *gabbai*.

"Not so," the tzaddik insisted. "This was done by other hands."

They next summoned that *shammes*, who appeared before the tzaddik in fear and trembling.

"It's true," he confessed. "Today someone else did it. I was pressed for time so I had to pass on the task to that young man, Zvi."

"His secret is out!" said the tzaddik. "And from now on, please, my bed is to be prepared only by Zvi."

❁ ❁ ❁

The time came for Reb Menachem Mendel to leave This World. Some of his disciples wanted his son Reb Nasan Leib to succeed him as their rebbe, but he declined. In fact so determined was he in his refusal that he even left Rimanov in order to ease the way for the appointment of Reb Zvi in his stead.

shir hashirim

When his friends challenged his departure from the town which his late father had made famous he explained: "From the day after Reb Zvi's wedding I could see what was going to transpire — that he would succeed my father as rebbe. Listen here: this is the story.

"The morning after Reb Zvi's wedding I walked into the House of Study and saw the bridegroom sweeping it as always. I didn't like this at all, for a bridegroom of course is not allowed to perform menial work during his seven days of festivities. So I entered my father's study and said: 'Father, what do you say to this beadle of yours, Zvi, who is desecrating his seven-day festival by sweeping the *beis midrash*?'

"My father's reply surprised me: 'You have gladdened my heart with your good tidings,' he said, 'for I was anxiously wondering how I would be able to pray today if my beadle Zvi did not sweep out the *beis midrash* during these seven days. You see, he sweeps out all the forces of impurity and leaves the air of the *beis midrash* clear of them. What a great thing it is to pray in there after he has cleaned it! Thanks for the good news.'

"I understood at once that if Reb Zvi knew how to sweep out all the forces of impurity — the *chitzonim* — from the *beis midrash*, then he for sure would be the one to succeed my father. And for the same reason you too, my friends, ought to accept him as your rebbe."

✦§ A Whisper

וְרֵיחַ שַׂלְמוֹתַיִךְ
כְּרֵיחַ לְבָנוֹן
The fragrance of your garments is like the fragrance of Lebanon (4:11)

Reb Simchah Bunem of Pshischah once said of his rebbe Reb Yaakov Yitzchak, the Chozeh of Lublin: "The rebbe had chassidim who were greater than I am — but I knew him better than they did. Once when he was not home I entered his room, and I heard his clothes whispering of his sanctity."

✦§ Worse than I Am

אֲנִי יְשֵׁנָה
וְלִבִּי עֵר
I am asleep but my heart is awake (5:2)

The last will of Reb Aharon of Karlin, reprinted at the opening of *Beis Aharon*, contains the following words: "I know not if there is anyone worse than I am." Chassidim explain that he wrote this in the wake of a certain incident. He once lay down in the bed of his rebbe שִׁיר Reb Dov Ber, the Maggid of Mezritch, and slept for הַשִּׁירִים three whole days in the rapt state of *dveikus*. His companions of the Holy Brotherhood wished to rouse him. The Maggid did not allow them to do so.

"He is now putting on the *tefillin* of the Master of the Universe — תְּפִלִין דְּמָארֵי עָלְמָא," he said.

But because during that period of sustained ecstasy Reb Aharon refrained from performing the mitzvos, he wrote in his will the words which appear there.

◆§ The Prayer which Heaven Ignored

Reb Menachem Mendel of Rimanov had a distinctive way of going to sleep. On a table near his bed he would prepare the volumes which he was studying at the time. After five or ten minutes' sleep he would wake up and pour the water of *netilas yadayim* over his hands. His attendant, who sat near his bed, then took out the vessels, and the tzaddik would spend five or six minutes in the hasty study of one of his books. He would now lie down to sleep for a few minutes — and so on, for several hours, until midnight.

Now this attendant, who was a learned fellow, once got it into his head that the tzaddik obviously could not be doing any serious or profound study in these intermittent bursts. He therefore took note of which tractate of the *Gemara* the tzaddik was studying at the time, and took himself another copy of it to the adjoining room where he used to retire while the tzaddik was studying; here he listened, so that he could observe how earnestly he in fact dealt with it. He soon heard the tzaddik repeating the name of a certain *tanna* cited in the *Gemara*, several times over. He could not tell whether he did this out of a special fondness for that ancient Sage, or because of a difficulty he experienced in comprehending his quoted statement. While he was still pondering these two possibilities the tzaddik appeared in his room, showed him a seeming contradiction between two statements of the Sage cited, and returned to his study. The attendant investigated the statements and found that there was indeed a real problem involved. So despite the

Pessach / פסח [385]

shir hashirim many interruptions in his study, the tzaddik was able to delve into his subject profoundly.

❊ ❊ ❊

Midnight was always the time for Reb Menachem Mendel to gather the strength of a lion for the service of the Creator (as the Sages expressed it). For from that hour until the morning prayers he would start his day with vigorous study and tranquil meditation. Reb Chaim of Zanz said of him that each night at midnight a voice from heaven would call him: "Menachem, wake up!" But once he heard something different: "Reb Menachem, wake up!" He was so grieved that he should be thus addressed that he undertook fasts, and prayed that he be called simply by his name. The gates of heaven were barred before him, however, and his prayer was not accepted.

৶ Some Sleep Faster

Reb Chaim of Zanz, remembered as the author of *Divrei Chaim*, used to sleep for an exceedingly short time — and even that was not continuous. After a very brief snatch of sleep he would awaken in awe, wash his hands, speak inspired words regarding the service of the Creator, take another nap, and so on — the whole of his sleep amounting to about two-and-a-half hours.

Asked once how he managed to maintain his physical health with a regimen like this, he replied: "Sleeping, you see, is like studying. An ordinary scholar might take six hours, for argument's sake, to plow his way through the legal material set forth in a section of *Choshen Mishpat* together with the commentaries of *Sifsei Kohen* and the accompanying authorities; a scholar with a strong head might master it in two hours. I, thank God, have a strong head, and the amount of sleep that others do in six hours, I manage in two ... "

A certain prominent scholar once complained to Reb Chaim that he was unable to overcome his desire to sleep, and asked the tzaddik what *segulah* he used to enable himself to make do with so little sleep.

"If you can sleep — good for you," replied the tzaddik. שִׁיר
"As for me, though, there's something that doesn't *let* הַשִּׁירִים
me sleep ... "

◆§ The Sleep of the Just

In the days before Reb Yeshayahu of Krastir became known as a rebbe he once spent *Shabbos* as a guest of Reb Shmuel of Dorog, who a little earlier had received a letter which attacked the young guest bitterly. After the midday meal on *Shabbos* Reb Yeshayahu lay down on a bench for a nap. His host took the malicious letter in hand and sat down next to him. He read a line or two, gazed upon the face of the saintly young man — and shook his head. This he did repeatedly, each time shaking his head in disbelief.

When at length he finished the letter he said: "If a person can sleep like this, then it's all a lie."

◆§ In Another World

The following episode was recounted by Reb Yaakov נַפְשִׁי יָצְאָה
Kaidaner, the celebrated chassid of Reb Dov Ber of בְדַבְּרוֹ
Lubavitch, the son of Reb Shneur Zalman of Liadi.
My soul
departed
❊ ❊ ❊ *when he*
spoke (5:6)
I was once privileged to accompany the rebbe Reb
Dov Ber on his travels, and one morning we arrived at a certain town. The rebbe delivered a memorable discourse on a mystical subject in chassidic philosophy, and then we went to have breakfast. Immediately thereafter the rebbe's attendant came to me in great haste and said: "If you want to gaze upon the rebbe's face, now is the time!"

"I don't want to," I said, "because I know that the rebbe in his modesty dislikes such conduct."

The *meshares* assured me: "I promise you that the rebbe won't see you at all."

So I followed him to the rebbe's room. The attendant opened the door and then I saw the rebbe — standing in the middle of the room with no visible sign of motion, his face burning like a fiery brand, his eyes wide open.

Pessach / פסח [387]

shir hashirim   Being certain that he could see me I was afraid he might express his disapproval, so I stepped back. But the attendant took me by the lapel and said aloud: "There's nothing to fear. Right now he neither sees nor hears, because he is up there in higher worlds."

"How do you know that?" I asked. "After all, you're just an ordinary fellow, aren't you?"

"I'm not speaking from what I understand," he said, "but from my experience, because I've seen the rebbe in this state more than once or twice."

I looked closely upon that holy countenance and saw that even though his eyes were open the rebbe indeed neither saw, nor heard, and none of the physical senses were awake. From ten o'clock until three I stood there. Servants were going in and out all the time, but the rebbe stood motionless.

At three o'clock the attendant said to the wagon-driver: "Set the table, because the rebbe hasn't taken anything into his mouth all day."

When the wagon-driver had done this he brought a vessel filled with water and stood in front of the rebbe so that he could wash his hands in readiness for his meal. The rebbe however did not notice him.

"Wake him up so that he will wash his hands," urged the attendant.

But the wagon-driver was afraid to touch the rebbe.

"I don't care what happens to me," said the attendant, "I must wake him up."

He then took hold of the rebbe's sleeve and said: "Rebbe, would you please wash your hands?"

Instead of answering, the rebbe walked across from the middle of the room to the wall, and stood there as before. Since I could now no longer see his face I retired to my room.

The next day the attendant told me that the rebbe had remained standing there until four o'clock, when he had of his own accord walked over to the table and sat down to his meal in a spirit of elation.

The attendant had asked him: "Rebbe, would you be good enough to reveal to me the cause of your joy?"

And the rebbe had replied: "Such joy I have never experienced before, for my father the Baal HaTanya ap-

[388]   *A Treasury of Chassidic Tales on the Festivals*

peared to me as soon as I began expounding this morning. When I stood there in the middle of the room I repeated the discourse for my father and from its words he revealed some wondrous insights into mystical truths that are beyond the grasp of mortal intellect. And it is these new teachings that have granted me this joy."

שִׁיר הַשִּׁירִים

❧ Flashback

At a festive repast held in honor of Rosh Chodesh, Reb Yitzchak Aizik of Zhidachov once referred to an allegorical passage in the Midrash.

There is a verse in the *Song of Songs* which says: לֹא יָדַעְתִּי, נַפְשִׁי שָׂמַתְנִי, מַרְכְּבוֹת עַמִּי נָדִיב — "I did not know; my soul set me upon the chariots of my noble nation." What the tzaddik quoted was the comment of *Midrash Rabbah*, which understands this verse as reflecting the astonishment of Israel at her elevation to grandeur: "We may compare Israel to a king's daughter who was gathering sheaves with her companions. One day the king passed by and recognized her; he sent his friend to bring her and seat her with him in the carriage. Her astonished friends exclaimed: 'Yesterday she was gathering sheaves, and today she is sitting in the royal carriage!' She replied: 'Just as you are astonished at me, so too am I astonished. To me may this verse be applied: *I did not know; my soul set me upon the chariots of my noble nation* — for I marvel indeed at my elevation.'"

לֹא יָדַעְתִּי נַפְשִׁי
I did not know...
(6:12)

Having quoted this passage from the Midrash, Reb Yitzchak Aizik turned to his son Reb Eliyahu, and said: "A time will come when you will need to make use of this passage."

Standing behind the rebbe's chair at the time was a learned chassid called Reb Meir Shalom of Skoli, and he overheard the rebbe's remark to his son.

Years passed, and Reb Yitzchak Aizik's stay in this world came to an end. It was then that his son Reb Eliyahu, who in his father's lifetime had been exceedingly retiring, suddenly revealed his hidden gifts, and most of his father's chassidim now regarded him as a worthy successor. Reb Meir Shalom was one of the many who made the journey to Zhidachov to gaze upon the wonder

<small>shir hashirim</small> — that Reb Eliyahu should accept the position of rebbe. While he was standing in astonishment, and thinking, "Is this indeed the same Reb Eliyahu of a year ago?" — the young rebbe sensed his puzzlement, and turned to him with these words: "Just as you stand there astonished, so too am I astonished. To me indeed may the verse be applied: 'I did not know; my soul set me upon the chariots of my noble nation ... '"

The flashback of an instant opened the chassid's eyes to what the late rebbe had alluded to in his enigmatic words years earlier.

◆§ A Time and a Place

When I would find You outdoors I would kiss You: Even when occupied by affairs of the temporal world, outside the portals of the House of Study, I cleave to you *(Sforno).*

<small>אֶמְצָאֲךָ בַחוּץ
When I would find You outdoors (8:1)</small>

Reb Shmuel of Lubavitch used to demand of his chassidim that when they walked in the streets they engage their minds in sacred thoughts.

A peddler once asked him: "But how is that possible?"

"If it is possible to think all kinds of irrelevant thoughts while praying *Shemoneh Esreh,*" replied the rebbe, "then it is possible to think holy thoughts while out in the street ..."

From that day on that man's mind was free of extraneous thoughts while he was praying, and out in the street he occupied his mind with holy thoughts.

◆§ Protection through Piety

If she be a wall: If their merits will suffice to protect their generation *(Sforno).*

<small>אִם חוֹמָה הִיא
If she be a wall (8:9)</small>

Whenever Reb Yisrael of Ruzhin visited Lvov for medical treatment he called on the local *rav*, Rabbi Yaakov Meshullam Orenstein, the author of *Yeshuos Yaakov.* Though this sage was a *misnaged* who was known for his antipathy to chassidim and rebbes, he used to receive the tzaddik of Ruzhin with all due respect.

Once Reb Yisrael asked him: "What are the roofs in your town made of?" שיר השירים

"Iron," replied the *rav* curtly.

"Why iron?" asked the guest.

"In order to give protection from fire," was the reply.

"If so," said the tzaddik, "then they could have been made of tiles ... "

With that he took his leave and went on his way.

Bemused, the sage later remarked: "So this is the great luminary to whom the masses flock?!"

When this comment reached the ears of Reb Meir of Premishlan during a visit to Lvov he cried out excitedly: "The rebbe of Ruzhin was right! Just as a roof protects a house, so should a *rav* protect his city — but he should have the contrite and broken heart of a humble man, like a fragile tile, and not a heart as hard as iron!"

܄§ Vantage Point

Early in the pastoral career of Reb Yisrael Meir of Ger, before he moved there from Warsaw, his followers decided to build him a house with a spacious *beis midrash* nearby for his chassidim. His previous residence could simply not cope with the tens of thousands who thronged from afar to knock on his door. The tzaddik approved of the plan, and chose a site on the outskirts of Warsaw, at quite some distance from the Jewish neighborhoods. Some of his elder disciples thereupon pointed out to him that no Jews lived in that area, which was regarded as virtually beyond the city limits.

"And that is exactly why I chose that spot," answered the rebbe.

When the work of construction was over the tzaddik was visited by the learned *rav* of Warsaw, Rabbi Dov Beirish Meisels, who was no adherent of Chassidism.

"You no doubt have a reason for having moved out so far from us," ventured the guest.

The rebbe held his peace.

"I think I understand your reason," resumed the *rav*. "Your intention was to set up a fortress in order to protect our city, and this of course must be done outside *shir hashirim* the city limits. Besides, sometimes one has to fire from the fortress into the city itself ... "

The tzaddik smiled as if in concurrence.

לג בעומר
Lag Baomer

לג בעומר

✦§ Simple Arithmetic

Reb Zvi Hirsch of Zhidachov was once sitting at the table with his chassidim at a celebration in honor of Lag BaOmer, the anniversary of the passing of Rabbi Shimon bar (or: ben) Yochai. Among other things he pointed out a mystically meaningful equivalence based on the numerical value, or *gematria,* of the letters which respectively spell two phrases — one from a Friday evening hymn, the other the name of that sage.

The tzaddik, then, remarked to his disciples: "The phrase: יְדִיד נֶפֶשׁ אָב הָרַחֲמָן — 'Beloved of my soul, merciful Father' — is the numerical equivalent of רַבִּי שִׁמְעוֹן בֶּן יוֹחָאי, Rabbi Shimon the son of Yochai."

Now among those present sat a scholar, who began at once — as a conscientious *lamdan* perhaps should do — to mentally check the arithmetic of that assertion. And indeed he found an error of one, for the letters of the former phrase add up to 764, while the letters of the name add up to 765 ...

The tzaddik guessed at once what was bothering the scholar. He turned to him and said: "Come, now, *lamdan* that you are! Doesn't the Talmud always spell 'Yochai' without an *aleph* — יוֹחִי? So, you see, it all works out exactly!"

✦§ No Place for Deceit

It used to be the custom — before your time, perhaps — for the pious congregants of the towns and hamlets of Europe to go out to visit their local cemetery on Lag BaOmer. The excursion was always led by the members of the local voluntary burial society, who walked up and down the paths, taking careful note of which gravestones and fences needed attention. When they had completed their survey the members of the *Chevrah Kaddisha* were joined by their townsmen at a light meal of vodka, eggs and pastries; this would be waiting for them in a nearby house, or on tables set up in the open fields just outside the cemetery fence.

One township among many which observed this custom was Homil. The *rav* there was Reb Yitzchak Aizik, better known as Reb Aizel Homiler, the author of *Chanah Ariel* and a chassid of Reb Dov Ber of Lubavitch. When the townsfolk were ready to take up their places around the tables for the annual *seudah*, their custom was to send a carriage to bring their *rav* to join them. He would first visit the cemetery briefly, and then deliver a chassidic discourse at the table.

One Lag BaOmer, though, when he entered the cemetery he paused next to a certain tombstone. He read the inscription and stood awhile, lost in thought. Turning to the senior *shammes* of the burial society who accompanied him, he then said: "In the Heavenly Court they are demanding that this man explain where are all the wonderful traits that his tombstone speaks of!"

After a further pause he added: "Please go at once and bring me an ax."

Wielding the ax vigorously, the *shammes* utterly obliterated the inscription as he was instructed to do.

And as the *rav* joined the townsfolk who were waiting for him at the table he said: "I've just been doing a favor for a fellow Jew ... "

שבועות

shavuos

↦§ Words that Work

Reb Chanoch Henich of Alexander related that Reb Menachem Mendel of Kotsk once spent several months in Pshischah in order to study at the feet of Reb Simchah Bunem. He was so utterly penniless that he was dressed in tatters, but he was consistent in maintaining his principle of never requesting help from mortal man. One day he was approached by Reb Feivl of Gritza who told him that Tamar'l, the wealthy philanthropist from Warsaw, was due to visit Pshischah that day, and if he would simply call on her she would no doubt provide him with whatever he needed — for this was her custom.

The Kotsker heard and roared in disgust: "Money?! Pfui!"

Reb Feivl later testified that when he heard these two words from the mouth of the Kotsker, the desire for money aroused in him such violent disgust that for several weeks thereafter as soon as he heard the subject mentioned he would begin to vomit. Indeed it took him some months of effort until he was able to actually look at coins.

From this incident the tzaddik of Alexander derived a novel insight into a well-known Talmudic passage. The sages debate whether it was on the Wednesday or the Thursday before Shavuos that Moshe Rabbeinu commanded the Children of Israel to separate themselves from their wives. The two positions are expressed respectively as: בְּד׳ עָבִיד פְּרִישָׁה ("On the fourth day of the week he made the separation"), and בְּה׳ עָבִיד פְּרִישָׁה ("On the fifth day ... "). The term עָבִיד — "made the separation" — is puzzling; surely a more appropriate phrase would seem to be אָמַר לְהוּ מִצְוַת פְּרִישָׁה — "told them of the mitzvah of separation."

But, says the tzaddik of Alexander, what the Talmud is telling us here is that when Moshe Rabbeinu told the Children of Israel of the mitzvah of separation, they were no longer drawn to bodily desire, so that by his

שְׁלֹשֶׁת יְמֵי הַגְבָּלָה
The three days of separation before Shavuos

Shavuos / שבועות [399]

very words he in fact *made* the separation(עָבִיד פְּרִישָׁה) — just as Reb Menachem Mendel did for Reb Feivl in regard to the desire for money.

⋄§ Pity the Rebbe

עֶרֶב שָׁבוּעוֹת
The eve of Shavuos

Remember the dusty road that winds from Beshenkovitz to Lubavitch? Once a poor and humble *melamed* called Reb Peretz was trudging along that track all the way from Beshenkovitz to spend Shavuos with Reb Shmuel of Lubavitch, when the Rebbe, who happened to be riding by, noticed him in the distance.

Every time Reb Peretz came to Lubavitch, Reb Shmuel would show him marks of affectionate regard, for his grandfather had been a revered chassid of the rebbe's father, the author of *Tzemach Tzedek*. This time was no exception, for when Reb Peretz arrived, the *gabbai* in charge of proceedings did not intend to admit him for *yechidus*, since such a vast multitude of chassidim were already waiting in turn. Nevertheless, out of the blue, on the rebbe's orders, the *gabbai* called Reb Peretz to enter. Once inside he told the rebbe that he was like an empty vessel, utterly unworthy.

Said the rebbe: "In order to feel that, a person needs to develop awareness and some serious thinking. Tell me, do you recite *Psalms* with tears?"

"Yes," said the chassid.

"Then every day of your life," said the rebbe, "read two Psalms so earnestly that they bring you to tears."

Then he added: "But now you are setting out to receive the Torah — and that has to be done with joy!"

In later years Reb Peretz related that every year at Shavuos he recalled that *yechidus*, and saw the rebbe afresh; and he used to imagine what a degradation it must be for the rebbe to have to descend to This World from the loftiest levels of Gan Eden, just to see him.

⋄§ Varieties of Service

לֵיל שָׁבוּעוֹת
The night of Shavous

It is a widespread custom to mark the festival of the giving of the Torah by staying awake all night on Shavuos and reciting *Tikun Leil Shavuos*, which is made

[400]   *A Treasury of Chassidic Tales on the Festivals*

שבועות

up of selections from all the major sections of the Written and Oral Torah. Instead of doing this, a certain individual once spent that night sitting in the company of many other chassidim at the table of Reb Yisrael of Ruzhin.

A doubt crossed his mind: "But shouldn't I now be reading the *Tikkun*? And I'm certainly not fulfilling that obligation here."

The tzaddik read his thoughts and said: "The initials of תַּעֲרֹךְ לְפָנַי שֻׁלְחָן ('You set a table before me') are identical with the initials of תִּקּוּן לֵיל שָׁבוּעוֹת (*Tikkun Leil Shavuos*)."

~§ Which I Command You This Day

The day on which you stood before the Lord your God at Chorev (Sinai): In dread and awe, with trembling and quaking (Talmud, Tractate Berachos).

It was the eve of Shavuos, and Reb Shlomo Leib of Linchna was at the festive table with his chassidim — the kind of situation in which he would normally be expected to deliver some original Torah thoughts. (In Yiddish: *zogn* Torah — "saying Torah.") Instead he cited his rebbe, the Yid HaKadosh of Pshischah, as holding that on the eve of Shavuos, paradoxically, one does not "say Torah," because (as the Midrash teaches) דֶּרֶךְ אֶרֶץ קָדְמָה לְתוֹרָה — "Proper conduct (*derech eretz*) takes precedence over Torah" — and it would not be proper for a mortal to "say Torah" when on the morrow all are about to receive the Torah afresh.

Reb Shlomo Leib concluded by asking: "So what *does* one do this evening?"

And he answered his own question: "One prepares onself to receive the Torah 'with dread and awe, with trembling and quaking.'"

And as he said these words he was seized by an awesome shuddering. He then slumped on the table in such a state that his chassidim, terrified, carried him to his bed. At length, after resting awhile, he resumed his place at the table.

מתן תורה
THE GIVING OF THE TORAH

◆§ Two Requests

Just before Shavuos, Reb Baruch of Mezhibuzh left his home in Tulchin to pray at the holy resting-place of his grandfather the Baal Shem Tov, at Mezhibuzh. While in the township he did not call on his brother, Reb Moshe Chaim Ephraim of Sudylkov, who lived there at the time, but returned straight home.

Immediately after Shavuos he again came to pray at the graveside, but this time visited his brother. The latter thereupon asked him: "When you came to our grandfather's graveside before the festival why didn't you call on me? And why did you go there again straight after Yom-Tov?"

Reb Baruch explained: "I was told from Above that if I so desired I could receive the Torah on Shavuos with thunder and lightning, just as Moshe Rabbeinu received it at Sinai. So when I was at the graveside I asked our grandfather to intercede in heaven so that I be granted the strength to receive the Torah in this manner. I then returned, and indeed received the Torah on Shavuos with thunder and lightning. But now I see that I haven't the strength to bear that kind of revelation, so I asked our grandfather to intercede and have it taken away from me."

◆§ A Convincing Argument

> On the day of his wedding (Song of Songs): This alludes to the giving of the Torah (Talmud, Tractate Taanis).

Reb Moshe Yisrael, the *av beis din* of Reivitz and Klementov, once spent Shavuos as a guest of Reb Yissachar Dov, who was known by his contemporaries as the Sava Kaddisha ("the holy grandfather") of Radoshitz. מַתַּן תּוֹרָה

Being in a hurry to return home, he called on the tzaddik the morning after the festival in order to receive his blessings for the journey. When the tzaddik asked for the reason for his haste he explained that there was some urgent business awaiting him at home. The tzaddik thereupon wished him *Shalom*, and the *rav* went to his lodgings where he ate breakfast.

While he was still at the table the *shammes* of the tzaddik visited him, drew himself up a chair, and sent for two bottles of wine which he placed on the table in honor of his host. This was most surprising, because no *shammes* in history has ever been known to defer to even the most important-looking chassid.

"What's so special about today?" asked the *rav*.

The beadle replied: "When you left my rebbe's study he told me, 'Go and tell the *rav* of Reivitz that it's not the proper thing for the parents of the bridal couple — the *mechutanim* — to leave the place where the wedding was celebrated before the bride has been brought to *shul* (for the custom in those days was that on the first *Shabbos* after the wedding the bride would be led to the synagogue with pomp and ceremony). Now Shavuos, the season of the giving of the Torah, is the time of our marriage with the Torah. You remember, of course, what the Sages say on the words in *Shir HaShirim*, בְּיוֹם חֲתֻנָּתוֹ: 'On the day of his wedding.' This, they say, alludes to the giving of the Torah — זוּ מַתַּן תּוֹרָה. If so, then the *Shabbos* after Shavuos is the day when we have to lead the bride to *shul*. And since I heard from the mouth of the rebbe that you, sir, are a *mechutan*, I should like to drink *LeChaim* with you!"

Hearing an argument as convincing as this the *rav* decided to remain in Radoshitz for *Shabbos*. And when he entered the study of the Sava Kaddisha to receive his greeting, the tzaddik smiled and said: "It *is* proper for a *mechutan* to stay around for the *Shabbos* when the bride is brought to the synagogue!"

the Giving of the torah

◆§ A Pile of Dust

With him that is downtrodden and of a humble spirit (Isaiah): I dwell with the humble of heart. For as we see, the Almighty ignored all the hills and mountains and caused His Presence to dwell on Mount Sinai — yet Sinai did not wax proud! *(Talmud, Tractate Sotah)*

הַר סִינַי
Mount Sinai

Reb Avraham the son of the Maggid of Mezritch is known as the Malach — "the Angel." His grandson Reb David Moshe of Chortkov related that the Malach once visited his father-in-law, the learned Rabbi Feivish, in Kremenets. The whole town, led by their most honored scholars, turned out to gaze upon this man of God. As for the saintly guest himself, he did not as much as turn to face them. He simply stood looking through a window at a certain high mountain. Those who had assembled there longed to hear at least *some* Torah thought from his holy lips — but he remained in his place in earnest meditation.

Now among all those present there was a certain young man whose scholarship and distinguished lineage were equaled only by his conceit. He was as well a *misnaged*, and assumed that their guest, the pride of the chassidim, was not showing the assembled scholars the anticipated honor and reverence which were their due ...

This was too much for the young man to swallow.

"Esteemed sir," he began, "would you perhaps be so good as to explain why you are gazing so intently at that hill — which is, after all, only a pile of dust?"

"That is precisely what amazes me," replied the Malach. "How can a plain pile of dust blow itself up so mightily until it becomes a proud mountain? ... "

The arrogant young man had learned his lesson.

◆§ Leaning Tower

In an ill-advised moment, a certain sage who was no admirer of Reb Menachem Mendel of Kotsk sent him a message in which he claimed that his own stature was so

A Treasury of Chassidic Tales on the Festivals

towering that his apprehension of divinity soared up to the seventh heaven.

"Tell him," retorted the Kotsker, "that I am so *small* in stature that the seven heavens are brought down to me ..."

מַתַּן תּוֹרָה

~§ To the People, For the People

At first Reb Shlomo of Radomsk refused to undertake the burden of being rebbe. A week before Shavuos, when he saw that vast crowds of chassidim from all the surrounding towns had converged on his township in order to spend the season of the giving of the Torah in his company, he admonished them, and advised them brusquely to go home. He was no rebbe, he insisted, and would not admit them to his study. The next day he saw that not only had the chassidim ignored him: the crowds were growing by the hour. This was clearly a time for deeds, not words. He promptly left the multitude behind him in Radomsk, and drove off in his carriage to spend Shavuos with Reb Yechezkel of Kozmir.

מִן הָהָר אֶל הָעָם
From the mountain to the people
(Exodus 19:14)

Reb Yechezkel received him in amazement.

"What have you done here?" he asked. "Is it not unthinkable that a person should leave a community of our brethren like sheep without a shepherd, and flee from them? You recall that the Torah writes: וַיֵּרֶד מֹשֶׁה מִן הָהָר אֶל הָעָם — 'And Moshe descended from the mountain to his people.' Here *Rashi* comments: 'This verse teaches us that Moshe did not turn aside to his own affairs, but went only from the mountain to the people.' Now I ask you: what kinds of affairs and business interests did Moshe have in the wilderness? But this comment of *Rashi* is to be understood as follows. Our forefathers were all occupied at the time with preparing themselves spiritually for the divine revelation which would mark the giving of the Torah — each of them according to his own spiritual level. As for Moshe Rabbeinu, it goes without saying that in keeping with *his* level of sanctity he would have liked to prepare himself more thoroughly than them all. Yet despite this, Moshe Rabbeinu did not consider his own spiritual needs and aspirations; he neglected his own affairs, and directed all

Shavuos / שבועות [405]

THE GIVING OF THE TORAH his exertions toward the needs of Israel — 'from the mountain to the people.' So tell me, then, how could you desert your brethren in your district and run away here?"

Reb Shlomo had an answer: "But Moshe Rabbeinu was at least *near* Mount Sinai, so he wasn't so sorely in need of self-preparation. But I too want to be near Sinai!"

To this Reb Yechezkel gave no reply, and his guest remained with him for Shavuos.

Among chassidim the memory of that *Yom-Tov* is fondly recalled. Indeed the elders of that generation used to say that he who was not in Kozmir during that Shavuos has never tasted the flavor of Shavuos in his life. In synagogue on *Yom-Tov* morning Reb Yechezkel honored his guest with the singing of the praises of *Akdamus*, for Reb Shlomo was renowned for his melodious voice. And when he stood up on the dais surrounded by the choir of eighty voices, and his sweet tenor was borne aloft on the crest of their swirling harmonies, soaring supreme, — the fretted windows of the wooden synagogue quavered in their frames, and with them the awestruck worshipers.

⋆§ A Peak Yet Loftier

Rabbi Shimon Sofer, the learned *rav* of Cracow, once asked his chassidic contemporary, Reb Chaim of Zanz, to explain a curious point in his conduct. For when Rabbi Shimon's brother, Rabbi Avraham Shmuel Binyamin Wolf Sofer, the celebrated author of *Ksav Sofer*, had visited Zanz, Reb Chaim had greeted him with no more than the conventional marks of respect, whereas when Reb Menachem Mendel of Vizhnitz had visited, Reb Chaim had gone out to welcome him and had honored him in every way possible.

Reb Chaim duly explained: "You will have observed that the *Beis HaMikdash* was not built on Mount Sinai, on which the Torah was given, but on Mount Moriah. Why so? Simply: Moriah is the mountain on which the patriarch Yitzchak allowed himself to be bound in preparation for self-sacrifice on the altar of the love of heaven; and this is more loved by the Almighty than מתן תורה Mount Sinai, on which the Torah was given. True it is that your learned brother is Mount Sinai — but Reb Menachem Mendel is Mount Moriah."

◆§ An Ungenerous Thought

Before the reading of the Torah in the synagogue on the first day of Shavuos, Reb Chanoch Henich of Alisk once retired to his home to rest a little. Utilizing his absence, a group of chassidim stepped up to the *bimah* on which the Torah would soon be read, so that they would have a convenient vantage point near the rebbe when he read the hymn known as *Akdamus*. The tzaddik entered, and indicated that he would like them all to leave the dais — all, that is, apart from one simple fellow to whom the tzaddik motioned that he could remain in his place.

"We scholars study Torah so conscientiously throughout the year," thought one chassid, "and the rebbe doesn't let us stand next to him. Yet to that ignoramus he gives permission! Strange, strange indeed ..."

The thought did not linger, though, for within a moment the rebbe had begun to recite *Akdamus* with such fervor that the attention of that chassid hung on every holy word he uttered.

Now the custom in that community was that after prayers the chassidim would visit the homes of the rebbe's sons and relatives for *Kiddush* and light refreshments. This particular chassid was at the table of the rebbe's son-in-law, Reb Anshel Ashkenazi. When he looked up and saw the ignoramus from the *shul* now sitting opposite him at the table, the ungenerous thought of the morning asserted itself afresh.

And at that moment he heard Reb Anshel saying: "We learn in the Midrash that when Israel stood at Mount Sinai, all the sick and ailing were healed. And since my father-in-law is a tzaddik, his *bimah* partakes of the qualities of Mount Sinai. So because a certain person is in need of a cure, my father-in-law allowed him to stand up there on the *bimah* during the reading of the Torah."

the Giving of the torah

זַכָּאִין כַּד שְׁמַעְתּוּן
Pure when you heard (Akdamus)

❧ A Corner in the World Above

A hoary chassid once posed a question to his fellows who had trekked from all directions in order to spend Shavuos with Reb Shalom of Belz.

"Our journey here to Belz," he argued, "is costly in money, exertion, and time — but in the World Above the rebbe will no doubt be in a place that is loftier than us by far. So tell me: what do we gain by our arduous journey here?"

His listeners decided at once to enter the rebbe's study together and to put their plaint before him. This was no trifling matter. For in Belz the very thought of entering that study was charged with such awe that the door was neither locked, nor closed, nor guarded — and despite that no man even dared to enter unless summoned. On this morning though, the first day of Shavuos before prayers, that elder chassid led his whole deputation into the rebbe's room.

When they had unburdened themselves of the question which they had been unable to answer the tzaddik replied: "Not only is it true that if a person hears Torah thoughts from his rebbe, and studies them, and distills from them practical guidance in his service of the Creator, then he without a doubt retains his bond with his rebbe and remains in his company in the World Above; more than that, even if a person completely forgets his rebbe's words, but *while he heard them* he was spiritually aroused, he too has a connection with his rebbe. A hint of this we may find towards the end of today's hymn, *Akdamus*:

זַכָּאִין כַּד שְׁמַעְתּוּן שְׁבַח דָּא שִׁירָתָא
קְבִיעִין כֵּן תֶּהֱווֹן בְּהַנְהוּ חֲבוּרָתָא.

'Pure when you hear the praise of this melody,
Your places will be fixed in this company.'

"That is to say, even those who are pure only when they hear, — they too will remain in the brotherhood."

His words were a balm to their anxious souls, and they left his study for the House of Prayer in trusting equanimity.

~§ Reliving Sinai — מתן תורה

At any time the prayers of Reb Yitzchak Aizik of Zhidachov were electrified by the literal dread of his Maker. But when he read the Ten Commandments from the Torah on Shavuos, and on the two Sabbaths when that passage appears in the weekly portions of *Yisro* and *Vaeschanan*, the entire congregation stood in awe and trembling as they listened: his very soul seemed in danger of being consumed by the fire of his fervor.

חֹשֶׁךְ עָנָן וַעֲרָפֶל
Darkness, cloud and fog
(Deut. 4:11)

It once happened that on Shavuos he was chanting *Akdamus* in his accustomed manner, and while he was carried away in his ecstasy one of his elder disciples, Reb Koppel by name, became so swept up with the reading that he lost his vision; only at the end of the reading of the Torah did it return to him.

Alarmed, he reported this phenomenon to his rebbe, who explained that it had come about because the soul of the chassid had become bound with that of the rebbe. And just then they had been passing through the חֹשֶׁךְ עָנָן וַעֲרָפֶל — the "darkness, cloud and fog" — which had enveloped Mount Sinai, and about which they had read at that moment.

~§ Short and Sweet

The morning prayers of Shavuos were over, and the chassidim of Reb Chaim of Zanz — some of them quite well-to-do — assembled according to their custom in the rebbe's home to receive his greeting of *Gut Yom-Tov*, and to recite *Kiddush* with him over wine and refreshments. They had to wait a little, however, for the rebbe was still in the *beis midrash*, lingering over his morning devotions.

When at length he arrived, the aged tzaddik whose compassion for the needy has become proverbial greeted them as expected and took his place at the table. But instead of proceeding with *Kiddush* he surprised them all by the following: "When I was a young man I used to deliver a closely-argued and learned discourse in honor of Shavuos to an audience of scholars. But I'm an old

the ten commandments man now. I no longer have the strength needed for the vigorous give-and-take of a scholarly *pshetl* of that kind. So, instead, gentlemen, I shall deliver for your benefit an exceedingly brief *pshetl*. Here it is: I need one thousand reinish for a needy cause, and I will not recite *Kiddush* until you settle amongst yourselves how much each of you is going to bring me — in cash, immediately as *Yom-Tov* ends."

He then left the room, indicating that someone should let him know when everything was arranged. There was little choice in the matter. Four of the wealthier chassidim present promptly divided up the amount in agreed proportions, and the rebbe returned for *Kiddush* and handed out cake and *kugel*. And as soon as *Yom-Tov* had passed the rebbe was given the required sum, which he handed over to a certain pauper who had to marry off his daughter.

עשרת הדברות
the ten commandments

The Ten Commandments (Aseres HaDibros) forms a part of the selection from the Torah which is read in the synagogue on Shavuos.

◆§ The Roar of a Lion

אָנֹכִי
I am...
(Ex. 20:2)

At the festive midday meal one Shavuos, Reb Shalom of Belz asked the chassidim who were at his table to sing a certain hymn which extols Israel at the foot of Sinai: וּבָאוּ כוּלָם בִּבְרִית יַחַד, "נַעֲשֶׂה וְנִשְׁמַע" אָמְרוּ כְּאֶחָד, וּפָתְחוּ וְעָנוּ "ה' אֶחָד" — "Together they entered the covenant; like one man they declared: 'We shall do and we shall hear'; and then they proclaimed: 'God is one!'"

After they had sung this several times the tzaddik expounded: "As our Sages teach us, Israel at Sinai responded *Yes* when they heard each positive commandment, and *No* when they heard each negative command-

עֲשֶׂרֶת הַדִּבְּרוֹת — ment. But, as we further learn, the first two utterances were pronounced simultaneously — אָנֹכִי וְלֹא יִהְיֶה לְךָ — בְּדִבּוּר אֶחָד נֶאֶמְרוּ; that is, the positive commandment of faith in One God ('I am the Lord your God ... '), and the negative injunction prohibiting alien worship ('You shall have no other gods ... '). Our forefathers therefore did not know how to respond. After consideration they accordingly proclaimed: ה' אֶחָד — 'God is One!' — for this response signified their assent to both of these commandments alike."

And when the tzaddik uttered the words וּפָתְחוּ וְעָנוּ ה' אֶחָד — "they accordingly proclaimed: 'God is One!' " — his voice resounded like the roar of a lion, and his listeners fell to the floor in dread.

◆§ Pride and Punishment

In a village between Liozna and Vitebsk there lived a widow with her three children — a son who went to school at the *cheder* in a nearby town, and two daughters who helped their mother manage her inn. In the course of time the elder daughter married a young man who was learned and observant, but intolerably conceited.

לֹא יִהְיֶה לְךָ
You shall have no other gods
(Exodus 20:3)

One of the persistent callers at the tavern was the parish priest. This individual was fond of spending long hours in religious debates with the young scholar, even though the latter consistently defeated him in argument — and grew more conceited into the bargain. They were once observed in action by a small group of bypassing Torah scholars who advised the young man to desist from these dialogues; he scoffed at them. Even when the local priest later brought along two of his colleagues from neighboring parishes the young man still held his own. The local cleric was now so impressed that he saw to it that his parishioners showed his talented sparring partner the same degree of respect that he himself showed him.

At one of their meetings the priest told the young man that he had made favorable mention of his name when speaking to the bishop in Vitebsk, and the prelate had indicated his desire to meet with him. The priest pointed out further that if the young scholar would vanquish the

the ten commandments bishop in argument, he would be honored beyond imagination. At first the young man would not even listen to such a proposition, but after some further artful persuasion the priest finally secured his assent.

The bishop as promised received him most flatteringly, and proceeded forthwith to propose points of faith for debate. After being out-argued point by point, the bishop reported to his colleagues that this young man was an outstanding scholar and an expert in Jewish thought. Hearing this, one of the senior clerics present invited the young man to stay in Vitebsk for several days so that all the higher clergy there would be able to sharpen their wits in debate with him. The young man agreed and stayed on for several days as a guest in the episcopal mansion, while buying himself food at the local market. He could never have hoped for more honor than what was now shown him in generous measure from all sides, especially as it rose to a dizzying crescendo of compliments when the clerics all assembled to farewell him.

Arriving home the young man uttered no whisper of where he had been. He satisfied himself instead with the private recollection of the honeyed phrases which had been his very own.

After some weeks several prominent Torah scholars visited the inn in order to rest from their journey. Overhearing their learned discussion the over-confident young fellow plunged into the thick of it, bestowing his unasked opinions right and left.

One of the venerable company smiled at this and observed: "A young man should learn to listen to what his elders have to say, and to regard Torah scholars with respect."

The opinionated young man not only took offense at these words: a spark of hatred flared up in his heart toward these men who did not show him the honor he felt was his due.

Soon after, the bishop and his ecclesiastical entourage paid a pastoral visit to those parts in order to dedicate a newly-built church in a neighboring village. While calling on the nearby townships he reached the village where our young man lived. He visited the inn and conversed with him at length, and from that time on the villagers from all around showed the young man ever-increasing respect — which in turn accelerated the growth of his ever-increasng conceit. עֲשֶׂרֶת הַדִּבְּרוֹת

After the festival of Sukkos he suddenly left his home for a few weeks, returned as if in a daze, and after several days disappeared again. In due course his family received a letter in which he informed them that he was lodging in the midst of the pomp and panoply of the episcopal mansion, where honors were being heaped upon him from all sides. Moreover, the bishop himself had assured him that if he would join him he would make a great dignitary of him.

The family did not know what to make of this strange letter, until one day the little boy who went to school at the *cheder* came home and cried out the news at the top of his voice: "Velvel is living in the bishop's mansion! He wants to apostatize!"

The household was thrown into turmoil, with weeping and wailing on all sides. Immediately after the *Havdalah* ceremony had signified the close of *Shabbos*, they set out by wagon to Liozna, where they burst into the House of Study of Reb Shneur Zalman of Liadi and shrieked their desperate plaint: "Rebbe, help us! Velvel wants to apostatize!"

The worhipers in the *beis midrash* were alarmed at the sight of the sobbing widow and her hysterical daughter. As for the rebbe, he said simply: "I cannot help you. All I can do is to tell you a story that took place during my stay in Mezritch.

"In the winter of 1769, while I was in Mezritch, a young man from one of the nearby villages was overcome by a spirit of folly, and took it into his head to be baptized. He went along to the local priest who duly received him in his home and undertook to arrange everything. His father ran in alarm to the Maggid of Mezritch and cried out: 'Rebbe! Rescue my son from baptism!'

"The Maggid listened to the story of the brokenhearted father, and after some minutes of rapturous concentration began to expound the verse: נֶפֶשׁ כִּי תֶחֱטָא וּמָעֲלָה מַעַל בָּהּ — 'If a person should sin, and

Shavuos / שבועות [413]

the ten commandments commit a trespass against God' " — and at this point Reb Shneur Zalman of Liadi repeated that entire discourse as he had heard it from the mouth of his mentor, Reb Dov Ber of Mezritch.

He then resumed his account of the incident: "When the Maggid completed his exposition, he instructed ten of his disciples to remain awake all night and to recite *Psalms* without a break until dawn. I was one of that *minyan*. At midday the young man in question came to the *beis midrash* of the Maggid. None of the disciples asked him what had happened. He stayed in Mezritch for a few days, called on the rebbe, and went home to his father."

Reb Shneur Zalman had completed his story. He recited the Grace after Meals and retired to his study.

As soon as he had left the room his disciples chose a *minyan* from amongst themselves who were to spend the night praying from the Book of *Psalms*. The widow and her daughter went home, and soon after a young man suddenly appeared in the *beis midrash* with a knapsack over his shoulders. Seeing a group of people intently reciting *Tehillim* he sat down too, and as he joined them in their supplication, his earnest words were chastened by the bitter tears of a penitent. The disciples well knew who this young man must be, but no man breathed a query.

This episode took place during Chanukah. Every evening after lighting the candles the rebbe delivered a discourse, which was promptly repeated and reviewed by his chassidim and students until they had mastered it word for word. The young man spent the whole week of Chanukah in Liozna, and the following week, after speaking privately with the rebbe at *yechidus*, returned to his home. Within a few weeks he had moved with his whole family to another township, and in due course became a chassid worthy of the name.

◆§ To Nourish the Soul

In a village near Apta there lived a wealthy and respected scholar whose sons were all prominent and learned citizens like himself. When he was already an old man he once thought to himself: "The Almighty has עשרת blessed me with everything; besides that, I study the הדברות Torah and distribute charity. What is there left for me to do?" Accordingly, he decided that in order to attain spiritual perfection he would have to begin to fast. He started out by fasting one day a week. This however did not satisfy him — for what was one day's fast worth? So he fasted two days a week, and so on and on, until he was fasting from one *Shabbos* to the next. This went on for a long time.

Late one *Shabbos* afternoon after the *Minchah* prayers, when he was about to sit down to his last meal in preparation for his week-long ascetic exercise, he suddenly turned to his pious wife and said: "Listen to this. I've had enough of our faith. I want to go the priest and baptize."

The poor woman was alarmed.

"What's come over you?" she cried. "Are you out of your mind? Some evil spirit must be tormenting you! Here, eat your meal before the long fast, and you'll feel better."

He did as he was told, and again fasted the whole week as usual.

The next week, at exactly the same time, on *Shabbos* before sunset, the impure spirit again began to stir within him, and he repeated the same words of the previous week.

His wife was sorely shaken by what she heard. She wept in her distress, and pleaded with him: "What kind of talk is this? We are believing Jews, aren't we? How can we ever show our faces when you talk like this?"

He ranted on like one possessed, against God and his anointed, and insisted: "I don't want to be a Jew any more! I'm going to the priest to baptize!"

This was no joking matter. She fell to the floor in her anguish, and begged him to have pity on her, to calm down and eat his meal, and fast again as always.

In the morning she decided it was time to tell her sons what had happened. Their hearts fell within them, for throughout the entire week there was no sign nor symptom of his malady: he studied and prayed as usual. For good measure, though, they decided to be on the alert for

Shavuos / שבועות

the ten commandments the coming *Shabbos*. The third *Shabbos* came, and late in the afternoon, without uttering a word, he cast off his festive garb and put on his weekday clothes, and ran breathlessly to the house of the priest. His wife rushed out to call her sons, who chased after him and caught up with him just before he arrived there. They seized hold of him and brought him home against his will. He shouted and screamed, and all the way discharged volleys of abuse against the faith of his fathers. He only wanted to return at once to the house of the priest. His sons however bound him with rope and arranged watchmen to guard him closely. When *Shabbos* came to a close soon after they harnessed their horses and led their father by carriage to Apta, where they related the whole bizarre episode to Reb Avraham Yeshoshua Heschel, the Ohev Yisrael.

"Follow these instructions at once," said the tzaddik. "Make the journey back to your village, and do not give your father any food whatever. Even if he is extremely hungry and asks for food, take no notice, and do not give him even a spoonful of water. Even if he appears to you to be at the point of death, give him nothing at all until tomorrow evening. When at nightfall tomorrow you see three stars, you are to open his mouth with forceps, and pour a little bit of something inside in order to revive him. If you act thus, then with God's help everything will be in order."

The sons at once prepared for the journey home.

"Food, food!" the father cried out. "Something to eat! I'm starving!"

And in between these cries he hurled forth his blasphemy in all directions. The sons however obeyed the rebbe, and paid no attention. By morning he was so weak and famished that he no longer had the strength to shout. At this point his sons unbound the rope, but still gave him nothing to eat. In the afternoon it seemed that his life was ebbing, but even now they heeded the tzaddik's stern warning. Then as soon as it was dark enough for three stars to be seen, they forced his mouth open and fed him some fluid, and only with difficulty did he again show signs of life.

He recalled at once what had transpired and was overcome by shame. He wept bitterly: Why had God done this to him? In the meantime he was so weakened by this one-day fast that he lay ill for several weeks. After he had gradually recovered he set out to Apta to visit the tzaddik, and with tears in his eyes asked him why he had thus been punished.

עשרת הדברות

"Let me explain," said the tzaddik. "Food contains two kinds of strength — material and spiritual. The material one gives vitality to the body, the spiritual one gives vitality to the soul. When a person fasts, this vitality is cut off from both the body and the soul — except that if he is fasting לְשֵׁם שָׁמַיִם, *purely for the sake of a mitzvah*, then his fast still provides vitality for his soul — though not for his body. Only if a person has a body like that of Reb Elimelech of Lyzhansk, then his body too can be sustained by a spiritual fast. If, however, a person fasts for an ulterior motive, then this fast can nourish his body — *but not his soul!* And this is what happened with you. Your fasts were not undertaken for the sake of heaven, but only to swell your pride. So the life-force to your soul was cut off, and all you were missing was the baptismal waters of the priest.

"And now you can understand why I told your sons not to let you eat all day. What I wanted was that your fast should bring you to its properly intended aim. And by virtue of this I set aright all your fasts and elevated them. This explains why you became so weak, for on that day all of your fasts were concentrated and compounded. And from today on, you will no doubt act differently."

Then, as the tzaddik guided him along the humble path of repentance, the once-proud man became his devoted chassid, and illumined his life by the lamp of his teachings.

⋅§ Out of Love Alone

לֹא תִשָּׂא
You shall not take the name of the Lord, your God, in vain
(Exodus 20:7)

A childless man once brought succor to the Baal Shem Tov in an hour of need. The tzaddik was on his way to the Land of Israel at the time (though later forced by a series of misadventures to return from Constantinople), and at one point, when he was left quite without all

Shavuos / שבועות [417]

<small>the ten commandments</small> that he needed for the approaching festival of Pessach, this man provided for him with a generous hand. In the fullness of his gratitude the Baal Shem Tov thereupon swore that his benefactor's wife would bear a son.

At that moment he heard a heavenly voice declare that he had now forfeited his entire portion in the World to Come, because by this oath he had (as it were) obliged the Creator to upset the order of nature, for this man was congenitally sterile.

The tzaddik was filled with joy.

"Thank God!" he exclaimed. "From now on I will be able to serve my Maker in truth, with no ulterior motive — for I no longer have even the promised rewards of the World to Come."

And turning to his benefactor he said: "I did not know that from birth you cannot beget children. Nevertheless, let your heart not fall within you, for, if God so wills it, as I swore so will it be."

Again a heavenly voice came to his ears, this time assuring him that the spiritual bliss of the World to Come would indeed still be his. At that moment it was revealed to him from Above that this incident had been a test — to see whether he would be able to serve the Creator without any expectation of receiving a reward. And he had stood up to its challenge.

ఆ§ Fire Consumes Fire

<small>זָכוֹר
Remember the
Sabbath day
to keep it
holy
(Exodus 20:8)</small> It was late on Friday night, and Rabbi Yitzchak of Hamburg (the grandfather of Reb Naftali of Ropshitz) was sitting alone by candlelight, deep in thought over his books. So engrossed was he that for an instant he put his finger to the flame, wishing to flick the ash from the wick — quite forgetting that on *Shabbos* this may not be done. He realized at once what he had done, and quickly withdrew his hand. But throughout the following week he could find no peace. To think that such a mishap could befall him! His heart ached at the thought.

When he visited the local bathhouse the next Friday afternoon to immerse himself in the purifying waters of the *mikveh* someone's hand slipped, and Reb Yitzchak was scalded by a kettle of steaming water. Everyone

[418] *A Treasury of Chassidic Tales on the Festivals*

rushed to his side to see if they could soothe the pain — but Reb Yitzchak's mind was elsewhere, and he repeatedly breathed the words: אֵשׁ אוֹכְלָה אֵשׁ — "Fire consumes fire."

עשרת הדברות

And he later revealed to his friends that only then had he found peace of mind from his distress at having inadvertently touched the candle flame on the previous Friday night.

❃ ❃ ❃

It was concerning this scholar that the Baal Shem Tov once remarked that a spirit of divine inspiration rested upon him from the beginning of the month of penitence, the month of Elul, until the regional fair in the month of Cheshvan — for at that time the clamor of the busy merchants distracted him.

⋞ Shabbos is Different

A worthy traveler from the Land of Israel was the honored Friday night guest of Reb Baruch of Mezhibuzh. This guest was one of those who constantly lament the destruction of Zion and Jerusalem, and whose typical frame of mind is melancholy. In the course of the festive *Shabbos* meal Reb Baruch sang one of his favorite table hymns — כָּל מְקַדֵּשׁ שְׁבִיעִי — to its usual melody. Then he came to the words: אוֹהֲבֵי ה׳ הַמְחַכִּים בְּבִנְיַן אֲרִיאֵל — "Those who love God and who await the rebuilding of Ariel (Jerusalem)." At this point he looked across at the face of his guest and saw that he was sighing and mourning, exactly as he was accustomed to do on weekdays. Reb Baruch interrupted his singing, and rebuked his guest by sternly quoting to him the words of that very hymn: אוֹהֲבֵי ה׳ הַמְחַכִּים בְּבִנְיַן אֲרִיאֵל, בְּיוֹם הַשַּׁבָּת שִׂישׂוּ וְשִׂמְחוּ — "Those who love God and who await the rebuilding of Ariel, on *Shabbos* you shall rejoice and be happy!" And the tzaddik then resumed the singing of his *zemiros*.

Shavuos / שבועות

the ten commandments

⋄§ Blessings upon his Head

Thousands of chassidim used to crowd into the *beis midrash* of the Chozeh of Lublin, so that on occasion a window pane would be broken inadvertently. Whenever this happened on a *Shabbos* (when breaking an object is ordinarily forbidden), the tzaddik would remark: בְּרָכָה לְרֹאשׁ מַשְׁבִּיר. In its context, this verse from *Proverbs* simply means: "Blessings upon the head of him who sells produce." But since the root שבר also connotes breaking, the remark was understood to mean: "Blessings upon the head of him who breaks." After quoting these three words from *Proverbs*, he would add: "And let him pay tomorrow."

Reb Chaim Elazar of Munkatsch explained this as follows: "What the Chozeh had in mind was that according to the law, כָּל הַמְקַלְקְלִין פְּטוּרִין — those who cause damage on *Shabbos* are not normally liable to punishment. However, in order to clear the accidental offender's acounts altogether the Chozeh had showered blessings upon his head. Having now come out of the incident *with a profit*, the offender could no longer be regarded as simply one who caused damage; and accordingly, he now might well be answerable in the Heavenly Court for his inadvertent transgression of the laws of *Shabbos*. And this is why the Chozeh used to add: 'And let him pay tomorrow' — for since he was now involved in a financial loss, he certainly reverted to the category of those who cause damage (הַמְקַלְקְלִין), and are thereby not liable to punishment."

⋄§ A Man of Truth

One Friday night, Reb Aryeh Leib of Shpola shared a somber thought with his chassidim who sat all around his long table. He was deeply grieved, he told them, because it seemed to him that he had lit the *Shabbos* candles later than was permitted. The chassidim thereupon vied with each other in finding ways of putting their beloved rebbe's mind at ease. Some quoted the verse, לֹא יְאֻנֶּה לַצַּדִּיק כָּל אָוֶן — "No evil shall happen to

[420] *A Treasury of Chassidic Tales on the Festivals*

the righteous." Others quoted the Talmudic statement: עֲשֶׂרֶת הַדִּבְּרוֹת הַשְׁתָּא בְּהֶמְתָּן שֶׁל צַדִּיקִים אֵין הקב״ה מֵבִיא תַּקָּלָה עַל יָדָם; צַדִּיקִים עַצְמָם לֹא כָּל שֶׁכֵּן! — "The Holy One, Blessed Be He, does not allow a misadventure to happen even through an *animal* belonging to righteous men; how much more certainly so in the case of the righteous themselves!" And so they continued in turn.

At the far end of the table sat Reb Raphael of Bershad. He was known to be man of truth, a man who would not budge a hairsbreadth from the naked truth. When all his colleagues had said all they had to say, he spoke out in these words: "It is certain that our rebbe must now repent. For is the possibility of the desecration of *Shabbos* to be taken lightly?"

The Shpoler Zeide was well pleased with his words. He turned at once to the other chassidim at his table and rebuked them sharply: "Fools that you are! Had I heeded you I could have died without first repenting!"

⇜ The Heavens are Changing

When Reb Yisrael of Ruzhin was a little boy he once dug himself a small garden in which to play.

Seeing him busy at work, his elder brother Reb Avraham reminded him: "*Shabbos* will be starting soon!"

The child looked upwards and said: "You're right."

"And how do you know that?" asked his brother.

"Why," said the youngster, "can't you see how the heavens are changing?"

⇜ Measure for Measure

It was a strange complaint indeed that brought a certain man to Reb Shmuel Abba of Zichlin. Every Friday evening, when the time came to declare the sanctity of the *Shabbos* by reciting *Kiddush* over a goblet of wine, such a fearsome slumber overwhelmed him that it was impossible to rouse him until morning. The first time it happened, his family thought he had fainted. The local doctors and apothecaries were urgently summoned and used every artifice and medicament to bring him to — but

the ten commandments

nothing helped. Since then the same disconcerting story had repeated itself every Friday night without fail, and nothing could be done about it. Being thus deprived of the mitzvah of reciting the Friday evening *Kiddush* the man was deeply distressed, and he wept bitterly as he asked the tzaddik to help him.

"What can I do for you?" said the tzaddik. "You have desecrated the *Shabbos*; that is why — measure for measure — this misfortune has overtaken you, so that you are unable to sanctify the *Shabbos*."

This reply made the man weep even more bitterly. He protested that he knew nothing of such desecration; on the contrary, he was always punctilious in observing the *Shabbos* down to its finest detail. But the tzaddik merely repeated his earlier assertion, bid him farewell, and spoke no further.

Brokenhearted, the poor fellow made his way home. He told his family exactly what had befallen him in Zichlin. They of course were dumbfounded, for they knew how careful he was in the observance of the holy day.

At this point one of his grown sons spoke up: "Father, I am sure you will forgive me if I say that the words of the tzaddik of Zichlin are not unfounded; in fact he speaks from רוּחַ הַקֹּדֶשׁ, for the spirit of divine inspiration rests upon him."

He went on to recount an incident that had taken place. One *Shabbos*, in the middle of the night, his father had woken up with an intense thirst. As he made his way in the pitch darkness from his bed to the jug of drinking water he quite forgot that it was *Shabbos*, and struck a match so that he could light his way with a candle. After drinking he extinguished the candle and went back to sleep. In the morning he had no recollection of this whatever. The son had seen what had happened, but in order not to shame his father had decided not to mention it for the transgression was obviously done unwittingly. Now however that the rebbe had made his extraordinary statement he felt it his duty to reveal the incident, in the hope that a remedy might thereby be found for his father's ailment.

No sooner had the father heard these words than he

turned around and set out again for Zichlin.

When he told the rebbe what his son had said, the tzaddik said: "Your son is right. That is exactly what happened. Now is it not inconceivable that a Jew should completely forget the sanctity of *Shabbos*? For our Sages teach us that זָכוֹר וְשָׁמוֹר בְּדִבּוּר אֶחָד נֶאֶמְרוּ — the divine commandments זָכוֹר (*'Remember* the Sabbath day') and שָׁמוֹר (*'Observe* the Sabbath day') were uttered simultaneously. We are further taught that זָכוֹר implies remembering the Sabbath day in *words*, that is, by reciting *Kiddush*; while שָׁמוֹר implies observing the day in one's *heart*, that is, the obligation to keep one's mind undistracted from the thought of *Shabbos* throughout the day. Since your attention in fact forsook the sanctity of *Shabbos*, *Shabbos* is now claiming its own, measure for measure."

The man was quite broken. He begged the tzaddik to prescribe him some means of penance for his transgression, and to cure him as well from his strange malady.

"There is no cure for you," said the tzaddik, "except for this: that if you are put to a test in the observance of *Shabbos*, and you withstand it, then *Shabbos* will be appeased after having been put to shame, and the Almighty will save you from misfortune."

Somewhat relieved, the man returned to his house, telling himself on the way that he would stand firmly in the face of any test to which he would be put; besides, it was clear that he would thus finally be saved from his weekly heartache.

Now this man earned his livelihood by working a mill which he leased from a local nobleman. Six days only he worked. On the seventh his millstones stood idle and silent, for he did not seek any legal contrivance whereby through a weekly contract of sale to a gentile he might find some means of having his mill operate on the Day of Rest. One day the nobleman's messenger summoned him. The gentile explained that he now planned to increase the size of the mill. The costs would be so great that he would no longer be able to tolerate a situation in which the mill worked only six days a week — for in addition to the annual rent he received a percentage of each day's proceeds. He therefore demanded that the mill *the ten commandments* work on *Shabbos* too.

The miller of course recalled at once what the tzaddik had told him during his last visit to Zichlin. He replied without hesitation that on no account would he ever agree to work on *Shabbos*.

The nobleman did not despair so readily: "Don't you Jews have ways and means of arranging things in such a way that through a contract of sale or whatever you will be able to rest on your Sabbath, yet I won't lose? Why should you be so unbending?"

The miller simply repeated his outright refusal. The owner of the mill thereupon gave him two months to decide — either to have the mill work on *Shabbos*, or to lose his lease on it. When the time elapsed the owner sent his messenger for an answer, which of course had not changed in the slightest. At whatever cost, the miller affirmed, he would never agree to the proposal. The owner evicted him from the premises forthwith, and the poor man's household was so bare and penniless thereafter that he had no bread for the little ones. To make things worse, he himself fell ill. Heartsore and ailing, he set out for Zichlin and poured out his woes to the rebbe.

"Be assured," said the tzaddik, "that your cure and your solution will reach you together. You have withstood your test, and *Shabbos* has been appeased of its disgrace. Within a short time your illness will leave you, and your livelihood will be restored to you, for the owner of the mill will ask you to take it over again."

The miller went home certain in his belief that the rebbe's blessing would no doubt be fulfilled.

In the meantime the gentile had greatly expanded the mill and had leased it to someone on the express condition that it would be worked on *Shabbos*. But day by day the most unexpected accidents were causing all kinds of damage to the mill. The circumstances were so unusual that the owner came to the conclusion that he was now being punished for having deprived his earlier tenant of his hard-earned livelihood. And so it was that when the poor fellow finally limped his way home from Zichlin the nobleman sent him a message: his new leaseholder had brought him no success whatever; on the contrary, the most surprising things were going wrong with the mill; and would he please come back and renew his lease as in happier days.

"But what about my *Shabbos*?" asked the little Jew.

"Don't worry," said the gentile, "I'll never again say a single word on that subject. After all the funny things that have popped up lately in my mill, I can see that God is with you. Do as you see fit!"

Back in his old mill, the man soon found that his livelihood and his health were restored to him together, exactly as the tzaddik of Zichlin had assured him.

עשרת הדברות

~§ Learning to Perceive Creation

During the period when Reb Yitzchak of Vorki was a disciple of Reb Simchah Bunem of Pshischah, he once set out on a journey in order to meet with Reb Mordechai of Chernobyl.

On his return to Pshischah, his colleague Reb Menachem Mendel of Kotsk asked him: "Well, what did you see over there in Chernobyl?"

"Why, I saw the Baal Shem Tov's table," said Reb Yitzchak.

"You saw a table that is about a hundred years old," countered his friend, "while our rebbe, Reb Bunem, constantly shows us things that are six thousand years old: he shows us the creation of heaven and earth."

כִּי שֵׁשֶׁת יָמִים עָשָׂה ה' אֶת הַשָּׁמַיִם וְאֶת הָאָרֶץ
For in six days God made the heaven and the earth (Exodus 20:11)

~§ It Takes Effort

Reb Yitzchak of Vorki was always particular about showing respect to his mother, and every year he would journey to his birthplace, Zloshin, in order to fulfill this commandment. When there he would sit at the Friday night table together with her, while the many chassidim who assembled in the house crowded around the table to hear his teachings.

Once his mother asked her son for a glass of water, but before he managed to move one of his chassidim promptly rose and fulfilled her request.

Leaving the glass on the table she said to her son: "Yitzchak, it was you I asked, not someone else."

כַּבֵּד
Honor your father and your mother (Exodus 20:12)

Shavuos / שבועות   [425]

the ten commandments

The tzaddik rose at once and ran to bring her another glass of water.

"The truth is that I don't really want to drink," she said. "I only wanted to give you the opportunity of being blessed with long life" — for this is the reward which the Torah promises those who observe this mitzvah.

Then she turned to the chassidim around her and said: "One isn't privileged to have a Yitzchak like this just from sitting and eating soup with noodles!"

ಆಕ No Contradiction

A circle of brilliant young men used to assemble regularly to hear the scholarly discourses of Reb Yitzchak Meir of Ger, the author of *Chiddushei HaRim*. One of the listeners was his son, Reb Avraham Mordechai.

On one occasion, after delivering a lecture that was extraordinarily complex, Reb Yitzchak asked his listeners whether they had followed his argument throughout. The answer all around was negative.

He then turned to his son: "And you likewise do not understand?"

Reb Avraham Mordechai shrugged his shoulders as if in assent. A moment later, however, when the tzaddik retired to an adjoining room, he overheard his son explaining to his friends every intricate step of the legal argument with remarkable clarity.

Returning to his students he challenged his son: "If you understand the *pilpul* so well, then why didn't you fulfill the commandment of honoring one's father and make me happy by answering, when I asked you, that you did in fact understand?"

"Father," explained Reb Avraham Mordechai, "if you had asked me whether I understood, I would have answered 'Yes'. But since you asked me whether I too did not understand, I fulfilled the commandment of honoring one's father by not contradicting your words."

◆§ Conspiracy

עשרת
הדברות

Two men called on Reb Meir of Premishlan and asked him to bless them with success. Having given them his blessing, the tzaddik handed them eighteen coins to prosper them on their way, and advised them to spend them on the first merchandise that was offered them at the big market in Leshkovitz. Off they went and met a man, apparently a gentile, who asked them in Polish if they were interested in buying a woolen cap with woven threads. When they had paid him six coins for it he told them he had more like it for sale, so they bought two more with their remaining twelve coins. They opened up their newly acquired merchandise and discovered that these caps were filled with precious stones. Not only that, but the stranger offered to sell them a whole sackful of similar merchandise. They told him that they had no more money. He simply answered: "So take it as a gift, because I've got more of this stuff than I need."

לֹא תִרְצָח
You shall not commit murder (Exodus 20:13)

Seeing that a vast treasure lay under their very eyes they conspired in Hebrew: "This person may go and tell people that we took all this from him, and for all we know it may be stolen goods. Let's go off with him near some pit and do away with him and throw him out of sight."

The stranger addressed them in Polish: "I too understand Hebrew, so I know exactly what you're plotting."

Within a second he had taken back whatever he had sold them, and disappeared. They were left high and dry, with neither their coins nor their purchases.

They returned to Premishlan. The tzaddik only said: "But that was the prophet Eliyahu!"

◆§ More Judgmental than the Judge

A prominent woman came to Apta to consult on some matter with Reb Avraham Yehoshua Heschel, the Ohev Yisrael.

As soon as she had stepped on the threshhold of his study he cried out aloud: "Harlot! Only recently you

לֹא תִנְאָף
You shall not commit adultery (Exodus 20:13)

Shavuos / שבועות [427]

the ten commandments

committed a grave sin — and now you come to my house?! Out of here!"

"The Creator," answered the woman, "is long-suffering; He does not hasten to being retribution upon the wicked; and He does not reveal their deeds to any creature in order that they should not be too ashamed to repent. Yet the *rav* of Apta sits on his chair and cannot desist from revealing that which the Creator has covered!"

The *rav* later commented: "Never has anyone had the better of me — apart from that woman!"

৵ Perception

A rich woman from Moldavia came to the house of Reb Yitzchak Aizik of Zhidachov, wanting to contribute a large sum of money as a *pidyon* to be used for the needs of the rebbe's household — provided that she be permitted to stand in the doorway of the tzaddik's study so that she could hear his blessing from his own mouth. Seeing the situation in the household at the time, a number of chassidim saw it as their duty to persuade the tzaddik's son, Reb Eliyahu, to ask his father to grant her request, even though visitors who had arrived before her were waiting in a long queue in the corridor. And the tzaddik agreed.

Now among the impatient visitors there was one particularly daring and sturdy fellow. When he saw that this woman was being admitted to the rebbe's study he forced his way through the jostling crowd until he stood right behind her in the anteroom. There, with restrained anger, he gazed intently ahead of him at the door which led to the rebbe's study. The door was opened from within. The woman stepped up to the threshhold and handed her contribution together with the *kvitl* detailing her requests to the rebbe's *shammes* who stood inside waiting. The tzaddik was sitting on his chair facing the far wall, with his back to the door. But as soon as the *shammes* handed him the woman's *kvitl*, he spun around to face the entrance, hurled the money at the door, and cried out: "Leave this place at once, you insolent one!" And he repeated a few words over and over: הֵן הִנֵּה הָיוּ

עשרת הדברות — having in mind the verse in which Moshe Rabbeinu speaks of the Midianite women who seduced the Children of Israel to idolatry: הֵן הֵנָּה הָיוּ לִבְנֵי יִשְׂרָאֵל בִּדְבַר בִּלְעָם לִמְסָר מַעַל בַּה׳ — "For it is these who caused the Children of Israel ... to deal falsely with God ... "

The woman hastily picked up her scattered coins from the floor and fled.

"Is this the kind of *pidyon* you bring into my house?" the tzaddik rebuked his son.

And the man who had forced his way in and had witnessed the whole incident turned to the chassidim who were waiting in the corridor and said: "Now I know that God is to be found in this place! I know this woman. And when I saw that with her disgusting money she found her way right up to the rebbe's study, while hundreds of waiting people were crowded in the corridor, I told myself: 'I really must see just how the rebbe will receive an unclean gift from this shameless woman, and how he will bless her.' And that explains why I made such strenuous efforts to push my way in there. Now I see that our rebbe is holy indeed!"

⋘ *A Slip of the Memory*

Reb Meir of Premishlan once came to his table, and washed his hands as usual before sitting down to eat in the company of his chassidim. Then, as expected, he began to recite the blessing which accompanies the washing of hands before a meal, and proceeded as far as the words: ... אֲשֶׁר קִדְּשָׁנוּ בְּמִצְוֹתָיו וְצִוָּנוּ עַל — "Who has sanctified us with His commandments, and has commanded us concerning ... " But at that point, instead of concluding: עַל נְטִילַת יָדַיִם — "concerning the washing of the hands," he broke off. He turned to the chassidim who sat around the table and ventured his last word — עַל — as a query, as if he had forgotten how to proceed and wanted to be reminded: "Concerning *what?*" No one said a word, however. They were certain that the tzaddik had not forgotten the concluding words of the blessing; it was clear that some intention lay hidden here.

Now in one corner of the house stood a stranger who

Shavuos / שבועות [429]

the ten commandments was not dressed in chassidic garb. When he heard the tzaddik stop short he decided to help him out, and glibly supplied aloud the missing words: עַל נְטִילַת יָדַיִם — "concerning the washing of the hands." The tzaddik, as if taking up a half-remembered cue, repeated the words after him.

When he had recited the following blessing, the one over bread, he asked his chassidim why none of them had reminded him of the concluding words. Again there was no answer.

So the tzaddik said, as if to himself: "Perhaps they too forgot, just as I did."

Then, indicating the one man who had in fact provided the missing words, he said: "But he did not forget; he remembered the blessing over washing the hands very well indeed. But something here is remarkable. The blessing, אֲשֶׁר קִדְּשָׁנוּ בְּמִצְוֹתָיו וְצִוָּנוּ עַל נְטִילַת יָדַיִם — he remembers; whereas the blessing, אֲשֶׁר קִדְּשָׁנוּ בְּמִצְוֹתָיו וְצִוָּנוּ עַל הָעֲרָיוֹת ('Who has commanded us concerning illicit marriages') — he has completely forgotten."

That was all he said, but everything was now clear.

◆§ Another Joseph

The following tradition was related by Reb Simchah Bunem, the son of Reb Menachem Mendel of Vorki.

"I am a tenth-generation descendant of the author of *Levushim*, Rabbi Mordechai ben Avraham Jaffe. When my forebear was a young man, and of handsome appearance, a certain noblewoman sought to seduce him to sin. He fled from her presence, and escaped by making his way through a drainage gutter, in the course of which all of his garments — ten in number — were of course soiled. At that moment it was ordained in the Heavenly Court that he was destined to write ten works, corresponding to his ten garments. And indeed, the title of each of his ten works begins with the word *Levush*, meaning 'garment' — as in *Levush HaTecheiles*, *Levush Ateres Zahav*, and so on. Nine of them have been published, and I would give all the world possesses to the man who would bring me the tenth.

"After having passed the test to which he was put, Rabbi Mordechai prayed that his children and their children after them should all be darkskinned. His prayer was accepted, and we of the house of Vorki, who are his descendants, are all dusky."

◆§ Thou Shalt Not Delude Thyself

עשרת הדברות

The first time that Reb Yechiel Meir of Gostynin went to study at the feet of Reb Menachem Mendel of Kotsk it was *Shavuos*, when the Ten Commandments are read from the Torah and expounded.

לֹא תִגְנֹב
You shall not steal
(Exodus 20:13)

On his return home his father-in-law challenged him: "Do you think it was really worth going all the way to Kotsk? Why, did they receive the Torah differently over there?"

"Of course," replied the young man.

"How is that?" asked his father-in-law.

"You tell me," returned Reb Yechiel Meir. "How were you taught to interpret the commandment, לֹא תִגְנֹב — 'You shall not steal'?"

"Simply and literally," said his father-in-law. "It means that a man must not steal from his fellow."

"But with us in Kotsk," said Reb Yechiel Meir, "this commandment means something else: 'You shall not steal *from yourself!*'"

◆§ How to Remove Suspicion

On the way home from the provincial fair the wagon of a certain merchant broke down. Since it was Friday he had no alternative than to spend *Shabbos* in a nearby township. He asked for the whereabouts of a certain man of means who he had heard lived in the town, and deposited with him the wallet with all his earnings until after *Shabbos*. But when the next night he came to claim his own, the local householder denied all knowledge of the deposit, and was deaf to the poor fellow's pleas and arguments. There had been no witnesses, so at length the merchant made his dismal way home, vexed and emptyhanded. Now in the course of time that rich man lost his fortune. He decided therefore to visit

Shavuos / שבועות [431]

the ten commandments

Reb Yehudah Aryeh Leib of Ger, the author of *Sfas Emes*. In the *kvitl* that he handed the rebbe he wrote two requests: that he be freed once and for all of the suspicion that had been unjustly attached to him — that he had meddled with another's money which was said to have been deposited with him; and that the rebbe advise him as to whether he should open a certain business in Lodz.

The tzaddik took a look at the face which confronted him and said: "Concerning that business, you should ask the opinion of experts in the field — for I am not acquainted with it. As to the deposit, without any delay whatever you should go and return the money to its owner!"

~§ Coveting Trifles

לֹא תַחְמֹד
בֵּית רֵעֶךָ
You shall not covet your neighbor's house
(Exodus 20:14)

Hearing that Reb Simchah Bunem of Pshischah was about to visit a certain town, his chassidim at once arranged for him to be the guest of a family who lived in an impressive stone mansion. On his arrival he sat on a bench in the lobby while his belongings were being unloaded from his carriage. Then quite unexpectedly he asked his attendant to accompany him: he was going to leave this house. Taken quite by surprise the chassidim did the best they could, and all they could find for their rebbe at this stage was a lean room in the home of the local *shochet*. To make things worse, it was midsummer, and it was unpleasant to stay in the confines of that crowded room.

When he returned to his home in Pshischah he realized that the chassidim had assumed that he left the first house because he had seen there something unsavory. Not wishing them to remain with this mistaken impression, he decided to explain to them what had happened.

"I left that mansion," he said, "in order not to transgress the prohibition against coveting. And it is to precisely such a case that the commandment chiefly refers. For it is inconceivable that a person should outright covet his neighbor's house. As far as lodgings are concerned, though, this could be a practical question —

עשרת הדברות

for since the accommodation is only temporary, one needs to be especially on one's guard."

Then he added: "— Especially since I gathered that the host agreed to the arrangement only after my chassidim had begged him to ... "

⋄§ That's All

Right from the start, Reb Yehudah Aryeh Leib of Ger made it a principle never to enjoy any financial benefit from his chassidim. His household was supported by the snuff shop which his wife ran, while he helped her with the accounts.

Once, when one of his sons became dangerously ill, the *rebbitzin* entered her husband's study and complained: "The whole world you help with your prayers. Can't you do something for our son?"

He replied: "Let's investigate closely. Perhaps in some way we have had some financial benefit from the chassidim?"

The *rebbitzin* immediately confessed that on one occasion when she was sorely pressed for household expenses she had accepted the gift of five rubles which a certain chassid had offered.

"Return it at once," said the tzaddik, "and please undertake that in future you will never again accept any financial help whatever from the chassidim. Then we'll no longer have any problems in raising our children."

It once happened that because of increased competition in the snuff trade his income dwindled to a pittance. The tzaddik thereupon summoned one of the wealthy householders who lived in Ger and described to him his financial situation.

The good man's heart was touched by this unadorned narration. Without a second thought he said: "Rebbe, have no worries! I have thirty thousand rubles; please take half, and the other half is ample for all my needs."

Smiling, the rebbe said: "What on earth did you think — that I would accept your money? I simply fulfilled an instruction of the Sages. For there is a verse in the Book of *Proverbs* which says: דְּאָגָה בְלֶב אִישׁ יַשְׁחֶנָּה — 'If there is a worry in a man's heart, let him suppress it.' And one

Ruth of the Talmudic interpretations of this verse understands it to mean: וְשִׂיחֲנָה לַאֲחֵרִים — 'Let him talk it over with others.' Now, you are the man whom I found to be appropriate for the task, and that's why I asked you to come and listen. That's all!"*

רות

RUTH

The Book of Ruth is read aloud in many Synagogues on the festival of Shavuos.

Why was Ruth called by this name? Because from her there descended King David, who with his Psalms and praises sated the Almighty (Hebrew: שְׂרִיָנְהוּ להקב״ה — the root letters of which are related to רות; *Talmud, Tractate Berachos*).

◆§ What Glistened in Heaven

In the days of the Baal Shem Tov it once happened that the Heavenly Court issued a decree of destruction upon a certain Jewish town. The Baal Shem Tov sent for two of his friends — Reb Mordechai and Reb Kehas, hidden tzaddikim both of them — so that he could consult with them as to how the decree could be annulled. Then, as his soul ascended to the World Above, he saw that this dread verdict could not be withdrawn.

At length, descending by stages through the heavenly palaces, he lighted upon a spiritual abode that radiated a rare luminosity. For whom could such a welcome wait in the World to Come? He gazed, and saw that in time to come this was to be the portion of a certain artless villager who recited the Book of *Psalms* five times each day. And what glistened with such brilliance in heaven above

---

* Additional stories relating to the Ten Commandments may be found in *A Treasury of Chassidic Tales on the Torah*, vol. 1, p. 229-245, and vol. 2, p. 474-479.

was the letters of his Psalms, the words of his earnest רנה pleas and humble praises.

Returned to This World, the Baal Shem Tov set out at once to find this villager, and asked him: "If you knew that by forgoing your portion in the World to Come you could save a whole town full of your Jewish brethren, would you be willing?"

"If I do indeed have a portion in the World to Come," said the villager, "I hereby give it as a gift to save that town."

And the decree was annulled.

⊷§ Words that Carry Weight

One of the chassidim of the Baal Shem Tov was a simple and God-fearing yokel who earned his bread by digging wells. He was known as Herschel Grebber — Yiddish for "Herschel the Digger." So great was his asceticism that from an early age he tasted no greater delicacy than bread and salt, and drank only water. At the same time, though, he provided his family with all their needs to the best of his ability. The Book of *Psalms* he knew by heart. He barely understood the meaning of the Hebrew words, and some of the obscurer verses were quite beyond the reach of his scant learning — but his lips were forever uttering the well-loved words, whether he was at work or walking on his way.

It was concerning this man that the Baal Shem Tov said: "In the World Above, the words of Herschel the Digger carry weight!"

⊷§ By Consultation Only

The following incident was recounted by Reb Shmuel of Lubavitch about his father, Reb Menachem Mendel of Lubavitch, the author of *Tzemach Tzedek*.

"One *Shabbos* I walked into my father's study and found him seated in his place studying the *Zohar*. A moment later we were joined by my eldest brother, Reb Baruch Shalom. My father closed the volume and said: "When the tzaddik of Ruzhin recites *Tehillim* the whole world opens up before him; and when he recites these same Psalms on *Shabbos* he sees the spiritual roots of all things in the universe, and then he is able to rectify matters by dealing with their spiritual sources. That being the case, the decree is being annulled — and I hereby agree to the steps proposed by the tzaddik of Ruzhin."

What lay behind these cryptic sentences?

As is known, there was a warm friendship between Reb Menachem Mendel of Lubavitch and Reb Yisrael of Ruzhin. Once, under the shadow of a threatened decree which the Czarist regime was about to promulgate against the Jewish population, Reb Menachem Mendel dispatched his celebrated disciple Reb Yitzchak Aizik of Homil as his envoy to Ruzhin, to consult with Reb Yisrael as to what could be done. Reb Yisrael gave him a warm hearing, and said: "Very well. Then let us read a few chapters from the Book of *Psalms* and the Almighty will open up for us the Gates of Light, and we will see what's going on."

The following *Shabbos* the tzaddik interrupted his Torah discourse, and asked all of his chassidim to leave the room: Reb Yitzchak Aizik alone was to remain. He then said: "My considered opinion is that we should send two emissaries to the capital where they should present such and such arguments, and the decree will be annulled, God willing.

"And by the way," he added, "your rebbe agrees with me."

≈§ The Power of Psalms

During the month of Tishrei in the year 1847 Reb Menachem Mendel of Lubavitch was in a stern frame of mind. Indeed he was exceedingly earnest even during the festive days of *Sukkos*. His sons and the elder chassidim were filled with foreboding, but no one dared ask him for the reason. On *Isru Chag*, the day after *Sukkos*, he summoned his eldest son, Reb Baruch Shalom, and instructed him to arrange that every morning, no later than by the fourth hour from dawn, a *minyan* of ten chassidim should recite the whole Book of *Psalms*. They were to continue doing so until he told them otherwise; and no one was to know that this order came from himself.

רות

Accordingly, this began forthwith, from Tuesday the twenty-fifth of Tishrei until the *Shabbos* on which the portion of *Vayishlach* was read — a total of fifty-three days. The rebbe's attendant reported that at that hour the rebbe himself likewise recited several chapters of *Psalms,* and after reading a few verses he would drop a few coins of copper, silver and gold, into the charity boxes that were in the drawer of his writing desk. On Friday the eighteenth of Kislev the rebbe again called for his eldest son Reb Baruch Shalom, and told him that his instruction was no longer in force, though those who so desired could of course continue as heretofore.

On the Nineteenth of Kislev, the anniversary which celebrates the release from capital sentence of his grandfather, Reb Shneur Zalman of Liadi, the rebbe was exceedingly joyful, and in the course of the day delivered three chassidic discourses. Soon after, during Chanukah, the first volumes of *Likkutei Torah* were delivered to him from the printer's, and this too brought him great joy.

On the twenty-fourth of Teves, the anniversary of his grandfather's passing, which fell that year on a Friday, the rebbe led the prayers, and at the *Shabbos* meal that evening his mood was the serene rapture of *dveikus.* Among the many pensive harmonies he sang at the table was the sublime Melody of Four Themes composed by his grandfather, the song of the worshiper who yearns to cleave to his Maker. One by one the chassidim around the table were roused to join him as the melody swelled from plaintive plea to imploring crescendo.

The last of its measured but stirring cadences had spoken its message; the gathering was left in silent repose. At length the rebbe spoke: "On the first night of Rosh HaShanah I saw that in the Heavenly Court a dire sentence hung over the heads of the People of Israel, and in particular over the Torah scholars. I was deeply distressed. I made every effort to see my grandfather, Reb Shneur Zalman, but this was not granted me. I did see my mentor and father-in-law, Reb Dov Ber, who warned me of the seriousness of the charges that were being pressed against the House of Israel, but told me too that

Ruth the verdict had not been sealed, so that there was an urgent need for strenuous efforts in prayer. This however was not to be made public, for thus only harm would be caused. Then, at the festive meal on Simchas Torah, while we were all singing my grandfather's *niggun* of the Four Themes just before the Grace after Meals, I finally saw my grandfather.

"His first words to me were a quotation from an instruction in the Talmud concerning the goblet of wine over which the Grace after Meals is pronounced. He said: 'כּוֹס שֶׁל בְּרָכָה טָעוּן הַגְבָּהָה טֶפַח מִן הַשֻּׁלְחָן — The cup of blessing should be raised one handsbreadth from the table.' He then went on to explain: 'The Book of *Psalms* is King David's cup of blessing. It raises a man aloft, a little handsbreadth up and above the straits and limitations of This World — and it annuls all the charges which the Prosecuting Angel may press in the Heavenly Court. See to it that every morning for fifty-three days, not later than four hours after dawn, the entire Book of *Psalms* should be recited secretly — and the Prosecution will be silenced.'"

Reb Menachem Mendel went on to tell his hearers: "If you only knew the power which the verses of *Psalms* sway in the heavens above, you would read them unceasingly. The *Psalms* shatter all obstructions between the House of Israel and their Father; they ascend without hindrance to the World Above; and there they arouse lovingkindness and mercy in abundance."

⇜§ If Only!

It once happened that all through the night Reb Menachem Mendel of Lubavitch studied earnestly, and at dawn he began his prayers, which occupied his concentration for a further few hours. Then, still wearing his *tallis* and *tefillin*, he resumed his study. All that day he fasted.

Now since it was market day, two simple villagers who lived not far away — Reb Binyamin Beines and Reb Yitzchak Shaul — came to Lubavitch that day to sell their wares. The first finished so early that he decided to walk into the local *shul* in order to wait until his friend had

completed his sales too, and then they would take a רוּחַ
wagon home. While waiting there he took out of his
greatcoat pocket a well-thumbed little volume of *Psalms*
and began to read from it in a voice that came straight
from the heart. This was the voice that reached the rebbe's ears in the midst of his concentrated study. He
looked around to see where it came from, and discovered
Reb Binyamin, the simple villager. Rising from his place
the rebbe walked across to a corner of the *shul* where he
wept bitterly.

A moment later an elder chassid called Reb Ephraim
Yaffe of Kopust entered the building. The rebbe turned
to him and said: "If only I could recite one verse of
Tehillim with the same unsophisticated simplicity with
which Reb Binyamin Beines does!"

⋘ Overtime

Foreboding hovered over the face of Reb Shmuel on his
return to Lubavitch from Petersburg. It was early in
the month of Nissan in the year 1880, and the rebbe had
just learned in the capital that a particularly influential
minister had proposed a new decree. The intended law
would impose even severer limits on the grudging permission granted to the Jews to support themselves
through commerce and on their right to live outside the
Pale of Settlement. While there the rebbe had almost succeeded in having these restrictions eased and in having
the date of the actual proposal to the Senate deferred by a
year. One of its members, however, who was an old
friend of the anti-Semitic proponent of the decree, in-
stigated the formation of a lobby of senators who
proceeded to demand from the czarist administration
that the proposals be presented and approved. Even
from his house in Lubavitch the rebbe now found no
rest, and continued to exert all influence possible
through emissaries and letters to well-connected communal figures among his chassidim.

A month after his arrival, on Tuesday the second of
Iyyar, the rebbe called for his son Reb Shalom Ber and
said: "From the day I arrived at Petersburg to work on

Ruth this matter I began to recite *Tehillim* more freely, completing the whole Book of *Psalms* by daily portions in the course of a week, in addition to completing the Book by daily portions in the course of a month. And today, the third day of the week, I came to the verse: כִּי מִכָּל צָרָה הִצִּילָנִי וּבְאֹיְבַי רָאֲתָה עֵינִי — 'For he has delivered me out of all trouble, and my eye has gazed upon my enemies.' At that very moment Ben-Zion, one of the attendants, walked in and handed me a telegram which informed me that that anti-Semitic minister had suffered a sudden stroke and died.

"But don't worry," added Reb Shmuel, "I went ahead and completed the whole of that day's portion of *Tehillim* all the same ..."

✥ In Kotsk it's Different

Two chassidim, one of Kotsk and one of Chernobyl, once met and began to discuss the various trends within Chassidism.

"With us in Chernobyl," said one, "three things are outstanding. We stay awake all Thursday night studying Torah; on Friday each of us gives as much charity as he can afford; and on *Shabbos* we all read the whole of the Book of *Psalms*."

"With us in Kotsk," said the other, "it's different. In Kotsk people stay awake studying every night; *tzedakah* is given every time we run into a man in need and whenever we have money in our pockets; and as for *Tehillim*, we haven't got the strength to recite the whole Book all at once. Instead, we say just a few Psalms, but with intent concentration. For is it conceivable that what King David of blessed memory toiled over the writing of for seventy years we should say all at once?"

✥ More than I can Take

"Praying from the Book of *Psalms*," Reb Yechiel Meir of Gostynin used to say, "is a shield that protects a man from all evil, and a salvation in hour of trouble."

A man once brought his seriously ill son to him in

order to request his blessing. When the tzaddik instructed the patient himself to recite the whole of the Book of *Tehillim* five times over, the father protested: "Rebbe, is it possible that my son who is dangerously ill should read through the whole of *Tehillim* five times?"

"Listen to me," said the tzaddik. "A few weeks ago a man came to me with his son who had gone (May we not know of such woes!) out of his mind. I told him too that he should recite the Book of *Tehillim*. Now I ask you, what value could there possibly be in the reading of *Tehillim* by one who is deranged? But I've arranged it in heaven that whomever I instruct to recite the *Tehillim* — if he obeys — will thereby be helped from Above."

And in fact whenever anyone came to ask his advice or to request his intercession for divine help, Reb Yechiel Meir would instruct him to recite the whole of the Book of *Tehillim*. As Biblical authority for this policy he used to quote the verse (from *Psalms*): מִי יְמַלֵּל גְּבוּרוֹת ה׳ יַשְׁמִיעַ כָּל תְּהִלָּתוֹ — "Who can utter the mighty acts of God? Who can declare all His praise?" This, at any rate, is the plain meaning of the words. In addition, however, Reb Yechiel Meir found in them a connotation on the level of *derush*. The verb יְמַלֵּל, he would say, comes from the same root as מִילָה, circumcision, and this signifies cutting. The noun גְּבוּרוֹת often means the stern judgments which may hang over an imperfect mortal, and which are motivated by the divine attribute of justice when not mellowed by mercy. The first half of the verse thus asks a question: מִי יְמַלֵּל גְּבוּרוֹת ה׳? — "Who can rend the stern judgments of the Almighty?" And the other half of the verse, instead of being another question, a mere amplification of the first question, gives an *answer* to that question, namely: יַשְׁמִיעַ כָּל תְּהִלָּתוֹ — "He who declares *all His praise*"; that is, he who recites the whole of the Book of *Tehillim* (literally, "the Book of Praises").

❊ ❊ ❊

It once happened that one of the young sons of Reb Yehudah Aryeh Leib of Ger took ill. He at once dispatched his brother to Gostynin to request the tzaddik to intercede in heaven on his behalf.

Ruth

Said the tzaddik: "To oblige the rebbe of Ger to recite the entire Book of *Tehillim* — that's difficult. But at least ten Psalms — that, even he has to read."

When the tzaddik of Ger received this message from his emissary he exclaimed: "*Ten* Psalms?! When I read *one* solitary Psalm my head aches. And he says *ten?!*"

৵§ The 'He' and the 'I'

Rabbi Zeira said: "The Book of *Ruth* contains no laws regarding impurity and purity, nor laws of what is prohibited and what permitted. Why then was it written? — In order to teach you the reward of those who do deeds of kindness *(Midrash)*.

May God grant reward for your deed (יְשַׁלֵּם ה' פָּעֳלֵךְ): Come and see how great is that which is wrought by those who do deeds of kindness *(Midrash)*.

יַעַשׂ ה'
עִמָּכֶם חֶסֶד
May God deal kindly with you as you have done (Ruth 1:8)

A wealthy chassid by the name of Reb Leib Posen lived in Vitebsk. He owned a number of stone mansions, and conducted his own household in fine style. He contributed of course to charitable causes and occupied himself with good deeds, though not allowing these to exceed the limits imposed by convention.

Among his acquaintances was one of the respected chassidim of Vitebsk, Reb Shmuel Brin, a scholar known both for his Talmudic erudition and for his profound grasp of the philosophical teachings of *Chabad* Chassidism. Though heavily engaged in business contracts which he had from the czarist government he devoted fixed times daily to advance his learning in both these fields. In 1880, however, a crisis overtook him: he fell prey to a band of swindlers, and was suddenly cast into weighty debt.

Before Pessach that year his wealthy friend Reb Leib visited Lubavitch. On meeting the rebbe Reb Shmuel there, he told the tzaddik in great detail of all his pending transactions and requested his blessing that they prosper. Then, having wound up his account, he sighed and said: "Poor Reb Shmuel Brin is in a very unfortunate situation indeed. Though it goes without saying רוח that the Almighty is righteous and his ways are just, so that if He brought this about then that is how it should be — nevertheless Reb Shmuel is to be pitied."

The rebbe covered his eyes with his hands and for a moment was sunk deep in thought. He answered not a word.

Soon after Pessach a fearful conflagration broke out in the street in which Reb Leib's linen storehouses stood and he suffered damage amounting to tens of thousands of rubles. At the same time a fire broke out in his house, where his large shop was situated; this too was destroyed, together with twenty thousand rubles worth of merchandise. To make matters worse, none of his property was insured.

A few days later he set out to Lubavitch to tell the rebbe of what had befallen him. As soon as he opened the door of the rebbe's study a bitter cry burst from his heart, and he told the rebbe that altogether his misfortunes had cost him fifty thousand rubles.

The rebbe looked at him with an eye that seemed to see through his entire being. Then he said: "When it came to the misfortune that struck Reb Shmuel Brin and left him penniless you managed to find consolation, and accepted the judgment of heaven with equanimity. But when it comes to your linen and your shop you raise a clamor, and do not find consolation in the two stone mansions that are still yours, and with the sums you have in investments and in government bonds. *The 'He' and the 'I' are apparently two separate things!"*

These words took complete possession of Reb Leib. After reflection he came to the conclusion that it was because of his sinful attitude to Reb Shmuel Brin's circumstances that he himself had been struck by misfortune.

For two whole days he walked about like a man out of his mind, not knowing what to do. Finally he entered the rebbe's study again in order to be guided in his repentance, asked to be given a penance, and solemnly undertook that in future his first thought would be another's need.

The rebbe said: "We have a tradition from the Baal

Ruth Shem Tov that when a person passes judgment on another, for good or for ill, he passes judgment on himself. And when a person piously accepts the judgment of heaven on his friend's behalf and is not distressed by his distress, and does not endeavour to arouse the compassion of heaven upon him, then he is in fact pressing charges against himself. Conversely, he who shares in the anguish of his friend is duly recompensed.

"And now," concluded the rebbe, "this is what you should do. Give Reb Shmuel Brin three thousand rubles as a loan, without any profit, in order that he should be able to buy merchandise and send it by raft to Riga. This money you are to give with an open hand and with pleasure, grateful to the Almighty for having given you the opportunity to do a kindly act. As for you, you should proceed to Moscow to buy up merchandise for your shop, and may the Almighty make good your loss in double measure."

The moment Reb Leib came home he took a walletful of money to the house of his friend, but Reb Shmuel Brin was out of town. He waited over a week for his return in order to carry out the rebbe's orders. He was anxious to set out to Moscow for his own purchases, but he was afraid to deviate from the order in which the rebbe had instructed him to act: first to give the loan to Reb Shmuel, and only thereafter to proceed to Moscow.

At sunset on Friday he went to *shul* in ample time for the evening prayers and there spotted Reb Shmuel, elated and outgoing, surrounded by an eager crowd of chassidim who were listening excitedly to his every word. For a moment Reb Leib envied him, thinking: "Happy the man whose lot is thus! It is now over two months that his luck has overturned. He is living in want, yet he looks as if he is the happiest man alive!"

A slap on the table jolted him out of his reverie. That was the *gabbai* drawing attention to his announcement: "Friends, let's have a little quiet, please! Reb Shmuel Brin is going to repeat the chassidic teachings that he heard from the rebbe!"

All conversations were instantly tucked away, and in the stillness that reigned Reb Shmuel reverently repeated the discourse that he had committed to memory. It was

רות based on the Midrashic exposition of the allegorical words from the *Song of Songs:* יוֹנָתִי בְּחַגְוֵי הַסֶּלַע — "My dove is in the clefts of the rock" — and Reb Shmuel repeated it in the very words he had heard, in the same sober singsong, in the same measured rhythm. At noon the next day, after the *Shabbos* morning prayers, all the congregants crowded into Reb Shmuel's home for *Kiddush* and light refreshments, and again their host made the occasion a festive one by repeating the same *maamar*. By late afternoon, worshipers from all the other chassidic prayerhouses in Vitebsk had converged on the *shul* which Reb Shmuel frequented in order to *davven* the *Minchah* service in his company and to hear him repeat the same discourse for the third time. And as may be expected, the joy of all present was unbounded.

That night Reb Leib was in two minds as to whether he should go immediately to see Reb Shmuel, or defer the visit to the next day — because wasn't there a folk belief that it is not advisable to give out your money on *Motzaei Shabbos*, even for household expenses, how much more so for someone who was not one of the family? But in a flash his imagination brought before his eyes the rebbe's holy face, gazing at him with that same penetrating look. He grasped the wallet, and stepped out into the street with the three thousand rubles.

Arriving at Reb Shmuel's home he found him deep in concentration over some complex question of jurisprudence in an outsize volume of the *Tur*, in the section entitled *Choshen Mishpat*. Looking up from his studies Reb Shmuel received him warmly. He then set about raising his spirits following the fires that had ruined him by offering an explanation of the common Yiddish adage that "after a fire one prospers." (This folk-saying has a mystical rationale in the Kabbalah.)

Listening to every word, Reb Leib was moved by his friend's spiritual stamina. For hadn't he himself just suffered financial ruin? Not so long ago he had planned to buy a certain stone mansion; now, not only had he lost whatever he owned, but he was left deep in debt and could scarcely muster the food needed for the next meal. Nevertheless, Reb Leib reminded himself, this man has just made the journey to Lubavitch; has returned exultant with a new *maamar* in his head which he heard from the rebbe's mouth; now repeats this discourse for all his friends in a voice that radiates joy; is sitting with undistracted concentration sorting out some classical legal riddle in *Choshen Mishpat;* and on top of that he has the courage to console *me!*

Turning to his host he asked him what he now proposed to do.

"As far as my situation is concerned," said Reb Shmuel, "you know there's an old wives' saying that at the beginning of the week one should talk only about happy things. So let's not talk about my financial situation now. But I'm full of hope that the Almighty will no doubt help me. I won't deny that before Pessach — when I discovered that I had been swindled, and had lost everything I owned as well as every ruble I had borrowed from others — I almost slipped into despair. I was thinking of finding myself some little shop, even in some quiet township. During the Intermediate Days of Pessach I walked around as if I was deranged. But I soon decided that I would put all my troubles out of my mind until the festival was over. Then the night on which the last day of Pessach ended, I came down with high fever. By the third day I was feeling a little better. That evening a *melamed* from Velizh called on me and told me that the day before he had come from Lubavitch. While he was there the rebbe had given him a message for me, but since he had found me ill he had waited until he could tell me about it.

"This is what the rebbe told him.

"'When you reach Vitebsk, call on Shmuel Brin and tell him that I know all about it, but I do not agree with his view. In fact I hereby order him to drop this thought. The brain rules the heart by its very nature — particularly so when one conducts oneself according to the ways of Chassidism. This is what you should pass on to him, and if you will have to wait a day in order to be able to do so, then wait.'

"When I felt better," Reb Shmuel Brin continued, "I went off to *shul* to *davven.* On my way home I met an acquaintance who lent me thirty rubles, and I took a wagon to Lubavitch. I spoke with the rebbe at *yechidus* for over an hour. At the end of that time he asked me רות about my situation. I described it in a very few words, exactly as it is. The rebbe turned to me and said: 'Shmuel, do not despair. Buy readymade rafts on the river, and the Almighty will set up for you good purchases and good merchants — as well as income on the side.'

"From there I went to Riga to see the readymade rafts. I examined a good number of fine samples at the river's edge in the hope that the Almighty would now do His part and arrange the requisite sums for me. When I climbed up into the train bound for home I met Reb Aharon Brodna. He was on his way from Smolensk in connection with some dispute between a magnate called Wittenburg from Dvinsk and another called Schwarcz from Smolensk. They had agreed to settle their differences through arbitration, and this Reb Aharon was on his way to Vitebsk to invite me to be the third person on the panel, because the two arbitrators chosen by the respective parties had both chosen me to be the third. We got off at Vitebsk and immediately took another train back to Smolensk. For four days we toiled away until we finally succeeded in sorting out and settling all the matters under dispute. They compensated me for my efforts, and in that way I honestly earned six hundred rubles. So far, then, the rebbe's blessing had already begun to be fulfilled — income on the side, in addition to the profits from my dealings. Now, thank God, I am able to pay the shops for my family's food, and a few hundred rubles will still be left over for my first business investments."

Reb Leib now asked his question: "But what are you going to do about the payment that you'll have to make in advance to the owners of the rafts, and to the boatmen who deliver them? That will add up to quite a tidy sum."

"Look here," Reb Shmuel reassured him, "the rebbe knows that one can't do business with empty hands. So if he gave me his blessing that the Almighty will bring good purchases my way, then included in that blessing is that the Almighty will bring my way whatever is needed to make those good purchases."

Reb Leib listened closely, without quite knowing how to broach the matter of the wallet which was still bulging

RUTH in his pocket.

Then he blurted out: "Don't worry about the money that's needed for trading. Here, I've brought you a certain sum just for that!"

And he took out a bundle of notes of one hundred rubles.

Reb Shmuel looked down at the bundle and up at Reb Leib; he could not work it all out. He knew Reb Leib as the kind of man one could approach for a loan when required — but not a sum like this! Yet Reb Leib spoke clearly: "I've brought you three thousand rubles as a loan until after you sell your rafts in Riga."

"Come, Leib," protested his friend, "I'm not going to take a loan of this size from you! Not only that: you are not even entitled to do such a thing, because even the most promising of business propositions can end up in either of two ways, and you certainly should not risk lending such an amount for someone else's investment. And anyway, I'm not going to accept this from you."

It was now clearly time for Reb Leib to narrate the whole story from beginning to end.

After listening intently, Reb Shmuel spoke up: "You have fulfilled what the rebbe told you to do, and as the Sages assure us, מַחֲשָׁבָה טוֹבָה הקב״ה מְצָרְפָהּ לְמַעֲשֶׂה — 'A good thought the Almighty reckons as if appended to a deed.' But as for me, I'm not accepting the money."

That same night Reb Leib drove off to Lubavitch, told the rebbe all about Reb Shmuel's refusal to accept, and deposited the bundle of notes on the rebbe's table.

Early Monday morning the rebbe's messenger arrived in Vitebsk with a sealed package for Reb Shmuel. Inside was a note which said: "I am sending you three thousand rubles with which to do business until you have sold the rafts in Riga. All success!"

Reb Shmuel accepted the money, bought and sold and dispatched his rafts, and in so doing earned a handsome profit.

At the same time Reb Leib went off to Moscow where he told the linen merchants what had befallen him. He had barely completed his story when they volunteered to share the loss with him. In the meantime they gave him a new consignment of merchandise on credit. Moreover, that summer he won fifteen thousand rubles in a lottery, and bought up more merchandise cheaply. In short, he prospered in all his ways, and in time both he and Reb Shmuel became very wealthy indeed. In his old age Reb Shmuel handed over his varied business interests to his sons-in-law, keeping for himself the income from the stone mansion that he bought, while his own house was always open wide to welcome needy chassidim and bypassing scholars.

רות

◆§ Whither Thou Goest

After the passing of Reb Yitzchak Meir of Ger, his chassidim appointed Reb Chanoch Henich of Alexander to succeed him as their rebbe. On the eve of the first Shavuos festival thereafter, in the year 1866, thousands of chassidim from Lodz and all the nearby towns began to converge on Alexander. When Reb Henich's son saw this great procession of carriages and wagons he entered his father's study and told him about it.

מִתְאַמֶּצֶת הִיא לָלֶכֶת
*She steadfastly sought to go
(Ruth 1:18)*

Said Reb Henich: "If so, we'll first have to recline a little."

From the ambiguous Yiddish verb — meaning "to recline" or "to lean" — his son understood that his father now planned to lie down a little, in order that he should be able to receive this vast crowd of chassidim with a rested mind. He accordingly began to prepare the sofa which stood in his father's study.

His father corrected him: "The only One on whom we must lean is our Father in heaven ..."

Then he added another thought: "In the opening chapter of the Book of *Ruth* we read of Ruth's insistence to go with Naomi, her aging mother-in-law. The words appearing there are: וַתֵּרֶא כִּי מִתְאַמֶּצֶת הִיא לָלֶכֶת אִתָּהּ — 'And she (Naomi) saw that she (הִיא) steadfastly sought to go with her.' Now the word הִיא, placed as it is, appears to be superfluous, for the preceding Hebrew verb (meaning 'steadfastly sought') is such that its subject is clearly implied even without this word. What then is the function of this word? — It refers not to Ruth but to Naomi. That is, Naomi felt at that moment that just as

Shavuos / שבועות [449]

Ruth Ruth desired to be close to her, so she too steadfastly sought to come close to Ruth."

◆§ It's All Explicitly Written

וְרָחַצְתְּ וָסַכְתְּ וְשַׂמְתְּ שִׂמְלֹתַיִךְ... אַל תִּוָּדְעִי לָאִישׁ
Then you shall wash, and anoint yourself, and put your dress upon you ... do not make yourself known to the man
(Ruth 3:3)

During the time that Reb Shalom of Belz was a young man and still supported by his father-in-law, a decree was issued by the government ordering that Jews be taken off to the army. Armed police used to descend upon Jewish houses and after a search would choose those whom they saw fit. Once his father-in-law sensed that the police were approaching his house in order to haul away Reb Shalom. He called out to alert him so that he would flee and go into hiding. The young man ignored him. He simply bathed himself in hot water, as if in preparation for *Shabbos*, dressed himself in his *Shabbos* clothes, took his place at the table and resumed his study. The police came soon enough. They looked into all the rooms, but not seeing him, went on their way.

Reb Shalom's father-in-law was stupefied.

"Tell me," he said, "how was it that they didn't see you at all here?"

"Why," replied the young man, "it's all explicitly written in a verse in the Book of *Ruth*. There we read: וְרָחַצְתְּ וָסַכְתְּ וְשַׂמְתְּ שִׂמְלֹתַיִךְ — 'Then you shall wash, and anoint yourself, and put your dress upon you.' *Rashi* explains that 'dress' here means *Shabbos* garb. And what is written thereafter? It says: אַל תִּוָּדְעִי לָאִישׁ — 'Do not make yourself known to the man.' That is to say: If you will act according to the instructions set out in this verse, then 'you will not make yourself known to the man' — no one will see you!"

◆§ On the Other Foot

שָׁלַף אִישׁ נַעֲלוֹ
Each man would take off his shoe
(Ruth 4:7)

A certain well-to-do chassid arrived in Belz to spend the festival of Shavuos there. Meeting a friend of his who was so poor that his shoes were badly torn, he took off his own shoes and gave them to his friend, while he put on the torn pair.

Word of this incident reached Reb Yissachar Dov of Belz, the son of Reb Yehoshua of Belz. He commented:

רוּת "There is a hint of this in the Book of *Ruth*. There it is written: ... וְזֹאת לְפָנִים בְּיִשְׂרָאֵל עַל הַגְּאוּלָּה וְעַל הַתְּמוּרָה שָׁלַף אִישׁ נַעֲלוֹ וְנָתַן לְרֵעֵהוּ — 'Now this was the custom in former time in Israel concerning redeeming and concerning exchanging ... a man would take off his shoe and give it to his friend.'"

This verse of course refers to the convention by which two parties would signify that they were bound by a certain transaction. Seeking however to derive another lesson from it, the tzaddik then went ahead to explain the words עַל הַגְּאוּלָּה וְעַל הַתְּמוּרָה — "concerning redeeming and concerning exchanging" — in the light of what the Talmud says about charity. Among the statements in the Talmud on *tzedakah* we find the following two. Firstly: גְּדוֹלָה צְדָקָה שֶׁמְּקָרֶבֶת אֶת הַגְּאוּלָּה — "Great is charity, for it brings the Redemption near." Secondly: גַּלְגַּל הוּא שֶׁחוֹזֵר בָּעוֹלָם — "There is a wheel that turns in the world." Today this one is poor and the other rich; tomorrow they can exchange places.

And this is what the verse is teaching us: that "concerning *redeeming* and concerning *exchanging*" — that is, *for reasons of charity*, "the custom in former time in Israel" was that "a man would take off his shoe and give it to his friend."

Shavuos / שבועות [451]

בין המצרים

the three weeks

בין
המצרים

⋧ Cleansed by Shame

It takes a notable celebration indeed to override the prohibition against eating meat and drinking wine during the Nine Days. For this period, at the end of the annual Three Weeks of Mourning which begin with the fast of the Seventeenth of Tammuz, culminates in the fast of the Ninth of Av, the anniversary of the destruction of both Temples. A notable celebration of this order might be the festive meal that follows a circumcision or marks the conclusion of the study of an entire Talmudic tractate.

It was the custom of Reb Yissachar Ber of Radoshitz to complete the study of a tractate in the *Gemara* and to celebrate the occasion with a *seudas* mitzvah complete with meat and wine every year on the fifth of Av — for this date is the anniversary of the passing of that giant among kabbalists, Rabbi Yitzchak Luria, the *Arizal*. And every year, in the midst of the gloom of the Nine Days, the Sava Kaddisha of Radoshitz would recount the same story to all the chassidim and students who had gathered for this festive meal. Here is the story.

✿ ✿ ✿

In a faraway town there lived a man who used to sleep so much that he was nicknamed "the Sleeper." The month of Elul arrived in all its awe. Seeing the Days of Judgment within reach, every Jew alive trembled, and roused himself in repentance. But this fellow slept. It was already Rosh HaShanah, and his wife rose early to join the congregation in prayer — but he slept on. When the morning service was underway she went home to nurse her baby, and while there tried to wake up her husband — but he neither budged nor stirred. Several times throughout the morning she interrupted her prayers and stole away from the synagogue. Nothing helped. But when the congregation began the reading of the Torah, and time was running out before the high point of the day's service, she ran home crying, and shouted at the top of her voice: "They're about to blow the *shofar!*"

He jumped out of bed in a flurry, grabbed some tattered garment strewn with feathers and threw it over his shoulders, bolted all the way to *shul*, and burst inside, puffing and panting, with slumber on his eyelids. The staid worshipers gaped at the comic spectacle. Some — and not only children — even snickered. The poor fellow felt so disgraced and humiliated that his burning shame flew up and appeared before the Heavenly Court. The verdict was pronounced forthwith: having been seared and cleansed by his shame, this humble Jew was now to have all his sins forgiven.

※ ※ ※

"So too with us," concluded the Sava Kaddisha of Radoshitz. "Here we are, in the depths of this period of mourning over the destruction of the *Beis HaMikdash*, sitting down to a festive meal. Why, this is such a *shameful* thing that on its account the Merciful One should forgive the sins of the entire House of Israel!"

And with this plea from the heart, the tzaddik wept so profusely that his tears fell into the wine goblet over which, in preparation for the Grace after Meals, he was about to recite the Psalm which laments the Exile: "By the waters of Babylon we sat, yea, we wept, when we remembered Zion ..."

⋄§ It's the Mood that Counts

This was good news indeed that reached the ears of Reb Yossele of Ostila, the son of Reb Mordechai of Neshchiz. He had heard that a celebrated tzaddik was soon to pass through his town and very much wanted to have him as his guest, for this was none other than Reb Yaakov Yitzchak of Lublin, known as the Chozeh ("the Seer") on account of his unusual powers of perception. Now he knew that when the Chozeh lay down on another's bed he would sometimes cry out: "It's prickly!" He therefore summoned to his home a God-fearing carpenter and instructed him to build a bed especially for the rebbe; to make sure that no one else should sleep on it; that he should immerse himself in a *mikveh* before working on it; and that he should entertain pure thoughts while working.

The carpenter was not at all enthused by this odd proposition, especially since this was the first week of Av, the mourning period for the *Beis HaMikdash*. On the other hand he could not quite bring himself to reject an instruction given by the rebbe. In the end he set about the work with a dejected spirit and a feeling of unworthiness, knowing full well who was the holy man who was soon to sleep on this bed. As soon as he received the finished bed, Reb Yossele stood it in a special room, made it up with bedclothes that were suitably spotless and ironed, brought in a chair, table and lamp, and locked the door. And in order that he should be certain that no one at all would enter the room, he kept the key in his own pocket.

A few days later Reb Yossele was overjoyed, for when he went out to greet his distinguished guest, the Chozeh in fact accepted his offer of hospitality. He conducted him to his room, showed him the bed which a God-fearing carpenter had constructed especially for him, invited him to lie down to rest a little, and left the room in calm satisfaction.

"Help! It's prickly!" — came the cries of alarm from within.

Reb Yossele did not know what to think. Perhaps he should offer the Chozeh his own bed? But then it would not be very pleasant if the same thing happened there too. Besides, if that were the case, how would the tzaddik rest after his arduous journey? Finally, however, he decided to ask the rebbe to sleep in his own bed, and the Chozeh agreed.

When he woke up he said: "Excellent! You have restored life to all my limbs!"

Reb Yossele was relieved — but he still had a question: "I was a little surprised, sir, that you said that the new bed was prickly, for a God-fearing man made it specially for you."

"Have no fear!" the rebbe reassured him. "The bed is kosher in every respect. Only one thing: it exudes a smell of melancholy, because it was built during the Nine Days of Mourning, and the carpenter, being a God-

the three weeks

fearing man, was lamenting the Destruction of the *Beis HaMikdash* while he was working on it."

⚜ Not Here Yet?

Reb David Moshe of Chortkov related the following description of the conduct of his grandfather, Reb Avraham the son of the Maggid of Mezritch, who on account of his piety was known as the Malach ("the Angel").

"On the anniversary of the Destruction of the *Beis HaMikdash*, on Tishah BeAv every year," he said, "my grandfather the Malach would sit with his head bowed between his knees, his eyes streaming tears. And from time to time in the course of the day he would raise his head, and out of the depths of his yearning for the coming of the *Mashiach* he would look around and ask: "Not here yet? Hasn't he arrived yet?""

⚜ Something to Rectify

Restoring peace between man and man and between husband and wife was a favorite mitzvah of Reb Raphael of Bershad, a disciple of Reb Pinchas of Korets. One Tishah BeAv he went off to a certain house in order to make the peace between a number of people who were quarreling there.

"But rebbe," he was asked, "can't you put off your visit until after Tishah BeAv?"

He replied: "The Temple was destroyed because of שִׂנְאַת חִנָּם — causeless hatred. That is why on the anniversary of the Destruction we should engage in the bringing of peace."

⚜ The Site of the Sacrifices

Someone mentioned to Reb Baruch of Mezhibuzh that a certain prominent scholar had written a learned work entitled *Mayim Kedoshim*, which comprised novellae on *Seder Kodashim*, the portion of the Talmud which deals with the sacrificial service in the Temple.

"I am surprised indeed," commented the tzaddik,

"that anyone finds it possible to write on this entire portion. As far as I'm concerned I know what happens to me every morning, as soon as I reach even the brief quotation from it in the *Siddur* which describes the places in the *Beis HaMikdash* where the sacrifices were carried out. For as soon as I say the words אֵיזֶהוּ מְקוֹמָן שֶׁל זְבָחִים — 'Where is the place of the sacrifices?' — I ponder on the lamentable state in which the Place of the Sacrifices lies, ever since it was destroyed on account of our sins; and I am then so distressed that I cannot read any further." בֵּין הַמְצָרִים

⋙ For Single Use Only

On the eve of Tishah BeAv every year Reb Avraham of Chechanov would have to buy a new copy of *Kinos*, the Book of *Lamentations*. For every year, as soon as the mournful service was over, he would stow away his copy in the *genizah*, the storehouse in the synagogue in which old and battered prayerbooks and unusable fragments of other sacred books were lodged, never to be removed, unless perhaps for ultimate burial. And each time he did this he would say: "I am sure that *Mashiach* will come *this* year, and then we won't have any further need for books of *Lamentations*."

⋙ Count your Chickens

Going from door to door on the fast of Tishah BeAv collecting *tzedakah* for some charitable purpose, Reb Levi Yitzchak of Berditchev was not a little surprised to enter one house where a group of frivolous folk were in the middle of eating generous servings of steaming chicken.

Now the word "*kapparos*" means both the ritual of atonement on the eve of Yom Kippur, and (in common parlance) the chickens used at that time. Reminding them therefore by suggestion that they would one day have to seek atonement for their present irresponsibility, he said: "If you eat your chickens now, then when it comes to the eve of Yom Kippur, *where will you find kapparos ... ?*"

the three weeks

◈§ In Your Own Interest

In 1868 an epidemic of cholera cast dread over entire Russian provinces. An emissary was therefore dispatched from Kremenchug in order to ask Reb Aharon of Chernobyl to intercede in heaven on behalf of the townsfolk. The emissary handed the tzaddik his *pidyon*, and stayed in Chernobyl over *Shabbos*. The portion that was read in the Torah that week was *Re'eh*, which begins as follows: רְאֵה אָנֹכִי נֹתֵן לִפְנֵיכֶם הַיּוֹם בְּרָכָה וּקְלָלָה. אֶת הַבְּרָכָה אֲשֶׁר תִּשְׁמְעוּ אֶל מִצְוֹת ה' — "Behold, I set before you this day a blessing and a curse; the blessing, if you will obey the commandments of God ..."

At the Friday evening meal the tzaddik began his discourse as follows: "Expounding the opening words of this week's *Sidra* on the plane of *derush*, the saintly author of *Or HaChaim* writes that Moshe Rabbeinu said to the Children of Israel, רְאֵה אָנֹכִי — 'Look upon me, and blessing will be given you.' Now I cannot say this; but something else I *can* say: וְהַקְּלָלָה אִם לֹא — 'If You, Master of the Universe, will not place this curse upon them, then I am Your guarantor that יִשְׁמְעוּ אֶל מִצְוֹת ה' — that they will obey Your commandments."

Then he added: "Look! You have already placed upon Your children (heaven forfend!) this curse of the epidemic. So what came out of that? — They were so weak and vulnerable to contagion that I myself had to instruct them to eat meat during the Nine Days of Mourning! And as to the fast of Tishah BeAv itself, I wrote telling them all not to fast. It is obviously preferable, then, Master of the Universe, that You should bring about the opposite situation: וְהַקְּלָלָה אִם לֹא — that this curse should be removed; and then You will see for Yourself: אֲשֶׁר יִשְׁמְעוּ אֶל מִצְוֹת ה' — that they will obey Your commandments. Almighty! Watch over all the House of Israel, and especially over the afflicted town of Kremenchug! Spare them from all disease and misfortune — and may we be found worthy of the final Redemption!"

[460]   *A Treasury of Chassidic Tales on the Festivals*

איכה
✥ Full Days

*Your years were long years, unlike mine
(Kinos, Lamentations for Tishah BeAv).*

On the way home from the funeral of Reb Yehudah Aryeh Leib of Ger (the author of *Sfas Emes*) in 1905, his eldest son Reb Avraham Mordechai who was soon to succeed him, commented to his brother, Reb Moshe Bezalel: "Our father had אֲרִיכוּת יָמִים — length of days."

"But he did not even reach the age of sixty!" his brother pointed out.

Replied Reb Avraham Mordechai: "Length of years he did not have, but he did have length of days."

איכה
Lamentations

Eichah, the Book of Lamentations, is read in the halflit synagogue in the undertone of mourners on the eve of Tishah BeAv, the ninth day of the month of Av, the anniversary of the destruction of both the First and the Second Temple.

✥ The Tears of Israel

On a visit to Kotsk, Reb Yaakov David of Amshinov complained to Reb Menachem Mendel that since the passing of his father, Reb Yitzchak of Vorki, he had not yet seen him.

"You will see him," Reb Menachem Mendel reassured him.

And indeed, while he was still in Kotsk, he entered his host's study and told him that he had seen his father.

בָּכוֹ תִבְכֶּה
בַּלַּיְלָה
She weeps sore in the night
(Lam. 1:2)

The Three Weeks / בין המצרים [461]

Lamentations

"In what state did you see him?" asked Reb Menachem Mendel.

"I saw him standing by a river," said the son, "leaning on his staff, as if he were gazing into the river."

"That river," said the Kotsker, "flows from the tears of Israel."

❧ Consolation for a Scholar

צַדִּיק הוּא ה׳
God is righteous (Lam. 1:18)

A prominent *rav* who was one of the opponents of Chassidism could find no consolation after his daughter had passed away, and in his distress he decided to travel to the rebbe of Kotsk, though without telling him anything of the circumstances that had brought him there.

On his arrival Reb Menachem Mendel confronted him with a difficult passage in the Talmud. The *rav* explained it.

The tzaddik challenged him: "But according to your interpretation, the commentary of *Tosafos* is puzzling!"

The *rav* cited and evaluated the various sides to the argument, and resolved the apparent contradiction. And so it was in the case of each seeming riddle or anomaly that Reb Menachem Mendel presented to him.

At length the tzaddik turned to him and said: "If indeed everything here proves to be in order and justifiable, then without a doubt the Almighty too is just, and His ways are righteous!"

The pain of the *rav* was eased by the balm of this consolation, and in due course he became a disciple of the tzaddik of Kotsk.

❧ Imported Inspiration

הִשְׁלִיךְ מִשָּׁמַיִם אֶרֶץ תִּפְאֶרֶת יִשְׂרָאֵל
He cast down from heaven to earth the glory of Israel (Lam. 2:1)

In the days when Reb Yitzchak Meir of Ger still lived in Warsaw, one of his chassidim came to request the tzaddik's blessing on the eve of his departure for Prussia on business.

As they parted the rebbe said: "I have heard that in Germany there are rabbis — known there as *rabbiner* — who are God-fearing. Could you please find out if this is so?"

[462] *A Treasury of Chassidic Tales on the Festivals*

On the eve of Rosh Chodesh Av, just before the **אֵיכָה** merchant set out on his homeward journey, he entered a synagogue in the middle of the sermon of the local *rabbiner*. The German rabbi had just quoted the words from the Book of *Lamentations:* הִשְׁלִיךְ מִשָּׁמַיִם ... אֵיכָה אֶרֶץ תִּפְאֶרֶת יִשְׂרָאֵל — "How has He cast down from heaven to earth the glory of Israel!" By a homiletical transposition of the words in the Hebrew original, the *rav* taught the following *derush:* "How has Israel cast down the values of *heaven* — spirituality, and in their stead has sought its glory in the values of the *earth* — worldliness!"

The first thing the chassid did on his return to Poland was to visit his rebbe.

"Well, what did you see over there?" the rebbe asked.

And when he was told this interpretation, he walked up and down his room in delighted agitation.

"Is it conceivable that a *rav* from Germany should propose such a thought?" he marveled. "It suits one of the disciples of the tzaddik of Pshischah, not a *rav* from Germany! It is clear that that *rav* over there must have a soul-root stemming from one of the tzaddikim of Poland ..."

✥ Two Kinds of Service

Driving through Krasna in his cozy carriage one bitter winter's night, Reb Moshe of Savran asked his coachman to draw rein in front of the cottage of Reb Yeshaya Leib, the aged local *rav*, who was exceedingly poor. Walking inside, he found his host huddled in bed and trying to protect himself against the freezing cold with a lean patchwork eiderdown — yet studying energetically.

קוּמִי רֹנִּי בַלַּיְלָה
Arise, cry out in the night (Lam. 2:19)

"Rav of Krasna!" he exclaimed. "Is it possible thus to serve the Almighty? For in the Book of *Psalms* King David writes otherwise: כְּמוֹ חֵלֶב וָדֶשֶׁן תִּשְׂבַּע נַפְשִׁי, וְשִׂפְתֵי רְנָנוֹת יְהַלֶּל פִּי — 'My soul is sated as with marrow and fatness, and my mouth praises You with joyful lips.' That is to say: when a man eats a square meal in the evening and sits in a warm house, *then* he can sleep, and rise at midnight to study afresh."

Lamentations

"And as for me," said Reb Yeshaya Leib, promptly quoting the very next verse in *Psalms,* "I say that *this* is what King David said: אִם זְכַרְתִּיךָ עַל יְצוּעָי, בְּאַשְׁמֻרוֹת אֶהְגֶּה בָּךְ — 'If I remember You upon my bed, and meditate on You in the watches of the night.' That is to say: when before retiring at night a man recites *Shema Yisrael* in a contrite spirit, *then* he can rise at midnight and study afresh."

As the guest now prepared to take his leave, his aged host told him regretfully: "I very much wanted to fulfill the mitzvah of escorting one's guest at least part of the way — but I am not adequately clothed for such weather."

"*Nu*, don't worry," Reb Moshe assured him. "After all, as you yourself say: 'If I remember you upon my bed ...'"

He then asked his coachman to bring a warm coat and furlined boots from the carriage, and handed them to Reb Yeshayahu Leib.

"But how shall I return them?" asked the elderly *rav*.

"When we reach the first inn along the highway," replied Reb Moshe, "I will ask my coachman to take you home in the carriage while I wait at the inn.'

When they finally parted at the inn door, Reb Moshe asked: "Well, sir, what do you say? Which is the better way to serve the Almighty?"

"It could be that you are right," conceded Reb Yeshayahu Leib, "but at my age I am not going to change my path."

Reb Moshe quietly warned his attendant not to bring the clothes back with him, and the carriage rolled down the highway on its way back to the cold cottage.

⥢§ Inspired Envy

שִׁפְכִי כַמַּיִם לִבֵּךְ
Pour out your heart like water (Lam. 2:19)

A striking boyhood memory has been recorded by Reb Yosef Yitzchak, the son of Reb Shalom Ber of Lubavitch.

"When I was a lad my father once laid down for me a course of study on the subject of a broken and humble heart. He wrote me a prescription, as it were. My studies on the sources he indicated on this subject took me some

three weeks, in the course of which my uncle Reb איכה
Nachum Dov came to stay with us as our *Shabbos* guest.

" 'Your uncle,' said my father, 'is truly a man with a broken heart' " — and it should be noted that this term in Hebrew (לֵב נִשְׁבָּר) does not describe a person overtaken by calamity, but one who is humble of spirit. "One weekday as I was on my way home for lunch after morning classes at *cheder* I dropped into the local *shul*, and was amazed at what I saw. Reb Dov, a villager who was the father of our attendant, was leaning against the table which stood in the middle of the synagogue, reading to himself in a quiet singsong from the Book of *Tehillim*, while my uncle, Reb Nachum Dov, was standing at a side wall gazing upon this villager with anguish written on his face, and his eyes streaming with tears.

"When I came home and described this scene to my father, he said: 'Your uncle in his humility envies that villager. There you truly have a man with a broken heart.' "

☙ There is Hope for the Learned

Snatched away from their home in early childhood, drafted into the rigors of the czarist army, coerced through torture to baptize, yet defying sustained brutality to assert their unsophisticated but unflinching loyalty to their Judaism, — these were the Cantonists. In the year 1843, when Reb Menachem Mendel of Lubavitch was in Petersburg for the famous Rabbinical Conference, six hundred of these Cantonists from the Petersburg region received permission from the authorities to meet in the capital and be addressed by him. The rebbe delivered a chassidic discourse in simple terms, which so affected them that many of those present shed tears of spiritual awakening.

טוֹב לַגֶּבֶר
שֶׁיִּשָּׂא עֹל
It is good for a man that he bear a yoke
(Lam. 3:27)

When he had concluded his words, fifteen of them approached him in the name of the whole group and said: "Rebbe! As Jews, we are maimed. We can't study, we know nothing. But we do stand by our faith, and we do know the words of the prayers for weekdays and *Shabbos* and *Yom-Tov*, and the Grace after Meals, and a few Psalms as well — though, mind you, we mightn't know the meaning of all the words."

The rebbe spoke reassuringly: "A Jew who believes in the Almighty — that He is the Creator of the universe, and gives life to it and all those who dwell in it through the Divine Providence which is directed to each individual created thing that exists; and that He gave us the Torah and the mitzvos; and if such a Jew knows the text of the prayers and the Grace after Meals and a few Psalms besides, — such a man is a strong and healthy Jew. Be well in body and in spirit, and may the Almighty bring you in peace to your homes!"

In the evening the rebbe told the communal leaders and chassidim who had gathered to meet him: "The decree conscripting the Cantonists resembles the war of the ancient Greeks, who in the time of the Hasmoneans waged a *spiritual* battle. As to the prayers of these Cantonists, their value is incalculable, being on a loftier rung than the prayers of those erudite and saintly folk who worship according to the mystical *kavanos* of the *Arizal* — for all their divine service is executed in the self-sacrificing spirit of *mesirus nefesh,* and out of simple faith. When *Mashiach* comes he will delight in the company of the simple *mesirus-nefesh* Jews. A unique spiritual palace will be theirs, and the most respected worshipers of a philosophical bent will envy them."

One of the chassidim present now spoke up: "Rebbe! How can one become אַ פָּשׁוּטֶער ייִד, אַ בַּעַל־מְסִירוּת־נֶפֶשׁ בִּתְמִימוּת — a simple Jew, of the kind who is capable of self-sacrifice out of simple faith?"

The questioner, Reb Chaim of Vitebsk by name, was at home throughout every tractate of the entire Babylonian Talmud, and expert as well in the philosophical and ethical teachings of Chassidism.

The rebbe replied: "That is in fact *more* difficult than becoming בָּקִי בְּשַׁ״ס — at home in the entire Talmud!"

But after a pause he added: "There is one remedy: קַבָּלַת עוֹל — divine service through the unquestioning acceptance of the yoke of the Will of heaven. For this *kabbalas ol* alters the essence of a man; and through *kabbalas ol* like that of a simple bondman, on whom the yoke of his subservience is apparent even when he is asleep, *even a scholar or a gaon* can aspire to the heights

attained by the Jew who out of simple faith serves his
Maker out of a spirit of self-sacrifice!"

איכה

◆§ In One Moment

A chassid of the Chozeh of Lublin once heard him expounding the verse: ה׳ מוֹרִישׁ וּמַעֲשִׁיר — "God makes poor and makes rich." Explained the Chozeh: "In one moment."

אַל יִתְהַלֵּל עָשִׁיר בְּעָשְׁרוֹ
Let not the rich man glory in his wealth
(Haftarah)

The chassid protested: "But how is it possible that 'God should make poor and makes rich' *in one moment?* If a man owns say a million gold dinars and property of all kinds, how is it possible that he should lose all his wealth *in one moment?*"

The Chozeh replied simply: "Go your way, and you will see what comes about."

The chassid took the road homeward. Halfway there, as he passed the house of a certain priest he knew, the Evil Inclination suddenly seized hold of him and persuaded him to abandon his faith — to baptize! Consumed by this raging conflagration which possessed him, he entered the house and boldly announced that he wanted to change his faith.

"You liar that you are!" shrieked the priest, for he had known him for years. "You're only here to make fun of me!"

"Not at all," insisted the Jew; "in all seriousness I mean exactly what I say."

"Then this is how your sincerity can be put to the test," the priest stipulated. "If you are in fact serious about what you say, then write me out a deed conveying all your proporty to me as an absolute gift."

And that is exactly what the man did.

The moment the document was signed, sealed and delivered, he awoke from his passing aberration and a spirit of sobriety returned to him. Intensely regretful, and shocked by his own treacherous thought, he fled from the house. The accursed document he left knowingly behind him, thinking: "It is worth losing all my wealth, so long as I do not lose my soul!" And since he soon realized that this misfortune had overtaken him on account of his having cast doubt on the teachings of

Lamentations his rebbe, he decided to return at once to Lublin, where he told the Chozeh the whole story.

"Well," said the rebbe, "now you doubtless realize that 'God makes poor' *in one moment* — for in one moment you found yourself naked and needy."

"But now," said the chassid, "I want to understand how 'God makes rich' *in one moment.*"

"Journey home," said the tzaddik, "and may the Almighty help you!"

The man did not even manage to reach his home, when a fire sent from heaven broke out in the priest's home. Everything he owned was burned — including the precious deed. The chassid was thus once more the owner of all his former wealth, and the assurance of the Chozeh, that *'God makes rich,'* was fulfilled — *in one moment.*

◆§ It is the Beloved who are Loving

בּשְׁנוּ מְאֹד
כִּי עָזַבְנוּ
אָרֶץ
We are ashamed indeed for we have forsaken the land
(Haftarah)

A chassid from Poland who went up to the Holy Land and settled in Jerusalem found himself unable to adjust to conditions of life there. Accordingly, he decided to return to Poland. Before leaving the Holy City he went along to take his leave of Reb Simchah Bunem of Vorki, the son of Reb Menachem Mendel of Vorki, who then lived in Jerusalem.

When he had explained his reason for leaving, the tzaddik sighed from the depths of his heart and said: "I feel very sorry for you. It seems that you did not find favor in the eyes of Jerusalem, for if you *had* found favor in her eyes, she would have found favor in yours ..."

These words trickled into that chassid's heart. He thought over his decision, and to the end of his days remained a loved and loving son of the Holy City.

Biographical Sketches

✑§ Introductory Note to the Biographical Sketches

1. The biographies appearing here are not alphabetized under surnames — because in the period under review (a) these are relatively few, and (b) they were commonly used imprecisely. For example: a place name earlier used descriptively to identify a person may at some indeterminable point in history begin to assume the formality of a surname.

2. In Yiddish, the mother tongue of almost all the heroes of these volumes, identification by locality is shown by the suffix *-er*, which in English is usually rendered *of*. (For example: "Kotsker" appears as "of Kotsk.")

3. In the Rabbinic world, such is the status of books that authors are often better known by the titles of their published works than by their own proper names. In these and similar cases, a *see* reference directs the reader to the desired entry.

4. An asterisk indicates the appearance in this section of an entry thus marked.

5. The alphabetization ignores parenthetical words.

6. To allow this section to also serve as an index to the personalities mentioned in this work, each entry is followed by a citation of pages on which the individual is mentioned. The following key is used:
T1 = *A Treasury of Chassidic Tales on the Torah*, vol. 1
T2 = *A Treasury of Chassidic Tales on the Torah*, vol. 2
F1 = *A Treasury of Chassidic Tales on the Festivals*, vol. 1
F2 = *A Treasury of Chassidic Tales on the Festivals*, vol. 2
For example: **T2**:379, 435. This entry refers the reader to *A Treasury of Chassidic Tales on the Torah*, vol. 2, page 379 and page 435. These page numbers indicate the *beginning* of the relevant story (or stories).

7. In order to help the reader who recalls the name of an odd character locate the story in which he appears, the listing below includes not only prominent figures, but virtually all the obscure individuals as well.

8. Passing mentions of the key personalities are generally noted side by side with their more significant appearances as protagonists. The aim here is to enable the astute and interested reader to marshal all these tangential but telling clues into a collective impression or collage of the figure in question; to enable him to trace the transmission of ideological traditions from master to disciple; to discern the appearance of family traits in father and son.

9. Throughout these four volumes of stories, the persons involved are referred to by either of two forms of address. If they belonged to the chassidic brotherhood, they are referred to as *Reb* — which is respectful, but relaxed and informal; if they did not, they are given the benefit of the more deferential title, *Rabbi*. In this Biographical Index, however, for the sake of simplicity, all the personages are referred to indiscriminately by the abbreviation *R.*, which can be pronounced in each case according to one's inclinations.

The Three Weeks / בין המצרים [471]

R. Abba
Chassid of R *Avraham of Chechanov.
T2:56

R. Abba'le (R. Avraham Abba) of Neustadt
18th-cent. kabbalist; disciple of R. *Simchah Bunem of Phischah and others.
T2:452

Adel
Daughter of the *Baal Shem Tov, and wife of R. *Yechiel Ashkenazi. Their children were R. *Moshe Chaim Ephraim of Sudylkov, R. *Baruch of Mezhibuzh, and Feige, the mother of R. *Nachman of Breslov. She figures in many chassidic stories as a selfless and saintly personage.
T2:459; F1:23, 223; F2:315

R. Aharon (Uren) Leib of Premishlan
Son of R. Meir the Elder of Premishlan, and elder disciple of the *Baal Shem Tov, and himself a disciple of R. *Yechiel Michel of Zlotchov and R. *Elimelech of Lyzhansk. He was the father of R. *Meir of Premishlan.
Died 1783 (2 Adar).
T2:328, 372

R. Aharon Marcus
German scholar, author of *Der Cassidismus* (1901).
Born 1843, died 1916.
T2:501

R. Aharon of Chernobyl
Grandson and student of R. Menachem *Nachum of Chernobyl, and eldest son of R. *Mordechai of Chernobyl, whom he succeeded as rebbe to thousands of Ukrainian chassidim. He was the son-in-law (by his first marriage) of R. Gedaliah of Linitz and then (by his second marriage) of R. *Aharon of Titiev.
Born 1787, died 1871 (8 Kislev).
T1:73; T2:561; F1:303; F2:337, 460

R. Aharon of Cracow
Disciple of R. *Shlomo of Radomsk.
T1: 269

R. Aharon ("the Great") of Karlin
R. Aharon HaGadol ("the Great"; not to be confused with his grandson, R. *Aharon the Second, d. 1872) was a disciple of R. *Dov Ber of Mezritch. He was the pioneer of Chassidism in Lithuania, as is evidenced by the fact that in contemporary sources "Karliner" became a local synonym for "chassid." He is remembered for the ecstatic and unrestrained fervor of his prayer, for his solicitude for the needy, and for the moral teachings embodied in his *Azharos* ("Warnings"). To this day the *zemiros* sung at the *Shabbos* table of chassidim of the Karlin dynasty are highlighted by one of the twenty or more melodies to which a classic hymn of his composition has been set. He was succeeded by his disciple R. *Shlomo of Karlin, after whose death the succession reverted to his son, R. *Asher of Stolin (d. 1823).
Born 1736, died 1772 (19 Nissan).
T1:112, 157, 221; F2:384

R. Aharon ("the Second") of Karlin
Son and successor of R. Asher of Stolin (d. 1823), the son of R. *Aharon ("the Great") of Karlin; he was the author of *Beis Aharon*, on the weekly Torah readings. During the period of his leadership groups of his chassidim settled in *Eretz Yisrael*, and the renowned repertoire of Karlin melodies came into being. Like his father, he spent his later years in Stolin, the town which gave the Karlin dynasty its alternative name. He was succeeded by his son, R. Asher ("the Second").
Born 1806, died 1872 (17 Sivan).
T1:208; T2:561

R. Aharon of Liozna
Elder chassid of R. *Shlomo Zalman of Kopust.
F1:34

R. Aharon of Ludmir
Chassid, contemporary of R. *Zusya of Hanipoli.
F1:194

Biographical Sketches [473]

R. Aharon of Titiev
Son of R. *Zvi, the son of the *Baal Shem Tov. His lifestyle was secluded and ascetic. R. Naftali Zvi of Skver was his son, and his sons-in-law were R. *Baruch of Mezhibuzh and R. *Aharon of Chernobyl.
Died 1827.
T1:134

R. Aizel Homiler
See R. Yitzchak Aizik of Homil.

Aizik
See also Yitzchak Aizik.

R. Aizik Mechadesh
Misnaged of Liozna, contemporary of R. *Shnuer Zalman of Liadi.
F1:225

R. Aizik (Eichenstein) of Safrin
His biography has no distinguished career to flaunt, yet his memory is revered for his saintly lifestyle, and for the exemplary upbringing he gave his five famous sons: R. *Zvi Hirsch of Zhidachov, R. *Moshe of Sambor, R. *Alexander Sender of Komarna, R. *Beirish of Zhidachov, and R. *Lipa of Sambor. Their home was in Safrin, Hungary (not to be confused with Savran, Podolia).
T2:431; F1:182

R. Aizik Reb Yekeles
Prominent banker and merchant, and communal leader in Cracow, Poland. The impressive synagogue which figures in the story, and which may still be seen, was built between 1638 and 1644, in defiance of ecclesiastical opposition.
Died 1653.
T2:606

R. Alexander Sender of Komarna
A child prodigy, he was reputed to have mastered and memorized the three tractates *Bava Kama*, *Bava Metzia* and *Bava Basra*, with their commentaries, by the age of seven. His mentors were his eldest brother, R. *Zvi Hirsch of Zhidachov, and R. *Yaakov Yitzchak, the Chozeh of Lublin. He lived a life of poverty and asceticism, and was succeeded by his son, R. *Yitzchak Aizik Yechiel of Komarna.
Died 1818 (21 Av).
T2:430, 431

R. Alexander Sender Yom-Tov Lipa of Zhidachov
See R. Lipa of Sambor.

R. Alter of Yazlivitz
Elder chassid of R. *Meir of Premishlan.
T2:372

Alter Rebbe
See R. Shneur Zalman of Liadi.

R. Anshel Ashkenazi
Son-in-law of R. *Chanoch Henich of Alisk.
F2:407

Ari (Arizal)
See R. Yitzchak Luria.

R. Aryeh Leib Heller
Galician scholar renowned as the author of *K'tzos HaChoshen* on part of *Shulchan Aruch*. After becoming *rav* of Stryy, he established a yeshivah there. Though the town was a stronghold of Chassidism, which he opposed, he was respected there for his erudition. His works, which also include *Avnei Miluim* and *Shev Shmaatsa*, have become classics in the yeshivah world.
Born 1745(?), died 1812 (27 Tishrei).
T:406

R. Aryeh Leib of Shpola (the Shpoler Zeide — "the Grandfather from Shpola")
A disciple of R. *Pinchas of Korets, the Shpoler Zeide figures in numerous chassidic stories as a miracle-worker who came to the relief of the common people in times of distress. He expressed misgivings about the teachings of his contemporary, R. *Nachman of Breslov. None of his writings have been preserved.
Died 1811 (6 Tishrei).
T1:37, 312; T2:331, 337, 453, 467, 546; F1:50, 56, 293; F2:332, 380, 420

R. Aryeh Leibush
Father of R. *Chaim of Zanz and *rav* of Tarnograd.
F1:146

R. Asher
Chassid of R. *Yisrael of Ruzhin.
F1:114

R. Asher
Relative by marriage of R. *Menachem Mendel of Lubavitch.
F1:237

R. Asher (Rabinowitz) of Pshedborz
Head of the Rabbinical Court in Pshedborz, and father of R. *Yaakov Yitzchak (the Yid HaKadosh) of Pshischah.
T1:162

R. Asher (Rubin) of Ropshitz
Son-in-Law of R. *Naftali of Ropshitz, whom he succeeded as rebbe in that town.
T1:36; T2:487

R. Asher ("the First") of Stolin
Son of R. *Aharon ("the Great") of Karlin, and studied as well under his father's disciple and successor, R. *Shlomo of Karlin, whom he in turn succeeded. Not to be confused with his grandson, R. Asher ("the Second") of Karlin (d. 1873), the son of R. *Aharon ("the Second") of Karlin. He guided communal leaders to the path of humility.
Died 1823 (26 Tishrei).
T1:157, 204; T2:343; F1:80

R. Avigdor
Rosh yeshivah of Vilna, ca. 1801.
T2:494

R. Avigdor Halberstam
Brother of R. *Chaim of Zanz; *rav* of Dukla (Galicia).
T1:252

Avnei Nezer
See R. Avraham of Sochatchov.

R. Avraham
Brother of R. *Yisrael of Ruzhin.
F2:421

R. Avraham Abele Gombiner
Polish scholar, author of *Magen Avraham*, a classic commentary on part of the *Shulchan Aruch*, and *Zayis Raanan*, on *Yalkut Shimoni*.
Born ca.1633-37, died 1683 (9 Tishrei).
T1:106

R. Avraham Binyamin Sofer
See R. Avraham Shmuel Binyamin Wolf Sofer.

R. Avraham Bornstein
See R. Avraham of Sochatchov.

R. Avraham Gershon of Kitov
See R. Gershon of Kitov.

R. Avraham HaKohen (ben Alexander) of Kalisk
A disciple of giants in the worlds of both the chassidim and the *misnagdim*, R. *Dov Ber of Mezritch and the Gaon of Vilna respectively. He emphasized *dibbuk chaverim* — group interaction — as a means of achieving spiritual awareness. The abandon with which his followers gave expression to their ecstatic joy during prayer roused the ire of the *misnagdim* of the day. He settled in Eretz Yisrael in 1777. His works include *Chesed LeAvraham*.
Born 1741, died 1810 (4 Shvat).
F1:73

R. Avraham Mordechai (son of R. *Yitzchak Meir) Alter of Ger
Suffered from illness throughout most of his life; worked as a shopkeeper and printer; father of R. *Yehudah Aryeh Leib of Ger; died at 39, during his father's lifetime.
Born 1816, died 1855 (26 Av).
T1:164; F1:152; F2:426

R. Avraham Mordechai (son of R. *Yehudah Aryeh Leib) Alter of Ger
A foremost Talmudic scholar whose diligence, alacrity, and purity of speech were legendary. Author of *Imrei Emes* on the Torah, but most of his voluminous writings on the Talmud, Halachah and Chassidism were destroyed during World War II. A gifted organizer who left his stamp on the influential community of

Gerer chassidim, first in Poland, where his followers were numbered in the hundreds of thousands, then in *Eretz Yisrael,* where he settled in 1940. He was one of the founders of the Agudas Yisrael movement, and was active in establishing schools and youth organizations, as well as in rescue and rehabilitation work during and after the Holocaust. In Jerusalem he founded the *Sfas Emes* yeshivah, in whose grounds he was buried during the siege of Jerusalem. Succeeded by his son R. Yisrael Alter of Ger (d. 1978). Born 1866, died 1948 (6 Sivan).
T1:164; **F1**:167; **F2**:368, 461

R. Avraham Mordechai of Pintchov
Disciple of R. *Elimelech of Lyzhansk, R. *Zusya of Hanipoli, and of R. *Yaakov Yitzchak (the Chozeh) of Lublin; father-in-law of R. *Yitzchak Aizik of Komarna.
F1:78

R. Avraham Moshe of Pshischah
Son and successor (for the remaining two years of his life) of R. *Simchah Bunem of Pshischah. Immediately after his father's death many of the chassidim regarded R. *Menachem Mendel of Kotsk as their leader — an attitude which R. Avraham Moshe encouraged, as is evidenced by an extant letter of his.
Died 1829 (1 Teves).
T1:186; **T2**:585; **F1**:176

R. Avraham (Landau) of Chechanov
Disciple of R. *Fishel of Strikov. Though invited to accept prominent rabbinical posts, he refused to leave the small community of Chechanov (Ciechanow, in central Poland) where he served as *rav* for 56 years. Wrote Talmudic and halachic works. His sons included R. Ze'ev Wolff of Strikov and R. *Yaakov of Yazov.
Born 1789, died 1875 (5 Adar).
T2:356, 620; **F1**:160; **F2**:345, 459

R. Avraham of Chmielnik
Mechutan of R. *Baruch of Mezhibuzh.
T1:131

R. Avraham of Kalisk
See R. Avraham HaKohen of Kalisk.

R. Avraham of Parisov
Uncle of R. *Pinchas Eliyahu of Piltz.
T1:35; **T2**:350

R. Avraham of Slonim
Son of R. Yitzchak Matisyahu Weinberg of Slonim; studied under R. *Noach of Lechovitch and R. *Moshe of Kobrin. He was active in disseminating Chassidism amidst the strongholds of the *misnagdim* in Lithuania, and exerted himself tirelessly for the spiritual and material welfare of those who had settled in *Eretz Yisrael.* His works include *Yesod HaAvodah, Chesed LeAvraham,* and *Be'er Avraham* on the *Mechilta.*
Born 1804, died 1883 (11 Cheshvan).
T1:262; **F1**:201

R. Avraham (Bornstein) of Sochatchov
Son of R. *Ze'ev Nachum, *rav* of Biala, and early recognized as a prodigy. Like his father before him he established yeshivos in each of the communities in which he served as *rav,* before finally settling in Sochatchov. His classic writings include *Avnei Nezer* (responsa) and *Eglei Tal* (on the laws of *Shabbos*). After ten years' study in the house of his father-in-law, R. *Menachem Mendel of Kotsk, until the latter's death, he became a follower first of R. *Yitzchak Meir of Ger, and then of R. *Chanoch Henich of Alexander, whom he eventually succeeded as the rebbe of thousands of chassidim. He was succeeded in turn by his son R. Shmuel (1856-1926). Born 1839, died 1910 (25 Adar).
T1:233; **T2**:364, 371, 426, 556, 577, 586, 619; **F1**:218, 302; **F2**:359

R. Avraham of Stretyn
Son and successor of R. *Yehudah Zvi Hirsch of Stretyn.
Died 1865.
T2:482; **F1**:285

R. Avraham (the Maggid) of Trisk
Born into the Twersky dynasty; a son of R. *Mordechai of Chernobyl. His

approachability and friendliness to all comers drew thousands of chassidim to the court which he conducted for some fifty years at Trisk. His *Magen Avraham* on the Torah and festivals enjoys great popularity among chassidim.
Born 1802, died 1889 (2 Tammuz).
T2:452; **F1**:121, 147

R. Avraham of Ulianov
Son of R. Yitzchak (Itzikl) Charif of Sambor; author of several Talmudic works including *Toldos Avraham*; highly regarded by his contemporaries, including R. *Chaim of Zanz, and his mentor, R. *Naftali of Ropshitz.
Born 1782(?), died 1814 (23 Tishrei).
F1:238, 301

R. Avraham Shalom of Stropkov
Son of R. *Yechezkel of Shiniva.
F1:210

R. Avraham Sheines of Shklov
Born into a rabbinic family of *misnagdim*, but became a prominent chassid of R. *Shneur Zalman of Liadi.
T1:231; **T2**:512

R. Avraham Shmuel Binyamin Wolf Sofer
Eldest son of R. Moshe Sofer, the author of *Chasam Sofer*, whom he succeeded in 1839 as *rav* and *rosh yeshivah* of Pressburg. Author of responsa and Torah commentary under the title *Ksav Sofer*.
Born 1815, died 1871.
F2:406

R. Avraham the Doctor
Of Liozna; contemporary of R. *Shneur Zalman of Liadi.
F1:225

R. Avraham the Malach ("the Angel")
Son of R. *Dov Ber (the Maggid) of Mezritch, who appointed his disciple R. *Shneur Zalman of Liadi to be his son's study companion: he was to teach Avraham *nigleh*, the revealed plane of the Torah, and to be taught in return *nistar*, the concealed, kabbalistic dimension of the Torah. Whilst a young man he chose an ascetic and secluded lifestyle, and on his father's passing in 1772 declined to assume leadership of the chassidic movement. He wrote a work entitled *Chesed LeAvraham*, and died at the age of 37. His only son, R. *Shalom Shachna of Probisht, was the father of R. *Yisrael of Ruzhin.
Born 1739, died 1776 (12 Tishrei).
T2:331; **F1**:132, 188, 258, 309; **F2**:404, 458

R. Avraham Yaakov of Sadigora
Son of R. *Yisrael of Ruzhin, whom he succeeded as rebbe at his father's last place of residence, in Sadigora. He married the daughter of R. *Aharon ("the Second") of Karlin. He was succeeded in Sadigora by his younger son, R. Yisrael, while his elder son, R. Yitzchak, founded the dynasty of Boyan.
Born 1819, died 1883 (11 Elul).
T2:390; **F1**:113, 147, 188, 309; **F2**:328

R. Avraham Yehoshua Heschel (the Ohev Yisrael) of Apta
Descended from R. Herschel of Cracow, *Maharam* of Lublin and *Maharam* of Padua, and studied under R. *Yechiel Michel of Zlotchov and R. *Elimelech of Lyzhansk. He delivered his celebrated sermons in fervor and ecstasy, and used his extensive influence to settle differences between conflicting chassidic groups. He was the author of *Toras Emes*, and of *Ohev Yisrael* ("the lover of his fellow Jew"), these being the only two descriptive words he agreed to have engraved on his tombstone. He is known to this day either by this epitaph, or as "the *rav* of Apta," this being one of the communities in which he served (in addition to Kolbasov, Jassy and Mezhibuzh).
Died 1825 (5 Nissan).
T1:93, 149, 296, 311; **T2**:345, 395, 413, 432, 448, 541, 555, 566, 603, 621; **F1**:100, 147, 194, 250, 282, 291; **F2**:328, 341, 370, 376, 414, 427

R. Avraham Yissachar of Radomsk
Son of R. *Shlomo of Radomsk; author of *Chesed LeAvraham*; father of R. *Yechezkel HaKohen of Radomsk.
Died 1892.
T2:465

R. Avraham Yisrael
Chassid of R. *Shneur Zalman of Liadi.
T2:572

R. Azriel, *rav* of Lublin
Son of R. Dov Halevi Horovitz; outstanding Talmudic scholar. After a lifetime of antagonism to Chassidism, he was buried next to its chief local exponent, R. *Yaakov Yitzchak (the Chozeh) of Lublin.
Died 1818 (22 Cheshvan).
T2:557

R. Azriel of Polotzk
Disciple of R. *Dov Ber of Mezritch, under whose direction he disseminated the teachings of Chassidism. Not to be confused with his colleague R. Yisrael (ben R. Peretz) of Polotzk, one of the leaders of the chassidic *aliyah* of 1777.
F2:323

Baal HaTanya
See R. Shneur Zalman of Liadi.

Baal Shem Tov
Founder of Chassidism. Born on 18 Elul to a poor family in Okop, an obscure village in Podolia, Ukraine; orphaned early; lived modestly as a teacher's assistant in a *cheder*. When in his twenties, in spiritual preparation for his lifework, he began a period of seclusion in the Carpathian mountains with his wife, supporting himself as a digger of clay. He had a son R. *Zvi, and a daughter, *Adel.

On his 36th birthday he revealed himself as a miracle healer and spiritual guide — a physician of both body and soul — to an ever-widening circle of followers which included scholars as well as common folk. His chassidim were inspired both by his teachings, whose roots often draw on the Kabbalah, and by his joyful and ecstatic mode of prayer. In the innumerable stories told of him, at times he appears in a state of mystical exaltation; at others, as a concerned shepherd, fearlessly and optimistically confronting the physical and spiritual anguish which was so often the lot of the community and the individual in eighteenth-century Eastern Europe. Ever since his time, his teachings and his personality have remained the chief inspiration for the hundreds of chassidic leaders who have — each in his own style — addressed themselves likewise to the challenge of tackling the physical and spiritual anguish of the Jewish community and the individual Jew, whether in the Old World in the nineteenth century, or in the New World in the twentieth.

For a brief summary of his teachings, see the entry on Chassidism in the Glossary of this volume.
Born 1698, died 1760 (6 Sivan).
T1:40, 62, 86, 89, 100, 109, 120, 122, 123, 125, 134, 170, 195, 247, 248, 254, 274, 285, 292, 295; T2:319, 337, 379, 402, 428, 439, 448, 449, 459, 499, 500, 515, 579, 597; F1:23, 39, 63, 98, 104, 118, 124, 183, 184, 196, 199, 223, 225, 243, 244, 245, 258; F2:315, 374, 402, 417, 435

R. Baruch
Father of R. *Aryeh Leib of Shpola.
T2:337

R. Baruch
Father of R. *Shneur Zalman of Liadi.
T1:116

R. Baruch David
Son of R. *Mordechai Dov of Hornisteipl.
T2:469

R. Baruch Frenkel-Teomim
Son of R. Yehoshua Yechezkel Teomim, and author of *Baruch Taam*. Served in an honorary capacity as *rav* of Leipnick in order not to break a continuous family tradition of 250 years. He was the father-in-law of R. *Chaim of Zanz.
Died 1825 (6 Tammuz).
T1:238

R. Baruch Mordechai, *rav* of Bobruisk
Chassid of R. *Shneur Zalman of Liadi; settled in *Eretz Yisrael* in the last year of his life.
Died 1852 (15 Elul).
T1:45; **T2**:494

R. Baruch of Gorlitz
Son of R. *Chaim of Zanz, and son-in-law of R. *Yekusiel Yehudah Teitelbaum, author of *Yitav Lev*. His five sons all continued the dynasty's teachings in various towns.
Born 1826, died 1906 (2 Adar).
T1:261; **T2**:393, 537

R. Baruch of Mezhibuzh
Grandson of the *Baal Shem Tov. Stressed the role of the tzaddik in the divine service of each individual, whose prime function was to destroy evil impulses. His manner was superficially brusque. Was in ideological conflict with various chassidic contemporaries. His teachings appear In *Butzina DiNehora* and *Amaros Tehoros*, and in *Chesed LeAvraham* by R. *Avraham the Malach.
Born 1757, died 1810 (18 Kislev).
T1:86, 89, 105, 131; **T2**:348, 456, 459, 476, 490, 507, 546; **F1**:23, 43, 190, 223, 270, 297; **F2**:402, 419, 458

R. Baruch (the Maggid) of Rika
Tutor in the household of R. *Levi Yitzchak of Berditchev.
T1:225

R. Baruch (Hager) of Vizhnitz
Eldest son of R. *Menachem Mendel of Vizhnitz; his writings were published under the title *Imrei Baruch*. Seven of his nine sons and three of his sons-in-law led their own followings of chassidim, each with their own traditions. He was succeeded in his hometown by his son, R. *Yisrael of Vizhnitz.
Born 1845, died 1893 (20 Kislev).
T2:354

R. Baruch Shalom
Eldest son of R. *Menachem Mendel of Lubavitch; did not serve as a rebbe with a following of chassidim.
F2:435, 436

Beirish
See also Dov Ber.

R. Beirish Meisels
See R. Dov Beirish Meisels, *rav* of Warsaw.

R. Beirish of Alisk (Alesk)
Chassid of R. *Mordechai of Neshchiz; colleague and (after his rebbe's death) chassid of R. *Uri of Strelisk.
T2:471

R. Beirish of Biala
Chassid of R. *Menachem Mendel of Vorki.
T2:443; **F1**:193

R. Beirish of Zhidachov
Younger brother of R. *Zvi Hirsch of Zhidachov.
T2:431

Beis Aharon
See R. Aharon ("the Second") of Karlin.

R. Ben-Zion of Bobov
Son of R. Shlomo (1847-1906), who was the son of R. Nasan Meir (founder of the Bobov dynasty), who was the son of R. *Chaim of Zanz. Martyred by the Nazis during World War II. After the war, his son R. Shlomo, שליט״א, found refuge in the United States where he has succeeded in rebuilding a vibrant chassidic community in the Boro Park section of Brooklyn.
Born 1873, died 1941 (4 Av).
F1:195

R. Ben-Zion of Ostrov
Born into a family of *misnagdim*, he was successively a chassid of R. *Menachem Mendel of Kotsk, R. *Yitzchak Meir of Ger, R. *Yehudah Aryeh of Ger, and (in his old age) of R. *Avraham Mordechai Alter of Ger. Was known for his scholarship; has been called the last Kotsker chassid.
T2:551

R. Ber of Radoshitz
See R. Yissachar Dov of Radoshitz.

Besht (acronym)
See Baal Shem Tov.

R. Betzalel (Shulsinger) of Odessa
Despite his total lack of formal musical education, this *chazzan* left his mark on synagogue music by singing original lyrical compositions which were committed to writing by his choirboys, some of whom grew to maturity as famous *chazzanim*. His old age was spent in Jerusalem.
Born ca. 1779, died ca. 1873
T2:394

R. Betzalel of Ozoritch
Chassid of R. *Menachem Mendel of Lubavitch.
T2:444

Betzalel Stern
Headmaster of the Haskaiah school in Odessa, and delegate to the 1843 conference on Jewish governmental schools in Russia. He cultivated his contacts with the czarist authorities in order to gain support for his reforms in curriculum which were opposed by the Orthodox leadership.
Born 1798, died 1853.
T1:131, 257

R. Binyamin Beines
Villager.
F2:438

R. Binyamin of Kotsk
Chassid of R. *Shneur Zalman of Liadi.
F1:205

Bnei Yissaschar
See R. Zvi Elimelech Shapira of Dinov.

Brahilov, tzaddik of
Contemporary of R. *Baruch of Mezhibuzh; author of *Mayim Kedoshim*.
F1:190

R. Bunem of Eybeschuetz
Chassid of R. *Yehudah Aryeh Leib of Ger.
T2:551

R. Bunem of Pshischah
See R. Simchah Bunem of Pshischah.

R. Chaikl of Amdur
Disciple of R. *Dov Ber of Mezritch.
F1:205

R. Chaim Avraham
Son of R. *Shneur Zalman of Liadi.
T2:450; F1:48, 175

R. Chaim Dov of Kremenchug
Chassid of R. *Shmuel of Lubavitch.
T2:525

R. Chaim Elazar Wax, *rav* of Pietrkov
Son-in-law of R. Yehoshua of Kutna and nephew of R. *Chaim of Zanz. Became *rav* of Pietrkov after losing his position at Kalish because of his refusal to defer to the communal magnate and the governor of the province. Had a special fondness for *Eretz Yisrael*, selling *esrogim* from there in Warsaw, and ultimately settling there in 1886. Author of *Nefesh Chayah*.
Born 1822, died 1889 (1 Tammuz).
F1:161

R. Chaim Eleazar (Shapira) of Munkatsch
Son and successor of R. Zvi Hirsch of Munkatsch from 1913; held strong views on secular and religious Zionism; his many works include *Minchas Elazar* (responsa).
Born 1872, died 1937.
T2:432; F2:338, 420

R. Chaim Eliyahu of Dubrovna
Prominent chassid of R. *Shneur Zalman of Liadi.
F1:225

R. Chaim ibn Attar
Born in Morocco, and studied under his father and grandfather, both of whom were kabbalists. Is known by the title of his classic *Or HaChaim* on the Torah, which he published in Italy on his way to *Eretz Yisrael*. Settling in Jerusalem in 1742, he established one yeshivah for the study of the revealed (*nigleh*) aspects of the Torah, and another for Kabbalah, the concealed (*nistar*) dimension of the Torah. His disciple, R. Chaim Yosef David Azulai, wrote that "whoever beheld his face took him for an angel of God."
Born 1696, died 1743 (15 Tammuz).
T2:531; F1:196

R. Chaim Kohen Rapaport
Son of R. Simchah HaKohen, the *rav* of Lublin. Sided with R. Yonasan Eybeschuetz in the great controversy; prolific author of responsa; took part in

[480]   *A Treasury of Chassidic Tales on the Festivals*

the historic debate with the Frankists (Lvov, 1749).
Died 1771 (13 Tammuz).
T1:246

R. Chaim Meir Yechiel Shapira of Moglenitz (Mogelnitz)
Son of R. Aviezra Zelig Shapira, av beis din of Grinitz; son-in-law of R. *Elazar of Lyzhansk; brought up and taught by his maternal grandfather R. *Yisrael of Koznitz; disciple also of R. *Yaakov Yitzchak, the Chozeh of Lublin, as well as of R. *Yaakov Yitzchak of Pshischah, R. *Avraham Yehoshua Heschel of Apta and R. *Yisrael of Ruzhin.
Died 1849 (5 Iyar).
T2:425; F1:160

R. Chaim of Kosov
Son and successor of R. *Menachem Mendel as rav of Kosov 1827-1854; author of Toras Chaim; father of R. *Menachem Mendel of Vizhnitz.
T1:65, 170; F1:188, 199

R. Chaim (Halberstam) of Zanz (Sanz)
Founder of a chassidic dynasty in western Galicia. Son-in-law of R. *Baruch Frenkel-Teomim. Became a chassid under the influence of R. *Yaakov Yitzchak, the Chozeh of Lublin; also studied under R. *Naftali of Ropshitz, R. *Zvi Hirsch of Zhidachov and others. Conducted his court modestly and was openly critical of the lifestyle of the Ruzhin-Sadigora dynasty. Famed for his exemplary practice of charity. His reputation as a scholar was worldwide; his various learned works (Halachah, responsa, and sermons) were all published under the title Divrei Chaim. (Not to be confused with R. *Chaim Tzanser of Brody.)
Born 1793, died 1876 (10 Nissan).
T1:106, 130, 201, 252, 260, 261; T2:349, 370, 393, 459, 528, 537, 592, 614; F1:33, 55, 117, 139, 140, 141, 146, 164, 192, 219, 301; F2:381, 385, 386, 406, 409

R. Chaim Shneur Zalman of Liadi
Son of R. *Menachem Mendel of Lubavitch (not to be confused with his great-grandfather, R. *Shneur Zalman of Liadi); led a community of chassidim; compiled Siddur Maharid (chassidic expositions of the prayers).
T1:114; F1:132

R. Chaim Tzanser
Head of the celebrated kloiz of Brody, and an opponent of Chassidism (not to be confused with R. *Chaim of Zanz). Of wealthy family, and famed for his hospitality. Prominent scholar in Talmud and Kabbalah. His halachic correspondents included R. *Yechezkel Landau, author of Noda BiYehudah. His soul was said (in the name of the *Baal Shem Tov) to have been a spark of the soul of R. Yochanan ben Zakkai.
Died 1794 (12 Adar I).
F1:143, 183

R. Chaim Yehoshua of Helochov
A chassid of R. *Menachem Mendel of Lubavitch.
T2:572

R. Chaim Zelig
A chassid from Vilna.
T2:494

R. Chanoch Henich of Alexander
Disciple of R. *Simchah Bunem of Pshischah and R. *Menachem Mendel of Kotsk; in 1866 succeeded R. *Yitzchak Meir (Alter) of Ger. Stressed Torah study and independent effort in divine service on the part of each individual chassid, without utter dependence on his rebbe, whose function is to guide him. His teachings were collected and published posthumously in Chashavah LeTovah.
Born 1798, died 1870.
T1:55,143; T2:606,617; F2:399,449

R. Chanoch Henich of Alisk (Alesk)
Son-in-Law of R. *Shalom of Belz; compiled the Siddur entitled Lev Same'ach, and sermons on the Torah under the same title.
Died 1884.
T2:531; F1:134; F2:407

Chayah Mushka
Daughter of R. *Dov Ber of Lubavitch.
F1:169

Chiddushei HaRim
See R. Yitzchak Meir of Ger.

Chozeh of Lublin, the
See R. Yaakov Yitzchak of Lublin.

R. David
Scribe in Hanipoli.
T2:488

R. David ben Shmuel HaLevi
Prominent halachic authority, better known as "the *Taz*", an acronym of the title of his classic work, *Turei Zahav*. Rav of Lvov; son-in-law of R. *Yoel Sirkes.
Born 1586, died 1667 (26 Shvat).
F1:177

R. David Leikes
Known as the Maggid of Bar; a chassid of the *Baal Shem Tov.
T1:157, 253

R. David Moshe (Friedman) of Chortkov
Son of R. *Yisrael of Ruzhin; author of *Divrei David*; attracted an extensive following; succeeded by his son R. Yisrael, author of *Tiferes Yisrael*.
Born 1828, died 1903 (21 Tishrei).
T1:134; **T2**:356, 405; **F1**:29, 51, 82, 115, 309; **F2**:333, 404, 458

R. David (Shapira) of Dinov
Son of R. *Zvi Elimelech (Shapira) of Dinov; author of *Tzemach David*; succeeded his father as *rav* of Dinov.
Born 1804, died 1874 (19 Adar).
T1:122

R. David of Lelov
Disciple of R. *Yaakov Yitzchak, the Chozeh of Lublin, to whom he introduced his friend (and later *mechutan*), R. *Yaakov Yitzchak of Pshischah. Mentor of R. *Yitzchak of Vorki, whom he took with him on his travels to the courts of the contemporary rebbes. Refused to see faults in his fellows, and showed compassion to dumb creatures. Father of R. *Moshe of Lelov.

Died 1814 (7 Shvat).
T1:104, 181, 222, 281; **T2**:319, 351, 397, 515, 527, 571, 588; **F2**:346

R. David of Mikliev
Elder chassid of the *Baal Shem Tov, and later of R. *Pinchas of Korets.
T1:248; **F1**:123

R. David of Nikolayev
Chassid of the *Baal Shem Tov.
T1:109

R. David of Skver
Son of R. Yitzchak, the son of R. *Mordechai of Chernobyl.
T1:157

R. David of Tolna
Son of R. *Mordechai of Chernobyl. Arrested by the czarist authorities because of the alleged inscription on his chair, "David King of Israel lives forever." His works include *Magen David*.
Born 1808, died 1882.
T1:56, 157, 248; **F1**:286

R. David of Zlatopol
Grandson of R. *Mordechai of Chernobyl.
T1:157

R. David Sirkis
Chassid of the *Baal Shem Tov.
T1:248

R. David Zvi Chein
Son of R. *Peretz Chein; chassid of R. *Shmuel of Lubavitch and of R. *Shalom Ber of Lubavitch; *rav* of Chernigov (Russia) from 1875 to 1925, when he settled in Jerusalem.
Born 1850, died 1925 (24 Kislev).
T2:321, 364; **F1**:275

Degel Machaneh Ephraim
See R. Moshe Chaim Ephraim of Sudylkov.

Devorah Leah
Daughter of R. *Shneur Zalman of Liadi, for whom she gave her life, entrusting her small son, who later became known as R. *Menachem Mendel of Lubavitch, to his care. Her husband was R. *Shalom Shachna.
Died 1791.
T2:317; **F1**:169

Divrei Chaim
See R. Chaim of Zanz.

R. Dov Beirish Meisels, *rav* of Warsaw
Rav of Cracow and Warsaw; a fearless leader in communal and civic affairs; joined the Polish Revolt in 1830 against Russian rule; elected to Cracow municipality and Austrian parliament. Published his *Chiddushei Maharadam* on Rambam's *Sefer HaMitzvos*.
Born 1798, died 1870 (15 Adar).
T2:398, 527; F2:391

R. Dov Ber of Lubavitch
Son and successor of R. *Shneur Zalman of Liadi; known as "the Mitteler Rebbe." Organized agricultural colonies so that his chassidim could be self-supporting; bought land in Hebron and established a Chabad settlement there; imprisoned due to slanderers in 1826. Works on chassidic philosophy include *Torah Or* and *Derech Chaim*.
Born 1773, died 1827 (9 Kislev).
T1:99, 145, 191; T2:364, 408, 423, 450, 498, 519, 525, 572, 578, 610; F1:37, 132, 169, 171, 174, 215, 239; F2:387, 436

R. Dov Ber (the Maggid) of Mezritch
Successor to the *Baal Shem Tov. Made Mezritch the center of Chassidism, which he endowed with an organized doctrine, drawing on the Lurianic Kabbalah. Unlike his rebbe he was not a man of the people — but he was the mentor of the founders of all the great dynasties. A major figure in both the revealed and the hidden aspects of the Torah, having been a disciple of the author of *Pnei Yehoshua*. His teachings are assembled in *Maggid Devarav LeYaakov, Or Torah, Or Emes*.
Born 1704 (?), died 1772 (19 Kislev).
T1:25, 45, 74, 83, 112, 191, 198, 220, 221, 268, 273, 289; T2:401, 402, 435, 439, 449, 483, 488, 490, 507, 516, 517, 543, 597; F1:32, 68, 72, 102, 135, 188, 198, 205, 225, 245, 257, 258; F2:374, 384, 411

R. Dov of Podheits (Podayetz)
Chassid of R. *Aharon Leib of Premishlan, and teacher of his son, R.

*Meir of Premishlan.
T2:328

R. Dov of Radoshitz
See R. Yissachar Dov of Radoshitz.

R. Dov Ze'ev of Kazivnikov
Chassid of R. *Menachem Mendel of Lubavitch.
T1:180

R. Dov Ze'ev of Yekaterinoslav
Emissary of R. *Shmuel of Lubavitch.
T2:572; F1:263

R. Elazar
Son of R. *Shalom of Belz.
F1:298

R. Elazar of Dzikov
See R. Eliezer of Dzikov.

R. Elazar of Lyzhansk
Son of R. *Elimelech of Lyzhansk, whose *Noam Elimelech* he published. Disseminated his father's teachings. Succeeded by his son, R. Naftali of Lyzhansk. Was the *mechutan* of R. *Yisrael of Koznitz.
Died 1806 (28 Tammuz).
F1:70

R. Elazar of Ternigrad (Tarnigrad)
Prominent scholar, colleague of R. *Yaakov Yitzchak of Lublin and of R. *Yaakov Meshullam Orenstein. Author of *Noam Megadim* on the Torah.
F1:120

R. Elazar Rokeiach of Amsterdam
Author of *Maasei Rokeiach* on the Torah, and other works. Great-grandfather of R. *Shalom of Belz.
Died 1815 (15 Elul).
F1:40

R. Eliezer
Father of the *Baal Shem Tov.
T1:62

R. Eliezer Dov of Grabovitz
Chassid of R. *Simchah Bunem of Pshischah.
T1:149

R. Eliezer (Horovitz) of Dzikov (Tarnobzeh)
Son of R. *Naftali of Ropshitz, whom

Biographical Sketches [483]

he succeeded as rebbe. Colleague of R. *Yissachar Dov of Radoshitz and R. *Zvi Hirsch of Rimanov. Succeeded in Dzikov by his son R. *Meir (Horovitz) of Dzikov.
Died 1860 (3 Cheshvan).
T1:35, 195; T2:404; F1:41, 55, 164, 215

R. Eliezer Zvi of Komarna
Son and disciple of R. *Yitzchak Aizik Yechiel of Komarna, and disciple as well of R. *Chaim of Zanz, R. *Yitzchak Aizik of Zhidachov, R. *Eliezer of Dzikov and R. *David of Dinov. His works include *Ben Beisi* (Scriptural commentary) and *Damesek Eliezer* (on *Zohar*). He was succeeded in Komarna by his son, R. Yaakov Moshe.
Died 1898 (24 Iyar).
F1:151

R. Elimelech of Lyzhansk
Disciple of R. *Dov Ber of Mezritch, and one of the pioneers of Chassidism in Galicia. Traveled extensively with his brother, R. *Zusya of Hanipoli, often in connection with the ransom of captives and other individual and communal needs. His *Noam Elimelech* expounds (among other things) his view of the relationship between rebbe and chassid. Succeeded by his son, R. *Elazar of Lyzhansk.
Born 1717, died 1786 (21 Adar).
T1:25, 47, 68, 77, 135, 181, 219, 225, 280; T2:372, 395, 396, 401, 410, 490, 621; F1:32, 41, 66, 68, 70, 95, 128, 194, 283, 301; F2:376, 414

R. Elimelech of Tlust
Chassid of R. *Shalom of Belz and of R. *Meir of Premishlan.
T2:202

R. Eliyahu, the Gaon of Vilna
One of the most prominent figures in the Torah world of recent centuries, his erudition covering (in addition to the natural sciences and mathematics) the entire field of Torah scholarship, on which he wrote some 70 works. Despite his extreme seclusion — his ascetic assiduity has become proverbial — he exerted a powerful influence on Jewish affairs. This is evidenced by his violent antagonism to Chassidism, which found expression in a series of excommunications, and instructions to his followers — the *misnagdim* — to burn the works of the new movement. Since his time, the Yiddish term *Litvak* ("Lithuanian") has come to stand for a scholarly and hard-core *misnaged* espousing the closely definable world-view whose prime ideologist and ideal personality is the Gaon.
Born 1720, died 1797 (19 Tishrei).
T1:54, 76, 118; F1:225

R. Eliyahu Moshe
Learned householder; in contact with the *Baal Shem Tov.
T2:579

R. Eliyahu of Viskit
Disciple of R. *Menachem Mendel of Kotsk.
T1:294

R. Eliyahu of Zhidachov
Son of R. *Yitzchak Aizik of Zhidachov.
Died 1875.
F1:284; F2:389, 428

R. Eliyahu Yosef of Drivin
Chassid of R. *Dov Ber of Lubavitch and of his son R. *Menachem Mendel of Lubavitch.
Died in Jerusalem.
T2:526

R. Eliyahu Zvi of Berisov
Grandson of R. *Eliyahu, the Gaon of Vilna; chassid of R. *Menachem Mendel of Lubavitch.
T1:54

R. Enzil (R. Yekusiel Asher Zalman Enzil) of Staria (Stryy)
Principal student of R. *Aryeh Leib Heller; author of responsa; outspoken *misnaged*.
T1:283; T2:400

R. Ephraim Fishel of Strikov
See R. Fishel(e) of Strikov.

R. Ephraim Michel of Shklov
Prominent chassid of R. *Shneur Zalman of Liadi.
F1:225

R. Ephraim of Sudylkov
See R. Moshe Chaim Ephraim of Sudylkov.

R. Feivish
Rav of Kremenets; father-in-law of R. *Avraham the Malach; author of Mishnas Chachamim on the Mishnah.
F2:404

R. Feivish (R. Meshullam Feivish HaLevi) of Zabriza (Zebariz)
Studied under R. *Yechiel Michel of Zlotchov and R. *Dov Ber of Mezritch. His Yosher Divrei Emes is a basic work on chassidic thought; his teachings appear also in Likkutim Yekarim. An authority on the laws of writing sifrei Torah. His disciples included R. *Menachem Mendel of Kosov.
T2:537

R. Feivl (Danziger) of Gritza
Disciple of R. *Simchah Bunem of Pshischah and of R. *Yitzchak of Vorki. Succeeded by his son, R. *Yechiel of Alexander.
Died 1849.
T1:149; T2:420; F2:399

R. Fishel(e) of Strikov
Disciple of R. *Dov Ber of Mezritch and R. *Elimelech of Lyzhansk; noted for his self-effacement and his love for his fellow. His colleagues referred to him by the reverent nickname of Olah Temimah ("the Unblemished Offering").
Died 1825 (9 Teves).
T1:281; T2:505

Gaon of Vilna
See R. Eliyahu, the Gaon of Vilna.

R. Gavriel ("the Likeable") of Vitebsk
Chassid of R. *Shneur Zalman of Liadi.
T1:309

R. Gershon of Kitov
Brother-in-law and ultimately disciple of the *Baal Shem Tov, some of whose correspondence with him is extant, and of great documentary value. In 1747 settled in Eretz Yisrael, living first in Hebron, then in Jerusalem.
Died ca. 1760.
F1:143, 144

R. Getzel
Grandson of R. *Zvi Hirsch Ashkenazi.
T2:429

Gnendl
Wife of R. *Zusya of Hanipoli.
F1:201

Gra
(Hebrew acronym for "the Gaon R. Eliyahu"), see R. Eliyahu, the Gaon of Vilna.

HaYehudi HaKadosh
See R. Yaakov Yitzchak of Pshischah.

Henich
See also Chanoch Henich.

R. Henich of Alisk
See R. Chanoch Henich of Alisk (Alesk).

R. Henick Schick of Shklov
Prominent rav; father of R. *Pinchas Reizes.
T1:144, 231

Herschele Ostropolier
Badchan ("court jester") of R. *Baruch of Mezhibuzh.
T2:348

Herschel the Digger
Villager.
F2:435

R. Herschele of Zhidachov
See R. Zvi (Hirsch) of Zhidachov.

R. Hillel Lichtenstein of Kolomya (Kolomei)
Disciple of R. *Moshe Sofer, the author of Chasam Sofer; prominent rav and preacher in various Hungarian cities, as well as in the Galician city Kolomei. Uncompromising opponent of Reform and of the introduction of secular studies in Jewish schools. His works (responsa, and sermons on ethics) include Maskil el Dal, Es Laasos, Mokirei Dardekei, Beis Hillel and

Biographical Sketches [485]

Avkas Rochel.
Born 1815, died 1891 (10 Iyar).
T2:349

R. Hillel of Paritsh
Chassid of R. *Menachem Mendel of Lubavitch; *rav* of Bobruisk; author of *Pelach HaRimon*; a seminal figure in *Chabad* Chassidism.
Born 1795, died 1864 *(Shabbos Nachamu).*
T1:109, 112, 156, 306; **T2**:472, 524

R. Hillel of Radoshitz
Grandson of R. *Yissachar Dov of Radoshitz, under whom he studied (as well as under R. *Shlomo of Radomsk) and whom he in part succeeded as rebbe. Renowned as an ascetic miracle worker.
Died 1901 (26 Teves).
F1:90

Hinda
Wife of R. *Aizik of Safrin.
T2:431

Hirsch, Hirschel, Hirschele
See also Zvi.

R. Hirschele of Radomsk.
Communal leader; father of R. *Shlomo of Radomsk.
T2:424

R. Hirschel the Watchmaker
Chassid of R. *Shmuel of Lubavitch.
T2:480

R. Hirsch (the Beadle) of Rimanov
See R. Zvi Hirsch of Rimanov.

R. Hirsch of Tomashov
Elder chassid and confident of R. *Menachem Mendel of Kotsk.
T2:352,356

R. Israel ben R. Eliezer Baal Shem Tov
See Baal Shem Tov.

R. Itzik'l Drohovitcher
See R. Yitzchak of Drohovitch.

Kedushas Levi
See R. Levi Yitzchak of Berditchev.

Kissele
Obscure opponent of Chassidism; contemporary of R. *Yaakov Yitzchak of Pshischah.
T2:414

R. Koppel
Nephew of R. *Zvi of Zhidachov.
F1:300

R. Koppel of Likova
Maternal grandfather of R. *Yaakov Yitzchak (the Chozeh) of Lublin.
F2:338

Ksav Sofer
See R. Avraham Shmuel Binyamin Wolf Sofer.

K'tzos HaChoshen
See R. Aryeh Leib Heller.

Leib, Leibish
See also Aryeh Leib.

R. Leibish Rokeiach
Elder brother of R. *Shalom of Belz.
T2:387

R. Leib Koshmirk
Chassid of R. *Shmuel Abba of Zichlin.
T2:415; **F1**:248

R. Leibl Eger of Lublin
Studied under his grandfather, Rabbi Akiva Eger, as well as under *Yitzchak Meir of Ger, through whom he became a chassid of R. *Menachem Mendel of Kotsk. While in Kotsk he became a disciple of R. Mordechai Yosef Leiner of Izbitza. First headed a chassidic congregation in Lublin, then after the death of R. Mordechai Yosef in 1854, led a chassidic following of his own, one of his disciples being R. *Tzadok HaKohen of Lublin. His works: *Toras Emes* and *Imrei Emes*.
Born 1816, died 1888.
T2:466

R. Leib Posen
Chassid of R. *Shmuel of Lubavitch.
F2:442

R. Leib Sarahs
Hidden tzaddik descended from the Maharal of Prague; devoted his life to collecting alms for his colleagues who were studying and worshiping in seclusion, and to the ransom of oppressed Jews imprisoned at the whim of the local landowners. Held in high regard by the *Baal Shem Tov.
Born 1726, died 1791 (10 Elul).
T1:153,270; **T2**:417; **F1**:54,125; **F2**:323

Leibele the Fool
Citizen of Ropshitz.
F1:198

R. Levi Yitzchak of Berditchev
One of the best-known and best-loved of all chassidic rebbes. Introduced to Chassidism through R. Shmuel *Shmelke of Nikolsburg; studied under R. *Dov Ber (the Maggid) of Mezritch. In 1785, after being dismissed from rabbinical posts at Zelichov and Pinsk due to the pressure of local *misnagdim*, he became *rav* of Berditchev, where he was deeply involved in all communal affairs.

In divine service he preached and practiced joy and fervor, and in his relations with his townsmen he exemplified the ideal of compassionate reproof which he extols in his *Kedushas Levi*. Always sensitive to the distress of his flock, and insisting at all costs on perceiving in them nothing but virtue, he even took the Creator to task, admonishing him in Yiddish — reverently but candidly — for His treatment of His children. Not without reason has "the Advocate of Israel" become immortalized not only in observant circles, but in the literature of self-styled secular Jewry as well.
Born ca. 1740, died 1810 (25 Tishrei).
T1:66, 70, 78, 98, 106, 107, 113, 136, 225, 301; T2:341, 432, 472, 476, 509, 518, 519, 546, 563, 613; F1:27, 42, 43, 66, 71, 72, 99, 107, 109, 113, 134, 135, 155, 157, 224, 253, 308; F2:328, 356, 367, 376, 459

Levush
See R. Mordechai ben Avraham Jaffe.

R. Lipa of Sambor
Son of R. *Aizik of Safrin.
Died 1883.
T2:431; F1:182

R. Lipman of Radomsk
Son-in-law of R. *Shlomo of Radomsk.
T2:448

Maggid of Bar
See R. David Leikes.

Maggid of Chernobyl
See R. Mordechai of Chernobyl.

Maggid of Dubno
See R. Yaakov Kranz.

Maggid of Mezritch
See R. Dov Ber of Mezritch.

Maggid of Rika
See R. Baruch of Rika.

Maggid of Trisk
See R. Avraham of Trisk.

Maharal of Prague
See R. Yehudah Leib ben R. Bezalel of Prague.

Maharash
See R. Shmuel of Lubavitch.

Maharshak
See R. Shlomo Kluger.

Maharsham
See R. Shalom Mordechai HaKohen (Shvadron), *rav* of Brezan.

Malach, the
See R. Avraham the Malach.

Mayer Amshel Rothschild
Frankfort merchant, and court agent to Landgrave William IX of Hesse-Kassel; founder of the Rothschild family fortunes.
Born 1744, died 1812.
F2:333

R. Meir Auerbach
Rabbi of the Ashkenazi community of Jerusalem, where he was known as the "*rav* of Kalish," the town in which he had previously served. Active in communal organization and in promoting agricultural settlement; one of the founders of the Me'ah She'arim quarter; author of *Imrei Binah (Halachah)*.
Born 1815, died 1878 (5 Iyar).
T2:415

R. Meir HaGadol ("the Elder" or "the Great") of Premishlan
Grandfather of R. *Meir of Premishlan.
F1:244

R. Meir (Horovitz) of Dzikov
Son of R. *Eliezer of Dzikov; author of *Imrei Naom* on the Torah.
F1:179

Biographical Sketches [487]

R. Meirke of Mir (Meir Mirer)
Prominent chassid of R. *Mordechai of Lechovitch.
T2:417; F1:36

R. Meir of Apta
One of the foremost disciples of R. *Yaakov Yitzchak (the Chozeh) of Lublin. His father, R. Mordechai, was a disciple of R. *Elimelech of Lyzhansk. Wrote *Or LaShamayim*.
Died 1827 (25 Tammuz).
T1:286; T2:595; F1:73

R. Meir of Constantine
Son of R. *Yaakov Emden; headed the rabbinical court of Constantine (Russia).
T1:219

R. Meir of Premishlan
Grandson of R. *Meir HaGadol of Premishlan, and son of R. *Aharon Leib of Premishlan. Lived in abject but patient poverty; exerted himself tirelessly for the needy and the suffering. His *ruach hakodesh* and his ready wit have become legendary. Wrote no works, but his teachings were collected and published by his chassidim after his death.
Born 1780 (?), died 1850 (29 Iyar).
T1:56, 58, 113, 115, 116, 119, 136, 139, 142, 202, 226, 237, 294; T2:325, 328, 372, 394, 459, 614; F1:29, 85, 141, 179, 237; F2:390, 427, 429

R. Meir Raphaels
Communal leader in Vilna; prominent chassid of R. *Shneur Zalman of Liadi.
T1:173

R. Meir Shalom of Skoli
Chassid of R. *Yitzchak Aizik of Zhidachov.
F2:389

R. Meir Shapira
Dynamic communal leader, brilliant Talmud scholar and educator; child prodigy, descended from R. *Pinchas of Korets; a gifted orator, and member of the Polish *Seim*. Originator (at the 1923 congress of Agudas Yisrael) of the *daf yomi* project, whereby the same daily page of Talmud is studied simultaneously around the world. Founder and head of the *Chachmei Lublin* yeshivah, which set new standards in yeshivah amenities and screening of applicants. A composer of melodies; asked his students to sing and dance around his bed as he prepared to breathe his last.
Born 1887, died 1934 (7 Cheshvan).
F1:309

R. Meir Yechiel of Ostrovtze
Disciple of R. Elimelech of Grodzisk, who said that he would account it a privilege if after his death R. Meir Yechiel would refer to him as his rebbe. Ascetic lifestyle; outstanding scholar, who led a following of learned chassidim. His sermons draw heavily on *gematria*. On account of their intricacy, his *pilpulim* have come to be known as *"Ostrovotze pshetlach."* They have been collected in *Meir Einei Chachamim*, and his teachings on *Bereishis* in *Or Torah*. Survived by his son, R. Yechezkel (d. 1943), *rav* of Nasielsk.
Born 1851, died 1928 (19 Adar).
T2:474

R. Melech (Elimelech)
Grandson of R. *Elimelech of Lyzhansk; lived in Rodnik.
F1:301

R. Menachem Aryeh
Hidden *tzaddik*; contemporary of the *Baal Shem Tov.
T2:579

R. Menachem Mendel of Fristik
See R. Menachem Mendel of Rimanov.

R. Menachem Mendel of Horodok
See R. Menachem Mendel of Vitebsk.

R. Menachem Mendel of Kosov
Son of R. Koppel Chassid, a disciple of the *Baal Shem Tov; himself a disciple (and later *mechutan*) of R. *Moshe Leib of Sasov; disciple also of R. Wolff of Charne-Ostro and R. Zvi Hirsch of Nadvorna, and brother-in-law of R.

*Uri of Strelisk. Conducted a modest business until persuaded by his contemporaries to become *rav* of Kosov, to which thousands now flocked. Founder of the Hager family and Vizinitz and Kosov dynasties. His eldest son, R. *Chaim, succeeded him at Kosov; his second son, R. David, was *rav* in Zablotov. His teachings are collected in *Ahavas Shalom*.
Born 1768, died 1826 (17 Cheshvan).
T2:368, 399, 534, 537

R. Menachem Mendel of Kotsk
Born into a non-chassidic family; early became a disciple of R. *Yaakov Yitzchak (the Chozeh) of Lublin, of R. *Yaakov Yitzchak (the Yid HaKadosh) of Pshischah, and ultimately of R. *Simchah Bunem of Pshischah. Superficially stern, he practiced and preached a zealous and unrelenting search for truth, whose prime enemy is self-centeredness. His oft-quoted aphorisms are characteristically pungent and unsugared. Stressed earnest Torah study. Spent the last two decades of his life in isolation. After his passing the majority of his followers recognized his disciple R. *Yitzchak Meir of Ger as their rebbe.
Born 1787, died 1859 (22 Shvat).
T1:35, 124, 149, 206, 207, 212, 264, 294, 304; T2:324, 352, 356, 365, 371, 419, 426, 491, 505, 535, 559, 577; F1:48, 55, 80, 191, 211, 236, 302, 303; F2:399, 404, 425, 431, 461, 462

R. Menachem Mendel of Linsk (Liska)
Rav of Linsk; father of R. *Naftali of Ropshitz.
F1:210, 251

R. Menachem Mendel of Lubavitch
Orphaned early, his principal mentor was his grandfather, R. *Shneur Zalman of Liadi; son-in-law and successor of the latter's son, R. *Dov Ber of Lubavitch. Prolific writer on *Halachah* and chassidic philosophy; known by the title of his classic collection of responsa, *Tzemach Tzedek*. Directed chassidim to Hebron. Prominent as a leader of Russian Jewry, particularly in his opposition to the Haskalah. Succeeded in Lubavitch by his son, R. *Shmuel of Lubavitch.
Born 1789, died 1866 (13 Nissan).
T1:45, 54, 71, 114, 125, 129, 131, 150, 170, 180, 229, 255, 257; T2:317, 375, 420, 439, 450, 472, 484, 498, 512, 524, 529, 543, 572, 578, 584, 588, 604, 610, 613; F1:31, 34, 48, 68, 132, 148, 169, 171, 175, 239, 245; F2:435, 436, 438, 465

R. Menachem Mendel of Nikolsburg
Rav of the Moravian town of Nikolsburg (Mikulov) in the eighteenth century; author of *Tzemach Tzedek*; not to be confused with the *Tzemach Tzedek* written by R. *Menachem Mendel of Lubavitch.
T1:81

R. Menachem Mendel of Rimanov
Disciple of R. *Elimelech of Lyzhansk and R. *Shmelke of Nikolsburg; lived for many years in Fristik, and sometimes referred to as R. Menachem Mendel of Fristik. His numerous disciples included R. *Naftali of Ropshitz and R. *Zvi Hirsch of Rimanov. His writings on the Torah are collected in *Menachem Tzion*, *Divrei Menachem* and *Ateres Menachem*.
Died 1815 (19 Iyar).
T1:64, 218, 229; T2:494, 501, 547, 569, 576, 584, 597, 621; F1:28, 100, 112, 166, 219; F2:382, 385

R. Menachem Mendel of Vitebsk
Elder disciple of R. *Dov Ber of Mezritch; one of the earliest of the chassidic rebbes; disseminated Chassidism. Accompanied by his disciple and colleague, R. *Shneur Zalman of Liadi, he made the journey to Lithuania to meet R. *Eliyahu, the Gaon of Vilna, in order to explain the tenets of the new movement, but they were not received. Headed the *aliyah* of three hundred chassidim and others who settled in Safed in 1777; after a few years moved to Tiberias, where he established a chassidic synagogue. His works on chassidic thought include *Pri*

HaAretz and Likkutei Amarim.
Born 1730, died 1788 (2 Iyar).
T1:158; T2:402, 449, 517; F1:72, 205, 224, 258

R. Menachem Mendel (Hager) of Vizhnitz
Son of R. *Chaim of Kosov; mechutan of R. *Yehoshua of Belz. At the age of 24, ten years after his marriage to the daughter of R. *Yisrael of Ruzhin, he succeeded his father as rav of Vizhnitz, and within a short time as rebbe attracted an extensive following. He organized funds for the relief of the poor of Eretz Yisrael. Succeeded by his son, R. *Baruch of Vizhnitz, who published his book Tzemach Tzaddik (a title which in gematria is the numerical equivalent of the name Menachem Mendel).
Born 1830, died 1884 (29 Tishrei).
T1:107; T2:354; F1:116; F2:406

R. Menachem Mendel of Vorki
Son and reluctant successor of R. *Yitzchak of Vorki; known as "the Silent Tzaddik," but nonetheless maintained meaningful communication with his chassidim, with whom he often sat in silence. Three things he praised — an erect bow, a silent shout, and a motionless dance.
Born 1819, died 1868.
T1:163; T2:398, 443; F1:193; F2:430

R. Menachem Mendel Schneerson
The Lubavitcher Rebbe; son and pupil of R. Levi Yitzchak Schneerson, rav of Yekaterinoslav; son-in-law and successor (in 1950) of R. *Yosef Yitzchak of Lubavitch. Directs the movement's worldwide outreach programs for the igniting of latent allegiance to the Torah and mitzvos. His Torah expositions and frequent statements on contemporary Jewish problems are heard on all continents by simultaneous telephone connection. Consulted on personal and national issues by countless Jews of all ideological shades of opinion.
Born 1902 (11 Nissan) — שליט״א.
T2:494, 578

R. Menachem Nachum of Chernobyl
See R. Nachum of Chernobyl.

R. Menachem Nachum of Stefanesti
See R. Nachum of Stefanesti.

R. Menachem Panet
Chassid of R. *Menachem Mendel of Rimanov.
T1:218

Mendel
See also Menachem Mendel.

R. Mendel of Bar
Disciple of the *Baal Shem Tov. His thoughts are cited in the writings of the early chassidic teachers, particularly in Toldos Yaakov Yosef of R. *Yaakov Yosef of Polonnoye.
T2:379, 518

R. Meshullam Zalman Ashkenazi
Head of the rabbinical court of Lublin, ca. 1840.
T2:429

R. Meshullam Zusya of Hanipoli
See R. Zusya of Hanipoli.

R. Michael Aharon HaKohen of Vitebsk
Chassid of R. *Shneur Zalman of Liadi.
F1:225

R. Michael of Nevel
Chassid of R. *Shalom Ber of Lubavitch.
F1:262

R. Michel of Zlotchov
See R. Yechiel Michel of Zlotchov.

Mirl
Wife of R. *Yitzchak Meir of Mezhibuzh.
T2:603

Mitteler Rebbe
See R. Dov Ber of Lubavitch.

R. Monye Monissohn
Chassid of R. *Shmuel of Lubavitch and later of R. *Shalom Ber of Lubavitch.
T2:604; F1:86

R. Mordechai ben Avraham Jaffe
Disciple of R. Shlomo Luria, the Maharshal, and R. *Moshe Isserles; talmudist, kabbalist and communal

leader in Prague, Venice, Grodno and Lublin; author of the classic ten-volume *Levush* (mainly *Halachah* and Biblical commentary).
Born ca. 1535, died 1612.
F2:430

R. Mordechai Bennet
Disciple of R. *Shmelke of Nikolsburg; a prodigy, producing learned commentaries at the age of 13; ascetic lifestyle. *Rav* of Nikolsburg, then of the whole of Moravia, author of *Parashas Mordechai* (responsa) and many other halachic works.
Died 1829 (13 Av).
T2:396

R. Mordechai Dov of Hornisteipl
Grandson of R. *Yaakov Yisrael of Chercass, direct descendant of R. *Zusya of Hanipoli, and son-in-law of R. *Chaim of Zanz. His works include *Emek She'elah* (responsa). Was highly regarded for his Talmudic erudition. His *derushim* on the Torah appear in *Emek HaChachmah* together with his grandfather's *Emek Tefillah*.
Born 1840, died 1904.
T2:353, 469, 616; **F1**:87, 286

R. Mordechai HaKohen of Birzan
See R. Shalom Mordechai HaKohen (Shvadron; *Maharsham*), Rav of Brezan.

R. Mordechai (the Maggid) of Chernobyl
Son of R. *Nachum of Chernobyl, and his successor as *maggid*; son-in-law of R. *Aharon ("the Great") of Karlin, and later of R. *David Leikes. Unlike his father, he conducted his court in grand style. Wrote *Likkutei Torah* (Biblical commentary).
Born 1770, died 1837 (20 Iyar).
T1:73, 157; **T2**:616; **F1**:82, 188, 250, 258; **F2**:373, 425

R. Mordechai of Kremenets
Son of R. *Yechiel Michel of Zlotchov; his four brothers and he were collectively referred to by their contemporaries as the "Five *Chumashim*." His disciples included R. *Meir of Premishlan.
Died 1813 (10 Tammuz).
T1:115

R. Mordechai of Lechovitch
Disciple of R. *Shlomo of Karlin; known for the fervor of his prayers. Exceedingly charitable, particularly toward the poor of *Eretz Yisrael*.
Died 1810 (13 Shvat).
T1:59, 60, 204, 261; **T2**:417; **F1**:36, 77, 139, 197, 210

R. Mordechai of Liepli
Chassid of R. *Shneur Zalman of Liadi.
T1:214

R. Mordechai of Nadvorna
Great-grandson of R. *Meir HaGadol of Premishlan, and son-in-law of R. Shmuel Shmelke Taubes, rav of Jassy. Orphaned early; ascetic; brought up by his uncle R. *Meir of Premishlan, like whom he gave away whatever he had to the poor. Chassidim from all over Rumania and Hungary flocked to Nadvorna to receive his blessing. His teachings were collected and published posthumously as *Gedulas Mordechai*.
Died 1895 (15 Tishrei).
T1:284; **T2**:592; **F1**:141; **F2**:331

R. Mordechai of Neshchiz
His ancestors included the *Maharal* (R. *Yehudah Leib ben R. Betzalel) of Prague and Don Yitzchak Abarbanel. Disciple of R. *Yechiel Michel of Zlotchov. The ill and the unfortunate came to visit him from long distances. Was never known to have uttered a negative word about his fellow. Actively supported settlement in *Eretz Yisrael*. His sons were R. *Yossele (Yosef) of Ostila, R. Yaakov Aryeh of Kovel, and his successor in his hometown, R. *Yitzchak of Neshchiz. His sayings were collected in *Rishpei Eish*.
Born 1740, died 1800 (8 Nissan).
T1:35, 216, 270; **T2**:352, 388, 457, 471; **F1**:102, 154

R. Mordechai of Pintchov
Disciple of R. *Yaakov Yitzchak (the

Biographical Sketches [491]

Chozeh) of Lublin.
T2:344

R. Mordechai Schatz of Zaslav
Disciple of the *Baal Shem Tov.
F2:371

R. Mordechai Shraga of Husyatin
Son of R. *Yisrael of Ruzhin, head of a dynasty in Galicia; his thousands of chassidim included many prominent scholars. Succeeded by his son R. Yisrael.
Born 1834, died 1894.
T1:285

R. Mordechai Yoel
Chassid of R. *Shmuel of Lubavitch.
T2:480

R. Moshe Aptzuger
Nephew of R. *Aizik Mechadesh; chassid of R. *Shneur Zalman of Liadi.
F1:225

R. Moshe Bezalel Alter
Son of R. *Yehudah Aryeh Leib of Ger. In his will, his brother R. *Avraham Mordechai designated him as his successor as rebbe of Ger. Perished in World War II.
F2:461

R. Moshe Chaim Ephraim of Sudylkov
Son of *Adel, the daughter of the *Baal Shem Tov; studied under his grandfather, whose teachings he collated and expounded in his *Degel Machanah Ephraim*. His later teachers were R. *Dov Ber of Mezritch and R. *Yaakov Yosef of Polonnoye. He was the brother of R. *Baruch of Mezhibuzh.
Died 1800 (17 Iyar).
F1:23; F2:402

R. Moshe Chaim Rothenburg
Brother of R. *Yitzchak Meir of Ger.
T1:207

R. Moshe Cheifetz of Chavs
Scholar; antagonist to the teachings of R. *Shneur Zalman of Liadi.
T2:397

R. Moshe Cordovero
Headed the kabbalistic community in Safed before the arrival of R. *Yitzchak Luria, the Arizal. Studied the revealed aspects of the Torah under R. *Yosef Caro, and Kabbalah under his brother-in-law, R. Shlomo Alkabetz. Eulogized by the Arizal, who referred to him as "my Master and my Teacher." His many works include *Pardes Rimonim*, *Or Yakar*, (an extensive commentary on the *Zohar*), and a *Siddur* with kabbalistic *kavanos*, *Tefillah LeMoshe*.
Died 1570 (23 Tammuz).
T2:442

R. Moshe Isserles
Foremost Polish halachic authority, better known by the Hebrew acronym *Rama*; colleague and humble mentor of the great Torah figures of the age. His *Haggahos* (glosses) to the *Shulchan Aruch* of R. *Yosef Caro added the equivalent Ashkenazi usage in cases of divergent rulings. The synagogue he built in Cracow in memory of his first wife survived World War II.
Born 1525 or 1530, died 1572 (18 Iyar).
T2:527

R. Moshe Leib of Sasov
Disciple of R. *Shmelke of Nikolsburg, R. *Dov Ber of Mezritch, and R. *Elimelech of Lyzhansk. His disciples included R. *Yaakov Yitzchak of Pshischah and R. *Zvi Hirsch of Zhidachov. Known as the "father of widows and orphans." Many of the stories involving him testify to his creative musical talent. Survived by his only son, R. *Shmelke of Sasov.
Born 1745, died 1807 (4 Shvat).
T1:114, 128, 133, 210, 211; T2:514; F1:102; F2:376

R. Moshe of Kobrin
Disciple of R. *Mordechai and R. *Noach of Lechovitch; founder of the Kobrin dynasty, though to his last day he argued that he did not grasp why people insisted on regarding him as their rebbe.
Died 1858 (29 Nissan).
T1:137, 148, 262; T2:433, 609; F1:216, 298

[492] *A Treasury of Chassidic Tales on the Festivals*

R. Moshe (Elyakim Beria) of Koznitz
Son of R. *Yisrael (the Maggid) of Koznitz; known for his humility. His many works include *Be'er Moshe* on the Torah.
T1:153

R. Moshe of Lelov
Son of R. *David of Lelov and son-in-law of R. *Yaakov Yitzchak (the Yid HaKadosh) of Pshischah. Declined to succeed his father as rebbe, considering himself unworthy of the position. Settled in *Eretz Yisrael,* where he strengthened the chassidic community. Buried on the Mount of Olives.
Died 1851 (11 Teves).
T2:415

R. Moshe of Rozvidov (Razvodov)
Son of R. *Eliezer of Dzikov, and great-grandson of R. *Naftali of Ropshitz. Had a numerous following.
Died 1894 (10 Sivan).
T1:159; F1:182

R. Moshe of Sambor
Brother of R. *Zvi Hirsch of Zhidachov; father of R. *Yehudah Zvi of Rozla. Disciple of R. *Yaakov Yitzchak (the Chozeh) of Lublin and R. *Yisrael of Koznitz. Author of *Tefillah LeMoshe* on the Torah.
Died 1840 (6 Iyar).
T1:92; T2:431

R. Moshe (Zvi) of Savran
Son of R. *Shimon Shlomo; *rav* in Berditchev, Savran (Podolia), and Titshlinik; exceptionally studious. Unremitting opponent of the followers of R. *Nachman of Breslov. Teachings published in *Likkutei Shoshanim.* Succeeded by his son, R. Shimon Shlomo (d. 1848).
Died 1838 (27 Teves).
T1:148, 227, 307; T2:508, 541, 601; F1:201

R. Moshe Plotzker
Chassid employed by *Tamar'l.
T2:585

R. Moshe Teitelbaum of Ujhely (Satoraljaujhely)
Headed a reputed yeshivah at 17; disciple of R. *Yaakov Yitzchak of Lublin. Famed among thousands as a scholar and wonderworker; spread Chassidism in Hungary; his descendants continued the dynasty of Sziget and Satmar. Author of *Heshiv Moshe* (responsa) and *Yismach Moshe* (derush). Daily awaited the coming of *Mashiach.*
Born 1759, died 1841 (28 Tammuz).
T2:410; F1:120, 219

R. Moshe Vilenker
Chassid of R. *Shneur Zalman of Liadi.
T2:520

R. Moshe Yisrael
Rav of Reivitz and Klementov; chassid of R. *Yissachar Dov of Radoshitz.
F2:402

R. Moshe Yosef Chodorov
Chassid; *mechutan* of R. *Moshe (Zvi) of Savran.
T2:601

R. Moshe Zalman Feldman
Musically gifted chassid of R. *Shneur Zalman of Liadi.
T2:520

R. Mottel of Kalshin (Kalshin)
Chassid of R. *Yitzchak of Vorki.
T1:200

R. Nachman Dulitzki
Chassid of R. *Shalom Ber of Lubavitch.
F2:346

R. Nachman of Breslov
Son of R. Simchah (son of R. Nachman of Horodenko) and Feige (daughter of *Adel, the daughter of the *Baal Shem Tov). From early youth he set out on his distinctive path in divine service — ascetic study, solitary meditation, fiery worship. His chassidim learned from him as well their lifelong quest for atonement, the impossibility of despair for the man of faith, and a unique concept of the nature and role of the tzaddik. After a brief stay in

Eretz Yisrael he settled in Breslov in 1800, but after the controversy which his radical teachings aroused among his contemporaries, he moved in 1810 to Uman. His burial place there, behind the Iron Curtain, has remained a place of pilgrimage for his chassidim to this day — for alone among chassidic dynasties, Breslov has continued without a successor to its founder. Most of his teachings were recorded by his disciple R. Nasan Sternhartz. His books include *Likkutei Maharan* (kabbalistic philosophy and moral teaching), and *Sippurei Maasios* (stories). Born 1772, died 1811 (18 Tishrei).
T1:37, 224; **T2**:605

R. Nachum
Son of R. *Dov Ber of Lubavitch.
F1:174, 225, 260, 268

R. Nachum Dov
Uncle of R. *Yosef Yitzchak of Lubavitch.
F2:464

R. Nachum (Menachem Nachum, the Maggid) of Chernobyl
Trained in Lithuanian yeshivos, he became a disciple of the *Baal Shem Tov and then of R. *Dov Ber of Mezritch; despite opposition he disseminated their teachings as an itinerant preacher. Engaged in the ransom of Jews imprisoned for debt by their local landowners. Wrote *Meor Einayim*, (on the Torah and *Tanach*, and selected Talmudic passages), which deals with the refinement of a person's moral attributes.
Born 1730, died 1787.
T1:307; **T2**:530, 532; **F1**:29, 188, 259

R. Nachum (Menachem Nachum) of Stefanesti
Son of R. *Yisrael of Ruzhin; led a following in Rumania. His teachings were never garbed in the conventional formality of talks and sermons, but were disguised in stories which to the initiated were pregnant with allusions. Succeeded by his only son R. Avraham Mattisyahu (1848-1933), with whose death the dynasty ended.
Born 1827, died 1869 (10 Kislev).
T2:405; **F1**:285

R. Nachum the Shochet
Chassid of R. *Mordechai of Lechovitch.
F1:210

R. Naftali Herz Suchstvir
Contemporary of R. *Shlomo of Karlin.
T1:246

R. Naftali of Ropshitz
Disciple first of R. *Elimelech of Lyzhansk, then of R. *Menachem Mendel of Rimanov, R. *Yisrael (the Maggid) of Koznitz and — particularly — R. *Yaakov Yitzchak (the Chozeh) of Lublin. Noted for his cheerful disposition and his witty and allusive manner of speech, which sometimes left his hearers pondering as to his meaning. Author of *Zera Kodesh* and *Ayalah Sheluchah* on the Torah and festivals. Succeeded by his son, R. *Eliezer of Dzikov. R. *Asher of Ropshitz was his son-in-law.
Born 1760, died 1827 (11 Iyar).
T1:35, 36, 82, 153, 193, 281; **T2**:388, 404, 487; **F1**:28, 73, 100, 164, 188, 198, 210, 215, 238, 251

Naftali Zahir
Misnaged of Liozna; contemporary of R. *Shneur Zalman of Liadi.
F1:225

R. Nasan David (Rabinowitz) of Shidlovitz
Grandson of R. *Yaakov Yitzchak (the Yid HaKadosh) of Pshischah. His following of thousands included disciples who were themselves rebbes, as too were his sons.
Died 1866 (7 Cheshvan).
F1:121, 192

R. Nasan Leib
Son of R. *Menachem Mendel of Rimanov.
F2:382

R. Nata of Chelm
Chassid of R. *Elimelech of Lyzhansk.
F1:128

R. Nechemiah Alter of Lodz
Son of R. *Yehudah Aryeh Leib (author of *Sfas Emes*) of Ger.
T1:223

R. Noach of Lechovitch
Son of R. *Mordechai of Lechovitch, like whom he prayed with intense ardor. Prayer occupies a focal position in his teachings. Disseminated Chassidism in provinces near Lithuania. Died 1832 (8 Tishrei).
T1:124; T2:381; F1:176, 298, 299

Noda BiYehudah
See R. Yechezkel Landau.

R. Nota Notkin
Scholar from Shklov, antagonistic to the teachings of R. *Shneur Zalman of Liadi.
T2:510

Ohev Yisrael
See R. Avraham Yehoshua Heschel of Apta.

Or HaChaim
See R. Chaim ibn Attar.

R. Peretz
Melamed from Beshenkovitz; chassid of R. *Shmuel of Lubavitch.
F2:400

R. Peretz Chein
Distinguished chassid of R. *Dov Ber of Lubavitch and of his son R. *Menachem Mendel of Lubavitch. In his childhood saw R. *Shneur Zalman of Liadi, in his old age saw R. *Yosef Yitzchak of Lubavitch, who was then an infant. *Rav* in Beshenkovitz, in Nevel, and (from 1866) in Chernigov. Born 1797, died 1883 (28 Iyar).
F1:275

R. Peretz of Pshischah
Chassid of R. *Avraham Yehoshua Heschel of Apta.
T2:458

R. Pessach
Chassid of R. *Shmuel of Lubavitch.
T2:480

R. Pinchas Eliyahu (Pintchi) of Piltz
Distinguished elder chassid of R. *Yitzchak Meir of Ger and later of R. *Yehudah Aryeh Leib of Ger.
T1:164, 223; T2:350

R. Pinchas (Halevi) Horovitz
Rav of Frankfort from 1771. His teachers included his brother, R. *Shmelke of Nikolsburg, with whom he visited R. *Dov Ber of Mezritch; it was there that he met R. *Shneur Zalman of Liadi. His fame however rests less on his connection with Chassidism than on his *Sefer Hafla'ah* (*pilpul*, Halachah) and *Panim Yafos* (*derush*, Biblical commentary). The celebrated *rav* of Pressburg, R. Moshe Sofer, author of *Chasam Sofer*, was his disciple. Born 1730, died 1805 (7 Tammuz).
F1:198, 270

R. Pinchas (ben R. Avraham Abba Shapiro) of Korets
Met the *Baal Shem Tov; differed from R. *Dov Ber of Mezritch, upholding the supremacy of the ecstatic prayer of simple request over contemplative prayer accompanied by the kabbalistic *kavanos* of the Arizal. His sermons appeared in various collections (such as *Midrash Pinchas*), including those of his disciples (such as *Bnei Yissaschar* by R. *Zvi Elimelech of Dinov). Born 1726, died 1791 (10 Elul).
T1:97, 123, 125, 260, 270, 292; T2:453, 490, 517, 518; F1:123, 150, 163, 201, 204

R. Pinchas of Shklov
See R. Pinchas Reizes.

R. Pinchas Reizes
Chassid of *Shneur Zalman of Liadi, and son of R. *Henich Schick, *rav* of Shklov.
T1:144; T2:520, 547; F1:169, 225

R. Pintchi of Piltz
See R. Pinchas Eliyahu of Piltz.

Rachel Leah
Daughter of R. *Shalom Yosef of Sadigora; second wife of her paternal uncle, R. *David Moshe of Chortkov.
T2:506

Biographical Sketches [495]

Rama
See R. Moshe Isserles.

R. Raphael of Bershad (or: Bershid)
Disciple of R. *Aryeh Leib of Shpola and R. *Pinchas of Korets; left no successor. On account of his unflinching devotion to the truth (Heb.: *emes*), he was known as R. Raphael der Emesser ("the truthful one").
Died between 1816 and 1826.
T1:69; **F1:**201; **F2:**420, 458

R. Raphael (HaKohen) of Hamburg
Prominent scholar, author of *Toras Yekusiel;* contemporary of R. *Shneur Zalman of Liadi; *rav* of Minsk and other major towns in Lithuania, and later of Hamburg; famed for his saintly conduct. His disciples included the celebrated R. Chaim of Volozhin.
T1:76

Raphael Wolf (or Wiltz) of Skoli
Chassid and chronicler from Galicia; died in Jerusalem in 1929.
T2:372; **F1:**56

Rashab
See R. Shalom Ber of Lubavitch.

Rav, the
See R. Shneur Zalman of Liadi.

Rav of Brezan, the
See R. Shalom Mordechai HaKohen (Shvadron; *Maharsham*).

Rav of Chodorov, the
See R. Yehoshua Herschel of Chodorov.

Rav of Libichov, the
Contemporary of R. *Chaim of Zanz.
T1:130

Rav of Merchov, the
Contemporary of R. *Levi Yitzchak of Berditchev.
T2:613

Rav of Skole, the
Disciple of the *Baal Shem Tov, from the Ukraine.
T1:86

Rav of Torchin, the
See R. Yechiel of Alexander.

Rav of Ulianov, the
See R. Avraham of Ulianov.

Rav of Volpa, the
Known only by this name; enigmatic contemporary of R. *Shneur Zalman of Liadi.
T1:45

Rav of Yanov, the
Contemporary of R. *Shmelke of Nikolsburg.
T1:297

Rivkah
Wife of R. *Shmuel of Lubavitch.
T2:529

Sarah
Daughter of R. *Menachem Mendel of Vizhnitz, and daughter-in-law of R. *Yehoshua of Belz.
T2:354

Saraph, the
See R. *Uri of Strelisk.

R. Sar Shalom of Belz
See R. Shalom of Belz.

Sava Kaddisha of Radoshitz
See R. Yissachar Dov of Radoshitz.

Seer of Lublin, the
See R. Yaakov Yitzchak of Lublin.

Sender
See Alexander.

Sfas Emes
See R. Yehudah Aryeh Leib of Ger.

R. Shabsai Meir of Beshenkovitz
Chassid of R. *Shneur Zalman of Liadi.
F1:225

R. Shabsai the Bookbinder
Father of R. *Yisrael (the Maggid) of Koznitz.
F1:110, 184

R. Shachna of Lublin
See R. Shalom Shachna of Lublin.

R. Shalom
Goldsmith; grandfather of R. *Shalom Mordechai HaKohen, *rav* of Brezan.
T1:115

R. Shalom Ber (Shalom Dov Ber) of Lubavitch
Son and successor of R. *Shmuel of

Lubavitch; known by the acronym *Rashab*; founder of the first chassidic yeshivah, *Tomchei Tmimim* (1897). In 1916 sent emissaries to found yeshivos in Georgia — a pioneering venture in the spreading of Chassidism among non-Ashkenazi Jewry. His discourses on chassidic philosophy and prayer are collected in numerous works including *Kuntress HaTefillah, Kuntress HaAvodah,* and *Toras Shalom.* Succeeded by his son, R. *Yosef Yitzchak of Lubavitch.
Born 1860, died 1920 (2 Nissan).
T1:119; **T2**:435, 449, 472, 485, 498, 520, 578, 604, 608, 613; **F1**:37, 103, 209, 237, 259, 306; **F2**:346, 379, 464

R. Shalom Mordechai HaKohen (Shvadron; *Maharsham*)
Prominent (and modest) Galician *posek*, known as the "Rav of Brezan" or as *Maharsham*, the acronym which serves as the title of the seven-volume series of authoritative responsa on which his fame rests.
Born 1835, died 1911.
T1:115

R. Shalom of Belz
Founder of the Belz dynasty; descended from R. *Elazar Rokeiach of Amsterdam. His mentors included R. *Yaakov Yitzchak (the Chozeh) of Lublin, R. *Uri of Strelisk, R. *Yisrael of Koznitz and R. *Avraham Yehoshua Heschel of Apta. Belz became the focus of Galician Chassidism for the thousands who recounted his wonders and heard his teachings, which stressed the centrality of Talmudic study; they are collected in *Dover Shalom.* Spokesman for Galician Jewry; active opponent of the Haskalah. Succeeded by his son, R. *Yehoshua of Belz; R. *Chanoch Henich of Alisk was his son-in-law.
Born 1779, died 1855 (27 Elul).
T1:194, 202, 206, 265, 311; **T2**:387, 391, 523, 531, 559; **F1**:33, 41, 100, 298; **F2**:333, 375, 408, 410, 456

R. Shalom of Probisht
See R. Shalom Shachna of Probisht.

R. Shalom Shachna
Son-in-law of R. *Shneur Zalman of Liadi; chassid of R. *Menachem Mendel of Vitebsk; father of R. *Menachem Mendel of Lubavitch.
T2:317

R. Shalom Shachna (ben R. Yosef) of Lublin
Rosh yeshivah in Lublin, which his erudition transformed into a major center of Talmudic study in Poland. Survived by no extant works, but by disciples — including R. *Moshe Isserles, his son-in-law. His letter of appointment (dated 1541) as chief rabbi of Lesser Poland, in which the government grants him jurisdiction for capital punishment, is still in existence.
Died 1558.
T1:82

R. Shalom Shachna (Friedmann) of Probisht
Son of R. *Avraham the Malach; father of R. *Yisrael of Ruzhin; his wife was the granddaughter of R. *Nachum of Chernobyl.
Born 1766, died 1803.
T2:483; **F1**:29, 309

R. Shalom Yosef of Sadigora
Eldest son of R. *Yisrael of Ruzhin; settled in Sadigora, and died in Leipzig, surviving his father by ten months.
Born 1813, died 1851.
T2:506

R. Shalom Yudel
Rosh yeshivah in Smilovitz.
F1:225

R. Shaul of Kazan
Chassid of R. *Shneur Zalman of Liadi.
F1:305

Sheindel
Rebbitzin of R. *Yaakov Yitzchak (the Yid HaKadosh) of Pshischah.
F1:191

R. Shimon Chaim
Son of R. *Yitzchak Meir of Ger.
T1:164

R. Shimon Eliyahu
Rosh yeshivah in Smilovitz; known as

"the *ilui* of Drutzin."
F1:225

R. Shimon Shlomo Savran
Father of R. *Moshe (Zvi) of Savran.
T1:307

R. Shimon Sofer
Son of R. Moshe Sofer, author of *Chasam Sofer; rav* of Mattersdorf, then Cracow. A founder of the anti-Haskalah Orthodox organization, *Machzikei HaDas,* which acted in harmony with the chassidic leaders of Belz and Zanz. Member of parliament in Vienna. Author of *Michtav Sofer (Halachah* and *derush).*
Born 1820, died 1883 (16 Adar).
F2:406

R. Shlomo
Son of R. *Uri Nasan Nata.
T2:579

R. Shlomo Kluger of Brody
Known as the Maggid of Brody, or by the acronym *Maharshak;* a prodigy; studied under R. *Yaakov Kranz, the Maggid of Dubno. Wrote hundreds of books and authoritative responsa; a vigorous opponent of the Haskalah.
Born 1785, died 1869.
T1:58

R. Shlomo Leib of Linchna (Lenchna)
Disciple of R. *Yaakov Yitzchak (the Chozeh) of Lublin and of R. *Yaakov Yitzchak (the Yid HaKadosh) of Pshischah. Never laid eyes upon a coin, nor uttered a needless word. In his childhood, administered an oath to the organs of his body that they would act only in harmony with the divine Will.
Died 1843 (19 Nissan).
T1:206; **T2**:488; **F2**:401

R. Shlomo of Dvort
Prominent chassid.
T1:147

R. Shlomo of Kanskivli
Wealthy chassid of R. *Yaakov Yitzchak of Lublin.
F2:358

R. Shlomo (ben Meir HaLevi) of Karlin
Disciple of R. *Dov Ber (the Maggid) of Mezritch,and of R. *Aharon ("the Great") of Karlin, whom he succeeded in 1772. No written works are extant, but his teachings and stories of his activities have been recorded. Most of the succeeding chassidic leaders in Lithuania (as well as R. *Uri of Strelisk) were his disciples. Succeeded by R. Asher ("the First") of Stolin.
Born 1738, died 1792 (22 Tammuz).
T1:54, 246; **T2**:343, 352; **F1**:205, 270, 281, 308

R. Shlomo (HaKohen Rabinowich) of Radomsk
Disciple of R. *Meir of Apta; *rav* then rebbe in Radomsk, where he concerned himself with the lot of his poor townsmen; author of *Tiferes Shlomo.* His manner of speech and melodiousness attracted thousands; his distinguished followers newly introduced to Chassidism included R. Avraham Chaim David Doctor of Pietrkov, and R. *Aharon Marcus. Succeeded by his son R. *Avraham Yissachar of Radomsk.
Born 1803, died 1866 (29 Adar).
T1:126, 169, 195, 256, 263, 269; **T2**:324, 424, 465, 595, 614; **F1**:52, 121, 309; **F2**:372, 373, 405

R. Shlomo of Strelisk
Son of R. *Uri of Strelisk, whom he survived by four months.
T2:365, 558

R. Shlomo Raphaels of Vilna
Chassid of R. *Shneur Zalman of Liadi.
T1:145

R. Shlomo Zalman of Kopust
Succeeded his father R. *Yehudah Leib of Kopust in this parallel branch of *Chabad* Chassidism. His *Magen Avos* includes an exposition of many concepts in *Chabad* philosophy. Succeeded by his son, R. Shalom Dov Ber of Rechitsa (cousin of R. *Shalom Ber of Lubavitch).
Born 1830, died 1900.
T1:129; **F1**:34

R. Shlomo Zalman Yosef (Frenkel) of Vilipoli
Disciple of R. *Meir of Apta and R. *Naftali of Ropshitz; known as a wonderworker. Lived an ascetic and secluded life, and directed that his scholarly writings be buried with him. Born 1804, died 1859 (13 Kislev).
F1:73

R. Shmelke (Shmuel Shmelke HaLevi Horovitz) of Nikolsburg
Disciple of R. Dov Ber of Mezritch; brother of R. *Pinchas (HaLevi) Horovitz. Philanthropy was one of the mainstays of his life and teaching. His numerous celebrated disciples included R. *Moshe Leib of Sasov, R. *Yaakov Yitzchak of Lublin, and R. *Menachem Mendel of Rimanov. Published works include *Divrei Shmuel* and *Nezir HaShem*. Born 1726, died 1778 (2 Iyar).
T1:43, 47, 81, 114, 210, 271, 297; **T2**:396, 472, 479, 483; **F1**:41, 42, 106, 120, 198; **F2**:333, 375

R. Shmelke (Yekusiel Shmuel Shmelke) of Sasov
When seven years old lost his father, R. *Moshe Leib of Sasov. Brought up by R. Avraham Chaim of Zlotchov, R. *Menachem Mendel of Kosov, and R. *Yisrael of Ruzhin. Returned to Sasov in 1849, and succeeded his father there. Died 1861 (18 Kislev).
F2:376

R. Shmuel
The last *av beis din* of Vilna; son of R. Avigdor, the *av beis din* of Prozna (d. 1771).
T2:494

R. Shmuel Abba of Zichlin
Rebbe in Poland; disciple of R. *Fishel of Strikov and R. *Simchah Bunem of Pshischah.
T2:415; **F1**:35, 82, 150, 152, 158, 248, 305; **F2**:421

R. Shmuel Brin
Chassid of R. *Shmuel of Lubavitch.
F2:442

R. Shmuel Eliyahu der Heizeriger
Chassid of R. *Shneur Zalman of Liadi.
F1:275

R. Shmuel Isaacs
Chassid of R. *Shmuel of Lubavitch.
T2:503

R. Shmuel Munkes
Elder chassid of R. *Shneur Zalman of Liadi.
T1:145; **T2**:363; **F1**:259

R. Shmuel of Dorog
Older contemporary of R. *Yeshayahu of Krastir.
F2:387

R. Shmuel of Kamenka (Kaminka)
The tzaddik referred to could be either R. Shmuel ("the Elder") of Kamenka (died 1831) or (more likely) his great-nephew, R. Shmuel ("the Second") of Kamenka, the disciple of R. *Levi Yitzchak of Berditchev and others.
T1:69

R. Shmuel of Karov (Kariv)
Rebbe, contemporary of R. *Simchah Bunem of Pshischah, and disciple of R. *Yaakov Yitzchak of Lublin.
T2:478; **F2**:358

R. Shmuel of Lubavitch
Youngest son and successor in Lubavitch of R. *Menachem Mendel of Lubavitch, like whom he often encountered the czarist authorities on behalf of Russian Jewry. Author of *Toras Shmuel* on chassidic philosophy. Born 1834, died 1882 (13 Tishrei).
T1:125, 170, 186, 227, 259; **T2**:321, 375, 420, 472, 480, 484, 485, 503, 525, 529, 572, 578, 588, 604, 608, 613; **F1**:31, 86, 148, 175, 215, 267, 306; **F2**:346, 375, 379, 390, 400, 435, 439, 442

R. Shmuel of Zichlin
See R. Shmuel Abba of Zichlin.

R. Shmuel Shmelke Horowitz
See R. Shmelke of Nikolsburg.

R. Shneur Zalman Aharon
Son of R. *Shmuel of Lubavitch; see R. Zalman Aharon.

Biographical Sketches [499]

R. Shneur Zalman of Liadi
Founder of the Chabad-Lubavitch branch of Chassidism. Born in Liozna (18 Elul). At 19, remarking that he knew "a little about learning, but nothing about prayer," he decided to study under R. *Dov Ber (the Maggid) of Mezritch, and with his son (see under R. *Avraham the Malach). On the Maggid's direction compiled an updated codification of the Halachah (Shulchan Aruch HaRav). Attempted to visit R. *Eliyahu, the Gaon of Vilna (see under R. *Menachem Mendel of Vitebsk). Arrested on charges of treason laid by Jewish opponents of his teachings; released on Yud-Tes (19th of) Kislev. His Tanya stresses individual intellectual endeavor in divine service, and Torah study. A Talmudic scholar and a spiritual leader of thousands, a philosophical systematizer and a mystic. Succeeded by his son, R. *Dov Ber of Lubavitch.
Born 1745, died 1812 (24 Teves).
T1:30, 45, 74, 99, 113, 114, 116, 136, 145, 173, 191, 198, 214, 220, 227, 255, 273, 309; T2:317, 336, 363, 364, 401, 423, 436, 439, 450, 485, 488, 494, 498, 500, 510, 512, 519, 520, 543, 546, 547, 552, 572, 578, 597, 610; F1:68, 75, 132, 169, 171, 205, 224, 225, 239, 257-278, 305; F2:340, 387, 411, 436

R. Shneur Zalman of Liadi
Son of R. *Menachem Mendel of Lubavitch, not to be confused with the author of Tanya (above), see R. Chaim Shneur Zalman of Liadi.

Shpoler Zeide
See R. Aryeh Leib of Shpola.

Shraga Feivl Danziger
See R. Feivl of Gritza.

R. Simchah Bunem of Pshischah
In his early days engaged in business and pharmacy, spoke Polish and German, and traveled considerably. Visiting R. *Yaakov Yitzchak (the Chozeh) of Lublin, he became a close associate and beloved disciple of R. *Yaakov Yitzchak (the Yid HaKadosh) of Pshischah, whom he eventually succeeded. Preached internalized preparation for mitzvos, including prayer; stressed Torah study; and cautioned against self-delusion in divine service. Succeeded in his hometown by his son R. *Avraham Moshe, but his main successor was R. *Menachem Mendel of Kotsk. Other prominent disciples include R. *Yitzchak of Ger and R. *Chanoch Henich of Alexander. Has been called "a rebbe of rebbes."
Born 1765, died 1827 (12 Elul).
T1:42, 43, 68, 70, 95, 138, 149, 152, 186, 222, 282, 286; T2:327, 346, 442, 452, 491, 493, 514(?), 535, 559, 596, 606, 617; F1:40, 46, 55, 112, 135, 163, 176, 191, 236; F2:378, 384, 399, 425, 432

R. Simchah Bunem of Vorki
Son of R. *Menachem Mendel of Vorki; settled in Jerusalem.
F2:430, 468

Tamar'l
Woman of spirit and great wealth which she directed to the support of needy chassidim. Before becoming recognized as a chassidic rebbe, R. *Yitzchak of Vorki was a clerk in one of her timber enterprises.
T1:244; T2:383, 585; F1:135; F2:399

Taz
See R. David ben Shmuel HaLevi.

Tiferes Shlomo
See R. Shlomo of Radomsk.

R. Tzadok HaKohen of Lublin
Often known by his contemporaries simply as "the Kohen." After joining the chassidic movement, his mentor was R. Mordechai Yosef (Leiner) of Izbitza (d. 1854). Recognized early as a child prodigy, he was later known as one of the outstanding scholars of his generation. His hundreds of original writings, including ten famous published works, synthesize the revealed and the hidden dimensions of the Torah.
Born 1823, died 1900.
T2:593; F1:121

Tzemach Tzedek
See R. Menachem Mendel of Lubavitch.

Tzvi
See Zvi.

R. Uren Leib of Premishlan
See R. Aharon Leib of Premishlan.

R. Uri Nasan Nata
Lithuanian scholar, known as the *Ilui* of Karinik.
T2:579

R. Uri ("the Saraph") of Strelisk
Disciple of R. *Shlomo of Karlin, and of R. *Mordechai of Neshchiz; brother-in-law of R. *Menachem Mendel of Kosov. His name "the Saraph" derives from the ecstatic fervor of his prayers. Author of *Imrei Kadosh*. His son R. *Shlomo of Strelisk survived him by four months, after which the succession passed on to R. *Yehudah Zvi Hirsch of Stretyn. Died 1826 (23 Elul).
T1:244, 246; T2:321, 352, 365, 368, 471, 522, 558; F1:115, 163

Vilna Gaon
See R. Eliyahu, the Gaon of Vilna.

Wolff
See *also* Ze'ev.

R. Wolff Kitzis
Elder chassid of the *Baal Shem Tov.
T1:89; T2:428; F1:39, 184

R. Yaakov Aryeh (ben R. Shlomo Guterman) of Radzymin
Founder of the dynasty; a disciple of R. *Simchah Bunem of Pshischah and R. *Yitzchak of Vorki; *rav* in Rychwal and Radzymin (central Poland); wonder-worker. His teachings were collected in *Divrei Aviv* and *Bikkurei Aviv*. Succeeded as rebbe by his son R. Shlomo (d. 1903).
Born 1792, died 1874.
T1:35

R. Yaakov David of Amshinov
Son of R. *Yitzchak of Vorki, and (at the age of 35) founder of the Amshinov dynasty; disciple of R. *Menachem Mendel of Kotsk. Imprisoned together with R. *Yitzchak Meir of Ger on the charge of inciting the masses to defy the newly enacted legislation which outlawed beards and *peyos*. He secured not only the revocation of the decree, but a certificate of protection as well. Succeeded in Amshinov by his son R. Menachem (1860-1918).
Born 1814, died 1878 (4 Kislev).
T2:398; F2:461

R. Yaakov David of Koznitz
Av beis din of Koznitz, disciple of R. *Shlomo Leib of Linchna.
T1:206

R. Yaakov Emden
Son of R. *Zvi Hirsch Ashkenazi. An outstanding and versatile scholar who maintained ideological independence in every controversial stance he adopted by occupying no official position for most of his life, and exploiting to the full his private printing press. He supported himself as a dealer in gems. Fled from Altona to Amsterdam for six months following his sensational allegation that the newly-arrived and respected *rav* of Altona, Rabbi Yonasan Eybeschuetz, was a clandestine Shabbatean. Apart from his polemical writings, his works on a variety of subjects include *Amudei Shamayim* (popularly known as R' Yaakov Emden *Siddur*, or *Beis Yaakov*), *She'elas Yaavetz* (responsa) and *Etz Avos*.
Born 1697, died 1776 (30 Nissan).
T1:219

R. Yaakov Kaidaner
Elder chassid of R. *Dov Ber of Lubavitch.
T2:408; F2:387

R. Yaakov Kranz, the Maggid of Dubno
Son of R. Ze'ev Kranz, head of the rabbinical court of Zetil. On close terms with R. *Eliyahu, the Gaon of Vilna. *Maggid* in Mezritch, Zolkiev, and Dubno. Author of *Ohel Yaakov*, *Kol Yaakov* and *Sefer HaMiddos*. Promptly produced an apt parable for every

need, including even an apt parable to explain how he always succeeded so promptly in producing apt parables.
F1:211

R. Yaakov Meshullam Orenstein
Head of the rabbinical court of Lvov; established his reputation by the publication of his *Yeshuos Yaakov* on the *Shulchan Aruch*. In such esteem was he held that after his passing his community decided not to appoint a successor to his rabbinic post.
Died 1839 (26 Av).
F2:390

R. Yaakov of Semilian
Chassid of R. *Shneur Zalman of Liadi.
F1:225

R. Yaakov of Yazov
Son of R. *Avraham of Chechanov. Born 1834, died 1894.
F2:345

R. Yaakov Shimshon of Kosov
Successor of R. *Chaim of Kosov as *rav* of the town from 1854 to 1880; succeeded as *rav* by his son R. Moshe (until 1925).
T2:509

R. Yaakov Shimshon of Shipitovka (Shepetovka)
Disciple of R. *Dov Ber of Mezritch, of R. *Pinchas of Korets, and of R. *Baruch of Mezhibuzh. Won a reputation among scholars for his halachic writings. Settled in Tiberias (1799?). Died 1801.
T1:270; T2:467, 507

R. Yaakov Yeshayahu of Chotemsk
Chassid of R. *Dov Ber of Mezritch and later of R. *Shneur Zalman of Liadi.
F1:225

R. Yaakov Yisrael of Chercass
Son of R. *Mordechai of Chernobyl; son-in-law of R. *Dov Ber of Lubavitch; author of *Shoshanas HaAmakim*.
Born 1794, died 1876.
T2:616; F1:219

R. Yaakov Yisrael of Kremenets
Maggid of Kremenets; author of *Shevet Yisrael*.
F1:102

R. Yaakov Yitzchak of Brizin
Chassid of R. *Simchah Bunem of Pshischah.
T1:151

R. Yaakov Yitzchak (the Chozeh, or Seer) of Lublin
One of the founders of Chassidism in Poland and Galicia. Disciple of R. *Dov Ber of Mezritch, R. *Shmelke of Nikolsburg, R. *Levi Yitzchak of Berditchev, and — notably — R. *Elimelech of Lyzhansk. Though founding no dynasty, his numerous disciples included the majority of the chassidic leaders of the next generation. The epithet by which he is universally known stems from the extra-sensory insight and perception to which his distinguished disciples testify. Saw his task as rebbe as including responsibility for the life and livelihood of his flock; some of his followers preferred to see the role of the tzaddik as giving clearer priority to guidance in the striving for spiritual perfection and *dveikus* which was the life-task of the chassidim.
Born 1745, died 1815 (9 Av).
T1:42, 61, 63, 82, 104, 105, 159, 160, 212, 220, 222, 245, 271, 286; T2:323, 344, 346, 406, 407, 414, 421, 422, 457, 515, 516, 522, 559, 577, 605, 621; F1:32, 46, 49, 78, 85, 102, 109, 111, 120, 135, 167, 249, 283, 286, 298; F2:358, 375, 384, 420, 456, 467

R. Yaakov Yitzchak (the Yid HaKadosh, or the Yehudi HaKadosh) of Pshischah
Founder of this branch of Polish Chassidism. Colleague of R. *Moshe Leib of Sasov and R. *David of Lelov. Demanded in others the moral integrity in constant self-improvement that he himself exemplified. Stressed Torah study together with fervent prayer. Became the closest disciple of R. *Yaakov Yitzchak (the Chozeh) of Lublin, but differences developed

between master and disciple, and between their respective followings. Soon after setting up his own court in Pshischah, the Yid HaKadosh died at the age of 48. Though his son R. Yerachmiel was his nominal successor, the standard-bearer of his school of thought was in fact his outstanding disciple, R. *Simchah Bunem of Pshischah. Other prominent disciples were R. *Menachem Mendel of Kotsk, R. *Chanoch Henich of Alexander, R. *Yitzchak of Vorki and R. *Yissachar Ber of Radoshitz.
Born 1766, died 1813 (19 Tishrei).
T1:35, 95, 162, 281, 286; T2:324, 346, 364, 407, 414, 424, 452, 457, 458, 475, 514(?), 515, 522, 559, 617; F1:32, 191, 200; F2:370, 373, 401

R. Yaakov Yosef of Ostro (Ostrog)
Known as R. Yeivi (an acronym for R. Yaakov Yosef ben R. Yehudah); a close disciple of R. *Dov Ber of Mezritch. A *maggid* living in poverty, and with a strong sense of social morality. Taught of the nearness to God which the poor can aspire to more readily than the rich. Took his professional rabbinical contemporaries to task for the allocation of rabbinical posts according to criteria other than scholarship and suitability. Works include *Mora Mikdash* (on synagogue decorum) and *Rav Yeivi (derush)*.
Born 1738, died 1791.
T1:125; F2:332

R. Yaakov Yosef of Polonnoye
Descended on one side from a family of kabbalists that included R. Shimshon of Ostropoli, and on the other side from a family of Talmudic scholars that included R. Yom-Tov Lippman Heller, the author of *Tosafos Yom-Tov*. In his own right a *rav* of repute. One of the earliest and closest disciples of the *Baal Shem Tov, many of whose teachings have been preserved only in the writings of R. Yaakov Yosef. His books include: *Toldos Yaakov Yosef, Ben Poras Yosef, Tzafnas Paane'ach*, and *K'soness Passim*.
Died 1784.
T1:233; T2:402; F2:353

R. Yaakov Zvi Yalles of Premishl
Disciple of R. *Yaakov Yitzchak of Lublin; *av beis din* of Dinov and Glogov; author of *Melo HaRo'im*, a learned compendium of topics which are the subject of Talmudic debate.
Died 1825 (9 Nissan).
F1:28

Yaavetz
See R. Yaakov Emden.

R. Yechezkel HaKohen of Radomsk
Son and successor of R. *Avraham Yissachar of Radomsk (and grandson of R. *Shlomo of Radomsk); author of *Kneses Yechezkel*.
Died 1911.
T1:195 (?)

R. Yechezkel Halevi
Son-in-law of R. *Yisrael (the Maggid) of Koznitz.
T2:445

R. Yechezkel Landau
Studied under R. Yitzchak Aizik Segal of Ludmir. Talmudic prodigy; studied in the *kloiz* of Brody. At 24 was a *posek* of widespread renown; *rav* of Yampoli and later Prague. Familiar with the literature of the Kabbalah — a fact which he did not make public. When elected *av beis din* of Prague he established a yeshivah there. Utilized the esteem in which he was held by the royal court to better the lot of the Jews. A prolific writer of responsa, best known for his frequently-reprinted *Noda BiYehudah*, by which name he is known.
Died 1793 (17 Iyar).
T1:120; T2:448

R. Yechezkel of Kozmir
Disciple of R. *Yaakov Yitzchak (the Chozeh) of Lublin, R. *Shmuel of Karov, and R. Yitzchak of Vengrov. Ascetic lifestyle; devoted himself to improving the lot of Jewry, in whose favor he was wont to speak up in the

hearing of the Heavenly Court. Founder of the Modzhitz dynasty. Died 1855 (17 Shvat).
T2:346,398; F2:343, 344, 405

R. Yechezkel of Ostrovtze
F1:82

R. Yechezkel of Radomsk
See R. Yechezkel HaKohen of Radomsk.

R. Yechezkel (Shraga) of Shiniva
Son of R. *Chaim of Zanz. Edited and published various kabbalistic works. His novellae, responsa and *derushim* were published posthumously under the title *Divrei Yechezkel*.
Born 1811, died 1899 (5 Teves).
T1:130, 260; T2:366; F1:149

R. Yechiel Ashkenazi ("der Deitsch'l")
Husband of *Adel, the daughter of the *Baal Shem Tov; father of R. *Moshe Chaim Ephraim of Sudylkov and R. *Baruch of Mezhibuzh.
F1:23

R. Yechiel Meir (Lifschits) of Gostynin
Better known as *Der Guter Yid fun Gostynin* ("the Good Jew from Gostynin"), or as *Der Tilim Yid* ("the Psalms Jew") — because of his constant instruction to those who turned to him for advice and support that they turn to the reading of the Book of Psalms. Disciple of R. *Menachem Mendel of Kotsk, who advised him to take up the position of *rav* of Gostynin, and of R. *Yaakov Aryeh of Radzymin, after whose death he became chassidic leader in Gostynin. His selfless and unsophisticated mode of living induced people to refer to him as "one of the 36 hidden tzaddikim." His teachings appear in *Merom Harim* and *Mei HaYam*. Succeeded in Proskurov by his son R. Yisrael Moshe. Born 1816, died 1888 (21 Shvat).
T1:25, 67; T2:524; F1:48, 303; F2:431, 440

R. Yechiel Michel of Zlotchov
Son of R. *Yitzchak of Drohobitch, with whom he visited the *Baal Shem Tov on several occasions; until this time practiced extreme asceticism; later became a disciple of R. *Dov Ber of Mezritch. His chassidic contemporaries spoke in glowing terms of his saintly lifestyle. The *misnagdim* of those parts burned a collection of chassidic works next to his house. Until the day of his death he was a *maggid*, first in Zlotchov, then in Yampol, his words having the particular power of arousing his listeners to repentance — perhaps because his sermons always opened with this preamble: "I admonish not only you, but myself as well." His *derushim* have been collected in *Mayim Rabim*. A melody which he once composed — the haunting expression of his yearning to see the Baal Shem Tov — remains one of the gems of the entire repertoire of meditative chassidic *niggunim*.
Born ca. 1731, died 1786 (25 Elul).
T1:219, 292; T2:335, 448; F1:63, 153, 203, 219

R. Yechiel (Danziger) of Alexander
Son and successor of R. *Feivl (Danziger) of Gritza; disciple of R. *Yitzchak of Vorki; father of R. Yerachmiel *Yisrael Yitzchak of Alexander.
T2:355, 398, 618; F1:161

R. Yehoshua Heschel of Chodorov
Son of R. *Lipa of Sambor.
F1:182

R. Yehoshua of Belz
Son and successor of R. *Shalom of Belz. Organized his chassidic community in a manner that made it the focus of Galician Chassidism. As one of the leading figures among Orthodox Jewry in Galicia, he was an outspoken opponent of the Haskalah. A founder of the *Machzikei HaDas* organization and of its newspaper, *Kol Machzikei HaDas*. Some of his teachings are published (under the title *Ohel Yehoshua*) together with his father's teachings in *Dover Shalom*.

Succeeded by his son R. *Yissachar Dov of Belz.
Born 1825, died 1894 (23 Shvat).
T1:198, 311; T2:354; F1:116, 298; F2:371

R. Yehoshua Zeitlin of Shklov
Scholar, antagonistic to the teachings of R. *Shneur Zalman of Liadi.
T2:510

R. Yehudah Aryeh Leib (Alter) of Ger
Son of R. *Avraham Mordechai (son of R. *Yitzchak Meir) Alter of Ger, who died young. In 1870, after the death of R. *Chanoch Henich of Alexander, the successor of R. Yitzchak Meir as rebbe of Ger, R. Yehudah Aryeh Leib succeeded him. A distinguished scholar, known by the name of his works of Biblical and Talmudic exposition as the "the Sfas Emes"; a powerful but modest leader; promoted Torah study. Succeeded by his son, R. *Avraham Mordechai Alter.
Born 1847, died 1905 (5 Shvat).
T1:55, 142, 164; T2:350, 400, 551, 609; F1:91, 152, 193, 201; F2:431, 433, 461

R. Yehudah Leib of Yanowitz
Brother of R. *Shneur Zalman of Liadi.
F1:169, 275

R. Yehudah Leib ben R. Betzalel (the Maharal) of Prague
As a thinker, Talmudist, and divinely-inspired kabbalist, he stands — like the awesome statue that dominates the entrance to the Prague Town Hall — a towering figure in Jewish history. Respected by the royal and ecclesiastical authorities, before whom he had occasion to defend his brethren. Opposed to pilpul, he based his works on logic and on the Kabbalah. They have been universally accepted as authoritative, and cover a wide range of subjects — Talmudic, halachic and philosophical — and include Or Chadash, Ner Mitzvah, Be'er HaGolah, Gvuros HaShem, Derech HaChaim, Netzach Yisrael, and a host of other classics.
Born 1513 (?), died 1609 (18 Elul).
T2:337

R. Yehudah Leib of Kopust
After the death in 1866 of his father, R. *Menachem Mendel of Lubavitch, R. Yehudah Leib (an elder brother of R. *Shmuel of Lubavitch) established an independent branch of Chabad Chassidism in Kopust. Following his death in the same year, he was succeeded by his son, R. *Shlomo Zalman of Kopust.
Born 1811, died 1866.
T1:114, 257; T2:420, 604; F1:239

Yehudah Zvi of Dolina
Son of R. Yissachar Dov of Dolina, and grandson of R. *Yitzchak Aizik of Zhidachov.
F1:182

R. Yehudah Zvi of Rozla
Son of R. *Moshe of Sambor.
T1:290; T2:400

R. Yehudah Zvi Hirsch (Brandwein) of Stretyn
Disciple and successor of R. *Uri of Strelisk, whom he resembled in the ecstatic nature of his prayer. He was succeeded by his son, R. *Avraham of Stretyn.
Died 1854.
T2:558

Yehudi HaKadosh, the
See R. Yaakov Yitzchak of Pshischah.

R. Yeivi
See R. Yaakov Yosef of Ostro.

Yekkele Rashes
Tailor from Kobrin.
F1:299

R. Yekusiel Asher Zalman Enzil
See R. Enzil of Staria (Stryy).

R. Yekusiel Shmuel Shmelke of Sasov
See R. Shmelke of Sasov.

R. Yekusiel Yehudah Teitelbaum
Grandson of R. *Moshe Teitelbaum of Ujhely; author of Yitav Lev.
F1:177

R. Yerachmiel
Son of R. *Yaakov Yitzchak (the Yid HaKadosh) of Pshischah.
F1:89

Biographical Sketches [505]

R. Yerachmiel Moshe of Koznitz
Great-grandson of R. *Yisrael (the Maggid) of Koznitz.
F1:97

R. Yerachmiel Yisrael Yitzchak of Alexander
See R. Yisrael Yitzchak of Alexander.

R. Yeshayahu Brlin
Chassid of R. *Shmuel of Lubavitch.
F1:86

R. Yeshayahu of Krastir
Disciple of R. *Zvi Hirsch of Liska, and of R. *Chaim of Zanz; active as a rebbe among the Hungarian Jewish masses, bringing many to Torah observance.
F2:387

R. Yeshayahu of Prague
Colleague of R. *Yitzchak Meir of Ger.
T2:614

R. Yeshayahu of Pshedborz
Contemporary of R. *Yitzchak of Vorki.
F2:378

Yeshuos Yaakov
See R. Yaakov Meshullam Orenstein.

Yid HaKadosh, the
See R. Yaakov Yitzchak of Pshischah.

Yismach Yisrael
See R. Yisrael Yitzchak of Alexander.

R. Yisrael
Son of R. *David Moshe of Chortkov. Born 1854, died 1934.
F1:309

Yisrael, the Baal Shem Tov
See Baal Shem Tov.

R. Yisrael Dov of Vilednick
Maggid and wonderworker; prominent disciple of R. *Mordechai of Chernobyl; author of *She'eris Yisrael*.
T2:433; F2:373

R. Yisrael Heilprin
Magnate from Berditchev (early 19th century).
T1:131, 257

R. Yisrael Kozik
Brother-in-law and devoted chassid of R. *Shneur Zalman of Liadi.

R. Yisrael Noach of Niezhin
Son of R. *Menachem Mendel of Lubavitch.
T1:114

R. Yisrael of Kalisz
Chassid of R. *Meir of Premishlan.
F1:181

R. Yisrael (ben R. Shabsai Hapstein; the Maggid) of Koznitz
Son of a poor bookbinder; disciple of R. *Shmelke of Nikolsburg, R. *Dov Ber of Mezritch, R. *Elimelech of Lyzhansk, and R. *Levi Yitzchak of Berditchev. His style of preaching has been described as "sweet persuasion, without harsh words," this attitude stemming from his belief that a *maggid* who reproves must have insight into the heart of each of his listeners, including the wicked amongst them. Ecstatic mode of prayer; involved in public affairs; disseminated Chassidism in Poland together with his friend R. *Yaakov Yitzchak (the Chozeh) of Lublin. He wrote scholarly works on *Halachah* (*Beis Yisrael*), Kabbalah (*Or Yisrael, Ner Yisrael*), and Chassidism (*Avodas Yisrael*). Born 1733, died 1814 (14 Tishrei).
T1:25, 27, 160, 217, 281, 286, 296; T2:320, 411, 420, 445, 519, 555, 621; F1:110, 111, 184, 196, 282, 291; F2:370, 380, 382

R. Yisrael of Modzhitz
Grandson of R. *Yechezkel of Kozmir.
F2:343

R. Yisrael (Friedmann) of Ruzhin
Son of R. *Shalom Shachna of Probisht, and great-grandson of R. *Dov Ber (the Maggid) of Mezritch. Became leader of an ever-growing chassidic following when extremely young, setting up an unusually well-appointed court, first at Ruzhin, then at Sadigora. Charismatic appearance and personality. Wrote no books, but his teachings appear in *Irin Kaddishin, Beis Yisrael, Tiferes Yisrael,* and other works. Six of his sons established chassidic dynasties with extensive follow-

ings: R. *Shalom Yosef of Sadigora, R. *Avraham Yaakov of Sadigora, R. *Menachem Nachum of Stefanesti, R. Dov of Leovo, R. *David Moshe of Chortkov, and R. *Mordechai Shraga of Husyatin.
Born 1797, died 1850 (3 Cheshvan).
T1:31, 40, 123, 148, 208, 213, 218, 226, 227, 292, 312; T2:321, 322, 356, 365, 390, 405, 425, 435, 448, 453, 483, 506, 523; F1:50, 51, 81, 82, 111, 113, 114, 118, 179, 188, 208, 245, 309; F2:390, 400, 421, 435

R. Yisrael of Skoli
Chassid of R. *Meir of Premishlan.
T1:139

R. Yisrael of Vizhnitz
Son and successor of R. *Baruch of Vizhnitz; attracted thousands of followers; established a major yeshivah called Beis Yisrael at Grosswardein (Nagyvarad), which he made into an influential center of Chassidism in Hungary. His works include Ahavas Yisrael.
Born 1860, died 1936 (2 Sivan).
T1:189

R. Yisrael Yitzchak (Danziger) of Alexander
Son of R. *Yechiel of Alexander. Earned the affection and loyalty of his chassidim by his style of leadership. This involved not only scholarly and spiritual guidance to the inner circle of learned disciples, but moral and material counsel to the whole gamut of his numerous followers as well. Author of Yismach Yisrael.
Born 1853, died 1910.
T2:474, 618; F1:195

R. Yisrael Yitzchak of Radoshitz
Son and successor of R. *Yissachar Dov of Radoshitz.
T1:223

R. Yissachar Dov of Belz
Disciple of R. *Aharon of Chernobyl. Son and successor of R. *Yehoshua of Belz, like whom he headed Machzikei Hadas, was accepted as a leader of Orthodox Jewry in Galicia, and was an uncompromising opponent of innovations and of Zionism. Spent the years 1914-1921 in Hungary, where he won many new adherents to Belz Chassidism, though becoming involved in a controversy with the Munkatsch dynasty. Succeeded by his son R. Aharon (d. 1957).
Born 1854, died 1926 (22 Cheshvan).
F1:90; F2:367, 450

R. Yissachar Dov of Radoshitz
Known as the Sava Kaddisha ("the Holy Old Man") of Radoshitz; miracle healer; lived in poverty as a melamed; disciple of numerous rebbes, principally R. *Yaakov Yitzchak (the Chozeh) of Lublin and R. *Yaakov Yitzchak (the Yid HaKadosh) of Pshischah.
Born 1765, died 1843 (18 Sivan).
T1:151, 223; T2:49, 145, 243; F2:366, 402, 455

R. Yissachar Horovitz
Chassid of R. *Simchah Bunem of Pshischah.
T1:149

R. Yitzchak
Brother of R. *Menachem Mendel of Kosov.
T2:534

R. Yitzchak Aizik of Homil
Author of Chanah Ariel; known as R. Aizel Homiler; chassid first of R. *Shneur Zalman of Liadi, then of his son and successor, R. *Dov Ber of Lubavitch. At the passing of the latter, R. Yitzchak Aizik was seriously considered for the succession, which in his humility he waived in favor of the ultimate successor, R. *Menachem Mendel of Lubavitch, who was many years his junior, and whose chassid he then became.
Born 1780, died 1857.
T2:336, 472, 610; F1:245, 271, 272, 275, 305; F2:395, 435

R. Yitzchak Aizik (Taub) of Kaliv
Disciple of R. *Smelke of Nikolsburg and R. *Elimelech of Lyzhansk. Pioneered the dissemination of Chassidism in Hungary. Suffered throughout his life from a painful skin disease,

but the soulful melodies for which he is remembered do not echo his private woes: they lament the Exile of the Divine Presence. A faithful shepherd of his poverty-stricken flock. His epitaph is telling — for instead of all the traditionally eloquent epithets of esteem, couched in classical Hebrew, the simple message which he allowed to be inscribed on his tombstone attests in homespun Yiddish: "He was an honest Jew" (erlicher Yid).
Died 1821 (7 Adar II).
T1:153

R Yitzchak Aizik (Yehoshua Yitzchak Aizik Shapiro) of Slonim
Contemporary of R. *Avraham of Slonim. One of the outstanding Talmudic scholars of his generation; his many works include *Emek Yehoshua*. His salty wit earned him the nickname R. Aizel Charif ("the sharpwitted"). Though his father, R. Yechiel, was a disciple of R. *Shneur Zalman of Liadi, he himself was an implacable *misnaged*.
Born 1801, died 1872 (Teves).
T1:262

R. Yitzchak Aizik of Zhidachov
Nephew and successor of R. *Zvi Hirsch of Zhidachov. Father of R. *Eliyahu of Zhidachov.
Born 1804, died 1872.
T1:96, 198; T2:616; F1:151, 166, 182, 192, 284, 285, 301; F2:368, 381, 389, 409, 428

R. Yitzchak Aizik Yechiel (Safrin) of Komarna
Son of R. *Alexander Sender of Komarna; disciple of R. *Yaakov Yitzchak (the Chozeh) of Lublin, founder of the Komarna branch of the Zhidachov dynasty. Published numerous works on Talmud, *Halachah*, and the *Zohar*; kept a diary of his visions. Succeeded by his son, R. *Eliezer Zvi of Komarna.
Born 1806, died 1874 (10 Iyar).
T:430, 431; F1:151

R. Yitzchak Dov
Scholar; contemporary of the *Baal Shem Tov.
F1:39

R. Yitzchak Halevi (Horovitz) of Hamburg
Head of the rabbinical court of Brody; later *rav* of Hamburg (hence the name R Itzikl Hamburger); contemporary of R. *Gershon of Kitov. His grandson was R. *Naftali of Ropshitz.
F1:144

R. Yitzchak Luria (the Ari)
Outstanding kabbalist; in 1570 left Egypt for Safed, where for the remaining brief period of his life he was the intellectual and spiritual focus of an unparalleled coterie of halachic and kabbalistic luminaries, including R. *Yosef Caro, R. Shlomo Alkabetz, and R. Moshe Alshech. Disciple of R. *Moshe Cordovero. His teachings were committed to writing by his disciples. Lurianic Kabbalah expounds the doctrine of *tzimtzum* ("withdrawal" of divine power in order to make creation "possible"), and the doctrine of *tikkun* (mortal participation in the work of Creation by revealing and elevating the divine sparks that are concealed in material things, and thereby bringing harmonious order and completeness into the universe).
Born 1534, died 1572 (5 Av).
T1:41, 109; T2:442; F1:219, 286

R. Yitzchak Meir (Rothenberg Alter) of Ger
Founder of the dynasty. His father R. Yisrael was a disciple of R. *Levi Yitzchak of Berditchev and the *rav* of Ger. R. Yitzchak Meir's mentors included R. *Yisrael (the Maggid) of Koznitz; R. Aryeh Leib Zinz, the *rav* of Plotzk; R. Moshe (the successor to the Maggid of Koznitz), for a brief period; R. *Simchah Bunem of Phischah; and (after the latter's death) R. *Menachem Mendel of Kotsk — whom he ultimately succeeded in 1859 as rebbe to the majority of the chassidim, like

him stressing Torah study. Best known from the title of his Talmudic and halachic novellae as *Chiddushei HaRim*, a classic work of *pilpul*. At the forefront of Jewish leadership in Poland, defying the *maskilim* and police arrest.
Born 1789, died 1866 (23 Adar).
T1: 77, 124, 149, 164, 184, 207, 264, 286, 295, 296, 304; **T2**:327, 341, 350, 356, 420, 492, 527, 614; **F1**:53, 152, 286; **F2**:426, 449, 462

R. Yitzchak Meir of Mezhibuzh
Son of R. *Avraham Yehoshua Heschel of Apta, whom he succeeded as rebbe in Mezhibuzh. He later moved to nearby Zinkov. There he was in turn succeeded as rebbe by his son, R. Meshullam Zusya of Zinkov (d. 1866), who published his grandfather's *Ohev Yisrael*. His daughter Rachel was distinguished for her familiarity with Talmudic scholarship.
Died 1855 (3 Adar).
T1:308; **T2**:395, 603; **F1**:291

R Yitzchak Meir of Zinkov
See R. Yitzchak Meir of Mezhibuzh.

R. Yitzchak Menachem of Shidlitz (Shedlitz)
Nephew of R. *Avraham of Sochatchov.
T2:619

R. Yitzchak of Drohovitch (Drohobitch)
Kabbalist; father of R. *Yechiel Michel of Zlotchov.
T1:219; **T**:335; **F1**:153, 203, 219

R Yitzchak of Hamburg
See R. Yitzchak Halevi (Horovitz) of Hamburg.

R. Yitzchak of Kalush (Kalish)
Brother of R. *Meir of Premishlan.
T1:129

R. Yitzchak of Neshchiz
Son of R. *Mordechai of Neshchiz; author of *Toldos Yitzchak*.
T1:98, 217, 253; **F1**:154

R Yitzchak of Skver
Son of R. *Mordechai of Chernobyl.
Born 1812, died 1895.
T1:157; **F2**:337

R. Yitzchak of Volozhin
Son of R. Chaim, founder of the Volozhin yeshivah; also known by the familiar diminutive form of his name as "R. Itzele Volozhiner." Prominent both as yeshivah head and as communal leader. Edited and published his father's ethical work, *Nefesh HaChaim*; his own *Milei DeAvos* was published posthumously.
Died 1849.
T1:131, 257

R. Yitzchak (Kalish) of Vorki
Founder of this dynasty in Poland. Through travel with his teacher, R. *David of Lelov, he became a disciple of R. *Yaakov Yitzchak (the Chozeh) of Lublin, of R. *Simchah Bunem of Pshischah, and of the latter's son R. *Avraham Moshe of Pshischah, some of whose chassidim later became followers of R. Yitzchak of Vorki — first in Pshischah, then at Vorki. His disciples included many acknowledged rebbes; R. *Menachem Mendel of Kotsk was his friend; and he often visited by R. *Yisrael of Ruzhin and R. *Meir of Premishlan. His public activities on behalf of his brethren who were often subject to oppressive and discriminatory legislation earned him the epithet "Lover of Israel." Novellae of his authorship and stories involving him appear in *Ohel Yitzchak* and *Hutzak Chein*. His son R. *Yaakov David of Amshinov founded a dynasty in that town, while R. *Menachem Mendel of Vorki continued the dynasty in his father's hometown.
Born 1779, died 1848 (22 Nissan).
T1:135, 138, 160, 163, 200, 244; **T2**:319, 383, 397, 398, 421, 429, 443, 526, 585, 588; **F1**:46, 191, 210, 217; **F2**:378, 425, 461

R. Yitzchak Shaul
Villager; contemporary of R. *Menachem Mendel of Lubavitch.
F:438

R. Yitzchak Zifkovitz
Wealthy chassid of R. *Shmuel Abba

Biographical Sketches [509]

of Zichlin.
F1:158

R. Yochanan of Rachmistrivka
Son of R. *Mordechai of Chernobyl.
Born 1802, died 1885.
T1:157

R. Yoel of Amschislav
Author of glosses on *Mishnayos* (in Vilna ed.); known as "R. Yoel Chassid" (lit., "the pious") on account of his saintly conduct; member of the circle of R. *Eliyahu, the Gaon of Vilna; opponent of Chassidism.
T2:510

R. Yoel of Tshopli
Chassid of R. *Mordechai of Lechovitch.
T1:204

R. Yoel Sirkes
Polish talmudist and *av beis din* in many major Polish towns; better known as *Bach,* an acronym of the Hebrew initials of his *magnum opus, Bayis Chadash,* a commentary on the *Arbaah Turim* of R. Yaakov ben Asher; it appeared over the years 1631 to 1639.
Born 1561, died 1640 (20 Adar I).
F1:177

R. Yosef Caro
Author of the monumental halachic codification, the *Shulchan Aruch* ("Code of Jewish Law"), which presents a simplified halachic summary of his own *Beis Yosef,* a commentary on the *Arbaah Turim* of R. Yaakov ben Asher. The *Shulchan Aruch,* incorporating the glosses of R. *Moshe Isserles, constitutes the basis of the *Halachah* today. Also wrote *Kesef Mishneh* on Maimonides' *Mishneh Torah.*
Born 1488, died 1575 (13 Nissan).
T2:526

R. Yosef Meir of Spinka
Founder of the dynasty. Son of R Shmuel Zvi of Munkatsch; disciple of R. *Shalom of Belz, R. *Menachem Mendel of Vizhnitz, R. *Chaim of Zanz, and R. *Yitzchak Aizik of Zhidachov, the last of whom he regarded himself as succeeding. Ascetic, and ecstatic in prayer. Works include *Imrei Yosef* (Biblical commentary and *derush*).
Born 1838, died 1909.
T1:198

R. Yosef Mordechai
Meshares in Lubavitch.
F1:148

R. Yosef Moshe
Son of R. *Avraham Yehoshua Heschel of Apta.
T2:555

R. Yosef of Shklov
Chassid of R. *Shneur Zalman of Liadi.
T1:145

R. Yosef (Yossele) of Torchin
Son of R. *Yaakov Yitzchak (the Chozeh) of Lublin.
F1:53; F2:366

R. Yosef Schiff of Tarna
Chassid of R. *Chaim of Zanz.
F1:33

R. Yosef Shaul Natanson
Celebrated *posek;* studied under his father, R. Aryeh Leibish HaLevi Natanson, a wealthy merchant of Brezan and erudite Talmudic scholar who published a work on *Rambam.* Appointed *av beis din* of Lvov in succession to his uncle, R. *Yaakov Meshullam Orenstein. In order to raise the morale of the local paupers for whom he established a soup kitchen, he made a point of eating there together with them. His fame rests chiefly on his *Shoel Umeshiv* (responsa).
Died 1875 (27 Adar I).
F1:85; F2:371

R. Yosef Yitzchak (Schneersohn) of Lubavitch
Only son and successor (in 1920) of R. *Shalom Ber of Lubavitch. Defying Stalinist oppression, he established and personally administered a vast underground network of educational

[510]   *A Treasury of Chassidic Tales on the Festivals*

and religious institutions and activities in the U.S.S.R. The day of his release (12 Tammuz) from Soviet incarceration (1927) is celebrated annually. Despite partial paralysis resulting from maltreatment at that time, he devoted the remaining ten years of his life (in the U.S.A., from 1940) to setting in motion an unprecedented revival of European-style Orthodoxy in the New World — to prove (in his own words) that "America is *not* different." Established ramified educational, publishing and welfare networks; in 1948 founded the Kfar Chabad chassidic village in *Eretz Yisrael*. His *Memoirs* and collected talks *(Likkutei Dibburim)* are an invaluable source not only for chassidic thought but for chassidic history as well. Succeeded as Lubavitcher Rebbe by his son-in-law, R. *Menachem Mendel Schneerson. Born 1880, died 1950 (10 Shvat).
T1:119; T2:435, 480, 485, 494, 532, 578; F1:31, 37, 209, 225, 257, 258, 262, 263, 270, 306; F2:464

R. Yosef Yitzchak of Ovrutch
Son of R. *Menachem Mendel of Lubavitch; maternal grandson of R. *Mordechai of Chernobyl; uncle and father-in-law of R. *Shalom Ber of Lubavitch.
F1:258

R. Yospe of Ostro
Householder who maintained a *beis midrash;* contemporary of R. *Yitzchak of Drohobitch.
F1:203

R. Yossele
See also Yosef.

Yossele Ganev ("Yossele the thief")
Contemporary of R. *Aryeh Leib of Shpola.
F1:56

R. Yossele (Katznelbogen) of Ostila
Son of R. *Mordechai of Neshchiz.
F2:456

R. Yossele of Tomashov
Chassid of R. *Chaim of Zanz, and famed chassidic leader in his own right.
F1:80

R. Yudel Kaminer
Mechutan of R. *Yitzchak Meir of Ger; chassid, Talmudic scholar, and wealthy businessman.
T1:164

R. Zalman Aharon
Son of R. *Shmuel of Lubavitch, following whose passing he was asked by the elder chassidim to assume the succession. He insisted on waiving it in favor of his younger brother, R. *Shalom Ber of Lubavitch, explaining: "I detest falsehood; he loves truth." Born 1853, died 1908 (11 Cheshvan).
T2:613; F1:37, 225, 260

R. Zalman Leib ("the Shmeisser")
Wagon-driver in the circle of the chassidim of R. *Shneur Zalman of Liadi.
T2:494

R Zalman of Cherbin
Chassid first of R. *Shmuel of Lubavitch, then of his son, R. *Shalom Ber of Lubavitch.
F2:346

R. Zalman of Dissna
Grandson of R. *Eliyahu, the Gaon of Vilna; chassid of R. *Menachem Mendel of Lubavitch.
T1:54

R. Zalman of Dubrovna
Chassid of R. *Shneur Zalman of Liadi.
T2:547

R. Zalman of Liadi
See R. Chaim Shneur Zalman of Liadi.

R. Zalman Senders
Chassid of R. *Shneur Zalman of Liadi.
T1:146

Zalmanyu
See R. Shneur Zalman of Liadi.

R. Zalman Zezmer
Chassid of R. *Shneur Zalman of Liadi.
T2:552

R. Zalman Zlotopolski
Chassid of R. *Shmuel of Lubavitch; from Kremenchug; had creative

musical talent.
T2:525

Ze'ev
See also Wolff.

R. Ze'ev Nachum of Biala
Disciple and *mechutan* of R. *Menachem Mendel of Kotsk; father of R. *Avraham of Sochatchov. *Rav* of Biala and head of a yeshiva there; author of *Agudas Ezov* (responsa).
T1:233; T2:426, 577; F1:302

R. Ze'ev of Zhitomir
One of the greatest of the disciples of R. *Dov Ber of Mezritch. His profound work *Or HaMeir* is one of the classics of chassidic literature. Revered in all branches of Chassidism; some of his thoughts are cited in the works of R. *Shneur Zalman of Liadi.
Died 1800 (14 Adar).
T1:272; T2:348,467

R. Ze'ev Wolff
Rav of Lyzhansk; on terms with R. *Elimelech of Lyzhank during the latter's tenure as *maggid* there, and wrote one of the approbations of his *Noam Elimelech;* expressed his reverence for him in his *Leshon HaZahav* (Talmudic novellae).
T1:135

R. Zelig of Shrintzk
Chassid of R. *Simchah Bunem of Pshischah, of R. *Shmuel of Karov, and of R. *Menachem Mendel of Kotsk; grandfather of R. *Yechiel Meir of Gostynin.
T1:106; T2:478, 524; F1:211

R. Zusya of Hanipoli
Disciple of R. *Dov Ber of Mezritch; friend of R. *Shneur Zalman of Liadi; brother of R. *Elimelech of Lyzhansk, with whom he was wont to wander on foot from one township to the next for reasons rooted in the secrets of the Torah. One of the best-known of all chassidic personalities — unsophisticated, longsuffering, saintly, and lovable. The following of chassidim that sprang up around him in Hanipoli grew further after the death of his brother R. Elimelech. Some of his teachings appear in *Menoras Zahav.* Succeeded as rebbe in Hanipoli by his son, R. Zvi Menachem Mendel; his youngest son, R. Yisrael Avraham (1772-1814) was rebbe in Charne-Ostro, his chassidim being led for several years after his death by his wife.
Died 1800 (2 Svat).
T1:25, 47, 68, 118, 225, 260, 289; T2:335, 347, 435, 467, 479, 483, 488, 490; F1:64-70, 194, 201, 258

R. Zusya of Shidlitz (Shedlitz)
Chassid of R. *Simchah Bunem of Pshischah.
T1:149

Zvi
See also Hirsch.

R. Zvi
Son of the *Baal Shem Tov. His sons included R. *Aharon of Titiev.
Died 1780.
T2:449

R. Zvi Elimelech (Shapira) of Dinov
Renowned scholar; disciple of R. *Yaakov Yitzchak (the Chozeh) of Lublin, and R. *Menachem Mendel of Rimanov; *rav* of Dinov and Munkatsch; prolific author, best known for his *Bnei Yissaschar,* which devotes a chapter to each month of the year. Succeeded as rebbe in Dinov by his son, R. *David of Dinov.
Born 1785, died 1841 (18 Teves).
F1:28, 104, 283; F2:367

R. Zvi HaKohen of Rimanov
See R. Zvi Hirsch of Rimanov.

R. Zvi Hirsch Ashkenazi
Halachic authority, better known as *Chacham Zvi,* the title under which his responsa were published (the Sephardi form of address dating from his days in Turkey). At different times in his stormy career, served as *rav* in Sarajevo, Altona, Amsterdam, and Lvov, where the reigning monarch invested him with juridical powers in-

cluding even capital sentence. R. *Yaakov Emden was his son. Born 1658 (1660?), died 1718 (5 Iyar).
T2:429

R. Zvi Hirsch of Chortkov
Father of R. *Shmelke of Nikolsburg.
F2:333

R. Zvi Hirsch (Friedman) of Liska
Son of hidden tzaddik, R. Aaron of Ujhely; disciple of R. *Moshe Teitelbaum of Ujhely, R. *Yisrael of Ruzhin, R. *Meir of Premishlan, and R. *Shalom of Belz. His halachic opinions are often cited in the responsa of his contemporaries. His works on chassidic thought include *Ach Pri Tevuah* and *HaYashar VehaTov*. Died 1874 (14 Av).
F2:330, 331

R. Zvi Hirsch ("the Beadle") of Rimanov
At first was attendant (whence the name R. Zvi Meshares) and disciple of R. *Menachem Mendel of Rimanov; ultimately (after R. Mendel's passing) his successor. Born 1778, died 1847 (29 Cheshvan).
T1:229; **T2**:537, 586; **F1**:28, 188; **F2**:382

R. Zvi Meshares
See R. Zvi Hirsch of Rimanov

R. Zvi (Hirsch) of Portziva
Chazzan; chassid of R. *Yosef of Torchin.
F1:53,55

R. Zvi (Hirsch Eichenstein) of Zhidachov
Founder of the dynasty; assiduous scholar; student of Kabbalah. Through his brother, R. *Moshe of Sambor, became a prominent chassid of R. *Yaakov Yitzchak (the Chozeh) of Lublin. His other mentors included R. *Moshe Leib of Sasov and R. *Baruch of Mezhibuzh. Insisted in his writings and teaching that the practice of Chassidism had to be firmly and openly based on a study of the Kabbalah of R. *Yitzchak Luria. His disciples included his nephews, R. *Yehudah Zvi of Rozla, R. *Yitzchak Aizik Yechiel of Komarna, and R. *Yitzchak Aizik of Zhidachov. The author of the classic Biblical commentary known as *Malbim* studied Kabbalah under him. Was succeeded in the dynasty by two of his brothers and then by his nephew. Wrote commentaries on kabbalistic classics. Born 1785, died 1831 (11 Tammuz).
T1:92, 245; **T2**:431; **F1**:192, 300; **F2**:395

R. Zvi Sanin
Chassid of R. *Shalom Ber of Lubavitch.
F2:346

Biographical Sketches [513]

Glossary

All terms are Hebrew unless otherwise indicated

Afikoman: last piece of *matzah* eaten at the *Seder* on Pessach.
Akdamus (Aram.): hymn chanted or sung before the Torah reading on the [first day of the] festival of Shavuos
Aleinu: initial word of the profession of faith with which each of the three daily prayer services concludes
aleph-beis: the alphabet
Avadim Hayinu: lit., "We were slaves"; opening words of the narration of the Egyptian bondage and Exodus, in the *Seder* service
av beis din: president of a rabbinical court

bahelfer (Yid.): lit., "helper"; teacher's assistant in *cheder*
bar-mitzvah: religious coming of age on thirteenth birthday
bedikas chametz: the household search for leavened products on the evening before Pessach begins
Beis HaMikdash: the (First or Second) Temple in Jerusalem
beis midrash: communal House of Study
bimah: dais in synagogue at which the Torah is read
biur chametz: elimination of the leavened products whose consumption and possession are forbidden on Pessach

Chabad: Hebrew acronym for the branch of Chassidism otherwise known by the name of the township Lubavitch
chametz: leavened products forbidden for Passover use
Chassidism: Movement within Orthodox Judaism founded in 18th-century Eastern Europe by Reb Yisrael, known as the Baal Shem Tov. Stresses emotional involvement in prayer; service of God through the material universe; the primacy of wholehearted earnestness in divine service; the mystical in addition to the legalistic side of Judaism; the power of joy, and of music; and the collective physical and moral responsibility of the members of the informal brotherhood, each chassid having cultivated a spiritual attachment to their saintly and charismatic leader — the rebbe or tzaddik.
Chassidus: the philosophical teachings of Chassidism. (Also: (a) a synonym for Chasidism, or (b) any particular branch or trend within Chassidism.)
cheder: elementary school for religious studies
Chevrah Kaddisha (Aram.): lit., "holy brotherhoo"; voluntary burial society
cholent (Yid.): stew cooked on Friday afternoon and kept simmering until the Sabbath midday meal
Choshen Mishpat: one of the four sections of the *Shulchan Aruch,* dealing with civil and criminal law

davven (Yid.): to pray
derashah: a sermon or discourse
derush: non-literal or homiletical interpretation
dveikus: the ecstatic state of cleaving to the Creator

Eichah: the Biblical Book of *Lamentations*
Eretz Yisrael: the Land of Israel
erev: the eve of (a Sabbath or festival)

Four Cups: the wine drunk as part of the *Seder* service in recollection of the four words by which the Torah expresses the promise of the redemption from Egypt

gabbai: (a) attendant of a rebbe; (b) master of ceremonies in synagogue
gartl (Yid.): belt worn in prayer
Gemara (Aram.): that portion of the Talmud that discusses the Mishnah; also, loosely, the Talmud as a whole
gematria (Aram.): system of interpretation by which each letter of the Hebrew alphabet has a significant numerical value

Haggadah: the book around which the *Seder* service is based
halachic (Eng. adjectival form): referring to the *Halachah*, the corpus of Torah law.
Hallel: a bracket of *Psalms* (113-118) recited or sung as part of the prayer service on festive occasions
Hasmoneans: in common usage, an alternative name for the Maccabees, whose successful revolt against the Seleucid invaders of *Eretz Yisrael* in the second century B.C.E. is celebrated on Chanukah
hiddur: the most beautiful or most punctilious manner of performing a mitzvah

Isru Chag: the day following any one of the three Pilgrim Festivals

Kaddish (Aram.): lit., "holy"; item of congregational prayer service, sometimes recited by a mourner
karpas: vegetable eaten as part of the *Seder* service
kavanos (pl. of *kavanah*): thoughts of devout intent
kazayis: halachic unit of measure equivalent to the volume of an olive
Kiddush: blessing over wine, expressing the sanctity of the Sabbath or a festival
kittel (Yid.): white gown worn on certain solemn occasions
kohen: descendant of the priestly tribe of Aharon
kvitl (Yid.): note handed to tzaddik, bearing name of supplicant and his mother's name, and the nature of the request
kugel (Yid.): a delicacy of baked noodles or potatoes traditionally prepared in honor of the Sabbath

Lag BaOmer: minor festival marking end of epidemic amongst disciples of Rabbi Akiva, and anniversary of the passing of Rabbi Shimon bar Yochai
lamdan: scholar of repute
LeChaim: lit., "To Life!"; greeting exchanged over strong drink

maamar: formal discourse in chassidic philosophy
Maariv: the Evening Prayer
maggid: preacher
Mashiach: Messiah
mashgiach: supervisor
matzah (pl. *matzos*): unleavened bread eaten on Passover
matzas mitzvah: *matzah* especially baked for the fulfillment of the commandment of eating *matzah* at the *Seder*
mayim shelanu: water kept overnight to cool in preparation for the baking of *matzah*
Mazel Tov: greeting of congratulation
mechutan (pl., *mechutanim*): the parent-in-law of one's son or daughter
melamed: schoolmaster or tutor
mensch (Yid.): upstanding person
meshares: attendant or beadle
mesirus nefesh: self-sacrifice
mikveh: pool for ritual immersion
Minchah: the Afternoon Service
minyan: quorum of ten men required for communal prayer
Mishnah: (a) the germinal statements of law elucidated by the *Gemara*, together with which they constitute the Talmud; (b) any paragraph from this body of law (pl., *Mishnayos*)
misnaged (pl., *misnagdim*; adj., *misnagdish,* — *er*): opponent of the teachings of Chassidism
mitzvah (pl., *mitzvos*): a religious obligation; loosely, a good deed

netilas yadayim: ritual washing of the hands
niggun: melody, usually wordless
Nine Days of Mourning: the period beginning Rosh Chodesh Av and culminating in Tishah BeAv

Orach Chaim: one of the four sections of the *Shulchan Aruch*, dealing with the respective commandments applicable daily, on Sabbaths, and on festivals

paritz: local squire in Eastern Europe
Pessach: the festival of Passover, celebrating the Exodus from Egypt
Pfui! (Yid.): expletive expressing intense loathing
pidyon (or *pidyon nefesh*): the contribution for charity which accompanies a chassid's request to his rebbe
pilpul: involved legalistic dissertation
piyyut: liturgical poem
posek (pl., *poskim*): one who rules on disputed halachic issues
pshetl (Heb./Yid.): brief original legalistic discourse

rav: rabbi
Rashi: the foremost Biblical and Talmudic commentator, d.1105

rebbe (Heb./Yid.): (a) a tzaddik who is spiritual guide to a following of chassidim; (b) a Torah teacher

rebbitzin (Yid.): wife of *rav* or rebbe

Rosh Chodesh: New Moon; i.e., one or two semi-festive days at beginning of month

Rosh HaShanah: the New Year festival

"Sect, the": derogatory nickname for Chassidism current among its early opponents

Seder: the order of service observed in the home on the first night of Pessach (in the Diaspora: on the first two nights), built around the narration of the Egyptian bondage and Exodus as set out in the *Haggadah,* and accompanied by various observances (such as eating *matzah* and bitter herbs, and drinking the Four Cups of wine) and the singing of hymns of praise and thanksgiving

segulah: spiritual remedy; talisman

Selichos: penitential prayers

Seudah Shlishis: the mystic Third Meal held at sunset on the Sabbath

seudas mitzvah: meal held in celebration of a religious obligation

Seventeenth of Tammuz: fast commemorating the breach of the walls of Jerusalem three weeks before the Destruction of the Temple on Tishah BeAv

Shabbas HaGadol: the Sabbath preceding Pessach: traditional time for learned discourse by *rav*

Shabbos: the Sabbath

Shalom: greeting — "Peace!"

shammes: sexton in synagogue or beadle in attendance on rabbi

Shavuos: festival commemorating the Giving of the Torah at Sinai

Shema Yisrael (or *Shema*): opening words of the Jew's declaration of faith

Shemoneh Esreh: prayer which is the solemn climax of each of the three daily services

shemurah: matzah which is guarded with the utmost stringency against any possible contact with *chametz*

Shir HaShirim: the Biblical Book of *Song of Songs*

shochet: ritual slaughterer

shofar: ram's horn blown on Rosh HaShanah

shtreimel (Yid.): fur-rimmed hat worn on *Shabbos* and festivals

shul (Yid.): synagogue

Shulchan Aruch: the Code of Jewish Law

Siddur: prayer book

Sidra: weekly portion of the Torah read in the synagogue

Tachanun: prayer requesting forgiveness, omitted on festive occasions

tallis: shawl worn in prayer

Talmud: the basic compendium of Jewish law, thought and Biblical commentary: comprises Mishnah and *Gemara;* Talmud Bavli — the edition developed in Babylonia; Talmud Yerushalmi — the edition of the Land of Israel

tanna (pl., *tannaim;* Aram.): authority quoted in the Mishnah

[518]   *A Treasury of Chassidic Tales on the Festivals*

tefillin: small black leather cubes containing parchment scrolls inscribed with *Shema Yisrael* and other Biblical passages; *tefillin* are worn by men, bound to the arm and head at weekday morning prayers; phylacteries

Tehillim: the Biblical Book of *Psalms*

Three Weeks: the annual period of mourning from the Seventeenth of Tammuz to Tishah BeAv inclusive

Tikkun Chatzos: midnight lament over the Exile of the Divine Presence

Tikkun Leil Shavuos: book of selections from books of the Written and Oral Law read during all-night vigil on the festival of Shavuos

Tishah BeAv ("the Ninth of Av"): fast commemorating the Destruction of both the First and the Second Temples; culmination of the Three Weeks

Tur, Turim: 14th-century codification of Jewish law by Rabbi Jacob ben Asher

tzaddik (pl., tzaddikim): (a) a saintly individual; (b) specifically, a chassidic rebbe

yarmulke (Yid.): skullcap

yechidus: private interview at which chassid seeks guidance and enlightenment from his rebbe

Yom-Tov: festival

Zohar: the basic work of the Kabbalah

Source Index

◆§ Source References to *A Treasury of Chassidic Tales on the Torah*, vol. 1:

page	
xv	As His children: *Maariv*, the Evening Prayer
xv	A tzaddik decrees: cf. Talmud, Tractate *Taanis* 23a
xvi	Signs and miracles: *Maariv*, the Evening Prayer
xvi	Our forefathers: *Psalms* 106:7
xvi	There was a man: Talmud, Tractate *Shabbos* 53b
xvi	The further a man: *Rashi* on Tractate *Taanis* 24b
xvi	A person for whom: Talmud, Tractate *Taanis* 20b
xvi	The miracle of Purim: *Torah Or* on Esther, s.v. *Yaviu Levush Malchus*; see also *ibid.*, s.v. *Chayav Inash*
xvi	Listen to the voice: cf. *Genesis* 3:8
xvi	Reb Shlomo Zalman: *Magen Avos* on Yisro, s.v. *Darash Ullą*
xvii	Now I know: *Exodus* 18·11
xvii	In recent generations: see Introduction to *Eser Oros* by Rabbi Yisrael Berger of Bucharest (Warsaw, 1913)
xvii	The many extant accounts: see Introduction to *Em LeBinah* by Rabbi Yekusiel Aryeh Kamelhar (Lvov, 1909)
xviii	This evaluation: quoted in *HaTamim*, *Kovetz* 8
xviii	When one hears: *Likkutei Dibburim* (Brooklyn, 1943)
xviii	When we used to hear: *ibid.*
xix	Reb Shlomo of Radomsk: *Tiferes Shlomo*, section on Chanukah
xix	The lengthy account: *Genesis* ch. 24
xix	The conversation: *Bereishis Rabbah* 60:8
xix	Offer praise: *Psalms* 113:1
xix	Reb Nachman of Breslov: *Sefer HaMiddos*, section on *Mashiach*
xix	It is given to him: *Likkutei Eitzos*, section on *Eretz Yisrael*
xix	Then they who feared: *Malachi* 3:16
xix	Their lips speak on: Talmud, Tractate *Yevamos* 97a
xx	To speak of the praises: *Shivchei HaBesht*
xx	Divine Chariot: cf. the kabbalistic interpretation of *Ezekiel* ch. 1
xx	You are not obliged: Mishnah, Tractate *Avos* 2:16
xxi	Words in *Deuteronomy*: 31:30
xxi	*Vayera*: *Genesis* 18:1ff.
xxi	*Eikev*: *Deuteronomy* 11:13
xxii	Yitzchak went out: *Genesis* 24:63
25	The classic dispute: Talmud, Tractate *Chagigah* 12a
25	For this reason: Talmud, Tractate *Sanhedrin* 37a
27	Dreams speak vanities: *Zachariah* 10:2
28	Not in the heavens: *Deuteronomy* 30:12

Source Index [521]

36	The Ten Commandments: *Exodus* 20:1-14
37	These are thy gods: *Exodus* 32:4
38	Goodly fruit: *Leviticus* 23:40
38	Give every man: Mishnah, Tractate *Avos* 1:6
42	The light ... illumined: Talmud, Tractate *Chagigah* 12a
43	I will sow: *Jeremiah* 31:26
48	Ingenious hairsplitter: Talmud, Tractate *Eruvin* 13b
53	Your friend: Talmud, Tractate *Kesubbos* 109b
58	Passage in *Exodus:* 18:17
60	If an emergency: Talmud, Tractate *Kiddushin* 40a
60	Avraham's alacrity: Talmud, Tractate *Chullin* 16a
61	One who offers a sacrifice: Midrash, *Vayikra Rabbah* 27:1
62	To extend hospitality: Talmud, Tractate *Shabbos* 127a
64	When a man and a wife: cf. Talmud, Tractate *Sotah* 17a
69	Rejoice, you barren one: *Isaiah* 54:1
69	The mother of children: *Psalms* 113:9
70	For everything: *Ecclesiastes* 3:1
71	The wicked have waited: *Psalms* 119:95
73	A man's legs: Talmud, Tractate *Sukkah* 53b (and see *Rashi* there)
73	To see what would become: *Genesis* 37:20
77	Gechazi: see *II Kings* ch. 5
81	*Where You Lodge: Ruth* 1:16
83	The Torah teaches us: Talmud, Tractate *Moed Katan* 18b
92	Speech connotes prayer: Talmud, Tractate *Berachos* 26b
96	*The Wellsprings of Salvation: Isaiah* 12:3
97	*Eyes that See Not: Psalms* 115:5
97	*The blind people: Isaiah* 43:8
97	Samson followed: Talmud, Tractate *Sotah* 9b
98	If a person gazes: Talmud, Tractate *Megillah* 28a
98	Honey and other sweet things: Talmud, Tractate *Yoma* 83b
98	See, I pray you: *I Samuel* 14:29
98	*The Grapes of Wrath: Deuteronomy* 32:32
98	*A Time to Die: Ecclesiastes* 3:2
109	Do not read: *Bereishis Rabbah* 69:7
113	Even loftier: In the Yiddish original, "Zein shlofn shteit hecher!"
115	The fourth generation: *Genesis* 15:16
116	A man is obliged: Talmud, Tractate *Berachos* 9:5
119	Just men: *Hosea* 14:10
121	One of his responsa: *Noda BiYehudah, Mahadura Kama, Yoreh De'ah* 93
123	God reigns: *Psalms* 93:1
125	Both these and those: Talmud, Tractate *Eruvin* 13b
128	If you repent: cf. Talmud, Tractate *Yoma* 86b
132	He who shames his fellow: Mishnah, Tractate *Avos* 3:11
134	Blessed is the man: *Psalms* 40:5

[522]   *A Treasury of Chassidic Tales on the Festivals*

135	Blessed is the man: *ibid.*
142	No individual ever subtracts: Talmud, Tractate *Yoma* 38b
143	Thou shalt not steal: *Exodus* 20:13
143	Relative liability: Talmud, Tractate *Bava Metzia* 34b
145	Their idols: *Psalms* 115:4
160	I have set: *Psalms* 16:8
173	I am not called: Talmud, Tractate *Pesachim* 50a
178	The wordly kingdom: Talmud, Tractate *Berachos* 58a
186	Yaakov shall not now be confounded: *Isaiah* 29:22-23
190	Just as it is a mitzvah: Talmud, Tractate *Yevamos* 65b
194	When will my deeds: Midrash, *Tanna Devei Eliyahu Rabbah* 25
197	I will make you: *Exodus* 32:10
197	Erase me: *Exodus* 32:32
197	When Pharaoh: *Exodus* 7:9
197	And the Children of Israel: *Exodus* 2:23
197	And their cry: *ibid.*
198	Then you shall be: *Genesis* 3:5
199	Midrash about a lion: *Bereishis Rabbah* 64:10
200	You, God: *Psalms* 36:7
200	For Thou: *Psalms* 23:4
201	The Ninth Plague: Midrash *Sh'mos Rabbah* 14:3
201	Rashi comments: on *Exodus* 12:6
201	And you were naked: *Ezekiel* 16:7
202	Who are those: *Exodus* 10:8
202	We will go: *Exodus* 10:9
202	Go, serve God: *Exodus* 10:24
202	Our cattle too: *Exodus* 10:26
206	And they believed: *Exodus* 14:31
210	*The Song of the Sea: Exodus* 15:1ff.
211	Then will he sing: cf. marginal caption to previous story; the Hebrew verb here admits of both translations
211	Whoever sings: Talmud, Tractate *Sanhedrin* 91b
213	The God of my father: *Exodus* 15:2
218	If you walk: *Leviticus* 26:3-4
220	Rav used to salt: *Shabbos* 119a
223	The Children of Israel: Midrash, *Sh'mos Rabbah* 26:2
224	A man is obliged: Mishnah, Tractate *Berachos* 9:5
225	Why does the Torah: Talmud, Tractate *Berachos* 64a
226	Treasure and wealth: *Psalms* 112:3
226	He distributed: *Psalms* 112:9
229	Thus shall you bless: *Numbers* 6:23
229	Observe the Sabbath day: *Deuteronomy* 5:12
230	And on the sixth day: *Exodus* 16:5
231	And they shall set: *Numbers* 6:27
233	Even if your intention: Talmud, Tractate *Bava Metzia* 61b

Source Index [523]

245	Wealth and honor: *I Chronicles* 29:12
246	The world will exist: Talmud, Tractate *Rosh HaShanah* 31a
246	The awe of your rebbe: Mishnah, Tractate *Avos* 4:12
247	And You fulfilled: *Nehemiah* 9:8
256	Love your neighbor: *Leviticus* 19:18
257	You know my folly: *Psalms* 69:6-7
259	Rabbi Judah HaNasi: Talmud, Tractate *Avodah Zarah* 10b
260	One of his responsa: *Divrei Chaim*, on Tractate *Bava Metzia* 49a
261	Support me: *Psalms* 119:117
263	If a deafmute: Mishnah, Tractate *Terumos* 1:1
263	A liquid: Mishnah, Tractate *Machshirin* 1:1
264	Shlah: in *Shaar HaOsios*
265	*A Shul with a Soul:* destroyed during the Holocaust; anguished traditions regarding its burning are current among Belzer chassidim today
268	The Ark: Talmud, Tractate *Yoma* 21a
269	He who wishes: Talmud, Tractate *Bava Basra* 25b
271	That he should never: Talmud, Tractate *Yoma* 7b
272	The girdle: Talmud, Tractate *Arachin* 16a
274	From this we learn: Talmud, Tractate *Pesachim* 59b
284	Just as they test: Talmud, Tractate *Sotah* 27b
284	Exalted indeed: Talmud, Tractate *Yoma* 86b
288	It is better: *Ecclesiastes* 7:5
289	Even to the undeserving: Talmud, Tractate *Berachos* 7a
291	Yirmeyahu the Prophet: Talmud, Tractate *Bava Basra* 9b, on *Jeremiah* 18:23
292	You shall not make: *Exodus* 20:4
295	Go, appear: *I Kings* 18:1
295	And Eliyahu went: *ibid.*, 18:2
305	There are such: Talmud, Tractate *Avodah Zarah* 10b
306	It is *Shabbos:* Talmud, Tractate *Shabbos* 12a
307	Hot beverages: Talmud, Tractate *Shabbos* 119b
310	Your harsh trials: Talmud, Tractate *Sanhedrin* 95a
311	Gavriel the Likeable: in Hebrew, *Gavriel Noseh-Chen*
311	A Woman of Valor: *Proverbs* 31:1
312	Return us: *Lamentations* 5:21
312	Return to Me: *Malachi* 3:7
312	Because of our sins: *Musaf* service
312	Covenant with Avraham: *Genesis* 15:13-14, and *Rashi* there

◈§ Source References to *A Treasury of Chassidic Tales on the Torah*, vol. 2:

318	Adam was created: Midrash, *Bereishis Rabbah* 17:4
318	And the man Moshe: *Numbers* 12:3
318	Struggle for mastery: Reb Shneur Zalman of Liadi, *Tanya*, ch. 12ff.

318	The name of Adam: *I Chronicles* 1:1
319	If any man: *Leviticus* 1:2
320	You have not called: *Isaiah* 43:22
320	Those who trust: *Isaiah* 40:31
321	The girdle: *II Kings* 1:8
323	And our lips: *Hosea* 14:3
323	The daily prayer services: Talmud, Tractate *Berachos* 26b
324	In order that my soul: *Psalms* 30:13
326	The pig: *Leviticus* 11:7
326	The camel: *Leviticus* 11:4
328	That allows itself: in the Yiddish original, *"vos es lost zich essen"*
328	That does not allow itself: in the Yiddish original, *"vos es lost zich nit essen"*
331	And David leaped: *II Samuel* 6:14
335	I will play: *II Samuel* 6:21-22
335	Nechunyah ben HaKanah: Talmud, Tractate *Megillah* 28a
338	Why do You forget us: *Lamentations* 5:20
340	Your friend: Talmud, Tractate *Kesubbos* 109b
341	And Avraham: *Genesis* 24:1
344	A man: *Leviticus* 13:2
345	He and I: Talmud, Tractate *Sotah* 5a
346	The whole world: *Isaiah* 6:3
346	The Sages of the Talmud: Tractate *Berachos* 5a
355	Before you pray: Talmud, Tractate *Berachos* 10b
357	Shoe-straps: Talmud, Tractate *Sanhedrin* 74b
359	Stand on ceremony: Talmud, Tractate *Pesachim* 86b
365	Redeemers will go up: *Obadiah* 1:21
365	My soul proclaims: from the *Hoshaanos* prayers
366	My heart: *Psalms* 84:3
366	Do not read: Talmud, Tractate *Rosh HaShanah* 24a
375	When you eat: *Psalms* 28:2
375	The Torah truly becomes: Talmud, Tractate *Berachos* 43b
379	Blessed is the man: *Jeremiah* 17:7
387	Has already been told: see vol. I, p. 265
387	Once a man: Talmud, Tractate *Kiddushin* 70a
388	You are the children: *Hosea* 2:1
389	One sin: Mishnah, Tractate *Avos* 4:2
392	From out of the depths: *Psalms* 130:1
394	From a Mishnah: Tractate *Shabbos* 1:3
395	My power: *Deuteronomy* 8:17
396	The Nazirite: Talmud, Tractate *Taanis* 11a
397	He Who makes peace: *Siddur*, conclusion of *Shemoneh Esreh*
400	Whence should I have meat: *Numbers* 11:13
405	It gave the man esteem: cf. Talmud, Tractate *Sanhedrin* 94a
411	From the example: Talmud, Tractate *Arachin* 15a

416	Be very, very lowly: Mishnah, Tractate *Avos* 4:4
416	Two *yuds* spell out: In the Polish pronunciation of Yiddish, the words for "two *yuds*" and "two Jews" sound identical — "*tzvai yidden.*"
421	The man Moshe: *Numbers* 12:3
423	The heads: *Numbers* 1:16
425	The rebbe of Moglenitz: Reb Chaim Meir Yechiel Shapira
427	Rabbi Tarfon: *Talmud Yerushalmi* 1:1
428	Will not abandon: *I Samuel* 12:22
430	The Torah truly becomes: Talmud, Tractate *Berachos* 43b
433	If one entertains: Talmud, Tractate *Sanhedrin* 110a
439	And to walk humbly: *Michah* 6:8
443	If someone tells you: Talmud, Tractate *Megillah* 6b
448	The passage: Talmud, Tractate *Bava Basra* 119a
449	Examples in the Talmud: Tractate *Menachos* 109b
453	Our Sages: Talmud, Tractate *Chagigah* 27a
456	The souls which they made: *Genesis* 12:5
459	Before I formed you: *Jeremiah* 1:5
465	A pauper is accounted: *Zohar II* 119a
467	There is no place: Midrash, *Bamidbar Rabbah* 12:4
467	Wherever ten: Talmud, Tractate *Sanhedrin* 39a
468	The prophet Yechezkel: *Ezekiel* 20:32
469	If you are willing: *Isaiah* 1:19-20
476	Abbaye was orphaned: Talmud, Tractate *Kiddushin* 31b
476	For in You: *Hosea* 14:4
480	The first Mishnah: Tractate *Berachos* 1:1
480	Raise your eyes: *Isaiah* 40:26
483	Love Him with both: Mishnah, Tractate *Berachos* 9:5
483	A man is obliged: *ibid.*
484	For whatever measure: *ibid.*
484	Whether it be a measure: *Rashi* on Talmud, Tractate *Berachos* 54a
485	Accepted joyfully: Talmud, Tractate *Berachos* 60b
486	Among the commentaries: on the paragraph beginning *Avadim Hayinu*
487	Of *them* shall you speak: Talmud, Tractate *Yoma* 19b
488	With a perfect script: Talmud, Tractate *Shabbos* 103b
491	I have set God: *Psalms* 16:8
492	Take care lest your heart: *Deuteronomy* 11:16-17
493	Raise your eyes: *Isaiah* 40:26
497	Ethics of the Fathers: Mishnah, Tractate *Avos* 3:1
498	Documentation from the Mishnah: variant readings of *Eduyos* 5:6
498	The Midrash: *Midrash Aggadas Bereishis*, Introduction 11
498	Baal HaTurim: on *Parshas Eikev*
498	The Arizal: *Shaar HaGilgulim*, Introduction 32
498	Shnei Luchos HaBris: on *Proverbs* 22:4
498	Because Avraham: *Genesis* 26:5
499	Praise by her relatives: Midrash, *Devarim Rabbah* 3:8

Page	Reference
505	In all their affliction: *Isaiah* 63:9
509	Remember the Sabbath day: *Exodus* 20:8
509	Guard the Sabbath day: *Deuteronomy* 5:12
509	Whoever is covered: Talmud, Tractate *Berachos* 20b
510	The righteous sit: Talmud, Tractate *Berachos* 17a
511	Claim in your book: *Tanya*, chs. 39-40
511	Torah without awe: *Tikkunei Zohar, Tikkun* 10
511	Rava pointed out: Talmud, Tractate *Pesachim* 50b
511	Unto the heavens: *Psalms* 57:11
511	Above the heavens: *Psalms* 108:5
511	To respect you: Mishnah, Tractate *Avos* 6:3
511	To ransom his teacher: Talmud, Tractate *Horayos* 13a
512	A statement from the Mishnah: Tractate *Shabbos* 5:1
516	A horse is a vain thing: *Psalms* 33:17
518	Words of our Sages: Talmud, Tractate *Berachos* 8a
519	And a redeemer: *Isaiah* 59:20
520	And all those who stand: *Siddur*, the *Nishmas* prayer
521	The Mishnah discusses: Tractate *Shabbos* 5:1, and cf. above, p. 512
522	When Rabbi Akiva: Talmud, Tractate *Berachos* 31a
525	A guest is obliged: Talmud, Tractate *Pesachim* 86b
525	Rabbi Eliezer: Talmud, Tractate *Bava Basra* 10a
526	But not outside: Talmud, Tractate *Berachos* 8a
529	And he shall surely heal: *Exodus* 21:19
529	Permits a doctor: Talmud, Tractate *Bava Kamma* 85a
529	An ignoramus is forbidden: Talmud, Tractate *Pesachim* 49b
535	Even a horse: Talmud, Tractate *Kesubbos* 67b
537	Fortune is a wheel: Talmud, Tractate *Shabbos* 151b
539	One mitzvah brings another: Mishnah, Tractate *Avos* 4:2
543	The Torah is wary: Talmud, Tractate *Rosh HaShanah* 27a
546	Mordechai and Esther: Talmud, Tractate *Megillah*, 15b and *passim*, on *Esther* 4:16
546	The city of Nineveh: *Jonah* 3:5ff.
552	No harm befalls men: Talmud, Tractate *Pesachim* 8b
555	He who is neither lame: Mishnah, Tractate *Pe'ah* 8:9
557	When King David: Talmud, Tractate *Menachos* 43b
558	Nor may one see: Mishnah, Tractate *Sanhedrin* 2:5
559	If a disciple: Talmud, Tractate *Makkos* 10a
560	The steps of man: *Psalms* 37:23
562	The Prophet Zechariah: *Zachariah* 10:2
562	A man is shown: Talmud, Tractate *Berachos* 55b
563	In the World: Talmud, Tractate *Kiddushin* 39b
573	Inscribe it ... on the horn of an ox: *Talmud Yerushalmi*, Tractate *Chagigah* 2:2
575	With me, in my abode: Talmud, Tractate *Berachos* 12b
577	Forty days: Talmud, Tractate *Sanhedrin* 22a

577	There is no marriage contract: Talmud, Tractate *Shabbos* 130a
578	Based on a Mishnah: Tractate *Nedarim* 10:4
579	He who quotes: *Talmud Yerushalmi*, Tractate *Shekalim* 2:5
580	No man's profit: Talmud, Tractate *Yoma* 38b
584	When a man: Talmud, Tractate *Gittin* 90b
587	A man is forbidden: Talmud, Tractate *Bava Basra* 89a
587	Is Shaul also: *I Samuel* 10:11
588	Know Him: *Proverbs* 3:6
588	Can the wife: *Isaiah* 54:6
589	And hide yourself not: *Isaiah* 48:7
592	If one brings: Talmud, Tractate *Kesubbos* 105b
594	Why is the price: *Proverbs* 17:16
594	And the Sages teach us: Talmud, Tractate *Yoma* 72b
595	The Torah absolves: Talmud, Tractate *Bava Kamma* 25b
595	Not a single donkey: *Numbers* 16:15
596	In his book: *Tiferes Shlomo, Parshas Ki Savo*
596	With our lips: *Hosea* 14:3
596	He who studies: cf. Talmud, Tractate *Menachos* 110a
599	In a place: Talmud, Tractate *Berachos* 34b
599	Examine me: *Psalms* 26:2
599	Be gracious: *Psalms* 57:2
599	Even the sparrow: *Psalms* 84:4
600	The lip of truth: *Proverbs* 12:19; *Tanya*, ch. 13
601	And Avraham fell: *Genesis* 17:17
601	The Midrashic commentaries: Midrash, *Bereishis Rabbah* 47:4
601	No verse: Talmud, Tractate *Shabbos* 63a
602	May the words: *Psalms* 19:15
602	The Midrash elaborates: Midrash *Shocher Tov* on *Psalms* 1
602	Seven people: Talmud, Tractate *Bava Basra* 17a
602	My flesh too: *Psalms* 16:9
606	A mystical discourse: *Likkutei Moharan*, ch. 21
609	Who is the man: *Deuteronomy* 20:8
610	This refers: Nachmanides' commentary on *Deuteronomy* 31:13
611	The world stands: Mishnah, Tractate *Avos* 1:2
612	A great deal of persuasion: cf. above, p. 450
613	Seven weeks: *Deuteronomy* 16:9
617	*For* Menachem Mendel, *read* Dov Ber
619	The Almighty: Midrash, *Pesikta DeRav Kahana*, on *Parshas Ki Seitzei*
619	How long: *Psalms* 13:2-3

◆§ Source References to *A treasury of Chassidic Tales on the Festivals*, vol. 1:

23	Even if one: *Midrash Talpiyos, Anaf Galus*
27	You shall not walk: *Leviticus* 18:3
30	Of Moshe Rabbeinu: *Psalms* 90:1
30	Of King David: *Psalms* 17:1
30	Of a pauper: *Psalms* 102:1
30	Heavy of mouth: *Exodus* 4:10
30	Sweet singer: *II Samuel* 23:1
30	Exalt God: *Rashi* on *Proverbs* 3:9
33	If a man pleads: Mishnah, Tractate *Berachos* 9:3
33	In the year 1856: *read*, 1855
34	Better is one hour: Mishnah, Tractate *Avos* 4:17
35	Who shall ascend: *Psalms* 24:3
35	He who has clean hands: *Psalms* 24:4
36	Twice the value: *Exodus* 22:3
36	Four or five times: *Exodus* 21:37
37	And the decree: *Esther* 1:20
37	And no razor: *I Samuel* 1:11
42	All her people: *Lamentations* 1:11
42	Why has the son: *I Samuel* 20:27
46	Happy is the People: *Psalms* 89:16
46	*Shofar*-blowing is a skill: Talmud, Tractate *Shabbos* 117b
47	And the two people: *Deuteronomy* 19:17
48	Happy is the People: *Psalms* 89:16
49	He who is angry: *Zohar I*, 27b
63	For this commandment: *Deuteronomy* 30:11-12
67	A head ... *tefillin:* Talmud, *Rosh HaShanah* 17a
69	You shall return: *Deuteronomy* 4:30
69	You shall be perfect: *Deuteronomy* 18:13
69	I have set: *Psalms* 16:8
69	Love your neighbor: *Leviticus* 19:18
69	Know Him: *Proverbs* 3:6
69	Walk humbly: *Micah* 6:8
71	If a person repents: Talmud, Tractate *Yoma* 86b
72	Rend your hearts: *Joel* 2:13
73	Sacrifice of a guilt-offering: *Leviticus* 19:20-22
80	One hour of repentance: Mishnah, Tractate *Avos* 4:17
81	He Who publicly humiliates: Mishnah, Tractate *Avos* 3:11
81	If a man marries: Talmud, Tractate *Kiddushin* 49b
81	Three who are forgiven: *Talmud Yerushalmi*, Tractate *Bikkurim* 3:3
83	These you have done: *Psalms* 50:21

83	In a place: Talmud, Tractate *Berachos* 34b
85	If you see: cf. Talmud, Tractate *Berachos* 19a
89	If all the judges: Talmud, Tractate *Sanhedrin* 17a
97	For my iniquities: *Psalms* 38:10
99	People out in the fields: Talmud, Tractate *Rosh HaShanah* 35a
100	The words are reckoned: Talmud, Tractate *Berachos* 15a
101	If our sins testify: *Jeremiah* 14:7
102	Is Ephraim: *Jeremiah* 31:19
103	In hidden places: *Jeremiah* 13:17
103	A heavenly voice: Talmud, Tractate *Berachos* 3a
103	*A Time to Weep*: *Ecclesiastes* 3:4
107	By this I know: *Psalms* 41:12
109	I have forgiven: *Numbers* 14:20
109	He who cites: Mishnah, Tractate *Avos* 6:6
111	I have forgiven: *Numbers* 14:20
111	Were I to know Him: Albo, *Sefer HaIkkarim II*, 30:206
114	The procedure followed: Mishnah, Tractate *Yoma* 3:1
114	Rashi quotes: cf. Talmud, Tractate *Yoma* 28a
115	A life for a life: *Exodus* 21:23
117	If I *am* a king: Talmud, Tractate *Gittin* 56a
117	Whoever saves the life: Talmud, Tractate *Sanhedrin* 37a
119	If you see: *Exodus* 23:5
119	The Talmud asks: Tractate *Bava Metzia* 33a
120	When the minstrel played: *II Kings* 3:15
120	The *Kohen Gadol* entered: Mishnah, Tractate *Yoma* 7:4
121	In order not to cause: Mishnah, Tractate *Yoma* 5:1
121	Those undertaking: Talmud, Tractate *Pesachim* 8b
122	Even when I cry: *Lamentations* 3:8
122	If one prays: Midrash, *Eichah Rabbah* 3:8
125	Hear O Israel: *Deuteronomy* 6:4
125	Blessed be His Name: Talmud, Tractate *Pesachim* 56a
125	The Lord: *I Kings* 18:39
127	The short prayer: *Psalms* 51:16
127	Nothing that can stand: cf. *Talmud Yerushalmi*, Tractate *Pe'ah* 1:1
127	In one hour: Talmud, Tractate *Avodah Zarah* 10b
127	The tenth shall be holy: *Leviticus* 27:32
134	You shall decree: *Job* 22:28
140	With righteousness: *Psalms* 17:15
141	For man is a tree: *Deuteronomy* 20:19
144	Whoever fulfills: Mishnah, Tractate *Avos* 4:11
147	There is nothing: cf. Mishnah, Tractate *Kelim* 2:1
147	You ... will not spurn: *Psalms* 51:19
150	An unwitting error: Mishnah, Tractate *Avos* 4:13
150	Turbulent waters: *Song of Songs* 8:7
160	The secret: *Psalms* 25:14

163	A man's income: Talmud, Tractate *Beitzah* 16b
166	The heavens: *Psalms* 115:16
171	The promise of the Prophet: *Isaiah* 17:10-11
173	The remembrance: *Psalms* 145:7
174	For with You: *Psalms* 36:10
174	For there God ordained: *Psalms* 133:3
174	Anniversary of ... Reb Menachem Mendel: read, Anniversary of ... Reb Dov Ber
175	The years of our life: *Psalms* 90:10
176	Here will I dwell: *Psalms* 132:14
176	If he prepared: Mishnah, Tractate *Beitzah* 1:4
178	A suit involving: cf. Talmud, Tractate *Sanhedrin* 8a
184	A man may not fill: Talmud, Tractate *Berachos* 31a
191	*Shabbos* table-hymn: *Dror Yikra*, by Dunash ben Labrat
191	Those who are abused: Talmud, Tractate *Shabbos* 88b
191	Do not converse: Mishnah, Tractate *Avos* 1:5
192	Famous interchange: *Leviticus* 10:16-20
199	Better to hear: cf. *A Treasury of Chassidic Tales on the Torah*, vol. 1, p. 288
201	An evil wife: Talmud, Tractate *Eruvin* 41b
202	The saving of another's life: Talmud, Tractate *Shabbos* 132b
202	Whoever saves: Mishnah, Tractate *Sanhedrin* 4:5
209	Man is always liable: Talmud, Tractate *Bava Kama* 3b
211	Be not hasty: *Ecclesiastes* 7:9
211	Not upon Me: *Isaiah* 43:22
212	And if not: *Exodus* 32:32
213	Has ever a nation: *Jeremiah* 2:11
218	I have set: *Psalms* 16:8
218	Women have been withheld: *I Samuel* 21:6
219	And He will hold back: *Deuteronomy* 11:17
219	He Who gives life: cf. Talmud, Tractate *Taanis* 8b
220	There are three partners: Talmud, Tractate *Kiddushin* 30b
226	A fiery law: *Deuteronomy* 33:2
227	One fire that consumes: Talmud, Tractate *Yoma* 21b
229	A mitzvah earned: cf. Talmud, Tractate *Berachos* 47b
231	Except for the lame: Talmud, Tractate *Chagigah* 1:1
233	From these wellsprings: Midrash, *Ruth Rabbah* 4:10
236	And is His sanctuary: *Psalms* 29:9
237	Render ... strength: *Psalms* 29:1
237	One may not mingle: Talmud, Tractate *Moed Katan* 8b
238	A man is obliged: Mishnah, Tractate *Berachos* 9:5
238	To accept joyfully: Talmud, Tractate *Berachos* 60b
244	When the *Beis HaMikdash*: Talmud, Tractate *Chagigah* 27a
244	And for a sin: Mishnah, Tractate *Shvuos* 1:4
244	The Psalm of that day: *Psalms* 104

245	A man goes forth: *Psalms* 104:23
245	All Jews are guarantors: Talmud, Tractate *Shvuos* 39a
247	The Torah ... started: *Rashi on Genesis* 1:1
247	This month is for you: *Exodus* 12:2
247	He has declared: *Psalms* 111:6
247	When the Almighty: Midrash, *Bereishis Rabbah* 8:7 on *Genesis* 1:26
248	Praise God: *Psalms* 117:1
248	For His kindness: *Psalms* 117:2
249	Praise ... become great: *Psalms* 117:1-2
250	The one to whom: Talmud, Tractate *Niddah* 31a
250	In the very place: Talmud, Tractate *Megillah* 31a
251	And they shall bring: *Isaiah* 66:20
257	The rejoicing overflows: Though the notification was made on the nineteenth, the release came into effect on the twentieth.
258	A name carries significance: cf. Talmud, Tractate *Berachos* 7b
259	Hide yourself: *Isaiah* 26:20
266	Because you did not serve: *Deuteronomy* 28:47
268	I am unworthy: *Genesis* 32:11
268	The great things: *Psalms* 126:3
268	Truth unto Yaakov: *Micah* 7:20
271	It was the Almighty: cf. *Psalms* 3:9
272	One of the pastoral letters: the final letter in *Kuntress Acharon*
276	And Yaakov sent: *Genesis* 32:4
276	Yehoshua said: *Joshua* 24:2
276	And he took of that: *Genesis* 32:14
277	Sang alone to the words: *Song of Songs* 3:11
277	You are my God: *Psalms* 118:28
277	He has delivered: *Psalms* 55:19
281	And He delivered us: *Psalms* 136:24
287	The Divine Presence: cf. Talmud, Tractate *Sukkah* 5a
287	If your wife: Talmud, Tractate *Bava Metzia* 59a
297	There is a passage: Mishnah, Tractate *Megillah* 2:1
297	From the *Haggadah:* cf. Mishnah, Tractate *Pesachim* 10:5
298	Whoever stretches out: *Shulchan Aruch* 694:3, based on Tractate *Bava Metzia* 78b
301	When Adar begins: Talmud, Tractate *Taanis* 29a
303	Whoever stretches out: *Shulchan Aruch* 694:3, based on Tractate *Bava Metzia* 78b
303	The Jews fulfilled: *Esther* 9:27
303	They now fulfilled: Talmud, Tractate *Shvuos* 39a
304	All the sick were healed: *Mechilta*, paraphrased by *Rashi* on *Exodus* 20:15
304	Wealth of Egypt: *Exodus* 12:36
304	Booty at the sea: *Midrash Tanchuma* on *Parshas Bo*, 8
304	The merest maidservant: *Mechilta*, paraphrased by *Rashi* on *Exodus* 15:12

309	His righteousness: *Psalms* 112:3
309	This alludes: Talmud, Tractate *Megillah* 16b
310	He fulfills: *Psalms* 145:19

৺§ Source References to *A treasury of Chassidic Tales on the Festivals*, vol. 2:

316	Wine in quantity: Talmud, Tractate *Berachos* 35b
316	Praise Him: *Psalms* 136:4 (in the "Greater Hallel")
321	Dreams speak vanity: *Zachariah* 10:2
325	Better is my death: *Jonah* 4:3
327	The righteous is delivered: *Proverbs* 11:8
330	In the evening: *Exodus* 12:18
330	You shall not steal: *Exodus* 20:13
331	*Shulchan Aruch:* Section 429:1
332	Now do you think: cf. *Rashi* on *Exodus* 18:7
338	To consume: lit., "eating," which though strictly speaking would be permissible *deoraysa* until the end of the sixth hour of the day, is in fact limited by Rabbinic ordinance until the end of the fourth hour.
338	... Neither Slumbers not Sleeps: *Psalms* 121:4
339	Be seen or be found: cf. *Exodus* 13:7
345	Let us fall: *II Samuel* 24:14
346	And you shall guard: *Exodus* 12:17
346	If the chance: cf. *Mechilta* there, cited by *Rashi*
348	The very soles: cf. *A Treasury of Chassidic Tales on the Torah*, vol. 2, p. 498
361	In the *Zohar: Parshas Emor,* on the verse *Uvachodesh harishon (Leviticus* 23:5), which deals with Pessach
361	*Song of Songs:* 5:2
362	His prophet, Hoshea: *Hosea* 2:21
362	Thus Amos asked: *Amos* 7:2,5
362	And so too Yirmeyahu: *Jeremiah* 31:19
368	At the head: Talmud, Tractate *Bava Basra* 58b
370	The very air: Talmud, Tractate *Bava Basra* 158b
371	Two phrases: *Exodus* 34:17-18
371	Judah was exiled: *Lamentations* 1:3
371	Because they ate *chametz:* i.e., instead of eating *matzah,* the "bread of affliction"
378	Elijah found Elisha: cf. *I Kings* 19:16, 19-21
379	A double portion: *II Kings* 2:9
385	*Tefillin* of the Master ...: cf. Talmud, Tractate *Berachos* 6a
386	Strength of a lion: Mishnah, Tractate *Avos* 5:20

Source Index [533]

399	Talmudic passage: Tractate *Shabbos* 87a (This interpretation is based on a variant reading: *avid* — "he made"; current editions give *avud* — "they made.")
399	Moshe Rabbeinu commanded: cf. *Exodus* 19:15
401	You set a table: *Psalms* 23:5
401	*Which I Command You: Deuteronomy* 6:6
401	The day at Chorev: *Deuteronomy* 4:10
401	In dread and awe: Talmud, Tractate *Berachos* 22a
401	Proper conduct: Midrash *Vayikra Rabbah* 9:3
402	Thunder and lightning: *Exodus* 19:16
402	Day of his wedding: *Song of Songs* 3:11
402	This alludes: Mishnah, Tractate *Taanis* 4:8
404	With ... a humble spirit: *Isaiah* 57:15
404	The Almighty ignored: Talmud, Tractate *Sotah* 5a
407	Sick and ailing: *Mechilta*, paraphrased by *Rashi* on *Exodus* 20:15
410	Israel at Sinai responded: *Mechilta*, quoted by *Rashi* on *Exodus* 20:15
413	If a person should sin: *Leviticus* 5:21
418	*Fire Consumes Fire:* cf. *Joel* 2:5
420	Blessings upon his head: *Proverbs* 11:26
420	Those who cause damage: Talmud, Tractate *Shabbos* 106a
420	No evil shall happen: *Proverbs* 12:21
421	The Holy One: Talmud, Tractate *Chullin* 7a
423	*Remember* the Sabbath day: *Exodus* 20:8
423	*Observe* the Sabbath day: *Deuteronomy* 5:12
423	Uttered simultaneously: Talmud, Tractate *Shvuos* 20b
423	We are further taught: *Toras Kohanim*, beg. *Bechukosai*, 26:3
426	The Torah promises: *Exodus* 20:12
429	For it is these: *Numbers* 31:16
433	If there is a worry: *Proverbs* 12:25
434	Talmudic interpretations: Tractate *Yoma* 75a
434	Why was Ruth: Talmud, Tractate *Berachos* 7b
438	The cup of blessing: Talmud, Tractate *Berachos* 51a
440	For He has delivered me: *Psalms* 54:9
441	Who can utter: *Psalms* 106:2
442	Rabbi Zeira said: Midrash, *Ruth Rabbah* 2:14
442	May God grant reward: *Ruth* 2:12
442	Come and see: Midrash, *Ruth Rabbah* 5:4
445	My dove: *Song of Songs* 2:14
445	Mystical rationale: Reb Menachem Mendel of Lubavitch, *Derech Mitzvosecha* (1953), p. 228
446	The brain rules the heart: Reb Shneur Zalman of Liadi, *Tanya*, ch. 12; cf. *Ra'aya Mehemna*, *Parshas Pinchas*
448	A good thought: Talmud, Tractate *Kiddushin* 40a
451	Great is charity: Talmud, Tractate *Bava Basra* 10a
451	There is a wheel: Talmud, Tractate *Shabbos* 151b

456	By the waters: *Psalms* 137:1
458	The Temple was destroyed: cf. Talmud, Tractate *Gittin* 55b
459	Brief quotation: Mishnah, Tractate *Zevachim*, ch. 5
460	Behold, I set before you: *Deuteronomy* 11:26-27
461	Your years: *Kinos*, para. beginning *Shomron kol titein*
463	My soul is sated: *Psalms* 63:6
464	If I remember You: *Psalms* 63:7
465	A broken heart: *Psalms* 51:19
467	Let not the rich man: *Jeremiah* 9:22
467	God makes poor: *I Samuel* 2:7
468	We are ashamed: *Jeremiah* 9:18

Subject Index

Key to Abbreviations
T1 = *A Treasury of Chassidic Tales on the Torah*, vol. 1
T2 = *A Treasury of Chassidic Tales on the Torah*, vol. 2
F1 = *A Treasury of Chassidic Tales on the Festivals*, vol. 1
F2 = *A Treasury of Chassidic Tales on the Festivals*, vol. 2

For example: T2:379, 435. This entry refers the reader to *A Treasury of Chassidic Tales on the Torah*, vol. 2, page 379 and page 435. These page numbers indicate the *beginning* of the relevant story (or stories).

Abraham, see Avraham
Adam, T1:30
Additional Festive Day of Diaspora, see Yom-Tov Sheni
Afikoman, F2:363
Agunah, T2:253, 254
Akdamus, F2:405, 408, 409
Alacrity, T1:60, 74; T2:498; F1:116, 157, 275; F2:346
Anger, T2:456, 457; F1:49, 148, 153, 157, 169, 210
Apostasy, T1:118, 274, 388; T2:586; F1:125; F2:370, 411, 414, 467
Appearances, T1:25, 40; T2:365, 411, 417, 442-445, 469, 484, 494, 604; F1:128
Arba'ah Minim, see Four Species
Asceticism, T1:281; T2:396, 474, 506, 507, 509, 527, 569; F1:70, 77, 194, 203, 204; F2:414, 435, 463. See also: Food and Drink
Aseres HaDibros, see Ten Commandments
Aseres Yemei Teshuvah, see Ten Days of Penitence
Avraham (Abraham), T1:55, 60, 62, 74; T2:428, 498, 597; F1:41, 128, 149, 150
Beard and *Peyos*, T1:156; T2:356
Bedikas Chametz, F2:333
Bikkurim, see First Fruits
Biur Chametz, F2:337
Blessing, T1:47, 50, 54, 73, 116, 218; T2:417, 466, 484, 594, 595; F1:23, 148; F2:427, 460

Blindness, see Eyesight and Blindness
Blood Libel, F2:315-328
Books, T2:364, 429; F1:177, 215; F2:379, 430
Brotherliness, T1:224, 227, 255, 285; T2:347, 350-354, 404, 411, 413, 416, 482, 485, 498, 566, 609; F1:154, 251, 267, 306; F2:442, 450
Burial and Burial Places, T1:81, 82, 116, 118, 156, 292; T2:398, 408, 410, 424, 432, 501, 620, 621; F1:56, 75, 174; F2:395. See also: Death and Mourning
Cantonists (child conscripts in czarist army), T2:572, F2:465
Cantor, see *Chazzan*
Chametz, F2:333, 337-340, 343-346, 370-372
Chanukah, T2:393, 572; F1:281-286
Charity, T1:47, 58, 70, 78, 115, 116, 130, 189, 255, 289, 290, 309; T2:336, 347, 368-370, 507, 525, 532-552; F1:98, 117, 139-141, 154, 204, 293, 299; F2:330-332, 409, 440, 450. See also: Gifts
Chazzan, T2:394; F1:28, 29, 55, 110, 116, 118; F2:405. See also: Singing and Music
Childlessness, T1:69, 73, 151, 164, 170, 309; T2:453, 584; F1:184; F2:417
Children, see Parents and Children
Circumcision, T1:59, 60, 61; T2:337, 341

Subject Index [537]

Clothes, T2:321, 347, 402, 449, 478, 485, 543; F1:64, 72, 189; F2:384, 450, 463

Confession, T2:390-395, 571; F1:35, 70, 73, 75, 78, 95, 112. *See also:* Repentance

Courtcases, T1:27, 78; T2:561, 563; F1:164, 177, 201, 210, 293

Cursing, T1:54, 55; F2:460

Dancing, T1:133; T2:331, 335; F1:184-188, 271, 360, 366. *See also: Hakkafos;* Singing and Music

Day of Atonement, *see* Yom Kippur

Death and Mourning, T1:98, 99, 114, 162, 170; T2:364, 394, 395, 432, 458, 531, 558, 563-572, 605, 613-616; F1:32, 33, 55, 90, 167-182, 196; F2:461, 462. *See also:* Burial and Burial Places

Discord, T2:397, 556, 577; F2:341, 458

Divine Presence, T1:35, 64, 225; T2:345, 346, 467; F1:102, 286; F2:315

Divine Providence, *see* Providence

Dreams, *see* Sleep and Dreams

Dveikus, T1:109, 112, 261, 271, 309; T2:317, 364, 365, 393, 406, 507, 512, 518, 520, 597; F1:34, 68, 164, 218, 285; F2:367, 384, 387, 436

Eating, *see* Food and Eating

Ecclesiastes, see Koheles

Elijah (Eliyahu) the Prophet, T1:43, 47, 77, 295, 296; T2:321, 372, 430, 547; F1:33, 41, 177, 308; F2:378, 427

"Enlightenment," *see* Maskilim

Envy, T1:141, 142; T2:395; F1:71; F2:464

Eretz Yisrael, T1:xix, 97, 99; T2:375, 428, 447, 458, 526; F2:368, 370, 371, 419, 468

Esrog, T1:37; T2:524; F1:153-161

Evaluating one's Fellow, T1:25, 37, 77, 78, 137, 186, 191, 193, 201, 289, 290, 292, 295; T2:415, 425, 435, 494, 515, 603 604; F1:87; F2:464

Evil Inclination, T1:35; T2:322, 467, 483, 527; F1:50, 197, 198, 208, 217, 224

Eyesight and Blindness, T1:97, 294, 307; T2:324; F1:211;F2:375

Faith, T1:78, 134, 135, 159, 200, 206, 207-210, 216, 217, 229; T2:375, 370-383, 505, 618; F1:27, 184, 211, 219, 225, 291; F2:328, 465

Fasting, *see* Asceticism

Fear, F1:37, 40, 54, 90

Feast of Weeks, *see* Shavuos

First Fruits, T2:592-594

Food and Drink, T1:27, 95, 214, 218-223, 252, 260, 261, 274, 280-282; T2:325, 327, 328, 355, 363, 396, 417, 452, 487, 493, 507, 527-529, 605; F1:23, 86, 145, 152, 195, 216. *See also:* Asceticism; *Shochet*

Four Cups, F2:368

Four Questions, F2:360

Four Species, F1:153-161

Gentiles, T2:356, 499-503, 588, 597, 606; F1:56, 109, 158, 211, 248, 249, 251, 265

Gifts, T1:56, 263; T2:478, 505, 592-594; F1:161, 284, 298

Gilgul, see Reincarnation

Haggadah, T1:xviii; F2:360-368

Haircutting, T1:128; F1:27, 43

Hakkafos, F1:217, 223, 225-238

Haskalah, *see* Maskilim

Health and Healing, T1:25, 71, 216, 217, 247, 306; T2:320, 343, 353, 355, 407, 424, 436, 439, 501-505, 528, 529, 579, 618; F1:102, 114, 116, 141, 182, 201, 225, 303; F2:363, 368, 407, 460

Heavenly Court, T1:25, 27, 181, 202, 274, 304; T2:390, 407, 411, 426, 453, 467, 488, 499, 501, 547, 579; F1:31, 32, 41, 43, 46, 56, 100, 109, 113, 123, 124, 132, 135, 149, 177, 200, 201, 203, 308; F2:315, 395, 434, 436, 455. *See also:* Reward and Punishment

Hidden Tzaddik, *see* Tzaddik

Honesty, T1:233-244, 259, 260, 270; T2:365, 367, 401, 422, 499, 586; F1:201

Honor, T1:124, 148-150; T2:335, 411. *See also:* Humility, Pretentiousness

Hoshana Rabbah, T1:216, 217

Hospitality, T1:58, 62-68, 104, 116, 129, 293; T2:325, 337, 572; F1:150, 167; F2:346

Humiliation, T1:130, 131, 138; T2:411, 421; F1:80, 106; F2:427, 455

Humility, T1:25, 43, 47, 56, 77, 123, 124, 129, 195, 204, 221, 229, 245, 268, 269; T2:317, 345, 401, 402, 415, 421-423, 425, 429, 449; F1:82, 106, 163, 189, 198; F2:340, 390, 464. *See also:* Honor; Pretentiousness

Husband and Wife, T1:56, 64, 70, 124, 213, 246, 265, 309; T2:319, 395; F1:153, 169, 184, 191, 200, 201; F2:341, 353, 370, 380, 455. *See also:* Matchmaking and Marriage

Hypocrisy, T1:93, 294

Ignorant, the, T1:41, 218; T2:375, 529, 597, 601, 603, 608; F1:95, 100, 107, 124, 157; F2:356, 367, 407, 434, 435, 438, 464, 465

Illness, *see* Health and Healing

Income, *see* Livelihood

Isaac, *see* Yitzchak

Israel, Land of, *see* Eretz Yisrael

Jacob, *see* Yaakov

Joy, T1:59, 69, 74, 114; T2:335, 483, 484; F1:103, 116, 118, 184, 237, 275, 291; F2:328, 387, 419

Kabbalah, T1:257; T2:442, 488; F1:144

Kapparos, F1:95, 97; F2:459

Kashrus, *see* Food and Eating

Kfitzas haderech (travel at miraculous speed), T1:248, 282

Kiddush, F2:360, 421

Koheles, F1:163-215

Kol Nidrei, F1:104-113

Korban, *see* Sacrifices

Lag BaOmer, F2:395

Lamentations, Book of, F2:459, 461-468

Leil Shimurim, F2:353

Lineage, T1:114, 157, 191-194; T2:317, 578; F1:132, 188

Livelihood, T1:56, 96, 142, 198, 270, 284; T2:395, 465, 474, 503, 505, 509, 526, 609; F1:128, 134, 135, 166, 184, 211, 219, 282, 303; F2:380, 421, 427

Mah Nishtanah, see Four Questions

Marriage, *see* Matchmaking and Marriage

Mashiach, T1:xix, 37, 158, 159, 206, 312; T2:428, 432, 439, 448; F1:40; F2:333, 366, 458, 459

Maskilim, T1:126, 257; T2:356, 493; F1:306

Matchmaking and Marriage, T1:83, 86, 89, 157, 311; T2:348, 367, 447, 563, 578-584, 588; F1:188. *See also:* Husband and Wife

Matzah, F2:315-328, 330-333, 340-346, 356, 367

Mayim Shelanu, F2:332, 333

Medicine, *see* Health and Healing

Megillah, F1:297, 298, 305-309

Melancholy, T1:145-147; T2:466; F1:36, 250, 275; F2:456

Melaveh Malkah, T1:274

Melodies, *see* Singing and Music

Memory, T2:419, 420, 509; F1:243, 273; F2:429

Messiah, *see Mashiach*

Mezuzah, T2:489, 490

Mikveh, T2:585; F1:23, 43, 121; F2:353

Miracles, T1:xv-xviii, 37, 135, 195; F1:225, 263

Mishloach Manos, F1:291

Misnagdim, T1:43, 47, 54, 55, 59, 73, 76, 109, 118, 120, 173, 212, 261, 262, 268; T2:322, 406, 423, 448, 478, 494, 510, 519, 557; F1:143, 216, 225, 243, 244, 268; F2:390, 391

Subject Index [539]

Mitzvah, T1:25, 59, 63, 64, 67, 78, 122; T2:368, 552, 585; F1:40, 42, 72, 116, 154-157, 281, 284, 298; F2:332, 339, 346, 367, 384

Modesty, see Humility

Moral Accounting, T1:30, 35, 40, 191-194, 251; T2:319, 421, 423; F1:55, 70, 81, 95, 107, 205; F2:468

Mourning, see Death and Mourning

Music, see Singing and Music

Names, T1:136, 151, 169; T2:432, 586; F1:113; F2:385

Ne'ilah, T1:123-134

New Moon, see Rosh Chodesh

New Year, see Rosh HaShanah

Niggunim, see Singing and Music

Nine Days of Mourning, F2:455, 456

Ninth of Av, see Tishah BeAv

Obstinacy, T1:297

Orphans, see Widows and Orphans

Parents and Children, T1:25, 116, 119, 130, 151, 157, 162, 164, 170, 186, 212, 231, 233; T2:317, 319, 337, 400, 426, 431, 459, 475, 485, 594, 610; F1:23, 99, 102, 132, 196, 282, 303; F2:425, 426

Patience, T1:62, 160; T2:324, 353, 457; F1:153, 184

Penitence, see Repentance

Penitential Prayers, see Selichos

Pessach, T2:453; F2:315-372

Peyos, see Beard and Peyos

Philanthropy, see Charity

Poverty, T1:35, 56, 104, 134, 181, 184, 244; T2:344, 430, 467, 483, 484, 569; F1:145, 216, 291; F2:330, 463. See also: Livelihood; Wealth

Prayer, T1:25, 42, 71, 92; T2:322, 323, 364, 365, 375, 397, 399, 494, 512, 515-525; F1:42, 55, 56, 100, 121-125; F2:385, 390. See also: Psalms, Reading of

Pretentiousness, T1:40, 123, 282; T2:321, 535, 601; F1:34, 194, 198; F2:404. See also: Honor; Humility

Providence, T1:31, 63, 82, 129, 170, 173, 181, 219; T2:379, 408, 410, 417, 465, 559; F1:23, 98, 167, 209, 249, 291, 306; F2:315, 372, 467

Psalms, Reading of, T1:40, 125, 186; T2:597, 601; F2:434-440, 464. See also: Prayer

Punishment, see Reward and Punishment

Purim, F1:291-309

Purpose in Life, T1:30, 35, 136, 170; T2:407, 426, 588; F1:55, 177, 195; F2:461

Ransom of Captives, T1:47, 50; T2:331, 572; F1:54

Rebbe and Chassid, T1:xviii-xx, 42, 73, 82-89, 226, 273; T2:321, 343, 344;
leadership, T1:256, 308; T2:449-452; F2:405;
foresight, T1:71; T2:388, 458; F1:102; F2:389;
confession, T2:390, 391; F1:82, 208;
chassid's perception of rebbe, T1:37, 40, 55, 163; T2:366, 433, 443; F1:82, 85, 128, 167, 199, 205, 376, 378, 420, 425;
relationship, T1:139, 144, 227, 274, 286; T2:399, 423, 452, 606, 609, 617; F1:32, 36, 218, 225, 238, 260, 305; F2:359, 442, 449;
bond after This Life, T2:408, 410, 572; F2:404, 408, 461. See also: Tzaddik

Rebuke, T1:47, 130, 248, 259-261; T2:324, 349, 350, 372, 466, 487, 586, 595; F1:73, 82, 143

Reincarnation, T1:25, 43, 170, 285; T2:337

Repentance, T1:27, 31, 73, 97, 126, 128, 133, 152, 274, 312; T2:469, 476, 518, 586, 597; F1:28, 29, 31, 68, 273. See also: Confession; Selichos; Ten Days of Penitence

Retribution, see Reward and Punishment

Reward and Punishment, T1:27, 47, 50, 62, 68, 129, 304; T2:411, 413, 459, 491, 492, 563-572, 603; F1:146, 149, 155; F2:333, 417, 421. See also: Heavenly Court

[540] A Treasury of Chassidic Tales on the Festivals

Ritual Slaughterer, see Shochet
Rosh Chodesh, F1:243-251
Rosh HaShanah, F1:23-56; F2:E848
Ruth, Book of, F2:434-450
Sabbath, see Shabbos
Sacrifices, T1:61; F1:73, 243; F2:458
Sarah, T1:69
Saving a Life, T1:25, 27, 301; T2:569, 571; F1:116, 201
Scroll of *Esther*, see Megillah
Seder, F2:353-368
Segulah, T1:69, 208, 274, 283; T2:341, 419, 482; F1:40; F2:372, 386
Self-discipline, T1:162, 272; T2:319, 400, 419; F1:153, 239, 260
Self-interest, T1:292; T2:510, 608; F1:298; F2:417
Self-sacrifice, T1:77, 131; T2:356, 364, 547, 569; F1:56, 64, 99, 139, 149, 155; F2:421, 434
Selichos, F1:28, 43, 104; F2:373
Seudah Shlishis, T1:261, 274; T2:425, 605; F1:166, 196
Shabbos (Sabbath), T1:62, 162, 219, 220, 223, 229, 248, 274, 301, 304, 306; T2:474, 571, 597, 603; F1:63, 166, 167, 184, 250, 271; F2:418-425, 450
Shavuos, F1:218; T2:399-409
Shema Yisrael, T1:186; T2:479, 480, 492; F1:167; F2:340, 367
Shemini Atzeres, F1:218, 219
Shidduch, see Matchmaking and Marriage
Shirayim, F2:363
Shir HaShirim, F2:373-391
Shochet, T1:27; T2:328, 363, 530
Shofar, T1:158; F1:39-53
Simchas Torah, F1:223-239
Sinai, F2:402-410
Singing and Music, T1:xviii, 133, 153, 211; T2:321, 394, 512, 520, 597; F1:34, 73, 120; F2:346, 373, 436. See also: *Chazzan*; Dancing
Sleep and Dreams, T1:25, 27, 86, 109, 112, 129, 297; T2:369, 404, 414, 415, 445, 450, 490, 561, 606; F1:104, 123; F2:315, 382, 385-387, 421, 455, 456
Song of Songs, see *Shir HaShirim*
Speech and Silence, T1:95, 180, 189, 223, 248; T2:319, 324, 353, 388, 439, 471, 488, 609; F1:153, 163, 190-193
Spiritual Fall, T1:45, 119, 245, 274, 281; T2:399, 492; F1:29, 125
Storytelling, T1:xv-xxii, 37; F1:199, 245
Students, see Teachers and Students
Suffering, T1:170, 224; T2:483, 484, 579; F1:102, 237
Sukkah, F1:139-152
Sukkos, F1:139-161
Supernatural, the, see Miracles
Synagogue, T1:113, 125, 265; T2:377, 387, 586, 603; F1:123-125, 225
Tallis and *Tzitzis*, T1:204; T2:356, 457, 592; F1:125; F2:368
Tashlich, T1:135

Teachers and Students, T1:71, 160, 264; F1:128, 167, 198, 303, 360; F2:374. See also: Rebbe and Chassid
Tefillin, T2:489; F1:66, 153, 309; F2:373, 384
Tehillim, see *Psalms*, Reading of
Ten Commandments, T1:229-245; T2:474-479; F2:410-433
Ten Days of Penitence, F1:63-91
Teshuvah, see Repentance
Theft, T1:142, 143, 233-244; T2:367, 476, 561; F1:35, 56, 78, 236, 299; F2:330, 333, 431
Three Weeks of Mourning, F2:455-461
Tikkun Chatzos, T2:337; F2:353
Tikkun Leil Shavuos, F2:400
Tishah BeAv, T1:98; F2:458-461
Torah Study, T1:36, 42, 58, 71, 125; T2:371, 372, 402, 406, 443, 472, 508, 510, 525, 603, 608; F1:23, 134, 164, 218, 224, 225, 245, 272, 282, 302; F2:340, 380, 381, 385, 440, 442

Subject Index [541]

Tzaddik, T1:xv-xx; 37, 56, 105, 106, 119; T2:405, 408, 410, 618-621; F1:111, 134, 150, 199, 225; F2:410;
  hidden tzaddik, T2:337, 439, 445, 579; F1:128. *See also:* Rebbe and Chassid
Tzedakah, see Charity
Tzitzis, see Tallis and *Tzitzis*
Ushpizin, F1:150-152
Vanity, T1:128
Vidui, see Confession
Wealth, T1:40, 56, 268; T2:606; F2:467. *See also:* Livelihood, Poverty

Widows and Orphans, T1:248-254, 459; T2:475, 559, 561; F1:104, 293

Wife, *see* Husband and Wife
Yaakov (Jacob), T1:55, 122; F1:267
Yichus, see Lineage
Yitzchak (Isaac), T1:55, 96
Yom Kippur, F1:95-135, 303
Yom-Tov Sheni, F2:368, 370
Yud-Tes Kislev, T1:30, 214, 257-275; F2:436
Zohar, T1:31, 42, 257; T2:510; F1:201; F2:368; 371
Zrizus, see Alacrity